I0678178

# DEAD MOURNER'S GROVE

GOLDENHEART MYSTERIES
BOOK 2

## M. PATRICK DUGGAN

ISBN: 979-8-9886047-0-9

Edited by Rachel G. Fain.

**MPATRICKDUGGAN.NET**

If you enjoy reading this novel, please go to the author's website and sign up for the mailing list.

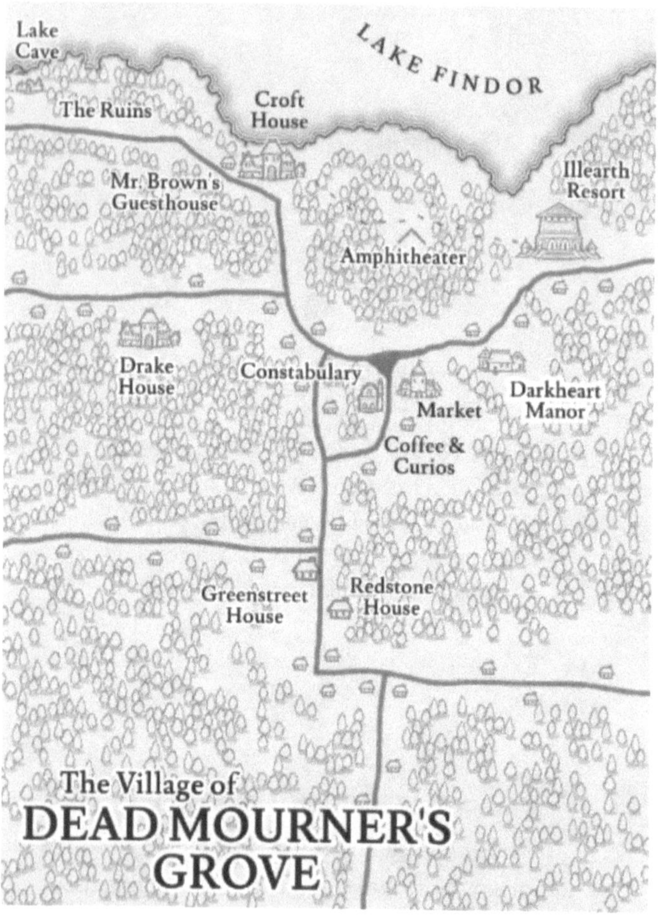

The Village of
# DEAD MOURNER'S GROVE

Lake Cave

Lake Findor

The Ruins

Croft House

Mr. Brown's Guesthouse

Illearth Resort

Amphitheater

Drake House

Constabulary

Darkheart Manor

Market

Coffee & Curios

Greenstreet House

Redstone House

The
# THREE
# REALMS
of Findor, Volusia, and Palas

# CONTENTS

# CHAPTER 1

# SHADOWS OF THE PAST.

Wet leaves covered the ground in a muted blend of red and gold. It was both slippery and cold at the corner of Hornbeam and Knox Streets. Georgia could feel the chill through her boots. The night was thick and humid with imminent rain. Autumn was to come, but the evenings were still warm. She checked the sword on her back and walked slowly. The sensation of wearing pantaloons was odd but liberating. This must be how it feels to walk like a gentleman.

"Now, this is an outfit," Lady Clara Gaye said, joining her. "I love that coat and bonnet. You look like a pirate princess from the old stories." Clara was dressed sensibly for the occasion in a sturdy black muslin dress and long overcoat. Her bright red hair was tied in black ribbon for a no-nonsense effect. It would have been a good choice for a brisk evening, were it not for the fact Clara was the Witch of Volusia and immune to the cold. She could have worn anything and felt comfortable, although it was not her way to draw attention. Thus, a dark muslin dress and coat.

"I feel like I'm going to a costume party," Georgia admitted.

"No, you look stylish." Lady Clara shook her head. "Granted, it is not the sort of thing one might wear at court, but the modified waistcoat is charming. I love the color scheme of black on black. It is almost as if one can see something, but one cannot, because it is all black."

"I think people will embrace being unable to see anything," Georgia answered with a wink. Lady Clara laughed.

"Those boots are adorable."

"No heels," Georgia said, pointing. "When Millie proposed I go flat-footed, I was skeptical, but I can run faster this way. She built the sole with little grooves for better traction. I feel... athletic."

"You lady's maid grows cleverer with each passing day." Lady Clara leaned over for a closer look. "Are those little gold hearts and stags sewn into the hem of the legs? Georgia, you are wearing your own heraldry. You are like a stylish patriot."

"Thank you, Clara." Georgia giggled despite herself. She felt dashing.

They would have said more, but the constables arrived. There were a few dozen of them, all armed with muskets. The wizard Mr. Blue, dapper in shades of cobalt tails and hat as always, walked with Chief Inspector Morris. As usual, Morris looked like a herd of cats dragged him through the street. Georgia wanted to push the man into the nearest barber shop. Still, he was serious about the work. That had to be respected.

"I want to help him with the nose hairs," Lady Clara murmured.

"Don't get me started," Georgia answered.

"Gents gather around. Fourteen souls were lost on this block in the last month. Everyone from children to derelicts to the local baker and a few of our own. We hunt a killer who follows no practical pattern, and who leaves almost no trace after the fact. We have found piles of gnawed bones here and there. We found a few bits of liquefied skin," Chief Inspector Morris called out. "Now, as you know, we are set to sweep Hornbeam back to Vix Avenue tonight. Stay alert. Whatever or whoever is causing these disappearances should not be underestimated. Keep an eye on your partner's back. In fact, do not lose sight of one another, do you understand? Here is the wizard with a bit more advice." He nodded to Mr. Blue.

The wizard looked around at the constables. "Move in groups of two," he instructed. "Each of you has proven your experience. You were hand-chosen by every Precinct Inspector in the city for your skill and judgment. Even so, after all the twists and turns this investigation has taken, I would feel better with an abundance of caution." In truth, he needn't have warned them. So far, four constables have been lost, vanished without trace over the past two weeks. Each went missing while patrolling within six blocks of where they stood.

"All right, listen up, lads. Tonight, Duchess Goldenheart and the Witch of Volusia join us," the Chief Inspector barked. "They ask you to treat them as you would any other constable, men. Waste no time bowing or whatever. These ladies are not shrinking violets. I have met them both. Just get on with the job. That said, Lady Clara, do you have any advice for the men?"

Clara gazed at the street. "Something old has returned. It is something wrong and evil. It has come to this place. I feel it in the air. It will take other forms, but it is in the ground and rising. Part of me wants to run screaming, even as I speak. This is not some mortal serial killer, gentlemen. This is something darker and fouler than we have seen before. It is a corruption from ancient times, and what we see today is a mere manifestation. Beware. Now, I know some of you are rolling your eyes, but look at the garbage pile. Where are the rats? Where are the birds in the trees? There are no stray dogs. No cats. Not even a squirrel. The natural creatures fled. This is a place of silence and death. At night. In the day, the locals walk in ignorance without fear because whatever this is hunts in darkness." Clara looked around at the constables. None of them rolled their eyes.

"Everyone takes a lantern," Chief Inspector Morris ordered. "Let's get this done."

They set out in pairs, as instructed. At first the constables noted Georgia's pantaloons with lifted eyebrows and a few low whistles. Chief Inspector Morris hushed them and urged the men to focus. Georgia moved down the street with Lady Clara at her side. Just ahead, Mr. Blue and the Chief Inspector walked. Behind them, the constables searched behind trees, in back yards, and on side streets.

Georgia was alert, her eyes darting from left to right. The street was gloomy and wet. The leaves on the ground were sticky. Was that frost? Even with Autumn coming, it was still a warm night. Why would the leaves stick to her boot? She pulled one up, but it resisted. Finally, the leaf tore apart. Her fingers were sticky. "Clara," she whispered. "Look at this. I do not think this is frozen."

Lady Clara bent down and poked at the ground. She blanched. "It is not frost, Georgia. It is a gummy fluid like a web."

"The whole block is covered. Look. The leaves are all flat to the ground, like they have been glued down."

"Georgia, draw your blade," Lady Clara whispered. Her breath began to steam as the air grew cold. "Something is about to happen. I feel it."

Georgia drew the sword from her back. The runes around the hilt shimmered with low light. "Something supernatural is... well... somewhat near," she breathed. "It is not here, precisely. But not far, either. Does that make sense?"

Clara nodded. "There is something below us. Underground." She gazed at the street again. "Georgia, were there not constables right behind us?"

Georgia spun around. Delicate flames sprouted along the blade of her sword. She felt the comforting song of the blade. She was mortal, but the greatest power of the sword was to drive off supernatural fear. With it in her hand, she would prevail as long as her motives stayed pure. The street was dark. She stared hard at the gloomy buildings along the road. Shadows seemed to drift. At the corner of her eye, something moved. She turned again, but there was nothing to be seen. "No lanterns," she whispered. "Where have they gone?" The shadows deepened. Her ear detected a low chittering.

"They are gone," Clara whispered in a stricken tone. She didn't have a magic sword, so she could feel fear.

A form stirred in the gloom. Georgia and Clara stepped backward as it approached. The light from their lanterns, and even the sword, barely pierced the darkness. Still, they could see something big was there. Eight indistinct points of red light formed, approaching slowly. Georgia thought they were lamps until she noticed they made a small circle... then the red lights blinked.

"Eyes," Georgia whispered.

The eyes sped up as a massive black spider the size of a wolfhound leapt from the dark with massive mandibles snapping.

"Clara, get down," Georgia hissed.

Clara did not need another warning. She dropped to the ground without hesitation. Georgia jumped ahead, slashing with her blade. No time to think. Act. She felt the power of the weapon in her hand and struck. The spider screamed with an almost human voice and twitched back into the shadows. A mere second later, the thing was at her again. It leapt from the dark, chittering with fury and snapping. Georgia ducked left and brought the blade around again. It sliced clean through one of the mandibles, prompting the spider to hiss and gurgle. The creature withdrew into the gloom.

Behind Georgia, Clara climbed to her feet again. "Sorry, I panicked," the witch whispered.

"It's okay," Georgia answered. "It is still there. The darkness hides it."

"There is more than one," Clara answered.

Some distance away, Mr. Blue called out, "Begone, thing!" The ground shuddered with a low explosion.

"There's more than one," Georgia said. "Clara, we need to gather our forces."

To the right, another huge spider appeared from the shadows. It leapt at Clara before Georgia could react. This time, Clara was ready. She slid away as if her feet were not on the ground, almost like an ice skater. The creature missed, chittering, and spun about to give chase, but the witch was moving too fast. When the creature leapt again, she ducked across the street. Georgia brought her blade down on the second spider's hind quarter. She ripped through the back half of the beast, and it screamed the same eerie wail as its mate had. Then it slumped as noxious green fluids poured from its severed back to sear the ground.

The odor almost undid Georgia's stomach. Somewhere in the distance, she heard muskets firing and men screaming. She heard someone cry out, "they are everywhere!"

Georgia sensed what would happen next. The original giant spider was sneaking up behind. She spun about just in time to ram her blade through its head. With a sickening gurgle, it went limp. Black blood pumped from the thing, staining the street. Around them, the darkness lessened. In the distance, Georgia could see four lanterns, along with a faint blue flame, which had to be Mr. Blue's wizardly walking stick.

"Clara, follow me," Georgia said. The witch fell in as she went down the lane. Patches of darkness were everywhere, but she could see between them. Another spider emerged. Clara screamed, but Georgia swept the blade around. The creature wailed and fell back. They ran, watching as the blue light flickered ahead. More muskets fired. A bullet passed Georgia's ear.

They passed through dark fog to find Mr. Blue and Chief Inspector Morris. Mr. Blue was gasping. His neck was covered in blood. Three constables with muskets gathered to form a circle. Nearby, inky smoke rolled off the burning corpse of a huge spider. When Georgia stepped from the shadow, the constables all spun and aimed. "Hold your fire, boys," Chief Inspector Morris cried. "Do you not see the Duchess?" Georgia did not blame the men. She could see the wild fear in their eyes.

Somewhere in the darkness, another woman screamed. "The creatures are going into homes," Lady Clara cried, as the blackness began to swirl around them.

"We need light. These creatures live in darkness," Mr. Blue said with a grunt. Georgia could see he was in pain. The blood on his neck was his own.

"You are injured, Mr. Blue," she said.

"One of the spiders caught him by the neck," Chief Inspector Morris said. "He fought it off, though."

"I will survive." With effort, the wizard swung his walking stick. Blue flames swirled in the air above his head, but it was not enough to pierce the darkness. He looked at Lady Clara. "Can you help us, Witch of Volusia?"

Lady Clara stared at the darkness. "I might be able to do something, but we are not technically in Volusia. I am somewhat limited."

"My lady," Mr. Blue said, "on your worst day, you are more powerful than any wizard or sorcerer."

"Kind of you to say that Mr. Blue. Perhaps I can be of use if I get some help from my sisters." She was breathing hard with fear. Georgia almost hugged her but held back. Clara gazed at the swirling shadows, then closed her eyes. More screams in the dark. The air grew ever more still around the witch.

Behind Mr. Blue, another huge spider appeared. He spun and struck it with his stick. Flames burned the thing's eyes, and it shrieked into the murk. The wizard was gasping. Georgia was about to go to him, but he shook his head. "I am alright, Georgia. Stay on guard."

Lady Clara stood very still and concentrated. She began to whisper. "Grey Lady, help me. Sisters of Findor and Palas, I need you. Lend me your power." Georgia felt something behind and whirled just in time to avoid massive mandibles dripping with acidic goo. She slashed and stabbed the great spider, driving it backward. Another spider appeared next to it, snapping at her. From behind, she heard one of the constables cry out.

Lady Clara looked up as if startled. All sound seemed to compress around her, and the world was muted for a moment. She raised her arms as argent light shimmered along her fingers.

The Witch spoke in a language older than any Georgia had ever heard. "*Naneyo Volusia. Tua na nin híril a galador. Lenda nina cín rod plural rodyna Palas a Findor. Hírilena mína baurshín aid.*"

A moment passed in utter silence. Clara began to glow as the light spread from her fingers. Pressure built in the air and moved outward. She threw her head back and white light exploded. All around, giant spiders were revealed. Screaming, the monsters fled. Clara swayed on her feet, but when Georgia turned to her, she nodded and smiled.

"Well done, Clara," Mr. Blue said, leaning heavily on his walking stick. "You spoke the ancient tongue of the Fay. The spiders are running away from the light. While we have the advantage, we need to figure out where they are coming from."

"They came out of a hole in the ground," one of the constables reported. "I was with Kerley, and we saw it.

The street opened, and they were all over us. Kerley did not make it."

"I am sorry, Cooper. I know you and Kerley started out in the constabulary together," Chief Inspector Morris said. "Where did you see the hole?"

Constable Cooper led them along the boulevard, wary in case the spiders returned. He took them to a pile of trash on a side street. "The hole is under there."

Mr. Blue and the constables kicked the garbage away to find a foot-wide crack in the pavement. Georgia leaned over it to shine the light from her sword and lantern down. The opening was barely wide enough for a child to get through. Of course, spiders were known for fitting through cracks. "Where does this lead, do you think?"

"Deep below the city. Well beyond any tunnel built in centuries," Clara answered. "I sense a long tunnel into darkness. Into another world. We must seal this. I do not know how else to keep these things from crawling up."

"Perhaps the city can fill it with mortar?" Mr. Blue asked.

"That does not seem like a long-term solution, Mr. Blue," Chief Inspector Morris muttered.

"I agree," Mr. Blue conceded. "But we cannot go crawling down there. Even if we could fit, we would be subject to constant attack by those spiders." He looked pale. Georgia could see he was barely on his feet.

"Very well," Morris said. "I will get the city to fill the crack."

"There could be more of them," Lady Clara said. "We need to figure out what prompted them to come here."

"Yes, of course, I was going to…uh," Mr. Blue started to say. He looked like he might say more, but instead his eyes rolled back, and he collapsed.

\*\*\*

At first look, parquet floors seem like a good idea. But then a piece breaks loose and the whole thing starts to fall apart. Georgia stared at the little cracks in the flooring of the old sitting room in the Order of the Blue chapter house. This was an incredibly old floor. There were spots of discoloration, along with tiny cracks and breaks. Some had a bit of black grit worn in over the years. Others were white with time and traffic. But each break was lovingly patched back together. She had been there for hours by then, waiting for news. Parquet. She remembered something from school. Small blocks built in opposing positions layered together could form a formidable barrier with the aid of gravity. Did that apply to laying them flat?

After Mr. Blue collapsed, Lady Clara took him to his order, and tended to his health. Georgia knew he could be in no better healing hands than Lady Clara's.

For her part, Georgia went with the Chief Inspector to instruct the city work crew. They had to block up the hole to giant spider land. She didn't know much but was sure Mr. Blue would want it managed before she checked on him. When the city crew was done, she went to the Order to check on her friend. That was 4 hours ago. The sun was up. It did not matter. Georgia slept out of habit or from emotion. She could go for weeks without rest. Such was her family gift. She was a bit hungry but could wait.

Lady Clara walked in. "Georgia," she said, looking tired. "I need to put my feet on that hassock. My heel is killing me. It is the boots. You will not tell anyone will you?"

"Sit," Georgia instructed. "Rest a moment, dear friend."

Clara threw herself onto the couch, unlaced her rather fetching leather boots, and stuck her feet up.

"Allow me to show you a little trick," Georgia said after a moment, slipping her boots off. She led Clara to the thickest plush rug in the middle of the room and rolled her toes against the ground. Clara followed suit, producing a rather satisfying crack.

"Oh, my heavens. You could bring peace to the Empire of Rhyn with that trick," the Witch whispered. "Georgia, where did you learn this?"

"The Cymbre School in my youth. There were days we had to stand for hours in the worst shoes," Georgia said, pointing for Clara to sit. Once she was comfortable, Georgia took hold of her heel and massaged just below the tendon. It was tight. Clara might be the Witch of Volusia, but this was proof of her humanity. She flinched, but still relaxed.

"Mother of pearl," Clara said. "How strong are you?"

"No one knows," Georgia answered with a grin. "How does your foot feel?"

"Much better. Thank you. I cannot repay you for this."

"My pleasure. You may recall you sang me out of a coma, a few months ago. I think I still have some work to balance that debt, my friend. How is Mr. Blue?"

"He is a wizard, so he will recover," Clara said, wiggling her toes. "There was poison in the mandible of the giant spider. For a moment, I worried he would succumb, but he is already on his feet. Of course, he will need to rest for the next week or so. I made a poultice to help him eject the toxin, but it will be up to him to take it. You know how men are. He may insist on suffering."

"I see," Georgia said, shaking. "I didn't want to panic."

"I know, dear," Clara said, looking at her. "You were remarkably quiet in here."

"There were others wounded," Georgia said.

"Yes, five constables and at least three local residents," Clara answered. "I have been with them for most of this time. Each suffers from spider poison. Two of them may not live past the day. They do not have a wizard's constitution, sadly. The other six will recover, I think."

Georgia nodded. She was so worried about Mr. Blue she almost forgot everyone else. Her face felt flush for a moment. Clara put a hand on her arm in a reassuring way and smiled, then pulled her boots back on. "Thank you so much for this and let us head upstairs. Now the danger is past, you should see him. Also, if you want to see the others…"

"Yes, to all of it," Georgia said, standing up. "If I can do anything. Boost anyone's spirits… I would like that."

Across the hall, they found Mr. Blue in a long medical gallery. Nurses bustled around beds at the other end of the room. It was like a hospital. The wizard looked tired and pale. His neck was wrapped in white gauze with an alarming blood stain. Georgia felt dizzy for a moment.

"You should be in bed," Lady Clara admonished. "Mr. Blue, you are still weak from the poison."

Mr. Blue shook his head. "I am about to rest, Clara. I promise. I wanted to wait until you and Georgia were here so we could talk. There are a few points to discuss."

"Very well," the Witch of Volusia answered. "After that, you must lie down."

"How did the cleanup go?" Mr. Blue asked Georgia.

"The city is filling the hole. Lord-Mayor Wyssop sent out teams to find if there are any other streets or neighborhoods affected the same way," Georgia said. "Chief Inspector Morris said it was not likely happening anywhere else. They would surely have gotten word, but agreed it was a good idea."

"Good," Mr. Blue said. "Those creatures were coming up on that street for months. I do not understand why people did not report it sooner."

"The capital is a busy place," Lady Clara said. "There is no other city quite this size, Mr. Blue. I think most people thought someone else was already reporting it. Or perhaps not. Either way, it is sad news."

"What were those creatures?" Georgia asked. "I mean, they were spiders, obviously… but like nothing I have ever seen."

"Children of the Flingan," Clara whispered. "Dark remnants of ancient powers long-gone. Some call them shadows now. The source of the evil died ages before the

Three Realms existed, but these monsters return from time to time, even in the modern era."

"They are an echo of something far older and rottener, it is true," Mr. Blue answered. "But I begin to wonder… is the original evil truly dead? Only months ago, we saw the return of the Winter Witch. What if there is more at work here? Why did they dig their way to the corner of Hornbeam and Knox of all places? It can hardly be described as anywhere important."

"That is merely where they reached the open air? So many questions," Clara said. "You think this is an ill of greater meaning spreading across the land? I will admit, I can feel Volusia, even from here. The fields are growing cold with the coming winter. But I sense no great evil growing there, only the change of season."

Mr. Blue nodded. "It is simply that. Clara, you know the significance of the date, though. What if there is more to this?"

"Today is October 15th," Georgia said. "What does that mean?"

"We are a couple of weeks from the start of a new millennium, according to an ancient calendar no one still follows," Clara said, touching Georgia's arm. "Based on some very old stories, this is when dark forces might stir and return."

"You're talking about the *Midnight King* children's books," Georgia said. "I remember. They were all about dates and they always went back to October."

"Yes, and as I mentioned before, those fairy tales were only part fiction," Mr. Blue said. "Is it a coincidence these creatures erupt from the earth so near the anniversary?"

Georgia smirked. "That is a trick question. We all know wizards abhor coincidence."

Mr. Blue smiled back. "Now we must make decisions. These spider creatures could be a lone incident, never to repeat. They might also be a sign of things to come. Clara and I must investigate."

"Very well," Georgia answered. "First, tell me about this new millennium of darkness or whatever name it goes by."

"There is an obscure text called *The Lungimiranza*. It is a prophecy of sorts. The Royal Library has a copy in the vault. The public cannot view it, as the document is more than five thousand years old; the library keeps it under glass, and one must have credentials to read it. The ancient folk of Gilder predicted the *Secolo del male* or *The Century of Evil* as we would say in the modern tongue," Clara said. "They spoke of five thousand years of peace, followed by a time when the celestial guardians would change. Sort of a shift change if you will. During that change, the world would be vulnerable. They could not predict what would happen."

"Shift change?"

Clara shrugged. "Perhaps not the best metaphor. Five thousand years ago, when the Midnight King was struck down by the free peoples, the remaining Fay Lords set a guard in a great tower to watch the world. We have come to the end of the time of the first guard. The next one will take his or her place eventually. Until then, the world is in a type of jeopardy."

"Why not plan ahead for this?" Georgia asked. "I mean, if they knew it was a five-thousand-year long shift, why is the next guard not ready to go? They had more than enough notice, surely."

"Five thousand years is a long time, even for the immortal Fay Lords," Mr. Blue said. "I would not be surprised if the next guard was not selected beforehand. The 'Century of Evil' may be a metaphor for the time when the next guard is selected. If there is a true Fay Lord left alive, they will seek a new guardian from the others who still live."

"Assuming, of course, the prophecy is legitimate," Lady Clara interjected. "It could be a legend with the original meaning or intent lost after all these millennia. We could be seeing dark shadow spiders because some sorcerer with the power to conjure beasts from the void wants it to happen. There could be players involved who want chaos to come so they can claim power for themselves."

"I see. It could be a product of the usual rubbish: folk seeking power and distracting us while they obtain it," Georgia said. "How do we proceed?"

"We keep our eyes sharp," Mr. Blue said. "One sign of the old prophecy is the tiny creatures of the world becoming large and terrible. Spiders today, perhaps mosquitoes tomorrow."

"Evil cannot create its own servants," Clara whispered. "Evil can only corrupt what is. There may still be spirits out there hoping to return to the living world. If the prophecy is true, those spirits... ones like the Winter Witch... will be emboldened and they will corrupt the natural world."

\*\*\*

When Georgia got home, Mr. Derry, her inscrutable butler, waited at the door. Despite being at least 80 years old, the man would have stood all night waiting for her to come back, and she knew it. Guilt clung to her as she entered the house. "My lady," Derry said with a bow.

"Welcome home." She could see he was tired. Behind him, Jasper the footman looked concerned.

"Thank you, Mr. Derry. Did you sleep last night?" She waved Jasper away with a quick gesture.

"Would you like something to eat, Duchess?" Mr. Derry asked, ignoring the question. "I can get you a bowl of lovely turkey soup and warm bread if you like. Mrs. Cotton outdid herself with it. The carrots in the soup are particularly delightful, and it will make you feel warm and drowsy. The bread is baked in garlic and rosemary, and still soft with just a slight crunch. I will roast it myself to make sure."

"That sounds nice," she answered. "Bring it to the library, please? I'll have a cup of the raspberry spice tea if it's not too much trouble."

"Of course, my lady."

"And then you take the rest of the day off, Mr. Derry."

"Yes, my lady. I wanted to make sure you were home before I went up." Mr. Derry was from the old school; a servant's servant who would never abandon her, and always anticipate her needs as the mistress. She watched him walk to the stairs, where Jasper helped him down.

Georgia went into the library. Her lady's maid, Millie, appeared at the door. "May I assist, my lady?" she asked.

"Thank you," Georgia answered. Millie helped her pull the scabbard off, and then got her out of her coat. Georgia stretched her arms and carried the sword over to its mount above the fireplace mantle.

"Millie, how do you do it?" Georgia asked.

"I beg your pardon, my lady?" Millie smiled.

"You look refreshed and alert at all hours," Georgia said. "I wonder if you can share your secret."

Millie shrugged. "Drink at least eight glasses of water every day, my lady. Wash your face with somewhat hot water before you sleep."

"Perfect," Georgia said with a gentle smile. "No advice on food, Millie?"

Millie laughed. "You always get a little rosy in the cheeks when you eat apples, my lady. It is a good look. Did Mr. Derry tell you about the soup? Somehow, Mrs. Cotton managed to keep the carrots slightly crunchy and sweet, even with the broth."

CHAPTER 2

# AN INCIDENT BOTH
# INCITING AND INSISTENT.

As the royal palace loomed into view, Georgia took a breath to calm her nerves. Millie peeked back from the front-board of the carriage. "I am alright," Georgia said, feigning confidence with a smile.

"You look wonderful, my lady," Millie said.

"Thank you, Millie." Sweet girl. Millie was actually a few years older than Georgia, but somehow, she always seemed younger.

Georgia could hear her own pulse. "You fought blood zombies and a winter witch," she whispered to herself, "they say you saved the Three Realms before anyone knew it was in danger. Journalists, artists, and writers follow you from party to party. You hail from a line of heroes dating back more than five thousand years. Who else in the Three Realms is a duchess with a magic sword?"

The magic sword hummed.

Georgia looked outside as the last lane to the palace ended. She could see the Queen's guards in their bright blue livery. No other royal guards were in attendance, which meant the Queen would be the main host. A queue of carriages blocked the way. The sword sang, asking for her state of mind. "I am all right," she whispered. "I mean, I think I am."

The sword laughed. Thousands of years of experience laughed with it. "Know yourself," it whispered in the tone of shimmering bells. "You can be frightened. You are still a young girl."

"No," Georgia answered. "I cannot be afraid."

"Sometimes life is surprising. Sometimes life is scary. There is so much to come. You still have time to make choices and mistakes. At your age, temptation and reward are everywhere in equal measure. You cannot control everything."

"I can control myself."

"Sometimes life is better without being in total control."

"Maybe," Georgia admitted. "You're starting to sound like Mr. Blue, sword."

"Apologies." The sword hummed.

"I do not think you are sorry," Georgia chided.

The sword chuckled.

The carriage stopped near the front doors to the palace. There were two other carriages ahead. Georgia waited her turn. She could have stepped out and walked, but that was not how it was done. She glanced at the invitation folded in her hands. It read:

*Her Royal Grace Queen Frederica Hart*
*Consort and Regent to his Royal Majesty King Robert Hart*
*Lord of the Three Realms of Findor, Volusia, and Palas*
*Grand Duke of Hildor and the Outer Marches*
*Requests the pleasure of your company.*

*Lady Georgia Goldenheart*
*Duchess of the House of Goldenheart*
*Knight-Protector of the Three Realms from Dragons*
*This invitation is for your Formal Presentation*
*to Court as a Lady of the Court.*
*We look forward to your attendance.*
*On October 17 at 6 pm*
*At the Royal Palace in Oradale City*

*A selection of known friends and associates have been invited, on your behalf, to attend.*

The carriage door opened, and cold autumn air poured in. Georgia let the air brush her face. A footman offered his hand. She enjoyed the sudden cold, but noticed the fellow was shivering. Georgia took his hand, even though she needed no help. She set her foot on the royal cobblestones and walked up the long row of steps to the palace. It was misty in the courtyard, but her eyes were sharper than the average person's. Georgia might be in turmoil, but her Cymbre training kicked in: always appearing serene and unaffected.

Millie fell in behind. In a lesser house, Millie would be directed to a side door or sent to a servant entrance in the back. Not in a palace like this where a host of guests might enter at once through the front. Ironic. All people, no matter their rank, set foot on the king's front step as equals… if only for a moment during the hike. Millie followed her mistress inside, and then down to the lobby past statues of the kings of old carved in the ancient black stone imported from the Far West. They crossed to a wide gallery of couches and tables. At one end was a massive fireplace carved to look like two gigantic stags rearing up with the hearth between. The Hart family, rulers of the Three Realms for more than three thousand years, kept the branches of the ancient forest on all the walls. In other realms, the people revered predators like kestrels, wolves, and lions. This was not the case in the Three Realms. The stag was fleet of foot, wise of eye, and always part of the greater whole where safety and security mattered most. Since the ancient days, balance and regard for the bigger world was most important. This was why three tiny and sometimes disparate realms held their own amidst the many great powers of the world: they stood together.

Millie helped Georgia out of her bonnet and checked her hair. There was no side room. Other ladies of note were with their maids right there. "Do we need to sit and correct?" Georgia asked. Millie shook her head.

"Hair is splendid and settled nicely on top," Millie whispered, fluffing a lock or two. Georgia checked the mirror. Her hair was coiled entirely up top. Millie fiddled with Georgia's modest tiara, a delicate silver hoop with an emerald mounted on top. Millie moved from there, checking the rest of the ensemble. Set in laurel green silk, Georgia's gown was high-waisted, in the style of the day. But instead of an open low neckline, Millie constructed a long, closed neck which split into four pointed white collars. The effect was akin to a flower framing her face. It was completely different from the modern trend. From there, Millie straightened Georgia's train of pale laurel green gauze. The magic sword was affixed to Georgia's back like an embellishment.

"You look perfect, my lady." Millie took Georgia's outer cloak, straightened her sword and scabbard, and inspected her once more before nodding her approval. Millie went to wait at the wall with the other maids. The footman guided Georgia to a gallery full of people. At the doorway, he announced, "Duchess Goldenheart of the House Goldenheart, Knight-Protector of the Three

Realms from Dragons. Hero of the Day against the evil winter witch."

At the door to the chamber stood the wizard Mr. Blue and Lady Clara Gaye, the Witch of Volusia. On a normal day, he would be clad in an odd blend of blue coat, vest, and pants. This day Mr. Blue was formal in a white tie and tails, with a bright blue sapphire on his lapel. As usual, his smile was broad and easy, and of course he held his walking stick. He was also recovered from the spider poison, apparently. Georgia could see no sign of fatigue or weakness on his face, even though it was only 48 hours since the attack.

Lady Clara Gaye was, as always, the height of elegance. She always wore all black and continued the trend with a sleek high-waisted silk gown trailing a foot behind on the floor. There were no frills or bows on her garment. It was all smooth with a square cut neckline. Her bright red hair coiled down from the shoulder. She wore only one piece of jewelry, a silver locket with an owl inscribed on the front. Despite the simplicity of her outfit, she was more glamorous than half the women in the room. As always with Lady Clara, less was more.

The sword on Georgia's back sang a happy tune the moment the wizard and witch appeared. "Hello, both of you," Georgia said, grinning. "Welcome to my entrance into proper society. Mr. Blue, I am so glad to see you in good health again."

Mr. Blue smiled. "Thank you. I too am glad to be healthy. Welcome, Duchess Goldenheart. The time has come to take your place in society, despite the fact you have been here all along."

"Long may you destroy everyone's preconceived notions," Lady Clara said. Mr. Blue laughed.

"If I haven't said it before," Georgia said, "thank you both for everything you have done. Upon reflection, I do not know how I survived last year, but I think you both had everything to do with my success."

"Oh, I think you would have found a way. But thank you. Let us hope we can do more," Mr. Blue said. "It looks like we are not your only admirers today."

Georgia's old friend, Lady Beatrice 'Bea' Irvingdale came over. "Georgia," she called out. Now that she was engaged to a Volusian Viscount, Bea was always dressed in black. It was Volusian custom to dress like a widow for the life of innocence before marriage and understanding. Behind Bea stood a small sea of ladies all dressed in hues of pale green and gold, the current colors of the late season. The wizard and witch stepped aside.

"Bea," Georgia said, "You came. Oh, I am so glad."

"Of course, I did," Bea said. "I brought Mum. The season may be over, but you are being presented." The proper way to present any Lady at court is by her mother, but Georgia's mother died when she was only 4 years old.

She was raised as a ward of her Uncle Raymond Goldenheart in the Cymbre schools. During that time, she spent holidays with the Irvingdales while Uncle Raymond was away on state business. If she were to select anyone as a substitute mother, she would choose Lady Breanna Irvingdale.

Behind Bea stood her mother. Breanna looked moderately healthy. Only two months before, she needed a cane to walk. Now she stood on her feet once more. "Lady Breanna, you are improving every day," Georgia said. "Is this all about the new diet?"

"It would appear so, Georgia," Bea's mother said, stepping from foot to foot as if doing a little dance. "We will not be so quick to brand Doctor Vestus a quack. He suggested I drink more water, less wine, and eat less beef. I have eaten my share of chicken this year, I must admit. That said, the swelling in my knees and feet is gone."

Georgia smiled. "When you fully recover, I will be happy to take my skepticism back. Oh, Bea, thank you for doing this. Lady Breanna, thank you so much for representing me. I am so honored to have you attend my formal entrance." Never mind Georgia spent the last year at every great party and gala of the season. Today was 'official.'

"Thank you, Georgia. I feel the same," Lady Breanna said. Her eyes twinkled and only teared up for a second.

"Now, I must tell you, there is potential in this affair for both family drama and perhaps an evolution."

"Do not tell me the Irvingdales have a new drama," Georgia said. "Has Lord Wickham done something outrageous?" Bea's brother-in-law, Lord Wickham, was not one of Georgia's favorites.

"Not Wickham," Bea whispered. "This is entirely of interest to you. You see, your kinsman from your mother's family, Sir Roger Whitestone, is just across the room. The Queen asked him to attend your formal entrance into society."

"Sir Roger Whitestone, heir to the Earl of Westfall?" Georgia asked. "I have not met him. Uncle Raymond had a falling-out with the Whitestones. They never spoke to me."

"Nevertheless, he answered the call of the Queen," Lady Breanna said, glancing past Georgia's shoulder. "And now we are clear of the doorway, he will come over."

Across the gallery, a middle-aged man in white tie and tails stood out. Sir Roger Whitestone was tall and hale with silver hair. He had the wind-burned face of one who lived in the western mountains where winter held for 9 months of the year. At the same time, he looked healthy. Happy. Georgia's mother had the same color hair. Even though Georgia was only four when her parents died, she could still remember her mother's hair. Most Findorians were black-haired like Georgia, but the Whitestones sometimes went another way. She remembered her mother's face and the faint pinkness of her cheeks. Her mother was from the mountains too. Uncle Raymond once told her pink cheeks and silver hair came from the unrelenting winter wind. Sir Roger was surrounded by folk in expensive finery, but there could be no doubt he was the most important person in the room. When Georgia turned, one of the people in his entourage tapped him on the shoulder. Sir Roger met her eye and approached without ceremony. "Duchess Goldenheart," he said with a nod.

"Sir Roger Whitestone," Georgia answered, also nodding her head. She made sure not to dip or curtsey, but also not be too brief in the head movement. Instead, she smiled and then looked down. The gesture showed deference without complicating the murky difference in their ranks. Georgia was technically a higher level of nobility, but Sir Roger was heir to the largest earldom in the Realm of Findor. He was also older, a man, and family.

When she looked up, Sir Roger was grinning. "My lady, you are as charming and glamorous as the papers report, and I can easily imagine you battling a pack of giant spider monsters. I hope you do not mind, but I look at this gown and all I can think of is you are the most elegant flower. At the same time, you wear the magic sword on your back like one of the heathen queens of old, right here in court." She had never met Sir Roger, but Georgia already knew he had a reputation as a flirt.

Georgia smiled back with a touch of frost in her voice. "It is tradition, sir. The Goldenheart must always wear it when appearing at court or any ceremonial function."

Sir Roger adjusted the tone. He was still smiling, but it was somehow less flirtatious. "I heard the same. Seeing it in person on a lady is another matter, I suppose. Forgive me, I speak out of turn. When I was a child, I saw your Uncle Raymond with that blade upon his hip at various ceremonies. My lady, may I ask you a blunt question? How is it that our families are estranged?"

Georgia blinked. "Uh… I do not know, sir. Uncle Raymond never explained what happened. He told me the Whitestones and Goldenhearts were not on speaking terms. I did ask him to elaborate, but he never did. He meant to tell me, but he never got around to it."

"I was a young man when the rift happened, but no one explained it to me, my lady," Sir Roger said.

"So, you do not know what happened, either?"

Sir Roger gazed at her for a moment, and she saw several expressions attempt to form on his face. "No," he said at last with a slow smile. "My father is not always concise or easy to understand. He prides himself on being a man of few words. Alas, that often means even close family find themselves wondering what he is thinking."

"What a night to meet," Georgia said. "And what a shame it has not happened sooner. Sir Roger, are you in town long?"

"Only for the night, I fear," he answered. "We were supposed to leave yesterday, but the Queen had other ideas. Tomorrow, I leave with Prince Eric to attend the Trade Summit in the Kingdom of Kaela. With winter approaching, we expect to be delayed for a few months in that part of the world. I hope to return in the Spring." He had no flirty agenda. In fact, Sir Roger kept looking to one side and the other, as if seeking someone else in the room. Finally, he nodded to a tall dark-haired woman across the room, and discreetly tilted his head when she saw him. She began to make her way across the gallery.

"I see," Georgia said. "When you return, I hope you will contact me."

"Mend the rift between families, I assume," the tall dark-haired woman said. She strolled over, clad in a stunning dark blue satin gown cinched in a toga style at the shoulder with a silver brooch. Her hair was black with streaks of grey, but her eyes had almost no wrinkles. She was in her middle years, but one would not see that at first. She smiled at Georgia. It was the wary smile of a woman whose husband occasionally wandered off the ranch. "Greetings, Duchess Goldenheart, I am Lady Alice Whitestone."

"Married to Sir Roger," Georgia said. She took Lady Alice's hand and gave it a tiny squeeze. "I am so delighted to meet you. I have, of course, seen your name in the Peer Registry, and I am on friendly terms with your sister, Lady Constance Greenheart, the Countess of Grandhall."

Lady Alice was surprised by the squeeze, which is what Georgia intended. She hoped it would impart the right amount of enthusiasm to her new acquaintance.

Fortunately, Lady Alice was all for it.

"Duchess Goldenheart, I cannot express my delight in full measure." Lady Alice squeezed her hand back and laid another on it for emphasis. "You are precisely what they report in the papers, and perhaps more. What a pleasure and an honor to meet you at last. I am so glad we did not leave the city when we heard about the spider monsters."

"The honor is entirely mine," Georgia replied. Suddenly she remembered one of the old etiquette lessons at the Cymbre School and employed it. She looked down at her hand clasping Lady Alice, then up… and then she blinked rapidly and smiled with her teeth. Suddenly she was the younger lady speaking to a regarded aunt or lady of note. Lady Alice almost cried. Well done, Georgia.

"The Queen is about to arrive," Lady Breanna said, breaking in. "We should move into the main gallery, Georgia. You should be first to present yourself. The longer you wait, the longer everyone else will wait."

"Right," Georgia said. She looked at Sir Roger and his wife. "Will you both join me when Lady Breanna presents me? It would be good to have some family there."

Lady Alice nodded with enthusiasm. Sir Roger looked amused. "We would be honored to join you, Duchess."

\*\*\*

Lady Frederica Hart, Queen of the Three Realms, strolled into the main gallery flanked by a dozen ladies-in-waiting. Nobles and courtiers bowed low as she passed. Unlike her husband, King Robert, she was not one for trumpets. Instead, the room went silent as she ascended the second throne. She was in her 50s with the body of a mother but clad in a modern high-waisted white silk gown with bright blue stags embroidered on sleeves and collar. Her salt and pepper hair coiled in a simple knot, and she wore the Queen's Crown designed to look like the branches of the Old Tree and strung with fresh white flowers.

Behind the Queen another woman followed. She was also of middle-age and dressed in white silk, but her gown was tied to the shoulder and gathered in folds at the elbow. Her arms were bare but covered in coiled rings. The fashion was from another realm, although Georgia was not sure where.

Following Georgia's gaze, Bea whispered in her ear. "That is Lady Amaris Bronte, Chief Lady-in-Waiting to the Queen. Amaris is also a bit of a political scientist. She is rumored to be a genius with a mind like a lexicon of familial ties, political alliances, and the ability to predict any consequence. I must admit I admire her. Rumor has it the Queen is also acting Regent since the King has grown ill of mind. Both princes are away and apparently refusing to return. The Queen must rule until one of them comes back. Lady Amaris is her informal chief of staff. Amaris hails from the Queen's homeland of Jendina. In fact, she is her second cousin."

"Interesting," Georgia whispered back. The Queen came to the Three Realms almost 35 years ago and married King Robert. The King was originally betrothed to her older sister, Princess Felicita, but broke the engagement when he met Frederica. The plan was to align the Three Realms with Jendina, eventually merging all of them together. Robert spent a winter in that foreign realm with their royal family. When Spring arrived, he formally rejected the betrothal and ran away with Princess Frederica instead. War nearly broke out. Both families were horrified. Eventually, Princess Felicita, the rejected daughter, made a public statement endorsing her sister's new claim. Despite the scandal, the realms restored their former alliance and grew stronger than ever. At the same time, it was agreed they would not merge. After that, the disgraced Princess Felicita vanished into obscurity. The new Queen-Consort Frederica would go on to establish herself in the Three Realms. She gave the king two sons, an heir, and a spare, followed by two daughters. Both daughters were married off to foreign kings, cementing new alliances. She became the mother of the nation, and over time revered. Eventually she was no longer Queen-Consort, but rather the Queen.

When recent rumors emerged of the king's failing mental health followed by the absence of the princes, Queen Frederica took the reins of the nation alongside Parliament. She might soon be formally titled Queen-Regent, following tradition and law, and maintaining the peace and prosperity of the Three Realms.

Queen Frederica took her place on the throne and activity resumed in the room.

Not wanting to hold everyone up in the queue, Georgia and her entourage approached. She was a duchess, after all. No one would go up until she did. "Please welcome Duchess Goldenheart of the House Goldenheart," the Queen's Valet announced. "She comes to present herself formally to the court and Queen. Her family friend, Lady Breanna Irvingdale, Dowager of the Baronet of Irvingdale, will present her, as her mother has passed. The Duchess is accompanied by her longtime friend, Miss Beatrice Irvingdale, heir to the House of Dale and fiancé to the Viscount of Simsley. In addition, Duchess Goldenheart is accompanied by her kinsman Sir Roger Whitestone and his wife, Lady Alice Whitestone. Behind them you will see Mr. Blue, head of the Order of the Blue. Next to him is Lady Clara Gaye, the Witch of Volusia."

"An impressive collection of friends, and from what I am told a darling of the independent press," the Queen murmured. She spoke with a faint trace of the Jendina accent, which made her voice sound almost sing-song. Georgia curtseyed deep, as one should for a queen. "Welcome, Duchess Goldenheart."

"Thank you for the invitation, Your Royal Highness," Georgia answered. "I am so honored to meet you."

The Queen looked at her Lady-in-Waiting, Lady Amaris. "She is a bit startling, yes? So thin and tall with that sword on her back like a heathen chieftess of old. Her face is quite lovely. Such cheekbones, but so gaunt? I remember her uncle Duke Raymond. He was tall and thin as well."

"It is a Goldenheart trait," Lady Amaris answered. "The family was blessed by the heathen gods of old. They are great heroes, my lady, and none of them fit an expected mold."

"She has a muscle protruding on her arm. I see it through her glove," the Queen said. "How is she so mannish and tall?"

"Part of what makes her a hero," Lady Amaris murmured.

"I beg your pardon?" Georgia said.

"One moment, Duchess," the Queen answered. "We are discussing you."

Oh.

The Queen looked at her lady-in-waiting. "Her family is the one mentioned in the old prophecy, yes? She is necessary to the Three Realms."

"Yes, Your Royal Highness," Mr. Blue said, stepping next to Georgia. "Forgive me for interrupting. The Goldenhearts will always be part of the Three Realms."

"I forgive you, Mr. Blue. My husband is fond of saying that wizards are like rain in the Spring."

Mr. Blue grinned. Georgia looked from one to the other. "Er... what does that mean?"

"Like a storm in the Spring, one can never tell when a wizard will show up and ruin your picnic," Mr. Blue answered. "The King is fond of metaphors."

Queen Frederica smiled, but it was a sad smile. "My husband is not as amusing as he once was."

"I am sorry to hear that, Your Royal Highness."

"Let us not get off the topic at hand." The Queen turned to gaze at Georgia, although she still spoke to the wizard. "Mr. Blue, the Goldenhearts hold a special place in the Three Realms according to the ancient writ. This is what I was also told. But my interpretation might quibble with your own."

"Oh? How so?"

"According to the writings, 'if the Three Realms stand there shall always be a Goldenheart. But only if there is a Goldenheart shall the Three Realms survive'," the Queen said. "I realize this is an old translation, but it seems clear enough."

Mr. Blue blinked. "How so?"

"Her existence is intertwined with the kingdom in some ancient and supernatural way. Does this not worry you?"

"Well, 'worry' is not the word I would choose," the wizard said with care.

"You are not worried that the entire kingdom's existence depends on the health of a girl not yet 20 years old, Mr. Blue?"

"When you put it that way—" he began to say.

"You took this girl, a mere 19-year-old, up into Volusia last Spring to fight the Winter Witch, did you not?"

"Well, yes, my Queen."

"Even though, as the last Goldenheart, imperiling her very existence might also imperil the fate of the Three Realms?" The Queen looked serious. "Mr. Blue, what were you thinking?"

"My Queen, this is what the Goldenhearts do.We needed to find the Winter Witch before she could complete her evil plot. She would have unleashed an army of blood zombies or worse upon the Three Realms if given time. Fortunately, Georgia was there to stop her," Mr. Blue answered.

"I went on that adventure willingly," Georgia said.

"One moment, Duchess. We are almost done with this," the Queen said in a dismissive tone. She turned back to Mr. Blue, "Would it not be more prudent to find a husband for this one last Goldenheart? We know you have long been a good and faithful counselor to the Crown, but we have been deep in thought, Mr. Blue. Duchess Goldenheart should reserve herself, if only for a time, for the expansion of her line. The Realms are at stake here in an existential way. If something should happen to her, would we not be on the outside of the Prophecy?"

Mr. Blue nodded. "It is possible, yes, but when I took Duchess Goldenheart into the north to find the Winter Witch, I had faith she would survive and be successful. To that end, I was right. She fulfilled her duty and saved us from the darkness before anyone knew it was there."

"Yes, it all worked out," the Queen answered, "but you could not have been sure it would. What if the Winter Witch had killed her?"

"There is precedent for her line surviving. The Goldenhearts have appeared to end before, only to restart with another heir."

Georgia wasn't sure if she should speak up for herself again. She was about to say something when Lady Clara caught her eye with a nearly imperceptible headshake. Frustrated, Georgia kept silent.

The Queen continued, as if Mr. Blue had not spoken. "After some thought, we have a solution to the problem."

"The problem?" Mr. Blue asked.

"Yes, Mr. Blue, there is a problem. We explained it to you only a moment ago. According to the law, Duchess Goldenheart is in an unusual situation. In fact, while being a product of tradition, she seems to defy all semblance of it. She holds her family title but cannot give it to the man she marries. That said, she is the last of her line. The ancient law says there will always be a Goldenheart. Even with the precedent of lost Goldenhearts being found, the act of voluntarily placing her in jeopardy seems most unwise. She must find a husband who is of a suitable family but willing to take the role of her mate and consort. He must be someone worthy of the only living virtual duchess, but also able to withstand the burden of being her lesser," The Queen answered. "To that end, we will personally take an interest in this affair. We offer the services of Lady Amaris and the full authority of the Crown to help Duchess Goldenheart procure a husband. By the next season, we expect to see a happy outcome. The Duchess will be married… or at the very least engaged… to someone suitable. Not long after that, we expect her to increase her line of heirs. Once that is accomplished with both her family name and the Three Realms are secure, she will be free to engage in your heroic endeavors, Mr. Blue. In the meantime, she is not to be put in harm's way. The very existence of the Three Realms depends on this outcome. The Duchess must be preserved until such time as she has legitimate heirs to take her place. Are we clear on this?"

"Yes, Your Royal Highness," Mr. Blue said with a bow. "We are clear. Although, I should tell you, the Duchess is currently involved in an investigation. In fact, she is integral to it."

Lady Amaris leaned over and whispered in the Queen's ear. "The disappearances in the North Canal Ward and the supernatural sightings in Hixby Ward."

"I see," the Queen murmured as Amaris continued to whisper. She looked back at Mr. Blue. "Yes, we agree this is an important investigation. Do you have the full support of the constabulary?"

"Yes, Your Royal Highness," Mr. Blue answered. "The city has committed all resources to assist."

"When are you expected to complete this investigation?"

"I wish I could predict it," Mr. Blue admitted. "As you know, last night we encountered an outbreak of Flingan Shadow Spiders. I am unsure how to describe them."

"I read the constable's report on the creatures," Lady Amaris said to the Queen. "Whatever is afoot, these are creatures of another era. A remnant of ancient evil. It is very serious, Your Royal Highness. We cannot afford to ignore the risk."

"Very well, you may continue to employ the Duchess in your investigation. But be careful, Mr. Blue. We cannot… I cannot stress enough my concern," the Queen answered. She turned to Georgia. "Good luck to you. Upon completion of your current mission, Duchess, I would ask you to set the sword aside and work on finding a husband. Until then, you have my leave to continue assisting against this remnant of ancient evil."

"Yes, Your Royal Highness," Georgia said with a curtsey.

∗∗∗

"Georgia, I have complete faith in you," Mr. Blue said as they walked away from the Queen. He looked put-out and a bit defensive. "Whatever part you have to play in this investigation, I know it is necessary."

"The Queen rattled you, did she?" Georgia asked.

"The Queen has been rattling me for the better part of a decade, ever since I took over as head of the Order of the Blue. I will recover from it," Mr. Blue answered with a wink. "Even so, there are those who believe she is little more than a brood mare for the king… a silly woman with far-fetched ideas, but I disagree. Queen Frederica is both a shrewd strategist and her fears are not unfounded. Last time the Goldenhearts died off, it took a decade before they found someone of the bloodline. During that time, the kingdom nearly plunged into civil war."

"In that case, let us honor her wishes and be especially careful about my own life," Georgia said, touching his arm.

"Duchess, may I speak with you?" Lady Amaris strolled up with a smile. After her formal introduction, Georgia and her entourage found their way to another part of the chamber to enjoy drinks and prepare for dinner. The Lady-in-Waiting was already upon her.

"Of course," Georgia answered. She looked at her companions and nodded, allowing them to go off and enjoy the evening.

"I thought we might compare schedules and devise plans," Lady Amaris said, looking efficient. "If I am to help you find a suitable husband, I will need your assistance, Duchess."

"What constitutes suitable?" Georgia muttered. "Based on the Queen's description, I suspect we will be searching until I am an old maid."

"This is my question as well," the lady responded. "My lady, this need not be unpleasant. I would prefer to help you find a man both suitable and agreeable to yourself. The Queen granted ample time to succeed. In her youth, she found a gentleman who was most agreeable you may recall. By coincidence, he turned out to be a prince. She married for love and would not bar you from such a life, provided we are not required to send you to a foreign realm. Obviously, this must be a marriage where you are allowed to live your life in the Three Realms. If you put your mind to this, I believe we can find someone you will come to appreciate. I believe we can find someone who is also useful to your family and any ambition you might have. The key is clarity of thought. This could be a bit like one of the investigations you have taken part in… except, we are not seeking a murderer so much as a partner."

"When you put it that way, it sounds much more appealing," Georgia admitted. Granted, it was never good to say 'murderer' and 'partner' in the same sentence, but she understood the intent. "I am sorry if I sound upset.

The Queen called me 'mannish' and implied I was... er... unpleasant to behold before she took Mr. Blue to task."

"The Queen was raised in a different generation and a different nation, Duchess," Lady Amaris answered. "She is not aware in full measure how you are seen by the public. In her day, a woman with a defined jawline was considered a sign of abject poverty or impending mortality. In her day, women of status were soft and often spoke of the weather in hushed tones. They did not run around with magic swords protecting the innocent from ancient dark powers. She would be the first to admit this. She was raised in a time when ladies of rank were in the background."

"She made her own way," Georgia said. "I find her inspiring."

"I do, too," Lady Amaris admitted, "but I am not attached to such outdated notions about ladies and the court.. Personally, I think you are stunning. You are not mannish. You look healthy to me, and it would be my privilege to help find a husband worthy of you." As Lady Amaris spoke, she had a fire in her eye. "Together, I think we can find a husband who would appreciate you for *everything* you are. I believe this firmly."

Georgia blushed. "Thank you, Lady Amaris. Though, I think we should seek a pleasant fellow who likes to garden and does not want to be anything more than the next Count Goldenheart and who may, on occasion, need to organize a dinner party. That might be all we can expect. I realize I cannot ask for some sort of warlord or hero of myth. Our roles are in reverse. It must be a fellow with sense who can live well in the space granted to him."

Lady Amaris's eyes narrowed. "If we found you a hero, what would that look like?"

"He would run alongside me, I suppose," Georgia admitted.

"Hm," Lady Amaris mused. "We may fall short of that goal, but I will aim for someone you like and who will respect you. In the meantime, I will send letters to all the great houses—Vexbury, Grandhall, Elton, and Cadwin asking them to recommend worthy sons. I will also reach out to the realms of Jendina, Kaela, Ubania, and Phaedros. It may be that a foreign lord's son will work where one of the locals will not. We will find someone, Duchess."

"I see," Georgia said. The prospect of reaching across the entire continent was a bit daunting.

"Will you be staying in the capital over the next month?" Lady Amaris asked. "If I make arrangements for interviews, will you be available?"

"As Mr. Blue mentioned, we are working on the investigation. If we turn nothing more up this week, we will set it aside until there are either other clues or another incident. In a week, I will be going to a baby shower in

Findor," Georgia answered. "It is in the country. I will be back in Oradale in a few weeks."

"Perfect," the Lady-in-Waiting said. "Enough time to send and receive the letters. I will contact you in about one month with news of what I have learned from the great houses. If our man is out there, we will find him."

# CHAPTER 3

# THE ONLY ROAD.

"We made a mistake," Bea said, her golden ringlets bouncing frantically. The coach hit another dip in the path, and she lost a handful of monogrammed wedding envelopes. "Are we even on a road? You know those clouds are following us, right? Why am I trying to write invitations in the carriage? Why did we not wait until tomorrow to make the trip?" Shaking her head, she gathered the papers from the floor of the cab.

"It is the only road to our destination," Georgia answered, glancing out the window. Towering pitch-black storm clouds rolled across the sky. Directly above, a gigantic thunderhead brimmed with barely contained fury. "They do not look too bad," she lied, closing the window in haste. "It is but a whiff of cumulus. As for why we are going today, Harriet's baby shower is in less than a week, and everyone else is there for the early parties. Even Lady Rebecca Drake arrived last week to tour the local attractions. We will appear rude if we wait any longer. Yes,

I realize there is a shadow spider monster problem in the capital, and I should be there, but Mr. Blue and Lady Clara have the situation in hand. They promised to send word if they need me back. Finally, you put off sending those invitations out for days. People are starting to talk." The windows flared brilliant white as lightning struck nearby, followed by a prolonged boom of thunder, as the coach almost keeled over by the force of it. Nearly deaf, Georgia stared at a tree erupting in flaming chunks.

"Wait. People are talking about me?" Bea went rigid, oblivious to the destruction outside. "William only proposed three weeks ago. We must still go through a whole year of engagement, and that is if everyone in each of the families agrees to the plan."

"Is everyone safe back there?" Mr. Reardon, the coach driver, called back from under a flimsy tarp. Crammed in with him were Georgia's lady's maid, Millie, and Bea's dour chaperone, Mrs. Macklin. Millie trembled, either from fear or the cold, and her hair dripped.

"Mr. Reardon, we're fine. Pull over and secure that tarp. While you are at it, send Millie and Mrs. Macklin back to sit with us."

"Very good, Duchess," Mr. Reardon said, looking pleased.

"Mr. Reardon will finally get some peace," Georgia said. "It must be terrible for him to be the only man in a carriage full of women... none of whom he can boss around."

"He is addicted to sour gum and tobacco," Bea countered, shaking her head. "Mrs. Macklin doesn't approve of such things, so he is abstaining. With her in the back, he can finally indulge himself."

"I do not approve, either." Georgia sniffed.

"Will you forbid him?"

"Oh goodness, no," Georgia declined, shaking her head. "Why would I tell anyone how to ruin their health? If it does not bother us back here, and no one of note sees my driver doing it… well, I see no reason to say anything."

They pulled over. Millie and Mrs. Macklin climbed into the cab. "Be careful," Bea said, "You are getting rain all over yourselves. We cannot have you getting sick and catching your death of cold, can we?"

"It's only a bit of water, my lady. It smells nice and feels good on my face," Millie said, smiling. "I don't mind the rain."

"That is what you say now," Bea chided. "You do not know about the terrible tale of Miss Marilyn Quickwood."

Georgia rolled her eyes. "Here we go again."

"What happened to Miss Marilyn Quickwood?" Millie blanched. Mrs. Macklin's expression did not change, but she leaned closer to listen.

Bea jumped right in, "The Quickwoods, once a notable family in south-central Findor, had all sorts of property and great respect. Alas, Mrs. Quickwood must have been a second wife. The first wife had a son, and he inherited their estate."

"What happened to the first Mrs. Quickwood?" Millie wondered.

"I wouldn't know," Bea shot back. "That is really not the point, Millie."

"Sorry, ma'am."

Bea smiled, "No, I am sorry, Millie. The rain makes me jumpy. Where was I? Oh yes. The first Mrs. Quickwood died. I never heard any story of a divorce or scandal. It was all very appropriate, of course. Mr. Quickwood found a second wife and had three beautiful daughters with her: Evelyn, Marilyn, and Martha. Evelyn was the smart one, Marilyn was beautiful, and Martha was probably notable, but for the life of me I cannot remember anything about her. In any case, everything was lovely for a time."

"Oh, that's not so bad," Millie said.

"It was fine... until he died," Bea said grimly. "He passed at the age of 90 in his bed with his family all around."

"It sounds like Mr. Quickwood had a fine life," Georgia said, smiling despite herself. This tale of woes had been around for a while, and this was not the first occasion she heard Bea tell it. The real question: how would Bea end the story this time? Not that she ever made up a new ending, of course, but several 'soft' landings might occur along the way, and any one of them could make her point.

"He did enjoy a have life, yes," Bea said, full of side-eye. "Anyway, when Mr. Quickwood passed, his son, the second Mr. Quickwood, inherited everything and threw the second Mrs. Quickwood along with her daughters... out of the house. The second Mrs. Quickwood wasn't his real mother, of course, so he had no use for her or his half-sisters."

"They went homeless?" Millie cried, growing pale. Mrs. Macklin rolled her eyes but remained silent.

"Actually, they had an annual pension and one of Mrs. Quickwood's cousins gave them a small five-bedroom house on the side of a lake. Also, they owned the lake. Marilyn's older sister, Evelyn, figured out a way to get non-local people to pay a toll to fish there. In fact, they sort of doubled their income and rescued the village from bankruptcy because the people in the region really liked fish."

"Oh. Well, that does not sound so bad," Millie said.

"That is what you say now, Millie, but it gets worse I promise you," Bea said with a dark look. "You see, Marilyn fell in love with a young man who was all wrong for her. What was his name?"

"Mr. Wilson," Georgia said, smiling. She went into her bag for her cross-stitch but decided against it. Perhaps read a magazine? These road trips were always such a bore.

"Right. Mr. Wilson was a franion and a lounge lizard," Bea pronounced.

"Really, Bea? Must you use such language?" Georgia asked, pretending to be shocked.

"I'm saying it like it is," Bea shot back, winking.

"What is a... er... a franion?" Millie asked, looking like she might panic and jump out of the carriage.

"A habitual pleasure-seeker," Mrs. Macklin answered blandly, "the kind of man who uses good ladies up and tosses them aside. Men like that are all bad pennies. They show up one day and decide to stick around. Like a bad penny, they are nearly worthless, but you wind up marrying them despite the counsel of wiser relatives. You cannot help yourself, for this is a man who possesses charm, wit, and the ability to speak to women. Usually, he is also appallingly attractive, and the sight of him... every so often the mere scent of him... sends one's mind into confusion. Years later, when your fingers are like raw eels from washing the wine stains out of his shirts, he dies... and you finally get your life back. Alas, you're too old to enjoy it. Although, to be fair, your memories of him will always be extraordinary, and you will live in a perpetual state of regret and non-regret."

The coach went silent.

"Right," Bea said. "Where was I?"

"Mr. Wilson," Georgia answered.

"Yes, that's it. Poor Marilyn had the worst taste in men. She passed over several acceptable suitors because she lacked common sense. Also, Mr. Wilson had a horse and was often found spouting poetry at impressionable young women. He was exciting but unreliable. As always happens with these stories, when he realized Marilyn did not have a penny to her name, he went and married someone with a massive dowry," Bea said, beaming. "And there you have it."

Millie appeared to be confused. "Er, what does that have to do with the rain, ma'am?"

"Oh, I completely forgot that part," Bea admitted. Georgia covered her mouth so as not to get caught chuckling. "Right. Very well. After Mr. Wilson left her to be a spinster, Marilyn was so despondent she took a walk in some garden, and it started raining. She foolishly ignored the weather and caught a terrible fever."

"Oh dear," Millie said. "She died of a rain fever."

Georgia took a breath. Steady. She gazed out the window to find Mr. Reardon tying down the tarp and happily smoking.

"Well, no. I mean, her mother and sisters nursed her back to health. Also, they had doctors," Bea said all in one breath. "She didn't die. In fact, she... well, she met some other fellow who was an elderly lord and married him instead. The lord died later, and she moved the whole family into his estate after inheriting a fortune. Shortly after, she met the old lord's nephew. The nephew turned out to be a widower who did not think he could love again. Marilyn healed his heart, they married, and had seven beautiful children. Listen, the moral of the story is the same: stay out of the rain."

"Yes, ma'am," Millie said.

Georgia called out, "Mr. Reardon, story time is done, and we're ready to go again. Are you quite finished with that tarp?"

"Very good, my lady," Mr. Reardon called back as wisps of smoke floated from the front cab. With a bump, the coach rolled back on the uneven path.

CHAPTER 4

# THE VILLAGE OF DEAD MOURNER'S GROVE.

The rain dwindled as they went deeper into the woods. "It is more like a charming forest now," Georgia noted, gazing at the dark trees. The path evened out as the already pale sun vanished in the canopy of leaves. "I thought Findor was all farmland, gentle rolling hills, and wine country. This is rather dark."

"You are thinking of southern Findor," Bea said, "We are near the Volusian border, where things are a bit more tangly and wild. The Findalon River, the border between the two realms, is only a mile or two away." Bea was now knitting a scarf, which looked interesting. Not interesting enough to learn, of course. Georgia glanced at Millie and Mrs. Macklin, who were both mending the hems on dresses or shirts... or something.

"My lady, we are almost there," Mr. Reardon called out. "I see the sign up ahead."

"Thank the heavens," Georgia whispered. "Ladies, get ready. Bea, do you have the letter for the rental house?"

Bea dove into her bag and pulled out a sheaf of correspondence. "Ah, here it is," she said. She read aloud, "Croft House is located at the end of Black Tree Lane. When you arrive, you will see a lilac bow tied to the gate. Pull your carriage around the far end where you will find a convenient carriage house and the 'rain entrance' to the house. Behind that is the pier to the lake. For the record, the pier is a perfect spot for dinner parties and wonderful evenings with friends. The staff will be waiting for your inspection. We hope you enjoy your holiday getaway. Sincerely, Sir Declan Wyclef, Lord of Dead Mourner's Grove and the surrounding boglands."

"Dead Mourner's Grove? What kind of name is that?" Georgia asked.

Bea shrugged. "It is probably derived from Old Findorian. Do not be surprised if the locals pronounce it 'Day-Mornay' or something quaint."

"I see," Georgia said, slowly. Off to one side, she spotted a bright red dome rising over the trees. "Um... what is that?"

Bea glanced over. "It appears to be the top of a hot air balloon."

"How extraordinary. I have never seen a hot air balloon," Georgia admitted.

"We are surrounded by innovation," Bea announced. "I read in an article that the kingdom of Ondara is now using hot air balloons to transport people en masse. They are calling them 'dirigible transports.' Except, of course, they say it in their own language. Allegedly, they can take people up to 20 at a time to locations beyond the horizon."

"Amazing," Georgia said. "Bea, do not pretend you do not speak Ondaran. What is the word for 'dirigible transport' in that language?"

"*Stýrilegar samgöngur*," Bea responded in perfect Ondaran.

Georgia grinned. "I knew it."

"All of these new inventions," Mrs. Macklin whispered darkly. "They will be the death of us."

"Probably," Bea said.

The carriage passed between two vast hedges, one to the south and one to the north. A moment later, they saw a sign in the north that read *Dead Mourner's Resort and Hotel - a place of rest and fun*. "That is where most of the other guests are staying," Bea noted. Georgia could see inside where carriages and sedans parked in a series. Beyond was a palatial hotel. It seemed quite modern.

"Should we have rented rooms there instead of taking the house?" She asked. "Are we missing the fun?"

"I think not," Bea answered. "All crammed into little rooms. You know how those new hotels are."

To the south, they passed another gate that read *Blackheart House*. "That sounds foreboding," Millie whispered.

"Harriet lives at Blackheart House," Bea said. "Trust me, there's nothing foreboding about it."

They rolled through the center of the village, which featured a cute little coffee and curio shop with a lively marketplace of outdoor stands and shops. Standing just beyond were a couple of young women in matching green hats who exuded sophistication in black wool coats each with a wreath of fresh mint entwined the length of the left arm. Georgia half-recognized them from the Cymbre School, where she and Bea grew up. "Bea, those two over there. We know them from school, but I do not recall their names."

Bea peeked out with a frown, "The Brady sisters. Nelda and Nora. Brady was their maiden name. A year apart in age, but inseparable in school."

"Oh, yes, right," Georgia said. "They both found solid marriages, as I recall."

"Correct. Mrs. Nelda Northbrook and Lady Nora Blacklock," Bea said. "Nelda landed a rather wealthy trade merchant, and Nora did even better. Some say Nora married above the line, although there are knights scattered amongst their ancestors."

"Lord Blacklock is a baronet or landed knight?"

"Second son to a baronet. He will not succeed his father's title, but his father bought honorifics for all the children and their spouses. Since then, Blacklock entered the Peer List on his own merit before the age of thirty. He served in the Intelligence Service with distinction, with a full Peerage, so Nora will rise either way. If she makes male heirs, she will manage their affairs as landed gentry, I suspect. Her background as a trade merchant's daughter may even be forgotten. She had refinement by the end of school. If anyone can pull off such a rise in station, it is Nora."

"That was kind of the father, a remarkable accomplishment by the son, and well done to her. Have they spotted us?"

"I cannot tell," Bea said. "Shall we stop and greet them?"

"Uh, let us do that later," Georgia said. "We will see them when we go to Harriet's Biscuit Party."

"Poor Harriet," Bea said, smirking. "She really lucked out with that new name."

Georgia blinked. "What do you mean?"

"Remember when we first met Harriet in Year Seven? She had terrible skin and blood red hair," Bea said.

"She is half Volusian," Georgia said. "They all look alike. I mean, you know, pale with reddish hair. It is not Harriet's fault."

"Oh of course, her skin cleared up and she can always dye her hair a sensible color. No, I mean her maiden name: Harriet Chalkbottom," Bea said. "What an unfortunate surname."

Georgia almost forgot Harriet's old name. "You're right, Bea. Mrs. Harriet Blackheart sounds so much better than Miss Harriet Chalkbottom."

"Bordering on heroically better. Have you met Mr. Blackheart?" Bea asked.

Georgia shook her head. "Harriet's family found him even before she graduated. They married a month after she finished school, as I recall."

"Oh right. So quick," Bea said, "and here I thought I was in a hurry."

"You had reason to hurry," Georgia admitted. "Your horrid brother-in-law was going to exile you to the cottage within a year rather than foot a proper dowry. After that, you might as well have given up and become a teacher."

"Right." Bea blinked. "Lord Wickham really is horrid. Still, one wonders why Harriet was in such a hurry."

Georgia shrugged. "Her family comes from trade. Those people do not waste time on long engagements. As I recall, Harriet was a plain girl growing up, even if her family had wealth. May I admit something? I was never clear how she got into the Cymbre School. Her family was not like either of ours... and do not judge me for saying that. I am happy for her. More than happy."

"Harriet's family is more than 'trade,' Georgia. The word 'wealth' does not even begin to describe them: they are rich. When I say 'rich,' I do not mean that in a laughing side-eye sort of way," Bea said. "The Chalkbottoms make both of our families look like paupers. They own almost a third of the farms in southern Volusia, and half of the silver mines in Hildor. That family owns a vast fleet of commercial ships, and controls sea commerce from Hildor to Phaedros. The governments of four nations rely on them to maintain regular sea trade. These are the kind of people who do not see a gentry title as worth having, because they are already in control across multinational boundaries. Money means nothing to Harriet's grandfather. Even so, she got into the Cymbre School on a scholarship completely of her own merit. She won the Findor Award."

"What do you mean she won the Findor Award? That is a grant for excellence in the arts. She would have had to be five years old when she won it. How is that even possible?"

Bea shrugged. "She was a child prodigy on the pianoforte. Her parents were parading her around the countryside almost before she could walk. Princess Edith Hart, may she rest in peace, was so impressed by little Harriet she sent a note to the award judges on her behalf.

They granted the award the next day, and Harriet was admitted into the Cymbre School."

"Amazing," Georgia whispered. "Wait. Princess Edith? The great-great aunt of King Robert? She was still alive when we were children?"

"That old woman lived to be 107," Bea said. "I met her once when I was a child. She was like a walking corpse."

"Oh, good heavens, Bea."

"Indeed. Anyway, Harriet was made Valedictorian of the class when she graduated the year after us and she was brilliant. Her grades were so high they opened an investigation at one point. She weathered it and answered every question from memory. Harriet proved herself so often in school the Dean apologized in person for ever doubting her. If she were a man, she would be overseeing something important right now. She would be a captain of industry, I'm sure of it."

Georgia blinked. "Instead, everyone is thrilled to pieces she found a husband. I am so glad you told me this, Bea. Now I feel like a bad person."

"You should," Bea said with a wink. "Get over it. The world is moving on."

Georgia laughed. "In all seriousness," she said, "do you really think Harriet would be a captain of industry by now? She only graduated last year, and now she is with child. For that matter, you and I only graduated the year before. Why do we talk about school as if it were a lifetime ago?"

Bea shrugged. "It does feel like a lifetime ago. Well, at times it does."

The coach took a long hill and pulled up to an ivy-covered wall with a metal gate and a waterlogged lilac bow. "That looks right," Georgia called out to Mr. Reardon. "There's supposed to be a carriage house around the other side." They rolled through, following a short, winding lane through massive oak trees. A moment later, the house loomed into view. Lord Wyclef was fond of referring to this as the 'little house', but there was nothing small about it. With 20 guest rooms and two separate living suites, it was a mansion to rival any other. They rounded the structure, noting the ancient Findorian granite columns and wide windows. Like many buildings in this part of the world, the great houses were built for maximum light and comfort. The fact that Dead Mourner's Grove appeared to be in perpetual rain was not apparently a factor anyone considered.

"How cozy," Bea whispered with a wink.

Sure enough, the carriage house loomed into view next to a secondary entrance. As they pulled up, a house butler, maid, cook, and footman lined up for inspection and greeting.

The butler was a young man. In fact, he might have been in his pre-teens. He was carefully combed and manicured, but the collar of his shirt was two-sizes too big, and he stood a head shorter than everyone else. The young fellow opened the coach door with a flourish, "Your Grace, welcome to Croft House."

Mr. Reardon hurried over with an umbrella to cover her from the rain. When he was in place, Georgia stepped out and smiled. "I am so sorry, my lady," Mr. Reardon gasped.

"Have no concern, Mr. Reardon," Georgia answered. She looked at the young butler. "Please use the formal 'Duchess' or 'Duchess Goldenheart' when addressing me. 'Your Grace' is too exalted. In future, wait for the driver to open the door when I am ready. Thank you. What are your names?"

The young butler winced. "Forgive me, Duchess. I was excited to meet you, and we were unsure what to call you. I opted for the most formal, just in case. Any error in this house must be attributed to me with the humblest apology." As he spoke, his voice cracked, going deeper for a moment before sounding like a flute the next.

Georgia smiled. "Young man, you speak well for yourself and this extraordinary house. I will assume nothing and endeavor to forgive everything, should that be necessary. I have a feeling you will foresee any problem going forward. Tell me more about this place and how you manage it?"

"I am Mr. Darkleaf. Mrs. Hensley manages the kitchen staff. Our senior housemaid is named Janet, Clyde is the first footman, and our chief gardener is Mr. Tremble. We used to have a Head Housekeeper, but she passed away last month. At that time, I was promoted from butler-in-training to Current Butler. This house is one part of a larger network of family houses held by our Lord Wyclef."

"And how did one so young come to be the butler-in-training here?" Georgia asked. She was not usually this inquisitive about domestic arrangements in guest homes, but he was not even able to shave. It was curious. In addition, she wondered if this was his first time running a house for someone at her station.

"My father is the Seneschal to Lord Baron Wyclef, Duchess. He has four sons, all of whom are in service to the estates and answer to him. My brothers all run the large houses. I run the small house for training. If you would prefer a more experienced butler or estate agent, I will go to my older brother, and he will serve you. Forgive me for any impudence." For a moment, she thought he might toss himself on the ground. Instead, he stood there awaiting her response with his eyes locked on the ground.

"Smart kid," Bea said, hopping out of the coach while Mrs. Macklin held an umbrella over her head. "Imagine if you had arrived and he called you anything below your rank. You might have had him arrested."

Young Mr. Darkleaf blanched. "She jests," Georgia said, gently. "We look forward to your lord's hospitality and I believe you will do fine, young Mr. Darkleaf. There is no need to call on your older brother to serve us just yet. If Lord Wyclef trusts the arrangement, then I am not going to question it. That said, do not be offended if I offer more advice. Thank you." In truth, she had heard of such arrangements with Findorian Seneschal families. There was a tradition. It was not uncommon to assign each son the duties of running a house within a larger network of estates. With that, Georgia strolled into the house. The structure was built on an axis of two massive foyers: the grand opening faced the front doors, with a more petite entrance to the carriage house. Both entries met in an enormous ballroom with a silver-white marble floor. Above soared a great domed stained-glass skylight. The walls were imprinted with a beautiful wallpaper pattern of white on off-white leaves that created a subtle feeling of wide but controlled space. The house was a bit chilly, and she suspected not all the fireplaces worked. Still, Georgia preferred the idea of staying in this lovely old space instead of the all-too modern resort up the road where every former Cymbre girl in Harriet's social circle would have instant access.

As the servants unpacked, Georgia wandered around
the first floor. The lower parlor was a bit snug for her
taste, and there was no library. On the other hand, the
solarium facing the lake was spectacular. The rain paused,
although it was still cloudy. Overall, the house was well-
positioned at the top of a hill facing the lake below. Off to
the north side of the yard was a series of paths into the
woods. Further down the hill was a rustic amphitheater
and a small stone building. Another side ended at a hedge,
but Georgia could see to the next yard. Distantly, she
heard a trio of violins from the neighboring home,
followed by the sound of someone laughing until they
coughed. Just beyond was the top of the hot air balloon.
Perhaps the neighbor owned it? She spotted Bea walking
to the gate. Unlike Georgia, Bea had no problem knocking
on a neighbor's door to say 'hello' without invitation, as
long as it was no longer raining, of course. Being the
daughter of a baronet, Bea had a certain latitude in the grey
area of protocol. She was a natural ambassador between
hedges and lawns.

Georgia turned back to her inspection of the house.
The central corridor featured portraits of former Wyclefs.
She knew the family was old, but this cemented it. Every
painting was a masterpiece with one arguable flaw: every
person on the wall had the same startled expression. It was
almost like they were looking at their own grave. The final
portrait was a rather modern photograph of her

acquaintance, Lord Wyclef. He too appeared startled, or perhaps had something in his eye. Across the corridor was a small den, comfortably laid out with couches and a few books on a table. "Ah, the reading room at last," Georgia whispered. Atop the mantle was placed a short sword on a stand. She read the plaque: *The blade is named 'Winterthorn.' It was a side weapon for Sir Augustin Wyclef until he fell storming the beaches of Hildor. The blade's mate 'Summerblaze' was broken that day.* That meant this blade was probably sitting on the stand for the better part of 10 years. She took it and felt the weight and balance. It was a small blade, which was to her liking, and surprisingly sharp. She put it back on the stand and continued to wander.

Young Mr. Darkleaf found her in the corridor of portraits. "Everything is to your satisfaction, Duchess Goldenheart?" he asked.

"It is lovely, Mr. Darkleaf," she answered. "We will have supper late. I think Miss Beatrice would prefer a walk before it gets dark. Feel free to surprise us with the menu. We are adventurous eaters."

"Very good, Duchess. In that case, on your first night, the menu will feature a variety of local dishes prepared to perfection. I should warn you Findorian cuisine can be rigorous and too spicy for those not accustomed. Shall I instruct the cook to hold back the spices?"

"Do not be concerned, Mr. Darkleaf. My mother's family is Findorian, and I enjoy spicy dishes. I would urge you not to hold back. As I mentioned, we are adventurous in this area, and I am keen to enjoy something local and authentic."

Mr. Darkleaf nodded and smiled. "In that case, Duchess, we will add a bit of local spice and pray you enjoy it as much as we might."

"I have no doubt we will," Georgia said, smiling. Personally, she could eat anything, and knew Bea would want the experience too. Bea had a remarkable palate, and she was always ready to try a new dish.

"If you plan to walk, there are many lovely trails along the west and northern sides of the property adjacent to the lake. If you go into the woods and turn north, you will find many pleasant sights," Mr. Darkleaf said. "You will find signs and landmarks along the way, as well. That said, if you need a guide, we can accommodate."

"Excellent," Georgia answered. She was about to turn away, then remembered something. "Oh, Mr. Darkleaf, perhaps you can answer a question?"

"Of course, Duchess."

"Tell me, how do the locals pronounce the name of the village?"

Mr. Darkleaf blinked. "Er… well, it is pronounced Dead… Mourner's… Grove. Just like that."

"I see." Georgia shook head. "And why, may I ask, is that the name of the village?"

"Twenty years ago, there was a terrible plague here. At that time, this place was called North Oaks Grove," the young butler answered. "A particular young girl, beloved by all in the village, lost her life to the plague. She died screaming in agony, as the story goes. Everyone was so upset they all went to her funeral in the old burial ground to weep and honor her memory. They locked themselves in with the body overnight. Unfortunately, they all caught the plague because they were all in the same place breathing upon one another. The local doctor bled them all to get rid of the ill humors, but they still died horrible deaths. The survivors renamed the village after that."

"I see," Georgia said, wishing she had not asked the question.

Upstairs, she found Bea returning from the yard to supervise the unpacking. "Have you seen the family portrait hall?" Georgia asked.

"The Wyclefs all look like they were painted during an existential crisis," Bea said. "Yes. I saw it. I can only imagine what a family reunion would hold. Georgia, we might have a problem. We cannot find your magic sword. Millie said you left it at home."

"Oh, yes, that's true," Georgia said. "We are only here for a week, Bea. The Queen ordered me to hang the sword up. I did as she instructed. Anyway, what sort of supernatural danger will be found lurking at Harriet Chalkbottom's baby shower?"

"I suppose not much danger," Bea said slowly. "Georgia, you do recall it was only days ago you fought an army of magical giant spiders, right? Before that you dispatched a warehouse full of blood zombies, the pack of ice wolves in the north, and a vampire bat creature in your own attic."

"Most of those creatures were under the control of the ancient sorceress Doria Nanette," Georgia said, shaking her head. "Mr. Blue said Doria Nanette is out of commission for at least a century or two. As for the giant shadow spiders, I think that was a fluke. We had our big adventure, Bea. From here on out, it is all parties and stuffy highborn types. You get married in a year… you know when you *eventually* meet your fiancé again. He cannot be on state business trips forever. You will do that, and I will continue to go to parties until some countess traps me with a suitable fourth or fifth or tenth son who will agree to take my name. I only pray he is a consenting adult and has all his teeth. Anyway, I want to have a normal holiday here in Dead Mourner's Grove. I want to feel like a real person for a bit."

"Right," Bea said, shaking her head. "You are the only female knight in the Three Realms with the authority to assemble an army, a duchess who owns a magic sword, with the physical strength of at least five big men..."

"Have we measured my actual physical strength?"

"No. But you understand what I am saying. You move faster than the eye can see when it suits you, and you are the scion of five thousand years of unbroken Goldenhearts dedicated to the destruction of supernatural evil. But we can *try* to have a normal week on holiday."

"Oh, Bea," Georgia laughed. "I am under orders. Even Mr. Blue is avoiding me now. The Queen made her thoughts known, and that is that."

"I miss him," Bea said, smirking, "and you like that wizard."

Georgia blinked. "What is not to like? He is smart and nice; helpful with advice about how to deal with monsters and the like."

"Obviously, he needs to re-think his core wardrobe," Bea said, "Even though he is charming. I have never seen anyone get away with blue suede shoes before. That said, when we attended the Hampton Gilmore Swim-For-The-Diseased Benefit, I did get a glance at him in his rowing attire. I saw a muscle or two. Not that it matters, of course."

"Really? I had not noticed," Georgia lied. She had, of course, seen the rowing attire. "Bea, he may not look it, but Mr. Blue is quite a bit older than you think, and for us to even discuss him this way is odd and inappropriate. Can we simply relax and enjoy our get-away? This week is all about Harriet and her child. No talk of monsters or wizards."

"Very well," Bea said, smiling. She knocked twice on an antique wooden side table. "Knock on wood. No monsters and no wizards. Just in case."

"Just in case," Georgia agreed, grinning. "You know, this is a beautiful old house, but there is no library. I hoped to see what Lord Wyclef keeps on his bookshelves, but he remains true to his bland self even here. Why would anyone want to rent a house with no library?"

"This is the 'little house'. The library is probably elsewhere. I think they are hoping we will go to the lake. It is a lake house, after all," Bea said. "Who needs a library when you can drown?"

"That makes sense. In that case, let us go for a walk by the afore-mentioned lake."

"We can't go for a walk," Bea said, pointing at the window. "It is raining again."

Georgia laughed. "Ah, but we possess these amazing marvels of technology, Bea. I do not know if you have ever heard of such strange new devices, but people call them... umbrellas."

Bea snorted. "I know what an umbrella is, but I cannot be dragging Mrs. Macklin through the woods while she holds it for me."

"Ah, as it happens, they have lighter umbrellas now. Umbrellas designed for a lady to hold in her own hand. The ribs are made of rubber reed so you will not break your back holding it. I took the liberty of procuring a few of them from *James and Leak* before the trip." She pulled two staffs wrapped in oiled silk from one of the chests. They weighed less than the ones favored by the men of business downtown. These umbrellas had a fine but sturdy Brownwood handle with nickel-plated tips. The cloth was a pleasant green, instead of the grubby black one might see on Market Street.

"Oh, fine," Bea said. "Give me your devil contraption."

"Duchess, a quick word?" young Mr. Darkleaf said as she and Bea walked out the door. "It's about the neighbor."

"The one with the hot-air balloon?" Georgia asked.

"The same, yes. His name is Mr. Brown. He is an elderly chap, a retired animal doctor, and a bit eccentric, but some of the locals go to him for their ailments too. You must have heard him playing the violin earlier?" Mr. Darkleaf said, smiling but also shaking his head in disapproval.

"We did hear him playing. He is quite talented," Bea said. "I spoke to him. He was rather sweet. I thought we might see his balloon tomorrow."

"If you will forgive me for speaking out of turn, I would not advise it, my lady," Mr. Darkleaf said in a low tone, as if avoiding an eavesdropper. "Some of the locals say he is a *sorcerer*. From what my father says, Mr. Brown is an asset to the community. Even so, he is a target of gossip. I am sure you would not want to sully yourself with an association."

"A sorcerer who helps farmers?" Bea asked dubiously.

Mr. Darkleaf shrugged. "A local washer woman claims to have seen Mr. Brown surrounded by gigantic rabbits who all were playing violins."

"I see. Do you happen to know if ergot mold grows locally?" Bea asked with a mischievous grin. "Is it possible the locals live too near bodies of still water?"

"Thank you, Mr. Darkleaf," Georgia said. "We will be careful with Mr. Brown." She glanced at Bea, as they wandered along the short trail away from the house.

"I do not think I shall be avoiding Mr. Brown," Bea said.

"Really?" Georgia asked. "This is such a surprise, Bea."

Two paths stretched beyond the backyard: one went in a direct line to the lake, while the other wound into the trees. The second path featured a sign that read, 'Frog Prince Trail'.

"We should follow the Frog Prince Trail tomorrow," Georgia said. "Why does that sound so familiar?"

"*Frog Prince Trail* is the name of a children's book," Bea said, leaning over the sign with her umbrella. "It says here, '…see the famous battle site of the Frog Prince, where he cast down the Cruel Princess of Dragonflies'."

"Interesting," Georgia said. "Do you think the author lived in Dead Mourner's Grove?"

Bea shrugged. "Either that or he came here on holiday. Ugh. *Frogs*."

"What is wrong with frogs?" Georgia asked. "In my experience, they seem innocuous enough. Most are content to mind their own business on their lily pads and the like."

Bea shook her head. "Nothing is wrong with them, I am sure. You know, we had a pond back at Irvingdale Manor. Well, we have several ponds, of course. When I was a girl, I was very fond of this one spot where the hummingbirds would gather. I used to go there and watch them."

"How lovely," Georgia said.

"It really was," Bea said, shaking her head. "But you know, Georgia, there was a big old bullfrog who lived in that pond. I used to see him paddling around. He would come up and give me the evil eye."

"The bullfrog gave you dirty looks?"

"He was a monster," Bea said. "Do not laugh. Anyway, I used to leave little bowls of honey and sugar water for the hummingbirds, and they would all gather around. Sometimes I would put some sugar water on my fingertip, and the birds would flit up and lick it off. It was wonderful."

"That sounds delightful, Bea."

Bea leaned in. "As I learned the hard way, nothing lasts forever and one day the hummingbirds stopped coming to the bowls. Instead, I found little patches of feathers... and that fat old bullfrog... he was nearly twice his size."

Georgia blinked. "What are you saying? He ate the hummingbirds?"

"I came out one morning especially early, just to check on them," Bea said, rubbing her temple, "and I found that fat horrid bullfrog with one of my sweet hummingbirds halfway in his mouth. He ate them all, Georgia."

"That is terrible."

"Yes, all frogs are terrible. Nothing should be amphibious. One should either live on land or be a fish. Everything in between is unnatural if you ask me."

"I had no idea you felt this strongly about amphibian-ism," Georgia remarked.

The lake was spectacular. Shades of deep blue were buried in a mist running toward the far shore. Near their shore, the water was turquoise with spots of lavender. Georgia took in the sweet air and wondered why she spent so much time in the big city of Oradale. In the rain and the mist, it looked like the ocean but was somehow more manageable. She lingered on the rocky beach and felt the downpour, snug in her black cotton bonnet and layered coat and shielded by the new umbrella. Beside her, Bea enjoyed the view from under her own umbrella.

"It feels strange holding this thing," Bea admitted. "But I think I like it. A parasol would not serve at all. I mean, this thing is heavier, but I can handle it and feel rather efficient."

"Agreed," Georgia said. "Look at that amazing lake. It is hard to imagine it is on a mere tributary of the river to the north. We can come out here any time we want and gaze at the world, Bea. Nobody tells us what to do."

"Nobody tells you what to do, Georgia," Bea said, gazing at the lake.

"The Queen tells me what to do," Georgia answered.

Behind them, someone coughed. Georgia glanced back to see two men carrying a large bundle down the path. One of them nodded. A moment later, they vanished into the mist. "What was that about?" she wondered aloud.

"Workers at the resort," Bea said, also watching them go away. "They are probably taking the trash out."

"Why are they taking their trash across the Wyclef property?"

Bea shrugged. "In Findor, the beaches are not private unless one owns the whole lake. This must be a short-cut."

"Public beaches on lakes? How barbaric."

Bea smirked. "It is almost as if we are living in the ancient dark times with these public beaches and horrid trash carriers."

They returned for dinner. Mr. Darkleaf proudly laid out an arugula, yellow tomato, and mushroom salad with a tangy dressing that managed to be both sweet and savory. In the local tradition, he served it with mild lemon water over ice. Georgia wondered where he got the ice. Her staff often had trouble finding fresh ice in the capital, let alone here in the wild country. After that, things got interesting, as the staff brought out a dish of sausage and cauliflower with a spicy Findorian sauce. Just in case, they had mild chicken with mushrooms on a side plate. Alas, the chicken went untouched as the spicy sauce dazzled, and there was a tray of warm flatbread to sop it up. Local tradition stated they use the bread like a spoon, so they did without embarrassment. The pepper felt like white-hot blinding fire on the first bite. It settled into something savory and comforting as they continued the meal. By the end, Georgia had an odd sense of spice euphoria, even though she had to blow her nose. After blowing their noses twice, they found themselves giggling. She felt strangely at peace with the world by the end of the meal.

"I must admit, I am enjoying Findorian food," Bea mumbled between bites of the bread. "It is so spicy, rustic, without being... what am I trying to say?"

"Too rustic?" Georgia asked. "It is lovely. We should eat like this all the time."

"Can you imagine blowing your nose this much in mixed company?"

"Honestly, I'm starting to sweat," Georgia admitted. "Findorians must have their own set of protocols."

After supper, they raided the wine cellar. Lord Wyclef might not be much of a reader, but he knew his vintages. Mr. Darkleaf took them on a quick tour of the cellar, where they were delighted to learn they could drink almost anything. "Lord Wyclef keeps only these three bottles in reserve," the young butler said, indicating a closed wine cabinet. "These three were acquired by his father in Jendina many years ago. I suspect they went to vinegar, but he keeps them anyway."

"Some sentimental memory, perhaps," Georgia murmured.

CHAPTER 5

# THE BISCUIT PARTY.

Harriet was not conventionally attractive. Her teeth were enormous, and her eyes were small. If you viewed her from certain angles, it was hard to tell where her nose began, and the rest of her face left off. Georgia remembered how some of the girls picked on her in school. They called her 'ox head' and joked how Harriet's vivid red hair was a sign she lacked a human soul. A handfull of those girls were now grown women celebrating Harriet's impending motherhood in that very room. There was also a joke with her name. Chalkbottom is not a pretty surname, and subject to all sorts of abuse by the adolescent mind. Georgia wondered if Harriet ever forgave those girls, or was she having this party to show them her success?

Standing outside the curio and coffee shop while Bea organized the gifts, Georgia gazed in and spotted the former Miss Chalkbottom sitting on a pile of cushions. Harriet's belly was immense with her first child as she held court for her old enemies and friends. Her midnight blue velvet gown was a modern marvel with no bows, fringes, or anything to distract. Her hair was immaculate, and possibly more blood red than ever before. It bordered on shocking, but somehow was fabulous. Her posture was perfect, despite her enormous belly.

Harriet looked like a queen. Of course, she was wearing a paper crown, so that added to it in a quirky way. Someone said something amusing, and Harriet clapped with delight. Jokes, songs, and poetry were a feature at these sorts of parties, so her guests were working to entertain. In fact, one of the ladies did a quick jig, much to the delight of the others. That was part of it all, of course. Those who pleased the expectant mother the most might be crowned the Queen's Emerald, which was a lucky honor. Naturally, one of Georgia's status would not be singing for her supper. She was almost jealous, though. Everyone looked like they were having fun.

Oh drat. Was the Queen right? Should she be enjoying her newfound celebrity more? Was she wasting time fighting monsters and solving murders? No. Of course not. She was a Goldenheart.

"People used to mock Harriet, but you never did," Bea said, walking up, arms laden with meticulously wrapped boxes. One of Bea's many talents was wrapping gifts.

"I never stopped them from doing it, either. Some of those women were terrible to her. I regret not saying anything to deter them. Caught up in my own world, I suppose," Georgia said. She looked at Bea. "You never had a bad word for her, though."

"Who has time for that?" Bea asked, rolling her eyes. "Even so, I never defended her either. I am glad she found Mr. Blackheart, though. Do you think he will come to the baby shower? I would love to see who Harriet landed."

Georgia shrugged. "I suspect we will see something of him, yes. If Harriet possesses any wits, she will parade him around the room and make everyone suffer for teasing her all those years."

Bea tilted her head in thought. "Also, not for nothing, but there are at least two women of note here today: you and Lady Rebecca Drake. I do not know what Mr. Blackheart does for trade, but most assuredly he will want to make contact. Men of business never miss those opportunities."

Georgia smiled. "Bea, you are about to marry a double-viscount, and you are the only graduate of the Cymbre school to leave with a perfect score in all nine disciplines. There are three women of note present."

"Ah, you are making me blush, Georgia. Let us not forget all but one of the women in that room is a full graduate of the Cymbre school in at least six disciplines.

Each of them managed to finish her education despite the expectations of the world at large. The only one who did not make it to Year Thirteen was Lady Rebecca Drake, but she had a good reason," Bea said.

Georgia nodded, remembering the drama. Her old friend, Rebecca, was the daughter of Lord Miles Drake, the Earl of Elton, and Princess Calliope Dahs, the niece of the king of Phaedros Isle.

Historically, Phaedros was the center of culture in the Eastern Sea. For nearly six thousand years, a millennia before the formation of the Three Realms, Phaedros was ruled by the House of Dahs, who valued scholarship, equality, and merit above all else. The line of kings in that land was unbroken until only recently, in the greater scheme. Alas, the ruling family fell into a pattern all too familiar and could not adapt to the changing times. The House of Dahs rejected any notion of a Parliament and maintained absolute monarchy, even as the neighboring states all evolved. At the same time, Phaedros was and still is famous for its universities, libraries, and academic centers. Unfortunately, access to those institutions became more and more limited. The general populace, once revered for their access to a thriving nationwide education system beyond all others... began to lose access over the last century. The latest generation became rabble rather quickly, and highly reactionary. The gap of wealth became more and more apparent until it reached a breaking point.

At the same time, the House of Dahs seemed to remove itself from reality. The last king in the line married his own sister in order to maintain 'the purity of the family'. All of that was a recipe for disaster.

Sadly, Phaedros fell into decline.

There was a coup. A group of reactionaries murdered most of Rebecca's extended family. Her mother was already married from a young age to a prominent earl in the Three Realms. In fact, Princess Calliope spent most of her life in the Three Realms. She only visited her cousins in their homeland on a few occasions. Even so, after the coup, she and her daughter were the only heirs to the old throne, albeit now in exile.

Rebecca left school to go into hiding. Despite that, her mother made sure she had private tutors on a par with the Cymbre School.

"Quite a few ladies of note," Georgia grinned.

"Yes, indeed. Let us go in before they see us loitering."

"Give me a moment," Georgia said. "Before I started gawking at the room, I had reason to pause. I am trying to see if Lady Rebecca is present. There she is." Across the room, Lady Rebecca Drake, Georgia's original roommate from the dormitories and afore-mentioned princess in exile, stood next to the fire. She was flawless, as usual. Clad in a high-waisted silk gown of jade green, perfect for the new season, Rebecca looked like a statue. Across her shoulders ran a stunning white lace shawl inlaid with silver beads and rare green pearls. In truth, such a garment was from a long-gone age, but Rebecca pulled it off. Placing green pearls on anything was the absolute most modern idea returned from the past. Georgia's friend, Sir Lionel Rance, the realm's most acclaimed dress designer had only the week before mentioned the idea of combining silver beads with green pearls to her over tea. He was excited, thinking he produced something new and bold. Now, a week later, Georgia gazed at an old friend who she knew had no connection to Sir Lionel already wearing the fashion. Sir Lionel would be so disappointed to learn he was not the originator of the fad. Rebecca's honey-gold hair was spun with pearls to match the buttons on her gown. The gown itself was the perfect shade to compliment her amber complexion. Georgia watched her until they locked eyes. Rebecca tilted her head in a minute greeting. Georgia responded with a quick gesture in a circle, touched her nose, pointed up, and then down. Rebecca nodded slowly, touched her earlobe, and gestured down.

"Very well," Georgia said. "Are you ready, Bea?"

"Wait, what just happened?" Bea asked. "The little hand twitch thing. You both did it. I saw it as clearly as the day."

"I asked her: do I come in as someone important, or do I come in as an old friend from school."

"I beg your pardon?" Bea asked. "You communicated via secret gesture with Lady Rebecca Drake through the window of a coffee shop?"

"We invented a language as young girls," Georgia explained. "In year two, she and I worked out a series of crude hand signals and gestures. Remember that winter when we were all stuck in separate houses? The snowstorms followed by that awful quarantine forced us to stay put. We were bored. It was a fun game. I am surprised she remembers, I will admit, but glad for it."

Bea was aghast. "You have a secret hand-gesture language with Rebecca Drake that you did not share with me?"

"We were children living through a plague when we invented it," Georgia said. "Come on, Bea."

"Of course that makes sense and well done you, but now I want to know the secret language too. You absolutely fail to see the potential of this. We could have been sitting in cafes and art galleries doing that finger twitch thing and gossiping about everyone," Bea said, blinking. "Opportunity is lost, Georgia."

"Oh dear," Georgia said. "You are right, of course. I will teach it to you. We had best get inside. They are all looking at us now. Let me open the door so we seem less formal." She pulled on the door and walked in.

Everyone got to their feet and curtseyed. "No-no let us not get into that here," Georgia said, sauntering in as though it were any old day of the week. "Today we are all Cymbre girls. We have all known each other since we were children. Let us keep our eyes on the real queen of the day: our sweet friend Harriet. That said, if someone is holding a glass of expensive red wine, I will take it out of your hands. Harriet, get back on your cushion. We are here to celebrate, not induce labor." Everyone laughed, relieved. Rebecca grinned and nodded. Harriet beamed.

Cymbre girls or not, Georgia was not about to miss a chance to show off a bit. She opened her fine wool coat to reveal her high-waisted silk dress. It was radiant blue, like the flag of the Three Realms. Her collar was sheer white lace sewn in the shape of stars that trailed down her back in a cape. None of the ladies present noticed how Millie weaved the lace into her jet-black hair, which was disappointing. Millie spent hours working on it, and Georgia felt certain one day this idea of hair-weaving-into-garment would provide an extraordinary view at a ducal or princely ball. Millie, always nearby, took her coat to the side room. Georgia strolled over to Harriet and kissed her cheek. "Congratulations," she whispered in Harriet's ear. "You deserve only happiness. Do not dare call me 'duchess' at this party, Harriet. Especially not in front of the Brady sisters or Fontina Williams. Am I clear?"

"Oh, they have all grown and changed, but thank you so much for saying that. And thank you for coming," Harriet answered, blushing, "...Georgia." As Harriet spoke, Georgia noticed something flash on the woman's right hand. It was a ring. Not just any ring, though. Her left hand bore the usual engagement and wedding ring combination. Both were extravagant. But the band on her right hand was something to behold. It was gold, but bore a white jewel of immense size, about as big as a dove's egg. It would have been gaudy, but was clearly a jewel of extraordinary value that glittered with a light of its own.

Georgia found herself staring, which was usually considered rude. Harriet noticed and held her hand up to show it off. "Do you like it?" she asked.

"It is amazing," Georgia answered, unable for a moment to tear her eyes away. Of course, she owned plenty of jewelry, but that ring was... something. She blinked. "Where did you get it?"

"Mr. Blackheart gave it to me, two weeks ago," Harriet whispered. "In honor of our first child. He said it will be an heirloom of our family. I must admit, it is the heaviest ring I have ever worn, and at first I did not like it so much. But now it has grown on me. I find it... precious." Georgia smiled, but also felt a peculiar desire to tear the ring off Harriet's hand and keep it for herself.

"Yes, it is remarkable," Georgia breathed, looking away. What was that about?

Bea followed Georgia, also revealing her new gown. Historically, Bea tended more toward pastels and soft colors, but now she was engaged to a Volusian Viscount. Correction: he was *the* Volusian Viscount. One of the most powerful and respected lords of the northern realm. Bea dressed as a Volusian noblewoman all in black with her arms covered. It was custom, and Bea was determined to follow it, albeit in her own style.

While Bea talked to Harriet, Georgia passed through the assembled women smiling and nodding. In school, she was popular, most likely because of her highborn family. Now they were out of school, her celebrity and title were evident in the papers. Despite telling them not to make a fuss, most of the ladies curtseyed. Georgia kept walking, rather than make something of it. At last, she arrived at the side of Lady Rebecca Drake, who held an extra glass of red wine. "This is for you, Duchess Goldenheart," Rebecca said with a smile. Behind her, Georgia noted two gentlemen in dark grey suits hovering. They wore coats big enough to hide musket pistols. They must be part of Rebecca's security detail. Next to them was a woman in a sensible dark grey dress, with a black bonnet. Not a lady's maid, but rather a personal assistant. It all made sense, as Rebecca was Lord Drake's temporary liaison to the court of the Three Realms. She was only 2 years older than Georgia, but already tasked with immense responsibility.

"Thank you, Lady Drake," Georgia answered, taking the glass. "You said to come in low," she gestured in their secret language.

"It didn't work," Rebecca whispered back. "Let's face it, that frock took the room off-guard, Georgia."

"Oh, this old thing?"

Rebecca laughed.

"How is your mother?" Georgia asked.

"Better," Rebecca answered. "I should tell you she did not come down with a flu like it said in the *Volusian Times*."

Georgia went cold. "Foul play?"

Rebecca nodded; her eyes wet with old grief. "The Sicarium will never stop hunting us, Georgia." Georgia remembered reading somewhere the Sicarium was a league of assassins, allegedly based in Phaedros, which of course was Rebecca's ancestral homeland. At the time Georgia read the article, she thought it a myth.

"You both renounced your claims to the Phaedros throne, and women cannot even rule there. Is that not enough for them?" Georgia asked, already knowing the answer.

"What if I marry and produce a suitably impressive male heir?" Rebecca asked. "I think they want to avoid the complication."

"I am sorry to hear this," Georgia whispered.

"It could be worse," Rebecca admitted. "On the other hand, my father has me at court where I have some protection. If he is infirm and cannot travel, I can fill in as heir-presumptive and liaison to the court." This answered another question. Georgia had wondered more than once how Lady Rebecca wound up acting as a court liaison. It was not a role often given to young unmarried ladies. Rebecca should have been looking for a husband, but she was too busy working. Not that she would have any trouble finding someone, of course. As the only child of the most powerful Earl in Volusia, she had a staggering dowry and her pick of suitors. Even so, her father would be the one to choose whom she married, and he did not appear to be in a hurry about it. He would decide who was most suitable. Now, that looked like no one.

"Lady Rebecca," Bea said, walking over. "It is always good to see you. How is your mother?"

"She is recovering," Rebecca said, discreetly wiping her eyes. "Thank you, Miss Beatrice. I will convey your well wishes."

"Of course," Bea said. She saw the tear almost fall but was too refined to comment on it without invitation. Instead, Bea positioned herself so the rest of the room had to move around her to see Rebecca. Georgia smiled.

"Congratulations on your engagement," Lady Rebecca said. "Who would have thought anyone could land our Viscount of Simsley. Not only did you land him, but you also cemented the alliance between the northern houses once again. Well done."

"Thank you so much. It was more of a group effort, but I will be glad to take the credit. Double bonus, he is a delight in person." Bea grinned. "Ladies, I hate to change the subject or sound crass, but did you see that bauble on Harriet's finger? The heirloom ring?" They might be too refined to comment on falling tears, but jewelry was another matter.

"How could we miss it? I hope she shoved it in all their faces," Rebecca said.

"She didn't need to. It shoved itself." Georgia shook her head, remembering the urge to grab the ring. What was that about?

Lady Rebecca's assistant, the woman in the grey dress, brought a tray of dainty drinks. "Oh, thank you, Emmaline," Rebecca said, taking one. "What is this?"

"Borage over ice, my lady," the assistant said. "With extra cinnamon and vermouth." She offered the tray to Georgia, who declined with a quick gesture.

"There appears to be ice in every drink in this village," Georgia noted.

"They have ice springs and frozen caves throughout the area. The volcanic history of coastal Findor features a rare geodesic phenomenon: frozen cave pockets near the lake and coast. The locals store water there to freeze, and use it in cocktails," Rebecca explained. "It is one of the regional lures for tourism."

"Clever," Georgia said. "Ice is difficult to get, even in the capital. I suppose I can see why they use it in everything here."

"The only problem, near as I can tell, is the frog eggs and other bacteria," Lady Rebecca said. "Apparently contamination is a recurring problem."

"Ew," Georgia said. "How common is that?"

Lady Rebecca shrugged. "I am repeating what I have heard, so my knowledge is limited. That said, I cannot imagine the locals would continue using their cave ice if frequent contamination were a problem."

"Canape?" Emmaline offered. She held up a tray of sweets and savories. Georgia realized Rebecca's security would not allow the wait staff of the café to serve their mistress. When she declined the tray, the woman returned it to a waiter. He looked put out, but what can you do?

"So, your secretary doubles as a waitress?" Georgia asked Rebecca.

"Who? Oh, you mean Miss Emmaline Sweet," Rebecca said. "My mother found her to help me keep track of things. I must say, I was skeptical at first, but Miss Sweet seems to anticipate my every need. She functions both as assistant and lady's maid. She even has medical training."

They were about to move to a more mundane topic when a group of loud young men entered the coffee shop. All eyes turned to the lead man, a dashing fellow with an overly chiseled jawline wearing black riding leathers and a ruffled shirt open at the chest to reveal a few too many muscles and wild black hair. "Wife!" he called out. "Where would Mrs. Blackheart be, this fine rainy day?" On the one hand, shouting in public cafes was something no one in this crowd might expect, but neither was the man himself. Two women in the back fainted. He was that virile.

Bea grabbed Georgia's arm. "Please tell me I am not hallucinating."

Harriet crawled off her pillows and laughed. "Husband!" she called out. "Your Mrs. Blackheart is here."

"Oh, this is too good," Lady Rebecca whispered. In their sign language, she gestured, "look around the room." Several refined women were gaping in dismay as Harriet dragged herself to her feet.

"Ah, my love," Mr. Blackheart said, rushing over to Harriet. "The lads and I have been out hunting pheasant. We brought back forty of them. Will it be enough for the party?"

"Oh goodness," Harriet said, looking a bit embarrassed. Given Harriet's former reputation as a 'plain girl', Georgia suspected the overt attention from Mr. Blackheart was on purpose, although she could not fathom how he thought this would help his wife. If anything, his behavior was likely to cement her status as 'trade'. "We bought 100 of them, my darling. No matter. We will just have to include them in the feast. Anything we do not eat we can give to the poor."

"I love your generous heart," Mr. Blackheart said, taking Harriet in his sweaty arms right in front of everyone and kissing her neck. Harriet giggled with delight and kissed him back, right in front of everyone.

"Good heavens," Rebecca whispered.

"Have we slipped into a romance novel?" Bea whispered, not taking her eyes off the spectacle.

Mr. Blackheart spun back to the loud men. "Let us go, lads. Leave the ladies to drink wine and gossip." He exited without so much as a goodbye, leaving everyone blinking.

Two other women drifted over to their group. Georgia recognized them from before: the Brady sisters. "Beatrice Irvingdale? Is that you, dear?" the taller of the two asked.

"Nelda Brady, do not pretend it has been so long since we last saw one another. I only graduated two years ago," Bea answered. "Or shall I say Mrs. Nelda Northbrook? How are you?."

"Oh, Bea," Nelda said, trembling with delight or the cold. Georgia could not be sure. "Or should I say Lady Beatrice?"

"I am not a formal Lady of the court yet," Bea admitted. "Perhaps we can maintain a bit less formality for the sake of old acquaintances. You remember Georgia and Rebecca?"

Nelda curtseyed to Georgia at once. "Of course. Duchess Goldenheart. You remember my sister, Lady Nora Blacklock?"

The other Brady sister curtseyed. "Duchess Goldenheart. It is a pleasure."

"Hello," Georgia said. "Nora, call me Georgia. That goes for you too, Nelda."

Lady Rebecca also nodded. "It is a pleasure to see you again, Nelda. Congratulations on your marriage last month."

"Thank you," Nelda said, smiling. "Even though Nora found a lord, I feel like I'm the one who won the prize."

"Well done you," Rebecca answered. "I've met your mother. I assume she is pressuring you for grandchildren already."

Nelda laughed. "I see you have indeed met her. After a month of marriage, I am expected… to be expecting. We shall see. What are we drinking, ladies?"

"Borage over ice," Bea said, crinkling her nose. "How did borage get to be such a popular drink?"

"I have no idea," Georgia admitted. "It is vile."

"Oh, I love borage," Nelda said. "All those cinnamon and nutmeg variations. It must be wonderful over ice. Festive for the coming holidays."

Lady Rebecca handed her glass to Nelda. "Enjoy it. I cannot stomach the stuff, but everyone is serving it these days."

CHAPTER 6

# A QUICK HIKE IN THE WOODS.

"That may have been the strangest pre-baby-shower party I have ever attended," Lady Nora admitted. "For a moment, I thought we were being attacked by pirates." After Mr. Blackheart's sudden appearance, Harriet claimed exhaustion and excused herself for a nap. The party broke and everyone went back to their hotel rooms to prepare for the next celebration: the formal godmother investiture. Although that ceremony would not be for another two days. As per Findorian tradition, the godmother's identity would be a secret until the ceremony. Practically speaking, if Harriet had a best friend or sister, that person would be the logical choice. Since she did not appear to have either, the question would linger in the air. Georgia knew the answer, of course. Harriet asked Bea to be godmother the month before, and of course Bea humbly accepted. This was before Bea was engaged to the viscount. Harriet would never have asked if the proposal were done. It would be inappropriate for a lady of Bea's rank to sponsor the child of a trade wife. Even if said trade wife was the richest in three provinces. That said, it spoke volumes of Harriet's regard for Bea.

In the meantime, Georgia kept the secret.

The respite gave them another day to enjoy the quaint village. Georgia and Bea returned to Croft House with the Brady sisters, who were keen to walk the trail along the lake. Lady Rebecca declined the invitation, as she had letters to write, and her security attaché forbade it. Georgia made a mental note to stay in better touch with her old friend. In any case, they would have other opportunities to visit during the week.

The Brady sisters arrived with their maids and other attendants for the night, so they were ready for anything. After changing clothes and a quick cup of tea, the group set off to explore the *Frog Prince Trail.* The path broke off from the back gate and meandered through a pleasant oak grove where patches of mist hinted at the coming winter. Still, it was warm enough to keep walking. The other ladies tightened their scarves a notch and steeled themselves for a rigorous hike, but Georgia was fine. Temperature rarely bothered her. "It looks like we have several hours of daylight," Georgia said, gauging the sky. "Hopefully, the path will not be too long."

"We can always turn back in an hour," Bea noted when they arrived at the correct path. Bea took the lead with Nelda at her side. Nora fell back to walk with Georgia.

"Watch your step, ladies," Bea called out. "The roots are sticking up and it gets narrow."

"Did you try the cucumber scented water at the coffee and curio shop?" Nelda asked.

"No, I did not see it," Bea answered.

"Oh, that is a shame. It was most refreshing. I would never have thought to infuse the two together, but I believe I will in the future. I must admit, I love the city, but these Findorian country folk are so clever with their home-spun recipes." Georgia bit her tongue. Cucumber water was a famous delicacy, yes, but it originated in the Realm of Palas, not Findor. Most likely, someone introduced it to the locals.

"How are you settling into your exciting new life, Georgia?" Nora asked.

Georgia smiled. "Right to it, as always, I see. I am glad you have lost none of your directness, Nora."

Nora blushed. "I hope I do not presume, my lady." She touched her face and looked like she might cry.

"Forgive me," Georgia said with an encouraging smile. "I hoped you would laugh at that remark. It would appear my tongue is as sharp as ever, except now people are listening when I speak. Do not worry, Nora. We are in the private company of old friends. I hope you will not think I am easily offended, just as I hope not to be offensive."

Nora grinned. "Oh good. I'm sorry, Georgia."

"No need to apologize."

They marched along the trail, which continued to narrow, even as the trees grew larger and more twisted. The woods grew creepier.

Nora managed to stay quiet for all of ten minutes before speaking again. "I can't take it anymore. You have forgiven my impertinence, and I intend to take you at your word. I have a million questions," she admitted.

Georgia stepped over a tree root in the path. "Ask away. I have a feeling I know what you want to know."

Nora looked at her. "Where to begin? We read in the papers how you went off and destroyed an ice witch? You promenaded with wizards and conjurers all last season? Then there were the other investigations, all sorts of talk about vampires and ghosts. All of it as that trade family, the Hamptons, went through a public downfall. Just shocking."

Georgia shrugged. "From what I understand, 'Ice Witch' is a misnomer. She is a nature spirit corrupted by dark powers. She has lived since before mankind walked the world and will return to cause mischief again. I did not destroy her. Lucky for you and me, it is unlikely she will be able to regain her form in our lifetime." The look on Nora's face almost made her laugh. Georgia knew better than to invoke the name of the ice witch/nature spirit, a.k.a. Doria Nanette, here in the woods, or anywhere with which she was not familiar. Despite that, she noted shadows darting through the trees in the distance, and the wood grew quiet like the trees themselves knew to whom she referred. Of course, even if she had said the name, it was unlikely anything would happen. That said, her friend Lady Clara Gaye warned her there were forces still in nature we could not see, and not all of them are friendly. Best not to push one's luck.

"How extraordinary," Nora said, finally. "I will be honest. I was not sure if it was some elaborate fiction piece or evolved popular literature in the papers. I feared everyone else knew it to be fiction, and we would humiliate ourselves by asking about it."

Georgia smiled. "Oh, Nora. You and I have the same schooling. You read the old books. I am a Goldenheart, and my family history is real. The stories in the papers are mostly true. Ignore the romance section of the *Townsend Journal,* of course. The wizard Mr. Blue is a wise friend and counselor, but nothing more. My attorney, Mr. Stackhouse, will be ridding us of that rag and its salacious tales soon enough."

"I see. That is a relief," Nora breathed. "So, you own a magic sword, and your family was blessed by the old heathen gods?"

Georgia shrugged. "I do not know about the old gods, but the sword is very real. I would show it to you, but I left it at my house in the city." From the corner of her eye, she spotted something moving through the trees: a flitting shadow that seemed to grow, and then diminish. Above, a bright red Oriole with a vivid orange breast flew through the branches to perch. Georgia gazed up as the bird looked at her sideways.

"Beyond incredible," Nora said. Georgia assumed she was talking about the magic sword, not the bird above.

"See, Nora? I told you," Nelda said, stepping over another gigantic root in the path. For a moment, she snagged her hem on it and did a little dance to free the cloth without tearing anything. Once free, Nelda sighed. "I swear, I am the world's biggest klutz."

Above, the oriole watched without judgment    .

"You know my husband is Lord Blacklock," Nora said. "He works as an attaché to the Marshall of the Three Realms."

"I knew his title, but not where he worked," Georgia admitted.

"Lord Blacklock told me... in wartime you, of all people, have the authority to seize regimens in battle. He said you can call out the City Guard without a Royal Writ. He told me you could do it on a mere whim," Nora whispered. "Is he joking?"

"Oh, I see," Georgia said. "No, Nora, he is not joking. I am the Knight-Protector of the Three Realms. I will admit, I would not know how to go about seizing a military regimen, but I have it on good authority that it is within the scope of my rights. I mean, we would have to be at war for that to be a reality. I am sure if that happened, someone would explain how or, you know, fix it."

"That is incredible." Nora whistled. "Georgia, I also read you never presented yourself to court as a debutante. You never joined the season in the formal sense? I mean, I read after I did not see you present yourself at court. Of course, I read the story about the Queen's admonishment and how you must find a husband. I do not know how these reporters get their stories. One would think if the Queen gave someone a lecture in private, it would remain that way."

Georgia looked at Nora with a bit of side eye. "Nora, when you start digging, you really do not stop."

Nora chuckled. "Forgive me, it is a habit. It is also public knowledge. You know there are six Brady sisters. That's a lot of weddings for our papa to pay for, and we are all a bit too aware of the social registry. I wondered why you were not already taking suitors. Forgive me. We Bradys are a nosy bunch. Mum is a master of matchmaking, and she has so far succeeded with three upward pairings. I looked you up, because I didn't remember seeing you when my family presented me… even though we are the same age."

"Logical," Georgia admitted. "It is true. I did not present at court in the usual way. Instead, when we finished school, I began training as the last Goldenheart in earnest."

"My mother presented Georgia to the Queen-Regent last week," Bea said from the front of the line. "Georgia is a duchess from one of the oldest families in the realms, and would normally choose for herself when, if ever, to do it. The court would honor her choice, as is tradition. Although, this time yes, the Queen insisted on a meeting."

"Really?" Georgia asked. "How extraordinary."

"I looked it up," Bea offered. "You did present yourself, so it is moot now… but you did not technically have to do so. You could have refused the Queen. I know that sounds ridiculous, but no one sponsors you without your direct permission."

"I get to come out when I choose," Georgia repeated to Nora with a wink. "Not that it matters, Lady Irvingdale was kind enough to function as a proxy for my deceased mother. It was an honor for me, and I think she enjoyed doing it."

"Enjoyed it? She was beside herself with pride for you," Bea admitted.

"That is marvelous," Nora said in a tone that almost sounded sarcastic. No doubt, the thought of a woman having that sort of agency alarmed her. "But… what about the other thing?" Above them, the oriole took flight and vanished into the leaves.

"What other thing?"

"Marriage, of course. I mean, I read an article about your family. You cannot take another surname. You are the last of your kind, and any man who marries you must take your name instead. For that matter, you retain all properties and entails. He must stand as consort. Who will marry you? Honestly, nowhere in the article could I find even a mention of your mother's family, the Whitestones. What do they think of all of this?" Nora blinked, lost in the horror of it. A moment later, she seemed to remember herself. "Forgive me. What a question. I'm so sorry."

"Do not be sorry," Georgia said. "I knew how it would work, and my mother's family understood from the beginning. They stepped away from my life early on. I do not know what resentment festered between them and my Uncle Raymond, but it was enough to make them strangers. I have considered it, and I encountered my cousin, Sir Roger Whitestone, in the capital last week. He was amenable to some sort of reconciliation. But in any case, they live all the way up in Northfast at the edge of the Three Realms. They have their own world up on that mountain, and do not come down from it. I have come to not only accept my situation, but often relish it. I hope that does not sound silly."

"You have more agency than any woman I know," Nora said quietly. "That does not sound silly at all."

"What about you?" Georgia asked, changing the subject. "I see you and Nelda both found matches. I assume all is well there."

Nora nodded. "Our mother arranged husbands for both Nelda and me and our family prospered."

"That is wonderful," Georgia said. Nora did not look pleased, though. "What is wrong? Did something go amiss?"

"No. Yes. Maybe," Nora shrugged. "Nelda and I did not speak for several months after it was done. I must admit, I was heart-broken."

Georgia blinked. "Heart-broken? Oh Nora, what happened?"

"The great irony, Georgia: when my mother forged the unions, she placed me with Lord Blacklock... but I was smitten with Mr. Northbrook. I begged my father to intercede and find a way to switch positions with Nelda, but he refused. The deal was struck, and I had to live with it. I asked Nelda to help, but she saw no reason for it. I must admit I was resentful."

"Oh, my goodness," Georgia breathed. "I am sorry, Nora."

Nora shook her head, "Do not feel bad, Georgia. As it happens, Lord Blacklock **is** a perfectly civil and pleasant husband. He is a decent man who, to my surprise, treats me well and values my counsel. In hindsight, I think my mother was wise."

Georgia was about to answer, but there was a delay ahead. "Drat," Bea said. "We lost the path." Above, the sky rumbled ominously. Bea glanced at Georgia.

"I have an umbrella," Georgia said, holding it up. "We will not be caught in the rain and catch our death of fever today."

"Well, the path must be here somewhere. Let us back-track our steps," Nelda said, casting about. They turned around to find there was no path. "Good heavens, we are lost." All around, the woods grew dark. The great oaks towered in silence, and one could barely see a glint of light beyond the next ten feet.

"Let us see," Bea said. "The house is to the south. What direction is south?"

"I think it is that way," Nora said. "No. It is that way." She pointed left, then right.

Georgia gazed at the trees. Far above, the wind ruffled the leaves. Through the trees, the clouds were growing dark, even though it could not be past 2:30 in the afternoon. She could almost smell the impending rain. "As we cannot gauge our direction with the sun, we should walk in a great circle and always keep an eye on this one tree," she said, finally. "The trail will either appear, or we will eventually find the lake and make our way from there." Carefully, they made their way in an arc. All the while, the trees held out the light. It was hard to tell where they went, and they lost their marker tree at least twice, only to find it again.

"What if we do not find our way out?" Nelda asked, her voice an octave higher than normal.

"We are a quarter of a mile from the village," Georgia said in a calm tone. "We will find a way out of the woods." With the sound of fluttering wings, she spotted the red oriole again. The bird looked directly at her, hovering just overheard. It sailed above and Georgia saw a flash of wan sunlight in the distance. "Follow that bird," she cried. The oriole jumped from branch to branch, pausing long enough for the ladies to catch up. Finally, they spilled out of the wood to find a lovely glade. The sun poked through the clouds. It was pale but reassuring.

Not far away sat an old man in a dark brown cloak with a gnarled staff. He sat on a blanket with a picnic basket. "Oh, Miss Beatrice," he called out. "What a pleasant surprise."

"Mr. Brown," Bea said. "You are a sight for sore eyes."

"I see you were wandering in the woods." The old fellow stood with the aid of his staff. He opened the basket and brought out a bottle of red wine and glasses. "Do you need refreshment? I also have lemonade. No tea. Sorry, today's stroll includes only cold food options."

"Well, that does sound rather civilized," Bea said, grinning.

The ladies gathered on the blanket, and happily accepted the invitation.

"We thought we were lost for a moment," Nelda said. "The woods were dark, and we could not find the trail."

"Ah yes, oak trees," Mr. Brown said, shaking his head. "Acorn to sap, they never forget nor forgive. Whenever they get together, it is troublesome. They remember everything. Every little insult. Every ax. Every torch. Unfortunately, they rarely remember who did the insulting. That is a tree problem, though. You know, we folk with legs and feet come and go quickly, and we do not take root. It is confusing for them."

"I beg your pardon. You say the trees are angry?" Nora asked.

"Oh, yes. Every tree in this age remembers something of the times before. They whisper as the years roll by.

They remind one another with each passing day. You can hear it in the leaves on a windy day. They say, 'Do not forget. Fire, blade, and stone. Do not forget and never forgive'. Oaks pass the memory down from one age to the next. To them, it just happened, even if they cannot quite remember what started the problem," Mr. Brown explained, pouring her a glass of lemonade. "Of all the trees, oaks possess the most ridiculous memory. That is why they twist themselves all about. Birches, cottonwoods... they stand aloof. Still angry, of course. But less likely to do anything about it. Instead, they grow upward. Pines are different; they believe in a philosophy. They see themselves as helpful, so they don't mind becoming furniture for creatures who vanish within a few years."

Georgia got a better look at the old man. He was well-dressed in fine tweed and a sturdy cap, all of it shades of brown and tan. Mr. Brown's skin was a bit like old leather, and the same color as his vest. He might have been quite pale at one time and had the features of someone from another part of the world, but his entire life was spent outdoors. His eyes, startlingly green, stood out. Something in his demeanor reminded her of Mr. Blue, though. Perhaps it was the fact Mr. Brown carried a staff while speaking of trees like they were people? No wonder the locals thought he was a sorcerer. He certainly looked the part. She could see something in him they did not, though:

utter kindness. He was eccentric, but something about his face told her to listen to his every word. Even though they only met a moment before, she felt she already knew him.

The red oriole landed on the end of Mr. Brown's staff. "Ah, there you are, Kenneth," Mr. Brown said to the bird. "I take it you had fun annoying those mean old trees?" The oriole chirped gleefully.

"Oh, you have a pet bird," Nelda said, grinning. "How sweet."

"Kenneth is no pet, dear lady," Mr. Brown said. "Although, among birds, I suspect he is a luminary. You will never meet a more loyal friend than Kenneth. Even for an oriole, he is exceptional."

"I see."

"Mr. Brown," Bea said, turning back to the group, "allow me to introduce my friends. This is Duchess Goldenheart." She made a deferring gesture to Georgia.

"Duchess," Mr. Brown said, bowing at once, "What a delight. I met your uncle once. He was a good man, and I'm sorry I did not know him better."

"Thank you, Mr. Brown," Georgia said. "What a lovely thing to say. The pleasure is mine."

"These are our other friends, Lady Nora Blacklock and her sister Mrs. Nelda Northbrook," Bea said. Mr. Brown nodded to the sisters.

"Hello," Mr. Brown said. "In addition to lemonade and wine, I have some lovely cheese, sausages, and olives for a light repast. The olives are tangy in a spiced oil, and well worth a taste. I assure you they will remind you how good it is to be alive. Are you here for the same reason as Miss Beatrice?"

"Our school friend, Mrs. Harriet Blackthorn, is celebrating her impending motherhood, yes," Georgia said. "We plan to cheer her on."

"What a wonderful tradition," Mr. Brown said, pulling a small bag of cheese out of the basket. "We have two cheddars and a charming provolone. It's saltier than one might expect, but not in a tiresome way." He drew a glass jar full of olives in a fragrant oil. The smell of it made Georgia's eyes sharpen, which was amazing.

"Do you take these tiny picnics often?" Nora asked. "It seems like a bit of fun."

"Not that often, no. In my childhood, I would wander for days at a time. Today I hoped to catch my friend, the Widow Wendelin, on her way through to town. We have not spoken for months. Alas, she appears to be delayed," Mr. Brown said, squinting at the nearby trees--as if the widow might appear at any second. "Where does your path lead today, ladies?"

"We are looking for the Frog Prince Trail," Bea said, munching on a bit of provolone. "Oh, this is salty. I think we lost our way, though."

"You will find it over there," Mr. Brown pointed north. "Take that path back toward the lake. There will be a bit of mud after yesterday's rain, so be careful where you step. You will find the sign for the trail, and not far beyond is the old amphitheater. The stones are old and uneven; it is beautiful, and worth the view. They used to hold the *Frog Prince* plays there, although the site itself was built on an even older one. Before it was an amphitheater, it was a market. Before that it was thought to be a religious site; a temple to one of the old heathen gods. You might find it interesting and informative to read the plaques. Just be prepared to learn that not all that glitters is gold."

"What an odd thing to say," Nora whispered. "Is that a local expression, Mr. Brown?"

"More of a statement about the world, Lady Blacklock. That little amphitheater is older than the village. You will find it charming if you do not look too closely, but a discerning eye will spot troubling details. Shadows bending the wrong way, or sudden movements one cannot explain. These are signs of something older and more sinister."

"Thank you for that. It sounds fascinating," Georgia said, shifting the subject. She could see the other ladies getting uncomfortable. "Mr. Brown, may I ask? Do you own the hot air balloon out in the eastern field? We saw it on the way into town."

"I do, indeed, Duchess," the old man said, looking pleased. "It is a marvel of technology, but also quite expensive to maintain. I hope to use it for a long voyage when the winds change."

"Oh? Where are you going?"

"Back to the west, where I was born. I have been too long in the east. I miss my family," he said, gazing at the edge of the woods again. "It is time to go home. That said, I will be in town for another few days at least. Perhaps we can enjoy another picnic, or maybe you would like to join Kenneth and me as we hunt for mushrooms."

"Mushrooms?" Nelda asked. "You mean here on the ground?"

"Where else would one find them?" Mr. Brown asked, his eyes twinkling. "Oh, I wouldn't know where to dig without Kenneth's deep skill. You realize he is a lord among birds. His folk, the Orioles, go back to the early days of the world. When the eagles were the kings of the sky, along with the magpie princes, it was determined by the royal court of birds there needed to be a sort of regular baron. Naturally, robins and cardinals and blue jays wanted their say. So loud, those birds. The mockingbirds had a say in everything. Woodpeckers and roadrunners were aloof, but even they would not yield without some leadership.

Finally, it was decided the noble oriole would be the gentle baron of birds. Kenneth is the direct descendant of that first oriole baron. I think we can see his noble visage, can we not? Just look at that proud beak."

***

"Mr. Brown wasn't kidding when he mentioned the mud," Nelda squeaked, pulling her leg free from a puddle as they arrived at the northern path. "It's all over the hem of my skirt now."

"Oh Nelda," Nora said, shaking her head. "It is like we are girls again. You've got soil running up the back of that boot now."

"Oh drat."

"When we get back to the house, they will clean that up in no time," Bea said. "I talked to the staff, and they seem quite adept at managing the aftermath of these muddy country lanes."

"What a strange old man," Nelda mused, picking her way along. "I don't quite understand what we just encountered."

"His best friend is a bird," Nora said, shaking her head. "It's really quite simple, Nelda. The world is upside down in Dead Mourner's Grove. Thank goodness we are only here for a week."

"I suppose so. I mean, I never thought of birds that way. I must admit, Kenneth the Oriole was rather charming, and he did have a noble beak." Nelda had a dry way of being funny Georgia did not always get. It was somewhere between cheeky and innocent, but always close to the vest.

The path turned north to a bluff overlooking the lake. It was dazzling in turquoise under a growing fog. Rain was coming again. Georgia was about to suggest they turn back, but there was the sign for the *Frog Prince Trail*. Just beyond, the path led to a low wall. They walked in and found a heavy mist clinging to a circle of ancient stones surrounding a ring of seats; essentially a wall within a wall. An ancient well dominated the center of the structure. It was the kind of well, built in days long gone by: little more than a hole in the ground, but surrounded by paving stones. Off to the side lay a massive circular granite cap. No longer was it on the well, but more of an ornament next to it. Upon the cap a plaque was inscribed. "Look at this," Bea said, reading the inscription. "'Here lies the site of the final battle of the Frog Prince and his greatest foe, the Princess of the Dragonflies. She who dared to speak and fly in her vulgarity of shimmering colors. Brought her down, he did. As all who think too highly of themselves are brought down. Vanity will always be destroyed by the purity of earnest men.'."

"Ew," Nora muttered. "What an odd inscription."

Nelda gazed at the trees. "I can see the roof of the resort over there," she announced. "It cannot be more than a thousand feet away from this very spot."

"What are you getting at, Nelda?" Nora asked.

"Maybe nothing," Nelda admitted. "It's just... well, how is it that we got lost in the woods earlier, yet we are literally within sight of the village now?"

The ground was layered with smooth stones inscribed with ancient runes. This was no mere amphitheater. It was a remnant of something older.

"Was all of this in the children's book?" Nelda asked.

"It was not," Georgia said. "I think we stand in the place where an older structure was rebuilt." She remembered Mr. Brown's comment about gold. From the corner of her eye, she spotted dark shapes moving in the trees. A cold wind arose. Normally, a chill in the air meant little to Georgia, but this wind seemed to cut through her. She pulled her shawl tight and shivered.

Nelda stepped closer to the well and leaned down. "Oh, look at this, the hole is full of tadpoles." At her feet was a writhing pit of black shapes.

"Frogs?" Bea asked. "Nelda, step away this instant."

"Ew, they're all over my hem," Nelda said, swatting at her feet.

"Let us go home," Georgia said, feeling a sudden dread. In the trees, the shadows were growing.

"I have something on my foot," Nelda said, swatting at herself.

"You've gotten a stain on your skirt," Nora cried. "Oh, Nelda. Why must you be so clumsy?"

"Oh, Nora, we were just tromping through the woods. We are all covered in mud."

The edge of the amphitheater grew darker and the temperature dropped rapidly. For an instant, Georgia thought she saw someone peek around one of the great standing stones. "We have to go now," she said, looking around. Shapes gathered at the edge of the amphitheater. "Everyone. Listen to me. We are leaving." She headed for the opening, turning to make sure her friends followed. They did, and she led them away from that place. As they went, she glanced back at the tadpoles. For a moment, it seemed like something bigger might crawl out of the well. When she turned to get a better view, it was gone. The mass of tadpoles receded.

"Georgia, what did you see?" Bea asked, hurrying to keep up.

"I saw frogs, Bea," Georgia said. "Let us get home and have dinner."

***

"What a strange afternoon," Nora said, as they walked up the path to the back gate at Croft House. "What an extraordinary walk. That Mr. Brown was a character. Do you think he met up with the widow he mentioned?"

"I think he was there for many reasons," Georgia said, mulling. Wizards. "Mr. Blue has on more than one occasion professed his dislike for coincidence."

"Mr. Blue?" Nelda asked.

"Georgia's wizard friend," Bea offered. "He's quite charming. Wait. Georgia, are you saying you think Mr. Brown is a wizard too?"

"Maybe," Georgia said. "He did not identify himself as one. But I felt a bit of magic in the air. Mr. Brown had just enough cups and charcuterie to accommodate our group of four ladies, and     he talked to birds and warned us about something in the amphitheater."

"That does sound pretty wizardly," Nelda agreed.

"And there was something in that amphitheater," Nora said, as they crossed into the yard at Croft House. "I felt it too. He said if you do not look too closely, it would be fine. But I confess that only made me study it harder."

"We all made it out alive, and had a little adventure," Nelda said, still shaking mud from her hem. "I think I should enter the house through the side door. I would hate to get any of this mud on that beautiful marble floor in the lobby."

"I am sure you will be fine," Georgia said.

"Hopefully," Nelda answered. "I heard you talking to Nora. She does not mind airing out our dirty laundry."

"Oh dear," Georgia said. "I hope I did not overstep."

Nelda shrugged. "Not at all. Nora is the one who brought it up. My sister has a way of enjoying regret more than other people. For her, it has a flavor."

"Ouch. Do you mind me asking? How did you and she patch this up?"

"The business with her coveting my husband?" Nelda asked. "We did not. We are sisters. In the end, that is all that matters to me. I waited for her to come to her senses."

"Nelda, you are wiser than people give you credit," Georgia said with a smile. "So, you two travel together and it is fine."

"Oh, no, we fight constantly." Nelda laughed. "Nora drives me up a wall. I know I sound flaky to her. I know she hears me talk and rolls her eyes. I love her, though. In the end, we have one another."

"That is wonderful," Georgia said.

Nelda shrugged. "You are not sisters, but you have the same relationship with Bea. You know of what I speak."

"I suppose I do."

The ladies returned from their walk ready to change their clothes. Young Mr. Darkleaf waited at the door and bowed. "Alas," he said, "the weather precludes a proper outdoor dinner. Instead, we moved the dining room to the main hall, if it pleases you, Duchess."

"That sounds lovely, Mr. Darkleaf, thank you," Georgia said. "We will be down in a bit." Millie followed her up to change into evening wear. An hour later, Georgia and Bea reappeared at the top of the stairs to start the party. The house was decked out in bright blue and white ribbons... and the air smelled of honey and spice. The main hall was populated with a small orchestra. Four violins, two cellos, one viola, one bass viol, and a pianoforte were the evening's entertainment. Nelda and Nora joined a moment later. The orchestra was lovely and subtle, and played in the background in a way that did not intrude on conversation. Instead, they seemed to enhance everything else.

Dinner was an elaborate affair. One of the things Lord Wyclef bragged about was the kitchen at Croft House. He was proud of the staff and their capabilities. For that reason and upon his recommendation, Georgia had not sent a menu, preferring instead to trust them to create meals. The first night had been a success with the rustic Findorian sausages, but that was only a prelude to the second night. As an ode to the night before, they started with tiny Findorian sausages in a savory sauce, with a side of crispy fried bread so delightful Georgia had to pause over it. She grinned at the other ladies; quite certain she had sauce all over her face.

"That's it," Bea said, crunching her fried bread, "I'm moving to Findor."

"How does Lady Rebecca Drake stay ahead of it all?" Nelda pondered aloud.

"Stay ahead of what?" Nora asked. "I mean, really, Nelda, I simply cannot keep up with you changing subjects."

"Oh, sorry," Nelda said with a laugh. "I was enjoying the dinner, of course. But then I started thinking about Lady Rebecca. I remember her in school. Always so focused and bright. When she left because of the Phaedros rebellion, I remember wondering how she would fare. Now we see her again and she seemed quite put together."

"She was always bright and creative," Georgia said. "Wiser than her years, I suspect. If she had been allowed to live like the rest of us, I wonder if she would have been bored?"

"Oh, no," Bea said. "I think she would trade in the existential threat of a Phaedros death warrant in a heartbeat."

"Good point," Nora said. "My husband knows her. He works on the Privy Council. You know she is a member, yes? A direct advisor to the Queen-Regent."

"I was not sure what it meant to be her father's liaison. It sounds like she carries his correspondence."

"She is more like his proxy than one would imagine," Nora said. "At least, that is what my husband says. He told me she speaks with nuance and surprising wisdom for a lady so young. In fact, he said the old men on the council listen to her whenever she speaks as if she were a man. The Queen listens. Not only because she is the daughter of the kingdom's most powerful Earl, but because she has a political savvy to be respected on its own. The general estimation is she is her father's child who learned statecraft at his knee. The fruit falls not far from the tree."

"I am not surprised they think that," Georgia admitted. "She was always smart and ready to learn. Even as a girl, one could see she was going to be someone of note, with or without her father. That said, you know she spent most of her early life at the Cymbre School, and barely ever saw her father. I think she learned statecraft from the teachers."

"You saw the bodyguards, right?" Nora asked.

"I did," Georgia said. "I do not envy her situation. I did not realize she was living in the capital now. I think I will invite her to a few parties. She must feel isolated with all that protection."

"I hope the crown can work out some sort of protection for her," Nora said. "You know what happened with her mother, yes?"

"Only what Rebecca mentioned this morning. She said it was not the flu."

"According to my husband, there are assassins working for Phaedros in the Three Realms," Nora whispered. Just then, the house staff brought the next course. She ducked her head until they were gone. "Lord Blacklock says they have a sect who disguise themselves. They have another assassin sect who specialize in poisons. Everything he told me was terrifying. The whole island of Phaedros lives in fear."

"All right," Bea said, "we might want to veer back to more acceptable topics. Lady Rebecca is thriving. We should not gossip or speculate."

"Of course, you are right," Lady Nora said. "I forgot myself."

After the sausages, they enjoyed a whole chicken wrapped in bacon with potatoes, carrots, and spring onion. Dessert was a festooned plate of crispy, sweet-bread apples and a side of buttercream for dipping. Georgia thanked her lucky stars there were no proper men around to witness her devour it. Manners dictated a more lady-like approach to the meal, but between her, Bea, and the Brady sisters there wasn't a crumb in sight by the end.

"Oh, now that was satisfying," Nora murmured, sipping her wine. "I think I am having a hot flash now."

"That was amazing, yes," Nelda agreed. "Forgive me, I'm so full. I think I might lie down for a bit." She went up to her room.

"If you do not mind, I would like to join the performers for a while," Nora said. "I may not be in the Harriet Chalkbottom league of playing, but that pianoforte is calling to me." Georgia remembered Nora as an excellent player, so of course she nodded. Nora joined the entertainment, sliding in next to the piano player with a genial nod. A moment later, the man bowed away in the face of her superior training and clapped to show his delight. Nicely done, Georgia noted. She also made a note to increase his tip for the evening, as technically it was not a polite move by a guest. He could have insisted on staying, or even pushed Nora away, although it might be different in Findor. The fellow enjoyed her performance afterward, and even took a glass of wine while she played. Of course, nothing like this would happen in the capital. They were enjoying the provincial life now, where a hired musician was well within his rights to grab a glass of wine, or so she imagined.

A moment later, Nora surprised them again when she began to sing. They played an old song often done only with instruments, but at another time, a man might sing to it. Nora sang the man's part. Her voice was surprising. It was strong but also a bit like velvet. Everyone who was not a musician stopped as she performed, effortlessly singing and playing the pianoforte at the same time. Georgia watched her move, and was amazed by her dexterity. Nora had no problem wielding both instruments at the same time. When she finished, even the musicians applauded. She blushed, because anything less would be vanity... but Georgia saw her almost glow in that moment.

"Nora missed her calling," Bea whispered.

"Did she have a choice in that?" Georgia countered. "She had to marry."

"Agreed. Georgia, now that the business of food is concluded and hopefully the music continues, I think we need to learn your secret sign language," Bea announced. Of course, she had not forgotten Georgia's special language with Lady Rebecca Drake.

"Of course." Georgia laughed. "It is not difficult, really. Bear in mind, we were young girls locked in a cabin when we invented it, so there was only so much to talk about."

Bea pointed at herself with two fingers, the way Georgia had at the window to the curio and coffee shop.

"Now, I recall you moved like this? I assume this means 'me' or 'I'?"

"Correct," Georgia said. "It must be two fingers with your pinkie bent just so. That way we know we are formally talking in code. To the untrained eye, it should be like one adjusting a button or a stray lock of hair." After that, she walked Bea through every gesture and connecting motion, carefully explaining the context of each. Not surprising, Bea was fluent in one lesson, such was her command of languages. By evening tea, when the orchestra finished, the staff went to bed, Nora went up, and only they remained, Bea re-taught Georgia how to say half the words again in a stealthier way than before.

By midnight, they spoke entirely with subtle ear-tugs, faint chinwags, and most brilliantly with variations tucking a lock of hair behind one's ear. Every gesture looked like the regular gestures a lady of means might engage in to maintain her appearance or appear modest. Instead of the odd pinkie position, Bea started a simpler finger-to-thumb gesture to show she was speaking. It made the whole process easier, while also more subtle to the eyes of those who did not understand the secret language. "It looks like you are about to adjust your collar," Bea said. "A gesture of genteel modesty. Instead, you open the communication with a starting gesture."

# CHAPTER 7

# NELDA HAS A MALADY.

In the warmth of her covers, Georgia dreamt of walking in faraway woods with the magic blade in her hand. She knew she was dreaming. Mist clung to the ground, and in her dream, Georgia felt alert and happy. It was as if she was off on some tremendously important adventure, like one of her ancestors. There was a man there. He smiled and had a magic sword of his own. Together, they were a team. The man said something terribly clever and made her laugh, even as they continued to stalk through the misty woods. A moment later, they were in some sort of vague danger, but it was thrilling. There was something in the shadows of the trees. It was following her. Where had her companion gone? Wait. Where was her magic sword? She woke at dawn. Her room smelled of fresh rosemary. From the corner of her eye, she watched one of the scullery maids silently exit the room after lighting the fireplace.

The godmother unveiling was still a day away, so Georgia slept in. After the decadence of the night before, she assumed the ladies would sleep in, too. Either way, they could fend for themselves. The staff would make sure no one went hungry with an abundance of tea and honey rosemary cakes waiting in each room. When she got up after 9am, the still crisp air hinted at impending autumn. Through the window, the morning looked wan and tinged with a strange gold. It made her feel oddly lonely. Millie checked on her a moment later. "Are we ready, my lady?" she asked.

"I suppose we are, Millie," Georgia answered, her mind went back to the man in the dream. He seemed familiar, like someone she knew. What had he said to make her laugh? Gone now, along with his face. How depressing. On the other hand, a tray full of hot tea and warm cakes with butter, cream, and marmalade called her name. She settled in with it as Millie went through her morning clothes.

Georgia arrived downstairs to find the dining room full of savory breakfast treats and the curtains thrown back to let in the golden morning light. A huge tray of bacon, eggs, tomatoes, beans, and sausages lay on the side. Bea sat pouring over the latest *Young Ladies Journal*. "How did you sleep?" Georgia asked.

"Barely a wink," Bea said, grinning. "Your secret language kept me up all night. Also, I had a bit of indigestion. Findor has wonderful food, but the spice has a way of lingering. Finally, I got up and found Millie down in the cellar washing your clothes. Georgia, I think we should teach her the secret language."

"I beg your pardon?"

Bea chuckled. "I had this thought: who better than your lady's maid to know your secret language? If you need a quick exit from a party or other function, she will know before anyone else. If you need a wardrobe shift without making a fuss, signal her across the way and she gets to work."

"Interesting idea," Georgia admitted, blinking. "I can see the usefulness of it. I know Millie can read, but can she learn languages? Forgive me, Bea, but not everyone has your ability to learn at the drop of a hat."

"There is only one way to find out," Bea said. "This will be good for you. Alas, Mrs. Macklin has no mind for it, but Millie is still young and so bright. And Georgia, she wants to make you happy. More than that, she is curious by nature. She might enjoy learning it."

"Very well," Georgia said, grabbing a plate full of bacon, eggs, and tomatoes. Having a silent language with one's personal maid no one else understands could be useful. "You are not eating?"

"Oh, they had to replace the plate of bacon before you got here," Bea said with a grin. "Nora and I made short work of it. She went up to get Nelda. We thought you two would sleep all day."

Another door opened and Mr. Darkleaf stepped in. He looked pale. "My lady," he said to Georgia, "there seems to be a problem with Mrs. Northbrook. She developed a fever in the night. Lady Blacklock is asking for a doctor."

"A doctor. That sounds serious," Georgia said.

"I have never seen anyone look like that," Mr. Darkleaf admitted. "Granted, yes, I am young, but I have seen ill people. Never like this, though."

"In that case, you should definitely fetch the doctor," Bea said, heading for the door. "I will check on her too."

"My lady, I am afraid the village does not host a regular physician, per se. Like many of these little country hamlets, Dead Mourner's Grove gets periodic visits from one doctor or another. If it is important, we usually go to the city."

"I suppose that makes sense," Georgia said. "It is only a day's ride to Oradale. Very well, let us get Nelda ready. If her sister cannot take her, we can send her in the carriage."

"Oh, Georgia," Bea moaned, shaking her head. "What if she is too sick to travel?"

Georgia blinked. "Right. A day-long ride through those woods might be worse than the illness. Bea, you had medical training in school. Perhaps you can help?"

"I will do my best," Bea promised. She turned to Mr. Darkleaf, "For a fever, we will need to cool her skin. Is there any ice left from the party last night?"

"We can get some from the ice cave below the basement."

"Bring it in a bowl, with a separate bowl of cool water and a few towels. You also stock ginger in the house. I tasted it in the cooking last night. Please make a pot of ginger tea," Bea instructed.

"Yes, my lady," Mr. Darkleaf said.

Bea turned to leave but hesitated. "Mr. Darkleaf, your neighbor Mr. Brown is a retired animal doctor. He might not be an expert on people, but is more experienced with illness in general than I am. Despite your concerns about his character, I think we should summon him."

"I will fetch him this instant," the young butler announced. "I will take your leave then."

"By all means," Georgia nodded. She turned to Bea, "Let's go see Nelda."

They found Nora at the top of the stairs weeping soundlessly. "Something is direly wrong, Georgia," Nora gasped.

Bea hurried down the hall with Georgia right behind. They entered Nelda's room without knocking. Nelda was in her bed, still in night clothes, her eyes wide and staring. That would have been startling enough, but her eyes were blood red and her lips black. Georgia gasped, despite herself. Nelda shook with intense fever and sweat. Even the sheets were wet. "What is this thing that builds our dreams," Nelda whispered hoarsely, "only to slip away?" She started to cry and coughed up a bit of grey spittle.

"Be still," Bea said, checking her forehead. "She is burning up, Georgia. Where are those towels?"

Nelda's maid came in with another house maid carrying towels, bowls of water, and ice. Bea snatched a towel and dipped it in the water. When she pressed it to Nelda's forehead, Nelda sighed and blinked. "Thank you," she whispered. "I don't deserve your kindness, Harriet. I know that but thank you all the same. And thank you for inviting me to your lovely party. Everyone looks so happy."

"Shush," Bea whispered, pressing the cool towel to her neck and face. "Nelda, you have a high fever, and I think you might be hallucinating. Do you understand what I am saying?"

"Oh, Harriet," Nelda gasped, grabbing Bea's wrist. "I saw him again last night. Do you know who I mean? You remember him, right?" She looked wild. The dark circles under her eyes were like wounds. "He's coming for you, Harriet. He is coming." A moment later, Nelda fell back and began to weep.

"Be still, Nelda," Bea said softly. "You must rest."

"No," Nelda gasped, blinking rapidly. "He has returned, Harriet. He brings the Blood Morning with him."

"What is she saying?" Georgia asked.

"Nothing sensible. The poor thing is dehydrated and rambling. We need to give her water," Bea said, shaking her head. "Georgia, she is soaked with sweat, and there is an odor. I cannot put my finger on it, but it is not right."

"You said it yourself, it is the fever," Georgia answered, taking a cup of water from a maid. "Give her this."

Bea nodded, carefully feeding Nelda. "Georgia, this is not normal."

The door flew open, and Mr. Brown entered slowly with his staff in hand. Fortunately, he had no bird perched on it. "Please, let me see her," he whispered. "Oh, poor girl. She was so charming only yesterday. Was she in the rain?"

Georgia shook her head. "We went to the amphitheater, and then walked a bit. I do not think she caught a draft, Mr. Brown. Last night, she had a fine appetite for dinner. Although, she did get tired right after. At the time, I assumed she grew drowsy from the food."

"I see," the old man said, leaning in close to Nelda. "Can you hear me?" He asked. His voice changed: no longer reedy or old. His words were momentarily like a song. Georgia had heard that tone before. Lady Clara

Gaye, the Witch of Volusia, sang to her like that once when she was ill.

Nelda jolted awake. "Oh," she gasped, "Oh no. Let me get away. I must not linger."

"Where would you go?" Mr. Brown asked, his voice still faintly echoing in the room.

"Somewhere else," Nelda said weakly. "Help me. He is near."

"Who? Who is near?" Mr. Brown asked.

"The shadow man," Nelda whispered. "You must warn Harriet. Will you tell her? I am so sorry, I forgot about him... over the years... I forgot...or I... I tried to forget." She trembled, and then began to cough flecks of blood. Mr. Brown turned to his bag and withdrew a vial of amber liquid.

"Swiftly," the old man said, his voice loud enough to rattle the window. "Make her drink this, Georgia. Do it now."

Georgia grabbed the vial, uncorked it, and pressed it to Nelda's mouth. At first, she spat and did not respond, but then began to drink it. A moment later, she settled into sleep.

Mr. Brown watched her. "Well done. That will give her strength if she has the will to live."

"I beg your pardon?" Bea asked. "Surely she will want to live."

"She may yet fail," Mr. Brown said in a quiet voice. "It is much like she is drowning in the air. You must keep an eye on her. I do not know what this ailment is. It could be an exotic fever, a brutal chill, or something worse."

"Worse? Like what?" Georgia asked.

"Poison? Infection? Infestation?" He looked at her. "Who knows? I only arrived a moment ago. I will examine her further, but it looks to these old eyes like an opportunistic infection. For all we know, she picked it up weeks ago in another location. I would urge you to wait and let her rest. When she awakes, feed her something plain like boiled oats and clean water."

"We will do that," Georgia said. "Mr. Brown, what was all of that talk of a shadow man?"

"Memories," the old man whispered. "Or guilt, Lady Georgia. Something from a time before I came to know this sweet young woman, when she had secrets. Whatever those secrets are, something haunts her."

"Other secrets?"

"Ask the one she calls Harriet," he said. "If anyone knows who this shadow man is, it must be her, yes? But Harriet must also know what guilt lays upon poor Nelda."

"What if all of this talk of a shadow man is dehydration and fever?" Bea asked.

"Then Nelda is in luck," Mr. Brown answered. "The illness will pass, and if she is strong, she will survive. Now leave us so I can do a more thorough examination."

"What if the shadow man is not a product of fever or imagination?" Georgia asked as he ushered them out. From the edge of her eye, the dark corners of the room began to deepen and she thought she caught a faint magical glow from Mr. Brown's hands. She regretted leaving her magic sword behind. She could never admit this to Bea, as she would never hear the end of it.

"I cannot say yet," Mr. Brown answered. "That said, you sense something here, do you not?"

"I do. I think I do," Georgia said, glancing around the room. A moment before, the shadows were moving. Now it all looked normal.

"You would not be wrong, I suspect. Now you should go. I need to sit with the patient."

They waited an hour downstairs, picking at the remains of breakfast before Mr. Brown appeared at the door. "Nelda may recover, but she is also growing weaker. She will sleep for a while," he said without preamble. "There is a toxin in her body. In the old days, they would call it an ill humor and bleed her, but I think it must be an allergic reaction to something she encountered on the trail yesterday. It is pulling her down. That said, I believe there is a remedy."

"Tell us?" Nora asked, jumping up. "A medicine from the city?"

"There is no time to go to the city, but there is a local herb called *Prince Robert Flower*. It grows in the woods nearby. If we boil and strain it, the infused water should help Nelda recover when ingested. At the same time, the fragrance will help her breathe easier. It will drive almost any natural poison from her body. I am going to search for it," Mr. Brown said. "The plant grows in isolated spots on the roots of ancient trees where the shade is deep and cool. The high wood to the east of the village is an ideal location."

"I will join you," Nora said without hesitation. "Sitting here useless will ruin me. Besides, two sets of eyes are better than one, are they not?"

"They are, indeed," Mr. Brown answered with a nod. "And a sister's eyes should be particularly sharp. I think Nelda will only survive for another day in her current condition, so we must act."

"One day," Bea echoed. "Good Heavens."

Nora jumped up. "Let us go then."

"Is there anything we can do while you are gone?" Georgia asked.

As Nora gathered her coat, Mr. Brown stepped closer to Georgia and Bea. "Duchess, I suggest you and Lady Beatrice check over the patient thoroughly. There is a faint odor of something on her person. It may be a cut or wound not healing. It would be improper for me to check her limbs myself. You and Lady Beatrice are beyond reproach. You are friends, women of note, and Bea has enough medical training to understand the situation and answer questions. I recommend you inspect Mrs. Northbrook... er, Nelda... to make sure she has no decay."

"Decay?" Georgia asked, aghast.

Bea leaned in. "She may be septic?"

"Something is off," Mr. Brown said. "She has more than one ailment. There is a fever, but something else is causing the scent, Miss Beatrice. It is like rot, but I can also detect something metallic in the air. Check her knees and ankles. The joints of the body are often the intersection of these ailments."

"We will do what we can," Georgia said, feeling her chest tighten. Bea did not wait for Nora and Mr. Brown to leave before going back to Nelda. Georgia paused for a moment to rub her eyes and think. Around her, shadows darted in the corners of the room. She raced upstairs.

"I will set up a bath for her downstairs," Bea said. "We will need to clean her."

"I think there are tubs on the second floor," Georgia said.

"The staff would have to carry hot water up in buckets. We have no time for that," Bea answered. "Downstairs, they have a furnace and plumbing."

Georgia nodded. "I will bring her down in a moment."

The instant Georgia lifted her from the bed Nelda began to scream. At the same time, Georgia was nearly overwhelmed by the odor.

"Let go of me," Nelda cried. "Don't take me. I want to live."

Bea ran back into the room and gaped. "Nelda," she said, "We are trying to help you. Now, you will go with us, old friend. Unless you do not want assistance?"

Nelda relented glumly. "Indeed," she whispered. "I do not feel well, though. What am I to do?"

Bea was firm. "You are to listen and agree. We will help you, Nelda. But only if you agree. That said, I cannot face your sister if you do not. Do you understand?"

"I think I do," Nelda said, trembling. "I agree."

Georgia was done waiting. She carried Nelda down to the bathing chamber. Followed by half a dozen maids and cooking staff, they got to the basement. Bea took over, helping Nelda out of her clothes. As they pulled garments away, Nelda screamed again, and one of the maids had to sit down. Rotting sores covered every joint on her body. The odor grew so potent Georgia wondered if she would ever smell anything else.

"What is that?" one of the maids squeaked, pointing at Nelda's face. Under the skin of her cheek... something wriggled.

Nelda coughed violently as blackish fluid rolled from her lips.

"She swallowed something," Bea said. She pulled Nelda's mouth open. "Cough," she said firmly. "Cough now, Nelda." Without waiting, Bea stuck her finger down the woman's throat. Nelda gagged, choked, and writhed. "Let it go. Martha, get a bucket. Do it now."

One of the maids shoved a wash bucket next to Nelda's feet. Bea kept her fingers in the woman's mouth and pushed her forward to hunch.

Bea flinched, but held her position. "Something just moved in her throat," she whispered.

With a violent lurch, Nelda gagged and coughed. For a moment, she seemed to calm, and Georgia thought the worst was over. Suddenly, the woman retched up thick bands of dark mucus. Bea aimed her head over the bucket, and they watched as Nelda filled it with bile. When she was done, she laid back breathing raggedly.

"Should we bleed her?" one of the maids asked. "You know, to rid her of the ill humors?"

"Absolutely not. Get her into the tub," Bea instructed. "Be gentle. She is covered in sores. But now I feel her skin cooling. We should keep her warm and clean her wounds.

Janet, we will need a soft cloth for this." One of the maids scurried away.

Bea turned back to the first maid. "Martha, while we manage the bath, check through that bucket."

"Check through it, my lady?" Martha wailed.

"Look for traces of blood or anything solid. Whatever she swallowed must be in there. Do not touch the mucus, though. If she has a disease, it could transfer on contact. Use one of those carpet beaters."

"Yes, my lady," Martha looked like she might be sick in a moment herself, but grabbed a stick off the counter, leaned in, and began stirring the bucket gingerly. Georgia laid Nelda in the warm water of the bath. The woman was trembling and alarmingly cold to the touch.

Bea stepped around Georgia to get a better look at Nelda's sores. Janet returned with an armful of fluffy towels. "We usually keep these in the master's room," she said in an uncertain voice.

"I am sure Lord Wyclef will understand," Georgia said. "If he asks, tell him I requested them."

"Yes, Duchess."

Martha gasped, almost dropping the bucket. "My lady... oh goodness."

"What do you see? Is there blood?" Bea asked.

Martha held up the bucket to show the mucus. It was writhing. "It is full of... tadpoles," she whispered. Georgia stared into the bucket.

Bea shuddered. "Cover it with a rag or something, Martha. Store the fluid... and tadpoles... until Mr. Brown returns. Perhaps he can shed light on what it means."

"I am pretty sure he will tell us that tadpoles in one's throat qualifies as unnatural," Georgia muttered.

"Probably," Bea agreed. "In the meantime, let us get Nelda cleaned up. Be careful of the sores on her wrists and knees. The sooner we have her back in bed the better. Is there another room we can put her in? Somewhere close to the tub in case we need to clean her again. I fear her malady infected the bed she was in before. We will need to clean the linens." She looked around for any of the maids to answer.

"There is an empty servant's room down here in the basement," Janet said. "It is not large, but has a window, and the bed is comfortable. Perhaps not as soft as the ones upstairs, though."

"We will make it work," Bea said. "Prepare that room. Use the softest linens you can find and be certain the area is spotless. No mold or dust. No perfumed cleaning oils with a strong odor. Do you understand? She must be able to breathe. This is all hands-on-deck. If you need help cleaning or carrying anything, ask someone. I do not care who you ask. Ask me. Anyone. Let us get it done, though."

"Yes, my lady." Janet nodded to one of the cooks. Together they hurried off.

***

"Once you finish cleaning upstairs, take whatever time you need. Rest. Cry. Take a walk. Whatever. Nothing about today has been normal for any of us, and it is still early," Georgia said to the maids. She turned to the cooks. "If you show me where the tea is, I can boil my own water. All of you need to sit down and put your feet up. I cannot imagine what Lord Wyclef will think when he hears about today's events, but from my point of view, you all handled yourselves admirably."

"We will not be far away, my lady," said Mrs. Hensley, the head cook. "If you need anything." She led Georgia and Bea into her private office adjacent to the kitchen, as it was close to the sickroom. The chairs had no cushions but were comfortable enough. A moment later, she returned with a tray of apricots, blueberries, sliced green apple, biscuits, tea, and honey.

Once Mrs. Hensley was gone, Georgia looked at Bea. "You managed that whole situation quite well."

"Thank you. I think, once again, I might be in my element bossing people around," Bea admitted. She stretched her legs under the desk and leaned back. Mrs. Hensley posted a footman at the door in case they needed anything. Otherwise, the regular house routine was effectively wrecked.

"Well, now we have the rest of the day to relax," Georgia said with a wry smirk.

Bea giggled. "Sorry," she said immediately. "I feel like my head is about to crack open. What a morning."

"When you were lecturing Nelda about cooperating, I was reminded of your old governess," Georgia whispered.

"Mrs. Donley," Bea said. "I suppose I was doing an imitation of her."

"'If you do not cooperate young lady, we will have to leave you in the bed to rot'," Georgia said, imitating Bea's voice.

"I did not say that," Bea gasped, trying not to laugh. "Why are we making fun here?"

Georgia shrugged. "I do not know, but if I do not laugh about something I may start crying."

There was a commotion from upstairs. "Duchess, the old man... Mr. Brown... he and Lady Blacklock have returned," said a footman, ducking his head in.

Georgia and Bea hopped up. Mr. Brown and Nora were in the main kitchen. They found them cutting up scraps of weeds into a boiling pot of water. "This will help Nelda breathe," Mr. Brown said. The air smelled like freshly cut grass. Across the room, Mrs. Hensley mashed more of the plants into a paste. "Mrs. Hensley, make two grades of the paste. First, the thicker one. We will treat Nelda's wounds with it. Make another batch right after but dilute it as if you were making milk and porridge. In fact, feel free to sweeten it with milk. We will feed the second batch to her," Mr. Brown instructed. Mrs. Hensley nodded and continued mashing. The old man turned to Bea. "Miss Beatrice, you cleaned her up?"

"We did, yes," Bea said. "I want to show you something, Mr. Brown. We got her to cough up the obstruction in her lungs."

"Well done, Miss Beatrice. You are a marvel, and I am heartened to see you took this on," the old man said, handing a taurine of the boiled plants to Janet the maid. "Put this on the night table next to Mrs. Northbrook. The aroma will help her breathe. Keep the window open." Janet took it away, with Nora following right behind.

"How can we help?" Bea asked.

"Rest, reflect, catch up on your correspondence, perhaps?" Mr. Brown suggested. "You have managed the crisis in my absence, Miss Beatrice. You still have a baby shower event to attend in the morning if I am not mistaken. If all goes well, Nelda will be out of danger by then. Your quick intervention likely saved her life. In the meantime, we can only wait and see, so distracting yourself with matters of the mundane world might be a welcome change after this morning."

"What about the tadpoles in her lungs?" Bea asked.

"Sorcery," Mrs. Hensley muttered.

"It may be from tainted water," Mr. Brown replied. "She must have drunk something with frog eggs in it. Somehow they were stuck in her throat or got into her lungs. They could have hatched within her, even as the infected water weakened her body. The tadpoles were dying immediately, but that would also explain them struggling. The entire experience would have been horrific, I am sure."

"Tainted water?" Bea asked, blinking. "If this is a mundane illness, I do not know what to think."

Mr. Brown shrugged. "It does not seem mundane to me either. But without some other evidence, we are speculating." He tilted his head at Mrs. Hensley, who was working on the weed paste. She looked quite pale and nervous. Mr. Brown leaned closer to whisper. "Let us not cause a panic until we are sure what we are dealing with, eh?"

"Good advice," Bea whispered back.

"Mrs. Hensley, you will want to check all the water barrels. Look for an oily sheen on top, and any offensive odor. You had ice from the basement cave. There was a bit of flooding and rain last week. In those conditions, frog eggs or other particulates could have slipped into the water supply without notice."

"Aye, sir," Mrs. Hensley said.

"Nelda had the cucumber scented water at the coffee and curio shop yesterday," Georgia recalled. "She mentioned it."

"And she drank that awful, iced borage," Bea added. "I remember her getting a second glass."

Mr. Brown nodded. "We should get young Mr. Darkleaf to send a message to them. If their supply is polluted, others are at risk."

"I will check our barrels just in case," Mrs. Hensley said.

"I will help you," Bea said, following the cook.

From there, Georgia went in to see Nelda again. Following Mr. Brown's instruction, Nora placed the pot of boiled weed water on the bedside table. Right away, Georgia could see Nelda breathing more easily. She looked almost comfortable on the little servant's bed. Nora sat nearby, quietly reading correspondence. "Nora and I will watch her now," Mr. Brown whispered, ushering Georgia and Bea back to the hallway. "You checked her over for sores and found the source of the odor, I take it?"

Georgia nodded. "We did. She is covered in them, Mr. Brown. I do not think we can transport her to the city in this condition."

The old man glanced at the door. "It may take her several weeks to fully recover. I would hate to move her from the comfort of this house. Even here in the basement it is better than elsewhere."

"I will write to Lord Wyclef and see if he will loan it to us a bit longer," Georgia offered.

"Good idea," Mr. Brown agreed. He tilted his head. "Duchess, you are somewhat more familiar with the supernatural world. I read about you in the papers."

"I know my fair share of wizards and witches, yes," Georgia admitted. Given Mr. Brown's affinity for Kenneth the Oriole, she wanted to ask him point blank if he was a wizard. Mr. Blue could talk to birds, as she recalled, horses. The problem with asking a question like that is always the answer. Either Mr. Brown says, 'oh yes, I am a wizard and I love it' or he looks at her like she is a madwoman. Granted, the latter seemed unlikely after the morning they just had.

Mr. Brown nodded. "As an animal doctor, I have had some experience with the, shall we say, unexplainable in my long life. It might sound silly, but animals walk in many worlds, and when you care for them... well, sometimes you see things you do not expect."

"I believe I understand you," Georgia said. So... not a wizard? Merely a veterinarian?

"There is something going on here that works outside the bounds of what we would call the normal world, my lady. I cannot shake the feeling that poor Nelda has been infected by a malady of supernatural origin. The tadpoles in her throat and strange sores. These are symptoms of something more than mere water contamination. Fortunately, we got to her in time. I think if she rests and continues to ingest the boiled leaves, she will recover from it."

"Oh dear," Georgia answered.

"I wanted to mention it to you alone, though," Mr. Brown whispered.

"Oh, I think Bea would understand. In fact, I suspect she would agree," Georgia said.

"I think so too. At the same, if I am wrong, we may need Miss Beatrice to keep a level head and see only the facts. I would hate to jump to a wrong conclusion," Mr. Brown admitted.

"Of course." Georgia almost told Mr. Brown about any one of Bea's many conspiracy theories, but opted to hold her tongue. It was one thing to tease her friend and quite another to say a word against her in private. "You think the supernatural malady would have killed her, but she is now safe?"

The old man shrugged. "I think she would have died eventually from it, yes... but not before something worse happened."

"Worse? Worse than death, Mr. Brown?"

Mr. Brown rubbed his eyes. "Perhaps I am a mad old man after all, Duchess. That said, I cannot shake the feeling that the tadpoles and sores were a sign of something quite awful. I think she was... well, I will just say it. I think she was transforming into something else."

One of the footmen, Clyde, appeared at the other end of the corridor. He looked somewhat alarmed but waited for her to finish her conversation.

"It would appear you have another crisis looming," Mr. Brown said. "Duchess, before you go, there is another thing. That metallic smell in the air. You got a whiff of it, yes?"

"Yes," Georgia said. "It was unpleasant." She wanted to go back to the 'Nelda transforming' discussion but was not sure where to start.

"I believe that odor is a side effect of poisoning," Mr. Brown whispered. "I think Nelda has at least two problems: the first being some sort of supernatural malady, and the second was that she drank some sort of poisoned substance within the last day."

"Wait," Georgia stammered. "Magic and poison together?"

Mr. Brown nodded. "On the bright side, she appears to be recovering from both. I should let you go. Your footman looks urgent."

"We will speak again," Georgia said. Mr. Brown returned to Nelda's room.

"Duchess," Clyde said with a bow, "I am sorry to interrupt."

"It is fine, Clyde," she answered. "We were just finishing."

"Of course, Duchess. There is a Constable Jenkins from the county here to see you. He said it is important."

CHAPTER 8

# THE PROBLEM AT REDSTONE HOUSE.

Constable Jenkins was a tall thin fellow with an impeccable black mustache. He looked like most Findorians with dark hair, olive skin, and brown eyes. Despite being so common, Georgia thought there was something charming in the way he held his hat in the study. Also, he had abnormally thick eyebrows, which she kept staring at. He was nervous but appeared resolute to meet her. When she entered, he fell into a bow that really was a bit too deep... but was almost endearing.

"Good morning, Constable," she said. Behind her, Clyde was on hand. She signaled him to bring tea, then sat down. "Please, sit with me. How may I assist you?"

"Your Grace," the Constable started.

Georgia winced. "Sorry. Please call me Duchess. 'Grace' is a royal honorific. You can also call me Lady Georgia if that is easier. I would not be offended." Once again, she waved to him to sit... which he did, hat in hand.

"Uh, Duchess, I am so sorry to bother you on your holiday. Um, it appears we have a violent crime in the village," he said.

"Oh?"

"Forgive me, we do not get these things in Dead Mourner's Grove. This morning, I was settling a dispute between Nordy Branwell and Nappy Whitefig. They own adjacent pig farms, and have a long-standing disagreement over who owns one section of mud. Last night a few sows crossed the line... there is no fence, of course. It was the most exciting thing to happen in these parts for months," he stammered. "But when I returned, I found out about the break-in."

Clyde returned with tea and holiday cakes. The Constable paused while the footman poured the tea. Constable Jenkins properly waited for her to take a sip, then did so himself. She nibbled the holiday cake, which had a pleasing sweet and spicy quality. The Constable also had a nibble, smiling in appreciation. Georgia waited patiently. When Clyde departed, she nodded for the story to continue.

"Of course, Duchess," said Constable Jenkins. "Where was I?"

"You returned from the pig farmer dispute to learn about a break in. Feel free to enjoy the cake while you talk. I am not a stickler about that."

"Oh, yes, of course. Well, I went to the scene, over at Redstone House. It is a residence owned by a famous anthropologist or... professor of antiquities named Lord Redstone. He is never there, as he is always traveling to exotic ruins in faraway lands. But his sister, Mrs. Crauford, comes and goes frequently. She lives in the city and uses the place as a getaway country home. Her maid arrived ahead of her and found the evidence in the library."

Georgia set her tea down. "I see. What sort of evidence?"

"This is where it all gets a bit murky," Jenkins said, "The maid did not want her mistress to be upset when she arrived, so she cleaned the room. Once that was done, she went to the Constable's office and filed a report."

"Astounding," Georgia said, setting her cup down. "She destroyed the evidence."

"According to the report, the maid cleaned up a significant amount of blood in one of the rooms. She also found a shoe and a knife." Jenkins shook his head. "She disposed of the blood, but kept the shoe and knife."

"People do strange things when they are unsure how to proceed," Georgia answered.

"When I looked at the room, I could not even find a blood stain on the floor. She is an excellent maid," Constable Jenkins admitted.

"She sounds a little too good," Georgia said slowly. "May I ask why you are bringing this matter to me, Constable?"

"I remembered reading in the *Oradale Chronicler* article, you said you would always be ready to lend a hand to the authorities in these situations." He looked miserable. "Oh dear, have I overstepped?"

"Taking it upon yourself to visit a duchess without notice? Maybe," Georgia admitted. "Then again, I did say that to the paper. You cannot be blamed for taking me at my word, Constable."

"Thank you, my lady. I have no experience with anything like this. As I mentioned before, we do not see that sort of thing in Dead Mourner's Grove. I was, of course, trained by the County Constabulary, but I fear this case is beyond my limited scope. We all read about your adventure last year with the murderous Hampton family, and I thought you could give me advice on how to approach this case. If it is not too much trouble. If you cannot help, I could send a letter to the City Constabulary and see if they will dispatch an Inspector."

"Yes, you could. And it might still come to that. I am not sure I can offer much assistance. Do you have any suspects?"

"Not yet, my lady. We are not even certain who was killed."

Georgia nodded slowly. "No suspect, no body, no evidence... only the word of a housemaid that anything even happened. This sounds like a challenge," Georgia said. "But I will try to assist as best I can." She stood up. "Constable Jenkins, we should go back to Redstone House together. I think I should look at everything."

Constable Jenkins stood and bowed again. "Yes, Duchess. I came here in a gig. It has two seats, if you are willing to ride in it. If not, I can get another coach."

"That will suffice," Georgia said. "Please, make yourself comfortable with the tea and cakes. I need to change clothes and then I will be ready." He bowed again as she left. Clyde was waiting in the hall with Bea. "Clyde, those cakes are a marvel. So sweet, but with the cheekiest hint of spice."

"Thank you, my lady," Clyde said, smiling. "I'll tell the cook you enjoyed them."

"You do that. I am going to leave with the Constable in a few minutes. I will be at Redstone House, and perhaps at the Constable's office... if anyone else needs me."

"Yes, Duchess," the footman bowed hastily.

"Do you want company?" Bea asked.

"Only if you are prepared for a ride sitting in my lap in a two-wheel gig, followed by a potentially vexing burglary investigation," Georgia said. "It might be grisly. It might not be. It has evidently begun in an unusual way, though."

"How so?"

"The housemaid destroyed some of the evidence. I will question her. Pray she was observant."

"Without seeing it yourself, you will be making guesses. I hate that. Very well, I will stay here and keep an eye on our guests," Bea said. "Will you be home for dinner?"

"I do not know," Georgia said, heading for her room. "I suspect I will make it back for tea, though. If you stay up, a late supper might be welcome."

"I will see it managed," Bea said, veering off toward the kitchen.

Georgia rounded up Millie, who was just finishing helping the chamber maids clean linens. "I know I should let you have a rest with everyone else, but I will need something sensible for detective work," she instructed. "Not without style, of course. But if I have to crawl around or peek under a table, I would like to be able to get up without assistance."

"I have just the ensemble, my lady," Millie said without hesitation, helping her out of her clothes. Georgia watched as the maid gathered parts of the outfit. Millie had grown in confidence since her first days in Georgia's employ. When they first met, Millie was like a mouse, even though she came from a noted service family. Millie's surname was Pepper. For generations, the Peppers were footmen, valets, housekeepers, butlers, and ladies' maids to noble and gentry families across the Three Realms. They had a pedigree of their own kind. To be a Pepper meant something, and other families in service aspired to be like them. Some, in fact, actively sought matches with the family. For that reason, it was odd to hear that Millie was being courted by a tradesman.

The tradesman in question was a fellow named Mr. Martin Edson. He was the proud owner of Edson Flowers, which was a thriving enterprise with three shops and a massive greenhouse in the West Town District. He first encountered Millie at Sir Lionel Rance's dress studio on Market Street. Mr. Edson was supervising a delivery, and Millie was there to pick up ribbons and other dressmaking supplies. They struck up a brief conversation. She found him pleasant, but he apparently could not stop thinking about her. Millie returned to the house with her supplies and thought nothing of it. Mr. Edson, on the other hand, spent the next month trying to track her down again… even going so far as to post an employee to watch the dressmaker studio in case she returned.

Sir Lionel Rance quickly grew tired of it all and invited them both to lunch on his patio. It was there he formally introduced them. Mr. Edson immediately obtained Millie's address and began writing polite letters. Millie, after some hesitation, responded. Over the next few weeks, Millie received a letter every day from Mr. Edson inviting her to dine with him. She eventually took him up on the invitation, chaperoned of course, and they formed a connection. Georgia suspected he would propose after they returned from Harriet's baby shower.

If Millie took Mr. Edson's advances seriously, Georgia wondered if it meant breaking in a new lady's maid. When Millie turned back to her, she put the thought out of her mind. It was too soon for that sort of thing. Millie switched Georgia out to a green muslin frock that lifted above the ankle for better movement. She found a pair of dark slippers with thick soles that were not too obvious. Once that was in place, Millie put her in a mid-length black wool pelisse. The arms were comfortable and loose so she could crawl around in it if necessary while maintaining modesty. For the final piece, Millie put Georgia's hair up in a high bun, then fit a snug black wool poke frame cap over it. Thanks to the pins in the cap, Georgia's head felt quite secure. She didn't have to worry about losing it in the Gig or knocking it off under a couch. The whole thing felt rather neat and clean, especially now with her infamous black hair contained.

"Perfect, Millie. You have outdone yourself. This ensemble is quite modern, do you not think?"

"I think so, my lady," Millie looked her over with a discerning eye. "Would you prefer to have a few locks of hair loose? It is, after all, a bit of a trademark now."

"My 'wild and enormous black hair'?" Georgia asked, quoting from a recent article in the *Oradale Chronicler*. Millie giggled.

"Here we are. A few locks of hair popping out the front." Millie fixed it, and Georgia was ready to go.

She went downstairs, found the Constable waiting at the door, and they set off on his Gig for the crime scene. Georgia climbed into the mini carriage without effort. "Once again, I do not know how much help I will be, Constable," she admitted. "If the scene is wiped clean, you may have an unsolvable mystery."

"Duchess, I feel better knowing you are here," Constable Jenkins said, guiding the gig out of the driveway. "Even if we cannot figure it out, at least we tried, and I am grateful for the assistance."

They crossed the village in a brisk wind that Georgia found refreshing. She was not accustomed to riding in carriages with no cover. If her hair had been loose, the whole trip would have taken a turn. Even so, this was lovely, particularly after the morning she just had. Redstone House was only about 8 minutes away, just past the main square. Georgia watched the coffee and curio shop blur past, and then they were down another side street. Minutes later, they cleared a lane of smaller houses with adorable little gardens, rolling into an area where the road opened a bit. Great cypress trees framed the new road, creating an elegant backdrop. As they went, she could see the houses were getting bigger, and then the hedges began to hide them altogether. That is how one knows the locals have wealth: you can no longer see their homes from the road.

"You are comfortable, Duchess?" Constable Jenkins asked, not taking his eyes from the horses and road ahead.

"Quite comfortable, sir," Georgia answered, reveling in the crisp wind as intermittent rain drops hit her face. Bea would hate this. The air smelled of juniper, which was lovely.

They arrived at a wide house surrounded by a well-manicured hedge with a wide open gate. They rolled in to find a long gravel driveway. The house was a type fairly common to the area: two-storeys with wide colonnades on the front to support a vast covered porch. In front of the house was parked a covered stagecoach. Two footmen pulled travel bags and crates out of it. "Mrs. Crauford has arrived," Constable Jenkins said. "I do not know how she will react. I have met her before, but she is always reserved."

Georgia hopped off the Gig, smoothed out her coat, and headed for the door. "Constable Jenkins, she knows something happened by now. Introduce yourself, explain the problem briefly, and then introduce me. I will take it from there." She looked at him. "My title will allow us entry. I am almost certain of it. If it is not allowed, you will probably have to insist. After that, we do the job."

"Understood," he said, scrambling ahead to make the introduction. Just before knocking, he glanced back at her. "Forgive me. I never had the gall to approach a highborn lady like you before today, and now I am swimming in self-doubt."

"Adapt. Trust you are the authority here," Georgia whispered. "Someone broke in. There must have been a scuffle. For all we know, someone is dead, even if there is no body. You did the right thing coming to me, and there is every reason to stand at this door, Constable."

He nodded and knocked. A moment later, a footman answered. "I am Constable Jenkins," the Constable said. "This is the Duchess Goldenheart. We are here to discuss the unfortunate event."

"Of course, sir," the footman said. "Mrs. Crauford is aware of the situation. Will you follow me to the sitting room?" He led them to an older woman waiting in a lavish room with tea. Georgia was struck by the décor. The walls were a pale blue with white damask drapes. The floor was covered with lush carpets of dark blue. The woman stood when Georgia entered and curtseyed a bit lower than necessary, but not in an exaggerated way. She paused at what would be an acceptable pose, then dipped a bit before coming up. It was a sensible movement, even if unnecessary. She came from a wealthy Findorian trade family, despite her married name, which was from the kingdom of Jendina. Georgia noted the telltale Findorian black hair and olive skin. Mrs. Crauford's hair was shot with white at the temples, which lent an air of dignity to her appearance.

"Hello," the woman said. "I am Mrs. Crauford. Welcome to Redstone House, Duchess."

"Thank you for welcoming me into your home, Mrs. Crauford. I am sorry to make your acquaintance under these circumstances," Georgia said.

"It is a pleasure to meet you, despite the circumstances," Mrs. Crauford agreed. That was a kind thing to say. She looked nervous. Not surprising, what with the whole burglary thing. Mrs. Crauford was also meeting a duchess for the first time. People in lesser stations were always nervous. Or did she have another reason? "Won't you sit for a cup of tea or coffee?"

"Thank you," Georgia said. "Do you mind if the Constable joins us? I am his assistant in this endeavor. You have a beautiful home."

"Thank you, my lady. This house belongs to my brother, Lord Redstone," Mrs. Crauford said, pouring the tea herself. "He allows me to stay here whenever I like as he is almost always away."

"He is an anthropologist?" Georgia asked.

"Archaeologist; an anthropologist is similar. From what I understand, the archeologist goes and investigates the past where the past happened. An anthropologist reads about it and teaches," Mrs. Crauford answered. Her hands were steady and practiced as she poured each cup. "Sugar?"

"No thank you," Georgia said. "Just the milk for me."

"Would you like sugar, Constable?" the woman asked Constable Jenkins.

"Yes, please."

"And your brother is away right now? Er… learning about the past where it happened?" Georgia asked.

"Yes. He is on one of his digs… er that is what he calls his expeditions. He calls them 'digs'. He is currently on an island off the coast of the kingdom of Jendina. It would appear he discovered an ancient ruin. He believes it proves the existence of the ancient Fay lords from mythology."

"You are certain he is there now?" Georgia asked.

Mrs. Crauford shrugged. "I think so. He said he would be there for several months."

"When did he begin the expedition?" Constable Jenkins asked.

Mrs. Crauford took a sip of tea before answering. "I dined with him a month ago, back in the capital. He was planning to sell a few of his artifacts from other expeditions to raise funds for this trip, and then he was going to go straight away. I suspect he boarded a ship some three weeks ago."

"You did not see him off?"

"Oh goodness no." Mrs. Crauford rolled her eyes. "Forgive me for chuckling, but my brother detests personal sentiment. The idea of being escorted to the docks, waving fondly as he sails away… it would never happen. No, he is a man who prefers to carry his own suitcase, jump across the plank or whatever they call those things on the side of the boat, and find the nearest liquor cabinet."

"Does he normally sell artifacts to fund his expeditions?" Georgia asked. "Forgive me, I know no archeologists. Is that how it is normally done?"

"Sometimes, yes," Mrs. Crauford answered. "Usually, he gets a royal grant or some sort of funding from the Academy in Phaedros, the History College in Oradale, or even a wealthy benefactor. This time, no institution seemed interested in proof of the Fay Lords of old and there were no benefactors, so he had to employ other methods. Honestly, I suggested he wait a year, and then see if they might become interested, but he was adamant. He had to get to those ruins as soon as possible."

"Why would he have to go so soon?" Constable Jenkins asked. "I mean, are the ruins in danger?"

Mrs. Crauford chuckled. "You make the same point I did, Constable. No, my brother works in a… shall I say… difficult field of research. He believes there are other adventurers who would swoop in and snatch away the glory of his discovery."

Right. The usual rubbish. 'Archeologist' is apparently a term akin to 'Adventurer'.

"You mentioned him leaving by sea," Georgia said. "Did he specifically say he was taking a boat the whole way to the island from the capital? I ask because if he opted to travel overland partway, then he might have come here while en route. This village is on the road to Jendina, after all… and there is a port in the town of Suncoast. Would he do that, or would he simply hop a ship in the capital?"

Mrs. Crauford thought about it. "He did not say how he was going to travel, I think. I mean, he would have to take a ship at some point, naturally. But you may be correct. If his funds were limited, he might go to Suncoast to rent a boat to the island, yes. If he did, I have seen no receipts for it. For that matter, I saw no receipts for a ship out of the capital, either. All of that said, he could have borrowed a friend's yacht."

"I see," Georgia answered. She watched the Constable jot it all down in his book. "When you dined with your brother, was that the last time you two spoke?"

Mrs. Crauford shrugged. "I received a letter from him just over a week ago, back in the capital. He said he would be in Jendina for at least six months. When he is away... which, I admit, is most of the time, I keep his affairs in order here and in Oradale. So, you think he may have come here along the way to the island?"

"It is possible," Georgia said. "Do you still have the letter and the envelope it came in? The envelope would have a postal mark on it. From that, we might determine his movements."

"Oh drat. I threw the envelope in the bin. I am sorry, I did not think to look at the postal mark. I kept the letter, though. I will fetch it." Mrs. Crauford returned a moment later with a satchel. "I keep all of the letters. Well, most of them. He put a few instructions on business matters there. I trust you to be discreet." She handed a page to Georgia, who was not sure how useful reading it would be. Perhaps he would mention something relevant?

"I will be, yes," Georgia answered. The missive was dated two weeks before. "Oh, terrible handwriting."

"That is how you know he wrote it himself." Mrs. Crauford chuckled. "Sometimes, he has an assistant with him, but not this time."

Georgia read the letter, despite the handwriting:

*Dear sister,*

*I hope this finds you well and in good spirits. Dinner was a fun affair, and I hope you were not (unreadable word) by my impertinent suggestion.*

"Impertinent suggestion?" Georgia said aloud.

"Oh, my brother thinks I should accept a marriage proposal from one of his dim-witted business friends. I see no point, though," Mrs. Crauford answered, touching her face in embarrassment. "Ever since my late husband passed, he has been urging me to move on."

"Ah, I see." Georgia continued reading:

*While I am gone, there will likely be several (unreadable) to the Oradale house. All of them will be from the Academy in Phaedros. Simply (something) Laurence put them in my office. I will go through them when I (illegible) return.*

*Of note, you will also receive updates from Mr. Fillmore on the state of my holdings in Nedwin. You already know the direction of those tenants. Once they are all evicted, Fillmore is free to proceed with the demolition. When I return, I will meet with the new contractors in person.*

*In the meantime, I trust you will check in at the house in Findor, as per usual. Otherwise, this should be a fairly quiet time while I am away.*

*Yours Always,*

*L. R. Redstone*

Georgia handed the letter to Constable Jenkins, who also read through it. She noted his dismay when he read the word 'evicted', but there was little of use that she could see.

"It does not rule him out," Jenkins said.

"Rule him out from what?" Mrs. Crauford asked.

"From coming to this house, two weeks ago," Georgia answered. "According to the date, that is when he wrote it. You received it one week ago. That means it spent approximately a week in transit. Mail from Jendina generally takes three weeks to a month to get to the Three Realms. But if he wrote it here and mailed it out, it might take only a few days in transit. The timeline may align."

"Oh, I see," Mrs. Crauford said, gazing at the floor. "It only takes a day to travel from the capital to Dead Mourner's Grove."

"The mail is routed through Grandhall's capital from Dead Mourner's Grove," Constable Jenkins said. "It generally takes a week to mail something to the capital from here. Literally, it is faster to take the letter and deliver it by hand, but of course that would be inconvenient, so no one ever does it, unless it is an emergency."

"Ah, well, that makes sense. I suppose he could have come through here on his way to Suncoast port, wrote the letter, and then went on his way," Mrs. Crauford said slowly. "I am still not sure why that would matter, though."

Georgia looked at the constable for confirmation, then turned back to Mrs. Crauford. "There was no apparent sign of a break-in: no broken door, no window left open, no sign of anything like that."

"So?"

"The alleged burglar did not break into the house with force," Georgia said. "The culprit either had a key or another access."

"Or the door was left open," Constable Jenkins added.

"Impossible. When we visit Redstone House, we make sure every door is locked and the property sealed tight before we leave. I am careful about that. My brother is very observant. Throughout my life, I have always made sure not to disrupt his comfort or work. This house is a symbol of his trust in me," Mrs. Crauford said, shaking her head. "The door could not have been unlocked." For the first time, her hands began to tremble; this was a point of pride. "And my brother would never leave the door unlocked. He is far too sensible for that." Georgia almost answered, but kept her mouth shut. Lord Redstone was too sensible to leave his door unlocked but had no problem racing to beat a gang of adventurers to a mythical island ruin in order to find proof of fairy tales.

Then again, Georgia herself owned a magical sword created by those same fairy tale creatures, so who was she to judge anyone?

Constable Jenkins leaned in. "Mrs. Crauford, we think your brother came here. He either stabbed someone, someone stabbed him, or someone stabbed someone else after he let them in." A bit more than Georgia would have admitted to the woman, but it was the truth. She glanced at the constable, who realized he might have said too much. Instead of chastising, she waited for him to look her way and gave him a slight nod of reassurance.

Mrs. Crauford went quite pale.

Georgia looked at the woman. "Until we know more, remain calm and hopeful, Mrs. Crauford." Mrs. Crauford took a breath and nodded.

"Perhaps we could speak with your maid, and see the room?" Constable Jenkins asked. "Ask her if she remembers any other details?"

"Of course. Forgive me, be gentle with her. She is a fine maid, but I think perhaps a bit delicate as a girl," Mrs. Crauford said. She picked up a bell and rang it.

\*\*\*

The housemaid was a woman named Marguerite from the Realm of Palas. Like many from that part of the Three Realms, she was tall with dark almond-colored skin, broad hips, and thick black hair tied in coils. She kept her eyes on the ground and waited for anyone else to speak first.

"Marguerite, I know you wanted to spare me an upset when you cleaned the room. I am grateful. Last month, when I had a dizzy spell, I saw how it unnerved you. I will not have an attack again, though. Dr. Branson gave me the tonic, and I am not so easily taken now. These people need to know anything you saw or did in the room. Can you tell the Duchess what you saw? Be honest about everything. We have nothing to hide." The tone of Mrs. Crauford with the maid was gentler than before. She cared for the girl. Maybe she viewed her staff with more affection than a typical employer. Georgia tried to remember the older woman's tone when speaking with the footman.

"Yes, mum," Marguerite said, meekly. She opened the door to the library. "I was dusting and found the... er... blood here, behind one of the couches."

The library was immense. The walls were lined to the ceiling with bookcases, all full of books. Now this was a library. The shelves ran the length of the room, which was about fifty feet by twenty feet. The only gap in bookcases was on the northern wall for the fireplace, which was stone. The maid obviously kept it tidy, but she could see it had been used frequently. Above the fireplace was a grand portrait of a man in a sailor uniform who was smiling. Georgia didn't see any ladders for getting at the higher shelves, which must be awkward. Or perhaps the ladders were in another room. The center of the library was dominated by a massive oak table on another thick blue carpet, with ten chairs. Two enormous leather couches were placed to the east and west. At the back of the room was a beautiful old desk covered in scrolls, other papers, and a tray of pens and quills. It was all neatly organized. Behind the desk was a sumptuous leather chair, slightly worn on the seat by long years of use. It looked very comfortable.

She turned back to the room. At the front of the library was a row of wide windows that brought in plenty of light. Set in front of them were two more leather chairs with side tables, no doubt for reading.

Marguerite guided them to the couch on the eastern side of the room, just in front of the desk. "I found the blood here," she announced, pointing down.

"Can you describe it?" Constable Jenkins asked.

"A big sticky black pool," she pointed to the ground. "And some other bits splashed over on this bookcase. These books are leather-bound, so I was able to wash it off them. That is when I found the shoe. It was on the floor over there. I found the knife near the desk."

"When you say it was a big pool, what does that mean?" Georgia asked. "Can you indicate the size of it? Where did it extend?"

Marguerite thought for a moment, then stepped closer to the couch. "It was not like a round pool so much as it was sort of an oval? And then there was sort of a trail that went over this way to the bookcase." She bent over and swept her arm around to show the approximate size of the pool. If she was not exaggerating, it would have been at least three feet by two feet.

"That seems like a lot of blood. More than two pints, I suspect," Constable Jenkins whispered. He turned back to Marguerite. "What did the room look like? Was it wrecked? Did you see signs of a struggle?"

Marguerite gestured around the couch. "No, the room was tidy, except for the blood... if that makes sense?"

"I think so," Constable Jenkins said. "Did you touch the blood? With your hand, I mean. Did it stick to you?"

"Yes, I did. The blood was almost dry in places, except near the rug, but also still sticky. Does that make sense?"

"Yes," Georgia said. "Under some conditions, blood can dry while still being sticky. If the… er… victim was a frequent imbiber of spirits." She was going to ask Mrs. Crauford if her brother suffered from gout or any other maladies, but the woman went pale and sat down.

Marguerite continued. "There was a bit of it under the couch too. Just a small spot, I suppose. But there it was still quite wet."

Georgia walked from the couch to the bookcase. "The static pool implies a great deal of blood loss in this one spot."

"A grown man would have about a gallon and a half in him," Constable Jenkins offered. "I think he lost almost a quart. Would that be fatal?"

"Possibly," Georgia answered. She looked at the maid. "Marguerite, when you said the blood went in a trail to the bookcase, what did it look like? Was it less thick than in the pool? Was it flowing toward the bookcase?"

Marguerite shook her head. "It was a smear. That would be more accurate, my lady. It was like when we would slaughter the pigs back home and drag the carcass to the chopping table. It looked like that, except in this case, it just ended over here. I could not find a trail that led out of the room. Not even spots by the door."

"You think the body was dragged over here, but then picked up and carried away," Georgia pointed.

Marguerite nodded, then hurried over to Mrs. Crauford, who was swaying in her seat. "I will fetch you some water, my lady."

"Find something stronger than water," Mrs. Crauford answered. She touched Marguerite's cheek in a rather tender way. "You were raised on a farm? I do not think I knew that."

Marguerite smiled at her mistress, then glanced at Georgia and the Constable… who both looked away without comment. The maid hurried out of the room.

"How often does Marguerite come into this room? How often do you come into this library?" Georgia asked Mrs. Crauford.

"I do not use this room," Mrs. Crauford answered, leaning back on the couch. For a moment, Georgia thought the woman might faint, but she did not. "Marguerite dusts it at least once every visit. I will not live in a dust-house, Duchess. She cleaned every room last time we were here."

Marguerite returned with a bottle of sherry and three glasses. She poured one for each of them. "Please forgive me," she whispered, "I would have decanted in the kitchen, but I thought speed might be preferable."

"You thought correctly," Mrs. Crauford whispered, accepting her glass first. In almost any formal situation, Georgia would have been offered the glass first. Then again, Georgia was not fainting.

"Marguerite, how often do you clean this room?" Georgia asked.

"I dust it at least once on every visit. I did this room last time we stayed."

"Do you remember what day?"

Marguerite nodded. "I usually do these extra rooms just before we go, so this was the final day of our last visit. Since this is supposed to be a short visit, I thought I would pop in and do a quick cleaning before the mistress arrived. Otherwise, I do not think I would have come in here for a while."

"A month or less," Georgia said carefully. "The blood dried on the floor, but still a bit sticky under the couch. We are coming to the end of the rainy season, so humidity could play a factor in keeping it wet. Marguerite, did you remove anything or put anything back where it belonged after you found the blood?"

"Oh, not much, my lady," the maid said. "I found a book under the couch. That's about it."

"A book? Where did you put it?" Georgia asked.

The maid went to one of the shelves and scanned through a long row of identical leather-bound volumes. "Ah, here," she whispered, sliding one out from the row. She handed it to Georgia.

"That is one of Lord Redstone's archaeological journals," Mrs. Crauford offered. "He keeps records from each dig in a different journal."

"Ever find one of these journals under the couch or out of place before?" Georgia asked the maid.

"No, my lady. I guess I have not. A year ago, we did find papers scattered around the desk. But the mistress said that was to be expected. The wind threw open a window that night," She looked to Mrs. Crauford for confirmation. The older woman nodded. "This is the first time I have seen a book on the floor."

"Show me exactly where you found it," Georgia commanded.

Marguerite scurried over to the couch. "It was just out of sight, but right there."

Georgia inspected the spot. Thanks to her sensible dress and coat, she was able to hunker down and look under the couch. She stood and dusted herself. "Very well, show me where the knife was? Was there blood on the knife?" They went over to the desk. Marguerite pointed at the floor. The area was swept clean, but Georgia noticed a small chip in the wood of the floor. She pointed it out to Constable Jenkins, who made a note in his book.

"The knife was not clean, precisely," Marguerite admitted. "I do not remember blood, though."

"You grew up on a farm," Georgia said. "You know what a dirty knife looks like."

Marguerite nodded, understanding. "It looked like someone wiped it but did not wash it, yes."

"But then they dropped it."

"They dropped the knife while carrying the body," Constable Jenkins whispered. "Surely, it was that, yes?"

"I cannot imagine they left it behind on purpose," Georgia answered.

"Oh, this is so grim," Mrs. Crauford moaned.

"The desk looked normal to you? You saw no drawers open or missing documents?" Georgia asked the maid.

"Yes, it looked like it always does," Marguerite answered.

"No," Mrs. Crauford said, standing nearby. She tilted her head, then came over and looked closer. "Something is missing." She poked around the ground, then riffled through papers.

"Do you know what is missing?"

"The ring," the older woman answered. "My brother keeps a small ring in a box here on top of the folders. You remember it, Marguerite. He always leaves it on the stack of papers."

Marguerite jumped. "Oh, goodness, you are right, ma'am." She opened the drawers and started looking through them.

"How much is the ring worth?" Constable Jenkins asked.

"Oh, it's worthless junk," Mrs. Crauford said. "Funny story about it. My brother was convinced it was a Fay Lord bauble from ancient times. He tried to sell it to several museums, but they kept rejecting it. They told him it was worth no more than a paper weight, so that is what he did with it. He kept papers from flying away in the breeze. I mean, it was oddly heavy for such a small piece of jewelry."

"It's not in the drawers, ma'am," Marguerite said.

Georgia glanced at Constable Jenkins, writing in his notepad. She looked back at the maid. "Did you notice anything else about the condition of the room, or anything you remember being out of place? Any windows open? Odd odors. Anything you can think of Marguerite?"

The maid pondered for a moment. "I do not think so."

Georgia looked at Mrs. Crauford. "May I borrow this journal for a few days?"

"Borrow it? Why?" the woman asked.

"It might be a coincidence, but perhaps your brother wrote something in it relevant to this break-in. Otherwise, why would it be out of place," Georgia said, holding the book up. It had no marking on the outside, but the first page stated it was *An Account of the Dead Mourner's Dig Site*. That was no coincidence, as they were in Dead Mourner's Grove, and it was the only item displaced in the library.

"Very well," Mrs. Crauford said slowly. "If you think it will help."

"That remains to be seen," Georgia answered. "Now, where did you put the shoe and knife?"

"I stuck them in a bag, my lady," Marguerite said. "I put the bag downstairs in a drawer."

"We will take it with us," Georgia announced. She looked at Constable Jenkins. "Do you have the facility to analyze fingerprints?"

"There is a Coroner's office in Grandhall. They have a man who can do that," Constable Jenkins said. "Almost a day's ride. I will get my deputy, Andre, to take it there."

Georgia nodded, then turned back to Mrs. Crauford and her maid. "Another question: have either of you noticed anyone out of the ordinary lurking around? Have you seen anyone standing on the street looking in at the house? Anyone in the yard? Think. Anyone you did not recognize? Anyone acting in a way you thought, even in passing, was odd?"

Mrs. Crauford and the maid exchanged glances. "No, I do not think so," Mrs. Crauford answered with some care. "Marguerite?"

"No one we do not know," Marguerite said. "I mean, many of the neighbors are nosy, but that is not so out of the ordinary." Nosy neighbors. Excellent.

\*\*\*

"What are your thoughts, Constable?" Georgia asked as they left the house.

"The old woman was helpful," he answered. "I think we can guess why she will not remarry."

"That is none of our business," Georgia answered.

"Agreed."

"She grew nervous when we spoke of her brother," Georgia said, mulling. "I wonder if that means she is innocent. Her motive being the most obvious."

"Based on the talk of inconvenience for Lord Redstone, I think Mrs. Crauford had nothing to do with the break-in. If she were involved, there would be no report." Constable Jenkins looked over his notes. "I talked to Reeve, the other footman. Mrs. Crauford's husband was from Phaedros, and successful in trade. She has all the money she needs. From what Reeve said, she is protective of her brother and uses the house with high respect."

"All right, before we head back to my rental home," Georgia said, "do me a favor? Take a walk around the perimeter of the property and check for anything out of the ordinary, will you?"

"Yes, Duchess," Jenkins said, veering off.

"I am going down the road to talk to the nearest neighbor," she said. "When you are finished, please find me." The Constable nodded and began moving through trees at the edge of the house.

Above, she heard a chirp. A bright red oriole sat on the branch of a nearby tree. "Hello, Kenneth," Georgia said. The oriole chirped again and took flight. He spun around her head a few times before landing in a tree up the street. She followed him, looking back to the house for line of sight. She could see the big windows of the library from a distance. She found herself at a neighbor's gate. Just over a hundred yards and still within sight of Redstone House, she noted. Georgia was about to knock when an old gentleman in a floppy hat and garden shears appeared. "Hello," he said. "Who might you be?"

"I am Duchess Goldenheart," she answered with a smile. "Are you the gardener or the owner of this house?"

"I am both," the fellow admitted. "It is a pleasure to meet you. I am Mr. Robert Greenstreet. Is 'Duchess' your name or your title?" He had a kind face and quick, mischievous grin.

"It is my title," Georgia answered.

"Never met a duchess before. I would bow, but you would have to help me up," the old fellow admitted. "I would think you would have a butler or guards with you."

"Best to stay casual. I am a duchess on foot today," she said. "Actually, Mr. Greenstreet, I wanted to ask you about the house up the street."

"Lord Redstone's house, yes," Mr. Greenstreet said. "Very cordial fellow. He is almost never home, but you might find his sister."

"Yes, I met her today. My question for you... over the last few weeks, have you heard any strange noises coming from there? Seen anything out of the ordinary?"

"Oh, my word," Mr. Greenstreet fanned himself, either from the heat or in surprise. "What happened?"

"There was a break-in, I am afraid," she said.

"Oh dear, a duchess and now burglary. When did it happen?"

"Sometime in the last couple of weeks," Georgia answered. "It looks like someone found their way in and there was a fight, but that is almost all I know."

The old man shook his head. "Our sleepy village is getting as bad as the capital. I always say that, you know. Well, of course you do not know, as we only just met."

"Did you hear or see anything odd over the last couple of weeks?"

"I did not. But I think my wife did," he said, swiveling around to scream. "TRUDY!!"

An old woman literally popped out of the hedge with a pair of her own shears. "Dammit, Robert, I'm right here. No need to scream. Oh, who is this?"

"This lady is a duchess," Mr. Greenstreet hollered. Given the woman practically sitting next to them, Georgia had to assume her hearing might be suspect.

Trudy... Mrs. Greenstreet, that is, curtseyed right away. "This is a pleasure, Your Grace."

"Please call me Duchess Goldenheart," Georgia said a bit louder than normal. She did not feel like explaining the difference between 'your Grace', 'my lady', and 'Duchess' again. She certainly did not feel like shouting the difference.

"You are the lady from the stories in the *Journal*. My goodness. Robert, we are talking to a bona fide hero of the realms. Well, they did say you were striking, and that is no myth, Duchess. You are quite a bit thinner than I would have thought. Oh, do you have your magical sword?"

"Thank you," Georgia answered. "No, I am without the sword today, Mrs. Greenstreet. May I ask you a few questions? Your husband said you might have heard or seen something strange coming from Redstone House in the last few weeks." Behind her, Georgia heard Constable Jenkins pulling up in his gig.

"Oh yes, I did," the old woman admitted. "Not so much a sound as a sight. I saw a strange man. Although, there were plenty of sounds coming from him. I came back from my late afternoon constitutional. Just before sunset when it's starting to cool, I like to take a nice walk up and down the lane before we settle in for tea and cocktails. Robert, when was that?"

"About two weeks ago, Trudy. The day before that big rain," Mr. Greenstreet said. "You were just back. She likes to go on a walk before we have tea. It gets her appetite up."

"Yes, thank you, Robert. That is exactly what I told the Duchess in front of you one minute ago," Mrs. Greenstreet said with faint annoyance. Apparently now she could hear just fine. "That sounds about right. Two weeks. Perhaps a day less than two weeks, but about that time, yes. I was coming up the lane when I heard a man scream. Or it might have been a bird crying out. I am still not certain. Right after, I saw the most peculiar fellow riding out on a horse..."

"Two horses," Mr. Greenstreet corrected.

"No, Robert, he wasn't riding both horses," she said, rolling her eyes. Then she looked back at Georgia, "The man rode one horse and held the reins of another horse running alongside. Both horses were fully saddled. He rode hard, too. I know because he only spotted me in the lane at the very last moment. He was looking behind him. Suddenly, he shouts at me, 'get out of the way, crone!' I barely scooted to the side before he went through. I was startled, of course, and barely had time to curse him back.

I said, 'I see you and what mischief you are up to. Run while you can'. I know. A bit dramatic, but I was upset."

"Goodness," Georgia said. "So, he went up that way to the left? Toward the market?"

"I think so," Mrs. Greenstreet nodded. "Although, he could have taken the right just before that, over by the Bluelake Farm. I was so flustered, I lost sight of him."

"Did you get a look at the man? Could you describe him?" Georgia asked.

Mrs. Greenstreet shook her head. "I don't know. He looked Findorian. Not a local, though. His hair was long. You know, I assumed he was one of those ridiculous Blackheart valets. Ever since Mr. Blackheart moved into the old manor just past Bluelake Farm, his staff have been riding all over the village on the most pressing errands. Always on horseback, and never a sensible carriage or on foot. Imagine running to the butcher like that."

Mr. Greenstreet cackled. "Oh, I simply must have a half pound of chicken salad with onions this instant. Now I'm off on horseback to deliver it to the master."

Mrs. Greenstreet chortled. "Oh, Mr. Butcher, we urgently need sausages. Now I must get back to riding like a crazy person on my horse." Mrs. Greenstreet looked back at Georgia. "Anyway, the only one with common sense is the wife, although I never met her. They say she is kind and friendly, despite being a northerner." The woman referred to Georgia's old school mate Harriet.

"I know Mrs. Blackheart, "Georgia said with a smile. "She is, as you say, exceedingly kind. Is there anything else you remember about the man with the two horses? Anything at all? Was he wearing valet livery? Is that why you assumed he was one of Mr. Blackheart's men?"

"Oh, dear. No, I did not see what he was wearing. Some sort of black overcoat, as I recall. He was rude. Whenever they are rude, I assume they are with Mr. Blackheart." Mrs. Greenstreet shook her head. "He was gone even as he appeared. In good faith, anything I say could be a mistake now. I'm sorry, Duchess."

\*\*\*

"Thank you for inviting me to work on your case, Constable," Georgia said as the gig pulled up to Croft House. "I must say, you were quite thorough on your own. I will be happy to assist again, but based on what I saw you need no help. Did you find anything on the property after we spoke to Mrs. Crauford?"

"Oh, Duchess, you honor me." Constable Jenkins blushed. "Thank you. No. It looks like the grounds have a gardener who keeps the outside up. If there was evidence of a break-in on the outside of the house, they fixed it or cleaned it up without saying anything."

They looked at the shoe and knife from the scene. "A man's shoe," Constable Jenkins said. "Expensive, too."

"It looks high quality, yes," Georgia agreed. "But look: the heel is worn. It is old and a little scratched up."

"I will go back to Redstone House and look in the closet. See if anything is missing."

"That sounds fine," Georgia said, "but if he was wearing the shoes, why would our attacker take his other shoe back to the closet?"

"Right. Of course," Constable Jenkins said with an embarrassed nod. "Forgive me. That makes more sense."

"It was not, on the surface, a bad idea, Constable," Georgia said in a kind tone. She shrugged, as if to give him the benefit of the doubt. "Check the closet just in case. I mean, it could have been a shoe left in the room for some other reason. If it was, we might rule it out."

Constable Jenkins rubbed his forehead. Georgia patted his shoulder. "There are no bad ideas... you know, until there are bad ideas. I have sat with wizards, detectives, witches, and all manner of experts, my friend. Chase every possible lead. You never know. Doubt yourself after the fact, but understand we all do."

Careful not to leave fingerprints, she took the knife out of the bag wearing a soft glove. She could see a smudge or two on the handle. Possibly fingerprints. To this day, she was dubious about that science. What good is it to be able to see fingerprints if you still do not know to whom they belong?

"Quality knife for hunting," Constable Jenkins murmured. "This is interesting." He pointed at the pommel.

Georgia looked and found scratches. "You see something?"

"People often monogram these little blades. The scratched-up area is where one would likely have their name or an identifying symbol, but it appears this one was scratched off."

"Intriguing," Georgia murmured. She wrapped the blade with care, then put it in another bag. "Can you send this knife, along with the shoe, to the Constabulary in Grandhall?"

"Right away, Duchess. We might even have an answer within two days if we are lucky."

"Perfect," Georgia said. "I just need to write a note to the coroner. Do you have a desk I can use?"

"Right this way, Duchess."

Georgia got back in time to change for dinner. She found Bea in the solarium. "I have something for you to read, if you are interested." Georgia held up the journal from Lord Redstone's library. "There is a possibility our burglar was after it. The maid found it under a couch next to a pool of blood."

Bea pulled the book open. "Lord Redstone's account of a Dead Mourner's Grove archeological dig from two years ago. Already interesting. What are you hoping to find?"

"A clue to why someone broke into Lord Redstone's house and left blood, a shoe, and a knife behind. The place goes without staff or residents for part of the year, so I cannot imagine he keeps anything of real value on site. Maybe this journal can give us some direction."

"Perhaps he keeps nothing of conventional value in the house. But what if it is unconventional?" Bea murmured, flipping open the first page. Her eyes began to dart along. "You ruled out coincidence, I assume? Oh. His handwriting is atrocious. This could take days. In the meantime, we should visit the archeological site tomorrow morning after the Queen's Emerald Party. The afternoon will be open, and according to this, the dig site is less than an hour west of the village."

"Let us make a lunch of it," Georgia nodded. "I am going up to change for dinner. I know you cannot resist a mysterious book, but my stomach is growling."

Bea put the journal down. "Now that you mention it, I am famished. See you there."

Half an hour later, they joined Nora, and the staff brought the first course. A delicate mushroom broth. The bowl was not as spicy or bold as previous courses, but instead showed another side to Findorian cooking. "According to Wyclef's menu notes, this broth is popular in far western Findor where mushrooms and clear broth are seen as an essential part of every meal. Rather than mix the spices, the western Findorians prefer to eat their peppers as a fiery side dish to compliment the umami of mushroom sauces," Bea said, reading one of the cards from the sideboard.

"How is Nelda?" Georgia asked Nora.

"She is recovering slowly, thanks to your generosity and the efforts of Mr. Brown and Beatrice. Mr. Brown stayed by her side all day, feeding her, talking to her, and being a great comfort," Nora answered as she fiddled with her soup. She sighed and gazed down. "Mr. Brown thinks she will recover soon and be much like her old self."

"That is good news," Georgia said. "Nora, I know you are worried, but you must be strong, if only to give Nelda something to focus on in recovery."

Nora's face spasmed, and she began to weep. "Oh Georgia, I am glad she is recovering but I feel such guilt. It was only a day ago I chided her about being a klutz and picked on her every faux pas. I have treated my sister shabbily. I resented her marriage and always made her feel like a fool." She went from a few fat tears to full-on ugly-face crying.

Georgia blinked.

Bea hurried over and put a hand on Nora's shoulder. "There-there," she said. "You mustn't be too hard on yourself, Nora. Sisters speak to one another in their own way. Why, I have four sisters, and not a day goes by that one of us does not lose patience with the whole lot. But then it always comes down to the same thing: family."

"You are right, of course," Nora said, wiping her eyes. "Sorry. Georgia, you were away today. Could you distract or cheer us with that? Were you working on the party tomorrow with Harriet?"

Just then the footmen returned with the next course for dinner. It was a lovely chicken and chickpea ragout with classic Findorian toasted bread. Rustic dining made it extraordinary. Once again, they eschewed southern spices in favor of western mushrooms for a savory palate. On the side lay a bowl of honey ham bites, a plate of exceptionally delicate asparagus in salty melted butter, and a bowl of spicy baked peppers.

Bea turned to the footman. "Clyde, we will manage pouring our own wine and sauces, thank you. I will ring when we need you again."

"Yes, my lady," Clyde said with a quick bow.

"Oh, I do not think you will be cheered by my movements today," Georgia said slowly, after the footman exited. "I went with a local Constable to assist in an investigation."

"How extraordinary," Nora said, blinking. "Why would he call upon you?"

"Georgia has experience in these matters," Bea said as she sat down. "He read the same articles you did, Nora."

"Despite being bright and attentive, he was somewhat out of his depth," Georgia explained. "The local authorities in the village rarely see burglaries, and this was complicated."

"How so?" Nora tilted her head. "You know, I think anything at this point would be a welcome distraction from Nelda. Even something awful like a burglary."

Georgia outlined the case, including the appearance of the journal, blood, shoe, knife, and discussions with Mrs. Crauford, the maid, and Mrs. Greenstreet.

"Surely, you do not think Harriet's husband is involved?" Nora asked with wide eyes. "If it was one of his men riding that horse... or both of those horses, I suppose I should say."

"Mrs. Greenstreet was startled by a horseman. She was not certain if he came from the house itself, or if he was only coming around it. She speculated the fellow worked for Mr. Blackheart but offered no proof. She had no direct evidence. For that matter, we cannot be certain her encounter is linked to the burglary," Georgia explained. "In a crime case, one must be able to prove everything with solid evidence or a confession. Now, we have none of that."

"Mrs. Greenstreet's word is not enough?"

"The woman could not swear to anything," Georgia said. "She saw a man riding two horses in a hurry. It happened sometime around the break-in, so the implication is there. But it will fall to me or the Constabulary to piece together the truth. If not, we might accuse someone of something they did not do."

"And being a Duchess, you could accuse someone, and it would carry a significant weight," Nora said softly. "I see what you are saying. In a way, you must be more careful than a constable."

"That is astute of you, Nora. We need more information. I must question Mr. Blackheart or his valets, if only to eliminate the suspects. For all we know, the man riding two horses may be a potential witness to get us closer to the real suspect," Georgia said. "In the meantime, there is the journal found at the crime scene. Bea agreed to read it and look for anything useful. Or, of course, if it is only a coincidence it was under the couch…"

"If the book had been under the couch before now, the maid would have found it sooner," Bea said, shaking her head. "Based only on your description of her work, she cares about her job and employer. So much so, she cleaned the crime scene before her mistress could see it. Of course, there is another reason she might have cleaned the scene."

"Oh?" Nora asked. "What other reason?"

"If she were somehow involved, she might contaminate the site in order to stymie the investigation, but the timeline does not work," Bea said. "If her account is to be believed, the blood pool was in that room for weeks. If the maid knew it was there before she arrived early this morning, she would surely get rid of it sooner. No criminal would leave the thing behind out of inconvenience. She would act before anyone saw it."

"Unless she did not know until she arrived... which was only hours ahead of her mistress arriving," Georgia said. "But that does not change the fact that she reported it to the Constabulary, even though she destroyed all the evidence. If she was an accomplice, she could easily dispose of the evidence in the time when she was alone with it... without reporting it. The authorities might never know."

"That would be the easiest course to take," Bea admitted.

"This is all very exciting and mysterious," Nora said. "Why all the discussion about timeline?"

"Because we have nothing else to work with," Georgia answered. "Someone was wounded in the library but vanished. If the victim is not Lord Redstone, then there is no obvious motive to kill someone in the house."

"Why would anyone kill Lord Redstone?" Nora asked.

"A detective always looks for the low-hanging fruit first," Bea answered. "Lord Redstone owns the house. Mrs. Crauford uses the house. Killing him might transfer the property to her, but we do not even know that for certain."

"You think this is about the property?"

Bea shrugged. "Always start with the most basic motive, Nora. People will kill for simple things before they do it out of passion. Then, if they do it out of passion, it is again for the simplest reasons. They are afraid they will lose something. Or someone."

"Once you eliminate the obvious, you move on to the more complicated schemes," Georgia added. "But the vast majority of crimes fall into the first category."

"How did you learn this?" Nora asked.

Georgia shrugged. "Last year was a crash course in crime, but I also had some training in school. Investigation is the 8th Discipline of the Cymbre School. They offered the classes in post-graduation."

"What?" Nora gaped. "We all went to the Cymbre School. There are six Disciplines for a proper lady's education: etiquette, history, the sciences, art and music, needlework, and optional culinary. I mastered all six."

"I did not take all the culinary classes. I did learn how to fry an egg and boil water, but that was about it," Georgia said. "My Uncle Raymond insisted the school teach me some elements of combat instead. I learned how to fence, shoot a bow, or if necessary, grapple with my fists."

"My word," Nora breathed. "When did this happen?"

"It was sort of on-going, particularly in my last couple of years at school." Georgia chuckled. "Bea mastered nine Disciplines. If you count the sub-groups within The Sciences, I think she must have learned twelve Disciplines."

"I did not take any courses in combat," Bea corrected. "That was all for Georgia."

"Oh, my word," Nora breathed. "The Sciences I learned were arithmetic, chemistry, and logic."

"Same here," Georgia said. "Bea also took medicine. I only made it to the 8th Discipline overall."

Nora scratched her head. "Wait. What are the 7th and 9th Disciplines?"

"The 7th Discipline is law and negotiation," Georgia answered. "The concept of balancing need against desire, how to bring about a mutual agreement, and how it conforms to governance. We were taught the principles of diplomacy and basics of the legal system."

"The 9th Discipline starts at the beginning," Bea said. "Languages. I learned languages all through school."

"Amazing," Nora whispered. "I always knew you two were smart."

"Aw, thank you. As it happens, I already have an immense ego but I appreciate you feeding it." Bea smiled.

Nora laughed. "Oh dear."

"Anyway, back to the case, I read the first few pages of the journal," Bea said. "It outlines Lord Redstone's plans for the Dead Mourner's Archeological Dig outside of the village. He is a specialist in old Fay lore. That said, he noted at the beginning of the journal that the local ruin he excavated just outside Dead Mourner's Grove was a human settlement. But he also said it was older than the Three Realms and hoped to find concrete evidence the Fay lords existed for real, and not mere myth. I am not sure yet how this would apply to our crime. That said, I am only getting started on the book. We shall see."

Georgia shook her head. "I already know the Fay lords were real. I own a magic sword created by them. I met a winter witch who tried very hard to kill me, and I have seen more than enough evidence to convince me magic is real."

"I am not sure that would hold up as evidence in the court of academia," Bea said with a wink.

"Good point," Georgia admitted. "Our last adventure proved the courts only want solid mundane evidence. Otherwise, we could have put Manx Hampton away right after he confessed."

"Wait," Nora said. "I read the entire story in the paper. Manx Hampton was guilty, was he not?"

"He confessed over dinner when we confronted him. He was tried, and convicted of several crimes, but murder was not one of them. The man used magic to kill someone. The law does not take that into account, as most people no longer believe in supernatural occurrences. He confessed again on his deathbed, two weeks later," Georgia said. "He tied himself to a kind of dark sorcery which eventually took his life. If he had succeeded with his plot, we might not have known. But he failed and the power turned on him. After that, he admitted everything and died. The dark magic was the end of him."

Nora shuddered. "I think I am done talking about this."

"Of course," Georgia said quickly. "We are about to have dessert anyway. Let us enjoy it." She rang the bell, the lemon souffle arrived a moment later, and they changed the subject for the night.

Right after breakfast tea, Clyde the footman announced the arrival of Deputy Constable Andre. Georgia met him in the parlor and invited him to sit. The poor fellow, still a bit sleep-deprived after his long ride back and forth from Grandhall, preferred to stand. That was the more appropriate protocol anyway, so Georgia let it be.

"I shall try to be concise with the questions, Deputy Constable," she said. "You look weary after your ride."

"Thank you, Duchess. I am fine," he responded. Andre was a proper constable. She did not need to explain her title to him in any way. His demeanor indicated excellent training.

"You went to the coroner in Grandhall, yes?"

"Correct, Duchess. As you instructed, I delivered the material there," he said. "After that, I returned to the village. Here is the receipt from the expert confirming everything. He said he will look into it as soon as he can." He handed it to her. Georgia noted it was only a confirmation. Obviously, they did not have time to do a proper examination, as it had only been a day.

"Thank you, Deputy Constable. When I see Constable Jenkins again, I will sing your praises."

Afterward, it occurred to her she might expedite things with a few targeted communications: one to the coroner, and another to the Countess of Grandhall. Quickly, she jotted the notes. The first to the Coroner's Office in Grandhall requesting they send her a copy of their investigation notes. If they had no plans to investigate, she urged them to at least send notes of anything they noticed about the evidence. She signed it with a Royal Writ Seal, as was her privilege. When engaged in enquiry, Georgia could invoke the King himself, if she felt it necessary. She did not go quite that far with this letter, merely affixing the overall Royal Writ.

Next, Georgia jotted off a note to her friendly acquaintance, Lady Constance Greenheart, the Countess of Grandhall, requesting she ask the expert to expedite his investigation. Georgia did not go into any detail on the case other than include the name of Lord Redstone and called it a matter of some interest to herself. She completed the letter with a vague invitation to lunch when next they might both be in the capital. She followed that with a salutation to Lady Constance's youngest son, Lucas.

That very last part, she hoped, would prompt the Countess to act on her behalf with the coroner. It was a slightly manipulative move by Georgia. If she had a shortlist of potential husbands, Lucas Greenheart would be at the top of it. Her letter would be arriving on the heels of the missive from Lady Amaris, and the Countess would likely interpret it as an invitation of significance. If she was indeed as keen to see her youngest son married as other sources might indicate, an answer would be quick.

According to the latest *Findorian Peer Registry*, Mr. Lucas Greenheart, or Luke to his friends, was still on the market to find a wife and recently entered as a lower peer. His father was the Earl of Grandhall and probably among the Top 5 most powerful lords of the Three Realms, but Luke was somewhere around 14th in line to the seat. With his older brothers already married and having families, he was quickly moving into a position many ladies like Bea understood all too well: extra weight. He could still prove useful to his family if they found a good match, but it was beginning to look like he might have to marry down if he was to find a wife at all.

Based on what Bea gleaned from the *Registry*, there were no ladies of parallel birth or family available to him in the Three Realms. It would be different if he had a sizable entail, but it looked like his father would only be leaving him with a few thousand crowns per year to live on. Enough to be comfortable, but with no room for excess. He would likely be welcome to stay in their house but expected to make something of himself. Perhaps he would go into the military. If not, his prospects were limited. He certainly could not go into trade or become a merchant.

His family would never stand for that. No doubt, they would rather he live in a guest house and fade into the background.

Then again, he could marry Georgia: a lady of great means and historic family. Her very existence placed her outside the normal rules.

Lucas was not going to inherit, but his pedigree was nothing to overlook, either. Lucas Greenheart was only 2 years older than Georgia, a suitable span. But would he be willing to take her name and let her grant him the title of Count Goldenheart? Georgia's attorney, Mr. Stackhouse told her she could always grant her potential husband a title in keeping with that of a high-ranking consort, but he could never claim to be a duke or outrank her. According to the law, her spouse could never outrank her. There was no way to know how such an arrangement would affect the man of the house.

Would his ego allow it?

Georgia cringed at the idea of even bringing the topic up. How would that even be done? She was not raised to ask those sorts of questions. Naturally, she could ask about blood spots and murder. She could in fact fight monsters... but this? This was a beast of another kind. Then again, that is what lawyers are for. She could have Mr. Stackhouse ask on her behalf and keep it all private.

Once done with the letters, she summoned her driver, Mr. Reardon, and sent him to Grandhall. "This is of the utmost importance," she instructed. "Please ensure delivery of both letters, first to the coroner's fingerprint expert, and then to the Countess... the moment you arrive, and make sure that moment is as quick as you can possibly go without endangering yourself or the horses. You understand?"

"Yes, my lady," Mr. Reardon said, tucking the letters into his coat. "I will see it done."

"Oh, Reardon," she said. "Before you set foot anywhere near the Countess, be sure to chew some mint leaves. You reek of sum gum and tobacco. I am sure they have a footman who will take the letter from you, but just in case. We do not want her to think I have pirates working for me."

"Yes, my lady," Reardon said with a grin. Afterward, Georgia spent the day doing almost nothing. It was remarkably relaxing, and she wondered more than once if she could have been more productive somewhere else. At the same time, she genuinely enjoyed the calm. Also at the same, she could not shake the feeling that this might be some sort of calm before a storm.

# CHAPTER 9

# THE QUEEN'S EMERALD.

The next morning arrived without rain. Without a coach, the ladies opted to walk the entire quarter-mile from Croft House to the resort for the Queen's Emerald Party. It took all of ten minutes, and then they spent another hour sitting in the party room.

"It is as if time has stopped. With everything else going on, it feels silly doing a..." Georgia said in the secret gesture language. "...beauty pageant," she whispered aloud, realizing they had not invented a gesture for 'beauty pageant' yet.

"It is not a..." Bea answered, also in the secret gesture language. "...beauty pageant," she whispered back. Then continued in secret gestures. "We are engaging in a..." She blinked, and said aloud, "...a talent show. It is a traditional Findorian pre-baby shower ritual. You know this. The mother-to-be chooses an emerald to shine at the dance and with luck find a good husband of her own. It is about good fortune and luck. Findorians are all about luck. Well, luck and spices, apparently."

"Delicious spices," Georgia concurred.

"Is it me, or does the name of our secret gesture language seem unwieldy?" Bea asked.

"Well, does it have a name?" Georgia asked back.

"I suppose not. It is just that every time I use it, some tiny part of my head calls it 'the secret gesture language'. Does that make sense?"

"Bea, I have known you for a decade at least. You always make sense in your own way. I had not considered the name for it… but now I have a feeling I will be thinking 'is this the secret gesture language?' every time one of us twitches or moves."

Bea smirked. "I am happy to see my thoughtful neuroses spreading to others."

"I would cake," Georgia admitted.

"Oh yes, cake would be delicious," Bea agreed. "Perhaps we should call it cake-talk? Cake speak? Pastry-patter?"

"Stop or I shall rip a seam laughing," Georgia gasped. She thought for a moment, "How about Cymbre Speak? Named after the school where it was invented?"

"Perfect," Bea said. "Cymbre Speak it is."

Cymbre Speak was not evolved enough to convey so much information. Georgia and Bea both imbued it with additional facial expressions and whispered words for the time being. At least until they fleshed out the grammar a bit more. They were sitting in the lobby of the Dead Mourner's Resort. The room was enormous with beautiful travertine floors and soaring pillars. Waiters served mint tea over ice and delicate saffron biscuits from the Realm of Palas as everyone loitered. Up the corridor, other groups of ladies waited for the Queen's Emerald Ceremony to begin.

Georgia rolled her eyes. "And ice, Bea. These people are obsessed with their ice caves. Whenever I look at them in the glass, all I can think about are tadpoles. Anyway, neither of us needs luck finding a husband. You are already engaged to a Viscount, and I cannot proceed on that front until I have a field of worthy candidates. I need third sons of foreign princes or someone very unusual and high-borne who would be willing to give up his surname in favor of mine. Which, by the way, describes almost no realistic man in the Three Realms."

"Other than Mr. Lucas Greenheart, whom you met once and he spoke in monosyllables," Bea added.

"And Sir Alfie Crighton, who was much the same," Georgia admitted.

"Fine, there are no realistic gentlemen in the Three Realms to marry you, except for the two we just mentioned and the Queen has her personal assistant hunting down more," Bea added.

"Were we not just talking about cake?"

"Wow. Nora really got to you," Bea answered. "Georgia, you do not need luck. You have only to wait long enough, and it will happen. Be patient."

"I suppose we will see. Anyway, Nora did not need to get to me," Georgia said in a flat tone. "I am already there, Bea. I do not feel any great need to find a husband today. My house is enormous, I have a staff, and a huge income from... well, I do not even know where all of the Goldenheart money comes from. Uncle Raymond actively invested when he was alive. My solicitor, Mr. Stackhouse said he was given instructions for investment in the future. He followed it, and my estate blossomed. I own a bunch of copper and tin mines in the Rust Mountains along with what I suspect is a ghetto of tenant farmers, called Thistley, somewhere in southern Volusia. At some point, I must tour the property and evaluate it. Mr. Stackhouse suggested I invest in olive oil from southern Findor. I did that, and it turns out there is a shortage on the continent so now I am making a fortune because everyone is paying top coin for it. Apparently, there are pirates dumping olive oil into the sea, so any ship getting through makes the most. Before that, I urged Mr Stackhouse to invest his own capital as he might see fit, and I think he did. Tell me if you want tips on investment. I will refer you to Stackhouse."

"I think I shall rely on the viscount for that sort of thing," Bea said. "Nothing gets a marriage off on the wrong foot like a wife too smart for her own good. I speak seven languages and my dowry includes the Dale estate. While I do not think his ego is threatened, I suspect I should draw the line somewhere. That said, if he puts us in the poor house with his own investments, I will take you up on that offer. You know, I might refer Stackhouse to my horrid brother-in-law, Lord Wickham."

"Absolutely," Georgia said. "Share the wealth. Stackhouse should author a book on investment planning for the public. I had him set up portfolios for my staff, too. They cannot all be in service forever, surely. Millie will hopefully marry that Edson fellow. He owns a successful flower shop, possesses pleasing features, and boasts an easy-going manner. Of course, that would not preclude her from continuing in my employ. But if she comes into the arrangement with her own entail, it will not hurt. And there's Mr. Derry who really needs to find a comfortable wind-down cottage somewhere. He will be 80 years old this year. I spend my mornings terrified we will find him passed-away in his sleep."

"Georgia, you astound me," Bea said, touching her face like it was hot. "Is this a sort of retirement scheme for your servants? What a thoughtful thing to do. Unequivocally, how many ladies in your position would even think of such a thing."

"Oh, well, thank you," Georgia blushed. "It was not really my idea, Bea. Lady Clara Gaye got to talking with Stackhouse about tax loopholes, and she suggested it. He followed up, and it looks like I can waive all sorts of gentry taxes merely treating my employees like human beings."

"Imagine it," Bea said. "I think you are doing something wonderful, and I'm going to see if I can pull it off too. Surely the Viscount will give me a bit of capital to play with."

Georgia smirked. "So much for a wife too smart for her own good."

Before Bea could answer, another voice interrupted. "Beatrice Irvingdale? Oh...my... word." The woman approaching was tall and resembled an emu. She had a pronounced neck and wild curly charcoal hair.

"Miss Octavia Potter?" Bea's head snapped up. "I haven't seen you since Graduation Day. How have you been?"

Octavia blushed. "You mean the day I called you a monster for beating me to Valedictorian? Oh, Bea, I have felt awful about that ever since."

"Octavia, I was a half-point ahead of you. We spent six years neck and neck to get there. I did not blame you for the name-calling then, and I do not blame you now. We both wanted that title. In fact, if our positions were reversed, I am certain I would have been far more horrible than you were," Bea said, fanning herself. As she did so, she gestured in the secret language, "She was a nightmare."

Octavia sank into a chair next to them. "Oh, Bea. Those days were awful. Everyone told me if I did not graduate at the absolute top of our class, there was no way a plain-faced third daughter of a knight like me could find a suitable match. I would have to teach or marry down. Or both. The thought of it consumed me."

"What a difference six months makes," Georgia whispered. "Bea was in a similar boat only a few months ago, despite graduating on top."

"It is true," Bea admitted. "As the fifth daughter of a baronet, luck and position were on my side in the end. My school marks meant nothing, Octavia. Have you considered teaching?"

Octavia nodded, "I have considered it, and may still do so. In hindsight, it is not the worst idea. I would have agency over myself if I did. I was almost engaged, last year, to an exceedingly kind older gentleman who was a knight. He retired from the Order of the Buck. I would have been his second wife, as he was a widower. Unfortunately, he passed away before he could propose. We spoke of it, in those last days. But he did not do it in the traditional way."

"Did this fellow do anything to spoil you?" Georgia asked.

"Er… I do not think so," Octavia answered. "I am desolate, though. I fear I will never find a happy match."

"Rubbish," Georgia scoffed. "Octavia, do not find yourself locked in a corner with some old man. Unless, of course, you have genuine feelings for him. I hope you forgive my bluntness. I do not know what to say other than do not give up. There is nothing wrong with you. You are barely 20 years old, and fortunately that old man did not lay a hand on you. You are worth more than this."

"Oh," Octavia said, "thank you. I... I don't know what to say."

"Tell Georgia to get over herself," Bea said.

Georgia laughed, startled. "Bea might be right. My life is bordering on a fairy tale, Octavia. You cannot depend on my advice in this matter."

"Perhaps. But I hope you are correct. My options are limited, and my brother wanted the connection most of all. I may have allowed panic to rule my choices. Now I fear I am running out of time."

"You have at least six more years before people start whispering the word 'spinster', and even then, it is not over," Bea said in a low tone. Georgia almost laughed, as only a year before Bea was beside herself over the very same worry. Bea gestured in Cymbre Speak, "Georgia, you can present her to the season. That is why she is here. Her family is no help."

"What? That sounds crazy," Georgia gestured back. Octavia did not notice the hand movements. She was looking down feeling sorry for herself.

"Maybe not. But you can help her," Bea gestured, ending with an emphatic ear-tug. The ear-tug, as per their expansion of Cymbre Speak, literally meant 'with emphasis'.

"Octavia, it may be that we can assist you, old friend. You know," Georgia said aloud, "I am going to hold a few events at the start of the season, this year. My Uncle Raymond used to have a wonderful picnic on Lady Day and another on Midsummer Sunday. I have been thinking about renewing the tradition at Wending Way. How about I invite you to both events? There will be a number of Volusian gentlemen of note." She shot a look at Bea, who would now be arranging the arrival of said Volusians with the help of her fiancée. Bea nodded, understanding. Octavia's family might not be the wealthiest, but they were respected gentry and lived in the capital.

"Oh, Georgia," Octavia said, blinking back tears. "Thank you. Thank you so much."

Yet another old school mate, Danica Forrest, approached. "We're preparing for the show, ladies. Octavia, will you not sing for us?"

Octavia looked up. "Oh, yes. Of course, the talent show. Forgive me, I must go. Duchess... Georgia, thank you." She curtseyed and hurried off.

Georgia turned to Bea. "That poor girl. Was she so terrible in school?"

"She was worse than terrible. We were deep rivals in those days," Bea said. "The difference, I realized, I have significant family advantages she and a few others do not. I realize if you look back a year ago, you could not say that to me. But obviously, things are different now. In the end, my family name and connection to you got me a viscount suitor and a massive dowry from another family whom I did not even know I was related to. Octavia has none of that. She has her wretched brother, whom you probably wiped from your mind the moment you met him because he is loon and a boor. Anyway, I treated her like some terrible rival, almost the most villainous, when we were teenagers."

"I do remember now," Georgia said. "She was a bit of a mess. Remember the case of the missing book?" Even in school, Georgia and Bea dabbled in the occasional mystery. During one of those mysteries, Octavia had been something of a suspect, but turned out to be more of a red herring.

"How could I forget? Anyway, the least I can do now is offer her a bit of help."

"You convinced me. Will you help me host the events I committed to?"

"Oh yes, I will, and I am honored," Bea said. "I did not know your Uncle Raymond hosted those events in the old days."

"He stopped doing them years before he died," Georgia admitted. "We were children. But I remember those parties. So much fun. Picnics and delicate creams and people laughing. There were many Goldenhearts back then. I remember them. I had distant aunts and uncles. It was wonderful. And yes, I can see the advantage of renewing the tradition. This will fix us in certain groups, and perhaps cement my reputation with the papers as someone to watch on the social scene."

"Agreed. I think we may need to solidify certain friendships with a series of smaller dinner parties before we start announcing the events," Bea said, making a note in her book. "You know, invite the Turners."

"Always wise to maintain a friendly relationship with the press," Georgia answered. Mr. Turner and Mrs. Smythe-Turner were both reporters for competing papers. Even so, they were both great friends to Georgia and Bea.

Bea grinned. "And let us not forget Lady Emily Gilmore. Perhaps Lady Johanna Price and her charming husband."

"Also agreed," Georgia said. "It would be nice to see them without worrying that one of them might be a murderer."

At the other end of the lobby, the quartet began to play, marking the start of the talent contest. Groups of young women began to wander into the ballroom. Some had violins in hand. One had a guitar. "We should get a good seat," Bea said. "Harriet will be here soon."

They settled in at their table. Harriet and her husband, Mr. Blackheart, arrived. Thankfully, the gentleman was not in his sweaty riding leathers this time. Instead, he wore a deep green velvet cutaway coat. His breeches were simple black cotton, tailored just tight enough to be fashionable without being vulgar. His collar went high and elegant with his long, ash-brown hair neatly tied back in the current style. Mr. Blackheart was a handsome fellow, with smoldery dark eyes. Not for the first time, she marveled at how well Harriet had done. The cynics in the room would imply Harriet acquired him with her family's staggering trade wealth. But Bea said Mr. Blackheart came from substantial trade wealth of his own. What if it was a genuine love match?

What a thought.

Georgia noticed the valets behind Mr. Blackheart. They were both southern Findorian with long black hair, olive skin, and at least as striking as their master in appearance. Neither looked like a servant. Both wore green velvet coats with tails almost identical to Mr. Blackheart, their breeches immaculate black, with high collars. One might assume they were in the gentry if one did not know better.

Could one of them be the rider of two horses Mrs. Greenstreet saw? Would she have recognized him if it were Blackheart himself?

Georgia was about to look away when it occurred to her: Mr. Blackheart, while having a Findorian name, was not Findorian. She looked at him again, standing next to his valets. His hair was not the local color. Findorians have coal black hair with a bit of curl. His hair was ash brown. It was wavy, but not what she would call curly. In fact, Georgia looked more like a native Findorian than he did. Then again, her mother was from Findor, so there was that. Mr. Blackheart had a tan, but his skin was not the same kind of olive complexion as the locals. She did not know what it was, but it was different. What if his family had Volusian roots? Dead Mourner's Grove was in northern Findor, near the Volusian border. It made sense. He was too pale to come from the Realm of Palas, and the wrong tone for Findor. It had to be a Volusian and Findorian mix. Or perhaps he had foreign blood? Then again, her own family hailed from across the Three Realms and she definitely had Findorian olive skin. She was a blend, but that showed through. Maybe it went another way with him.

As Emerald Queen for the day, Harriet was resplendent in a hunter green silk maternity gown clasped at the neck. She looked confident and happy. Once again, she wore the striking ring. It flashed and nearly glowed on her hand, and Georgia found herself idly staring at it. The stone seemed to blaze with a light of its own. Georgia realized she wasn't the only one staring. Half the people in the room were gawking.

When the Blackhearts were settled, the talent show began. One after another, young ladies of acceptable family and reputation, but who were still unmarried, went up and played their hearts out. Georgia would not be playing or prancing. That was not something a duchess did. Bea was engaged, so she was off the proverbial hook. They sat through an entire recital of mostly mediocre singing, pianoforte, violins, the one afore-mentioned guitar, and Miss Emma Brownfield doing bird calls to the accompaniment of a professional harpist. Four hours crawled by. All of the performances were balanced by the resort staff, who were quick with tea and cakes at every table.

At the end of the event, Harriet proclaimed Miss Rowena Rodale for her violin skills the winner. Georgia was not surprised. Rowena was a renowned musician in the capital, and about to start a tour across the eastern continent.

Normally, the Emerald Queen would reward the young Miss with a bouquet of flowers and good luck in the future. Harriet, however, opted to take the 'emerald' title a step further... and gave Rowena a broach worth more than anyone could imagine. "She just gave her half a dowry," Bea said quietly. "I mean, Rowena's life has changed. This is more than a wish for good luck. This success is ensured. Granted, Rowena is successful in her own way, but this will catapult her."

"Well done, Harriet," Georgia whispered. "Look at you."

For her part, Harriet was almost bland about it. She was, after all, Emerald Queen for a day and her family was beyond wealthy. Why not assist someone else? At the same time, Georgia felt anyone who mocked Harriet back in the day must surely be dying inside. Rowena nearly fainted. The party ended on a high note, with several ladies wishing they put more into their performances. Had they realized the stakes were so high, they might have trained or practiced more. A few had to flee, lest they be reduced to tears on the spot. Everyone else poured out of the resort looking excited.

"And so Harriet has another level of revenge," Nora whispered, rubbing her eyes.

"Oh?" Georgia asked.

"Rowena was another music prodigy in school," Nora whispered. "When the rest of us were being utterly terrible to Harriet, Rowena was always kind and often stuck up for her. I was not so kind on those days, until Rowena urged me to talk to Harriet. You know, we both played the pianoforte. I was talented, but nothing like Harriet."

"You could always sing, though," Georgia said. "I saw you the other night. You were marvelous."

"Thank you. Yes, I could sing and play at the same time. But I was always going to level out somewhere," Nora answered. "Rowena got me to talk to Harriet. Harriet worked with me for months. I excelled at both pianoforte and singing. She never held any grudge with me and I must admit I came to see her as a true friend. At the same time, those girls who are running out of the room right now… the ones in tears… they were terrible to her."

"Fascinating," Georgia said.

"More like the usual rubbish," Nora answered. "I wish I had stuck up for her more."

"Before anyone invites us to a picnic or who knows what, we should go see the ruins," Bea said, pulling the Redstone journal out of her bag.

Georgia agreed. "We should go." After the appropriate number of goodbyes and well-wishes, they hurried out to Georgia's carriage. Mr. Reardon was driving. "How did your mission go?" Georgia asked. She could see he had not slept. Despite that, the fellow was alert and present. Perhaps that was the real power of sour gum and tobacco? She would never know.

"The mint leaves helped, my lady," he said with a quick grin. "I delivered the letters. The fingerprint expert said they had not yet inspected the evidence but would do so and send their results to you immediately. They made me wait a moment while the doctor himself read your letter, and he seemed to understand your urgency."

"Excellent, Mr. Reardon. Any thoughts on the delivery to the countess?"

He shook his head. "The footman took your letter, and I came home, my lady."

"That is as expected," Georgia said. "Thank you, Mr. Reardon. Once we finish this ride, you must rest."

"Yes, my lady," he said, guiding the coach to the street. They rode west, headed for Lord Redstone's nearby dig site.

"When we get to the site, he's going to take a nap," Bea said.

"I would, too," Georgia admitted. "May I see the journal?"

"Of course," Bea said. "I read the next few passages. Lord Redstone found an ancient site just west of the village. He thought it might date a thousand years prior to the formation of the Three Realms. The people who settled there were refugees from some far-flung ancient Western realm. They came from a place far more evolved and civilized, but their homeland apparently sank into the sea in some sort of disaster."

"I see," Georgia said.

"They arrived in what is now Findor to start over and built a haven. According to Redstone's notes, he gleaned all of this from ancient scrolls and writings. He sent them to the Library of Phaedros before the revolution that destroyed their old government. The scrolls were lost in the uprising when the rebellion burned the library and the university," Bea said.

"So Redstone started the project here in Dead Mourner's Grove more than a decade ago," Georgia noted.

"According to the journal, he started exploring the local ruins almost 25 years ago," Bea answered. "He bought the house in Dead Mourner's Grove about 20 years ago, and then his sister started keeping track of his affairs about five years ago, after her husband died. He mentioned it in the journal, which spans a long time on its own. He basically handed it all off to her because he was afraid she was depressed and thought she needed the distraction from grief… which seems like a kind thing to do. After that, he began his own chronicle of his properties and his sister's progress managing for him. She is apparently quite efficient. He even has a will of sorts in the pages of the book where he repeatedly insists she inherit his property, titles, funds, investments, and everything in between. I do not know if it would hold up in court, but it is extensive. In fact, he had to take the journal to a printmaker to have it expanded on several occasions."

"Why not simply start a new journal?"

Bea shrugged. "He is an archeologist. He wanted his notes all in one document. That said, Redstone did wonder if it was a mistake to write it all in one book after the library in Phaedros burned down."

"Phaedros is a mess," Georgia muttered. "How could they have such exalted libraries and then burn them down? Who does that?"

"Angry people do that," Bea answered. "People with no hope."

"You mentioned he leaves everything to Mrs. Crauford. Should I re-evaluate her? What if she had something to do with the blood pool and whatnot?" Georgia wondered.

"According to the journal, he told her nothing of his wishes. He did mention that the entail is all with his attorney… one Mr. Stackhouse in the capital."

"Mr. Stackhouse," Georgia repeated. Her own attorney. Of course, Stackhouse would never break the confidentiality of another client. If she asked him about it, he would never tell her anything useful. Too bad. On the other hand, an attorney who values his clients' privacy above all else is a valuable thing.

"Still, I wonder if I should re-examine Mrs. Crauford."

"If she were that capricious and diabolical, she would have prevented her maid from making a report in the first place. No one would know," Bea offered. "I think the culprit dwells elsewhere. Also, after reading his thoughts on his sister, I think Lord Redstones trusts her for a reason."

Mist clung to the road as their carriage left the village. For a moment, Georgia feared Bea would insist on going back for fear of rain. Instead, she pulled their umbrellas out of the boot when they arrived and pulled on a warm coat and wellingtons.

"I hope we do not ruin these gowns wandering around the woods," Georgia said, hopping out.

"We may need to hike up our skirts," Bea said as they unfurled the umbrellas. "According to the map Lord Redstone drew in his journal, that little trail going north into the woods should take us straight to his old camp." Ahead stretched a small fence with a sign that read, *Redstone Property. Do Not Intrude.*

"One moment, my lady. I will just get my coat," Mr. Reardon said, hopping out of the carriage.

"No need," Georgia answered. "Mr. Reardon, you rode all night and now here. Relax. Tend the horses. We will not be long, I suspect."

"Are you sure, my lady?" he asked, looking concerned. He looked exhausted but was still worried.

"It is a short walk," Georgia answered with a smile. "Take a moment. I have asked enough of you over the last day. We will return soon. That said, if it starts to rain, come find us if you think the road will mud over, but otherwise do not worry. You know I can handle it if something goes awry."

"Yes, my lady." Mr. Reardon settled on the front of the carriage, and promptly dozed off, despite himself.

"Oh goodness," Bea whispered.

"He's been busy," Georgia whispered back. "Let us go."

They stepped over the fence on the little path, not much more than an indent in the grass. Georgia was not sure how Bea even spotted it from the road. No more than two hundred feet into the woods they found the remains of an overgrown camp site. Georgia could see where they had fires and tents placed at one time. An old cart lay in the brush. "According to the journal, this old cart lost a wheel at some point, so they left it behind. It marks the edge of the Redstone dig," Bea said, patting the book. She turned to the right. "That path leads to all of the good stuff."

"I see the remains of a road here," Georgia said, spotting octagonal flagstones amongst the grass. They followed it to a wide area of ancient buildings. Beyond were dozens of large pits.

"'Behold the 6,000-year-old remains of the easternmost settlement of the great realm of Gildernesse'," Bea said, reading from the journal. "According to Lord Redstone, the people who built these structures came from the ancient civilization we talked about on the way here. Guildernesse was a great sea power at the time and landed colonies at the edges of their known world."

"We are a bit inland, are we not?" Georgia asked.

"The river is attached to the lake, and all of it goes to the sea. That tributary is probably less than five hundred feet away," Bea answered. "They appear to have come right up to it."

"Amazing," Georgia said. The buildings were beyond old, but surprisingly structured for such a society before modern history. The people who built them were not primitive at all. "How could something like this exist so close to the capital without anyone knowing?"

"Oh, there are other ruins near the capital," Bea answered. "It's just... people do not really care about those things anymore. The world is too modern for something like this to matter."

Georgia remembered the Mountain of the Tree, just north of the capital. She went there with Mr. Blue barely a year ago. It too was an ancient ruin from a time before time was properly recorded, and in fact, sat overlooking the city of Oradale itself, albeit unnoticed by most people who lived within a mile.

Bea was still reading, "This settlement housed at least five hundred Men of Gildernesse and was likely a trade point."

"Just the men?"

"According to Lord Redstone's notes, 'Gildernesse' translated to 'The Men of Gilder' or 'Gilderians'. 'Men,' in this case, means 'people' or more likely 'humans.' He's very odd with the nomenclature, but I suspect it is a translation from an older language… or possibly Lord Redstone is a sexist," Bea said, flipping through a few pages. "That said, I think he is not. A sexist would not leave his sister in charge of his business dealings, would he? He called them 'Men of Gilder' meaning humans… to differentiate from the legendary Fay lords. The Men of Gilder traded with many groups in the area. Redstone speculates the existence of actual goblins, which he calls 'dark elves,' living in the woods nearby. He swears they are not a fairy tale but rather a diminutive race of indigenous humanoids who lived underground and only came to the surface at night. He said they would go to this settlement for trade. Redstone also speculated the people of Gildernesse... even the most common of them... were sorcerers. Cultists who worshiped dark gods of old. He mentions in the notes finding powerful artifacts, although most lost their meaning over time. Still, they belonged to a darker era when people often dealt with the unseen world in ways we cannot fathom."

"So, an ancient sorcerous kingdom nobody ever heard of had a colony here," Georgia said.

"Oh, we know a lot about them, actually," Bea answered. "Gildernesse was another name for the lost island of Naurland. The place of children's stories that ruled the oceans until the island sunk when their emperor offended the old heathen gods."

"Oh, I see. Interesting," Georgia said. Everyone knew about Naurland, of course. She looked around the edge of the ruin. Once again, the shadows in the trees seemed to move of their own volition. It reminded her of the amphitheater with its prehistoric stones and sense of dread. Not for the first time, she wondered if it had been unwise to leave her magic sword behind.

Bea squinted at the book. "His handwriting really is terrible. There's a bit here about a curse upon the region. Lord Redstone was worried about 'frog zombies' and apparently other shadow monsters. There is another bit about the coming of the 'Century of Evil'. That sounds bad. Frogs are bad enough. Frog zombies sound like my worst nightmare."

"Mr. Blue was just talking about the coming Century of Evil too," Georgia said, peeking over Bea's shoulder. The handwriting was nearly indecipherable; worse even than in the letter Mrs. Crauford showed her. "Does he say anything else about it?"

"Um… 'the dead shall rise with fallen faces when the guardian is away, the ground will open and that which is tiny and unnoticed will be corrupted to walk in shadow…' This is nonsense," Bea answered.

"That is… um, that is not nonsense," Georgia said. "Mr. Blue and Lady Clara said something very similar just last week: a new Century of Evil, right after the giant shadow spider monsters attacked."

Bea continued reading. "Then there is this: 'it will grow like a plague. The shadow will spread across lands where the folk are careless. The wise knew better, but they are gone now'. My word."

"That sounds important. It also sounds like a man with an over-excitable mind," Georgia said.

"We should copy these notes," Bea said. "Before we give the journal back, I mean."

"Agreed."

"And watch out for frog zombies." Bea winked. "Just to be on the safe side."

"I will keep an eye out," Georgia answered.

"The same language," Bea murmured.

"I beg your pardon?"

Bea was near one of the taller pillars inscribed with writing. "This is the same language we saw in the amphitheater," she explained. "It was carved on the ring of stones. Do you remember?"

Georgia nodded. "I remember the place, of course. Not sure I would recognize carvings from an ancient language like you would, though." At the edge of her vision, the shadows twitched. Behind them, she could feel it growing darker. Something was not right. "Bea, I don't know if I like this spot."

Bea glanced up from the stones. "This was a place of some evil at one time. I feel it too."

"And yet you aren't running for the carriage," Georgia said.

"Not with you here," her old friend said with a smile. "You remember the Cymbre school adages? *Learning comes at a cost.* Let us look at this place before it gets too creepy, shall we? I trust you will know when to leave. I trust you, Georgia."

Georgia looked at her old friend. Bea might have an irrational fear of the rain, but she had no trouble with the truth, and could be brave when she needed to be. They moved forward, examining the remnants of buildings. At the end of a row, they found a series of holes in the ground. "Is there a corresponding note to this in the journal?" Georgia asked.

"Yes, he has a map. There should be 26 holes in the ground," Bea said, holding up the journal. "Most were a waste of his time. He dug but found nothing of interest other than old pottery. He said there is one at the end where they found a tomb or burial compartment. After that, he lists a series of jars and things. Most of it is notations about wheat stocks and offerings to old gods." She looked around. "Maybe over there?" They wound their way amongst the pits looking for anything of promise. Eventually, they found a ramp down to an open stone doorway. "I have a lamp with a built-in shutter," Bea said, pulling a clunky device from her bag. "It is very modern. Much like an umbrella. But it sheds light, unlike an umbrella."

Georgia chuckled.

Bea fiddled with a flint and wick until a tiny light appeared in the lamp, and they passed the door into the dark beyond. The room was musty and old. Georgia could see faded footsteps in the mud. The walls were covered in strange writing.

"Oh, look at that," Bea said, pointing. On the wall was a carving of a frog.

"Well, we are only a half mile from the lake," Georgia said. "There are bound to be frogs… or frog zombies." She was about to turn away when she noticed something on the ground. The footprints went to the wall. In fact, one set was cut off by it. The prints were directly below a carving of a frog. The groove around the frog was more than an indent. It was a separate thing entirely. Slowly, she reached over and pressed it. The frog indented into the wall and stopped. A moment later, they heard a clicking noise.

"Georgia, what is that?" Bea asked, leaning in.

"A latch," Georgia breathed. "A hidden door."

The wall slid back as another room appeared. "What in the world?" Bea whispered. The footprints continued across the next room, where there was yet another frog carved in the wall. This time, Bea pressed it, and it slid open without sound. Faintly, they heard rushing water. The space beyond the second secret door was a rough-hewn stairway running downward.

"No dust on these stairs," Georgia whispered. The air grew chilly. She took the lantern from Bea and went in first. "Stay behind me."

"I have a bad feeling about this," Bea whispered.

"Stay behind me," Georgia repeated. Her eyes adjusted to the gloom. Bits of lichen and moss clung to the walls, and the passage was wet with an undercurrent of mold. Georgia shined the lantern ahead. It was dark. She wondered if they should turn back but spotted a faint light. They turned a corner, and the sound of rushing water grew louder. The stairs opened to reveal a larger, darker chamber with a small spot of light, a torch on a boat. It was some sort of underground port.

"A cave in the lake?" Bea whispered. She flinched, stepping in a puddle. "Ugh. Frogs everywhere." At her feet, tiny forms hopped across the cold wet gravel.

"I think this is a storage area," Georgia answered. She could see her breath. It was cold down there. To one side were stacks of crates. "Perhaps this is a storage point for shipping along the river?"

"Why would the storage point be a cave on the lake? Wouldn't it make more sense to use the village dock and the warehouse?" Bea asked.

"You are right. It must be a cave for smugglers," Georgia answered. She pulled the lid off one of the crates to find it full of hay and bottles. She took a bottle out and opened it. The scent of fresh olive oil filled the air.

Bea pulled open another lid. "Musket pistols. Many of them."

"Guns and olive oil," Georgia whispered. She gazed around the gloomy cave. There were hundreds of crates. Faint voices floated in her ear. "Bea, get down." Bea did not need to be told twice. She ducked behind the crates with surprising agility. Georgia followed, snapping the lantern shut.

For a moment, it was quiet until she heard feet crunching on the rocky floor. The flickering light of lanterns appeared at the far end of the crates. Georgia kept her head down. Men laughed and taunted one another in the idle way men do.

The light got closer. "Over here," Bea whispered. "Another room." They scooted away from the barrels and pushed past a curtain. It led to another cavern; this time significantly colder. Georgia looked around. It was an ice cave. The floor was frozen. Dozens of wooden canisters and glass jars lined the far wall. All of them were marked with a symbol like a flying seagull. She wasn't sure what company it represented but could see it was on all the canisters.

The voices got closer. There was no way out, other than back to the room with the barrels. They pressed against the wall in the darkest reaches of the ice cave, shivering silently. She hoped the men on the other side of the curtain were not coming this way.

"Har!" another voice laughed. "Good one, Dario."
They stumbled on the shale as if drunk.

Bea gestured in Cymbre Speak. "What do we do?"

"Wait a moment," Georgia gestured back. "Be still.
Maybe they will move on."

"What if they do not move on?"

Georgia shrugged. Aloud, she whispered, "I do not
know. If they linger, push them over and run?"

"You cannot... fight them?" Bea asked.

"Oh Bea," Georgia whispered. "Maybe? Never have I
fought a... normal person. Not for real, I mean. I fight
supernatural monsters. I have heard of men who punch
one another in their faces all the time in the market. But in
the real world? What would that entail?"

"We will figure out another way," Bea whispered.
"First chance, we run."

Georgia nodded. Fortunately, the men wandered off.
After a long moment, she and Bea crept back to the
passage to Lord Redstone's archeological site. Their
movement caused no reaction, so they made their way past
the frog doors, up the ramp, through the woods, and back
to Mr. Reardon. They found him at the edge of the site.

"My lady," he gasped when they appeared. "The
woods are full of strange men. Forgive me, I was worried."
He had a riding crop in hand, almost as one would hold a
weapon.

"Men in the woods," Bea whispered. "Are they the same as in the caves?"

"Caves?" Mr. Reardon asked.

"Much happened in the last hour. Thank you, Mr. Reardon. Let us head back," Georgia said. "We will need to swing by the local Constabulary on the way."

"Right away, Duchess," he answered, launching their carriage back onto the road. As they headed back to the village, Georgia glanced backward and spotted someone on the road behind. But when she looked again, they were gone.

They found Constable Jenkins at the Constabulary. "We do not have a solid update on the Redstone murder," Georgia told him. "That said, Bea and I followed a lead in Lord Redstone's journal to the archeological dig. There we found a passage to an underground cave next to the lake, where smugglers are hoarding stolen olive oil and muskets. You can find it at the last pit in the dig. I will write down instructions on how to open the secret doors."

"Good heavens," Constable Jenkins said. "What is happening with this village? Duchess, I will need to gather a group of constables from Grandhall. I would not put you at any risk. You and Miss Beatrice might want to return to your house and enjoy the rest of the day in comfort. I could come by after we raid the cave."

"Of course," Georgia said.

"Thank you both," the Constable said, tipping his little police cap.

They returned to Croft House before dinner. Bea went to the solar room to read more of the Redstone journal. Georgia checked her suite, then went to the basement to find Millie. She found her mending clothes in the servants' common area. "Don't get up," Georgia said to Millie and another maid. "This is an informal visit. Millie, I must ask you to go back to the city tomorrow and retrieve the magic sword. I know. I told you before I wanted a free week for relaxation, but life is not going that way. I would feel better having the blade nearby. In fact, the sooner it is strapped to my back the better. Mr. Reardon is going to rest now. In the morning, he will take you to the house in Oradale. I will send letters with you. Please deliver them to Lady Clara Gaye and the Order of the Blue offices. Once you deliver them and retrieve the sword, return as quickly as you can with it. Sleep in the carriage if you must but do not delay. If Mr. Reardon is too tired to make the journey back, ask him to get Francis to drive you back. I will detail this in a letter to Mr. Derry. I know, in my heart, you are capable of this trip. Will you do it for me?"

"Of course, my lady. I will be fine," Millie said. "How will you dress while I am gone?"

"Right," Georgia scratched her head. "Lay out my outfits for the next two days of parties, just in case. Set them along the dresser in the second room of the suite. I will ask Mrs. Macklin to assist if things get complicated, but I can dress myself for more casual events, and I think I can handle dinner for two nights if you plan ahead."

"My lady, what about your hair?"

Georgia gulped. "I will ask Mrs. Macklin for assistance."

"Very good, my lady. I will go as fast as I can."

"Thank you. I am sorry to put you to this."

Millie smiled. "Oh, my lady, do not be sorry. You will get through this. I will do everything I can to help. But you will succeed. I know it."

They assembled at 6pm for dinner. Nora, Nelda, and Mr. Brown joined. Nelda was pale and looked weak. The staff started with the safest dish: toasted bread fragrant with rosemary, salt, and butter. It was so comforting. She watched Nelda eat slowly, chewing as if for the first time.

"Oh, forgive my bad manners," Nelda gasped. "I forgot how delicious food is."

Tears rolled from Nora's eyes. "Nelda sweet baby girl, I am so glad to see you better."

"Not a moment too soon," Mr. Brown said, nibbling at his salad. "The wind is changing. Tomorrow I must climb into my balloon and fly to the west."

Nelda smiled. "Yes, you did mention it, Mr. Brown. I cannot thank you enough. I know I will recover, but I will miss hearing you humming in the corner while boiling your fragrant weeds."

"I'm so glad to see you up and about. Be careful, though. You are still recovering," the old man warned. "Boiling weeds indeed."

Nelda laughed, sounding almost like her old self.

# CHAPTER 10

# GOODBYE AND HELLO.

*Click. Click-click. Click-click…click.*

Georgia awoke. Where was the clicking coming from? She looked around. Nearby, her fireplace crackled, but it was not the source of the noise. Her room smelled delicious with warm rosemary breads and the lingering scent of ginger tea. A plate of fresh biscuits and butter waited on a nearby tray. Next to this was a steaming pot with a teacup and chopped lemon.

The clicking persisted.

Kenneth, the bright oriole sat on her windowsill pecking at the glass. Georgia pulled a robe around her shoulders and went over. The little bird chirped and tilted his head before pecking at the glass again. Carefully, Georgia pulled the window open, so as not to startle him. Kenneth blinked and said, "The old man goes home. Be careful, wingless thing." With that, he flew into the trees.

Georgia jumped. "I knew he was a wizard. What now?" She hurried down the hall, pulling her wool coat and autumn bonnet on. In the lobby, Millie and Mr. Reardon were about to leave. "Oh, my lady," Millie said. "We were going to wait before waking you."

"Never mind, Millie. I am awake now." Georgia came down the stairs. "Got everything you need to make the trip? I am sorry to make you go so quickly."

"My lady, it is like an adventure," Mr. Reardon murmured. Considering he just returned from an overnight trip, the fellow was being a good sport about things.

"As long as you are in no danger, that's fine," Georgia answered. "Mr. Reardon, how tired are you?"

"Not as tired as you might think, my lady," he answered. "I stand ready to serve you."

"I have your letters to Mr. Blue and Lady Clara," Millie said, pointing to her bag. "I have the notes for Mr. Derry and the staff. As soon as we make the deliveries, Mr. Derry will likely have the sword ready for transport. He is very efficient. Mr. Reardon thinks we can be back tomorrow night."

"Good," Georgia said. "You have both been in my employ long enough to know the Goldenhearts occasionally deal with unusual and... unnatural... things. I assure you there is something happening in this village. I do not understand it, but I think we must work together to prevent it."

"We understand, my lady." Millie smiled. To Georgia's eye, the maid looked small and vulnerable. Then she noticed Millie was grinning; they were about to enjoy their own little adventure.

"Thank you," Georgia answered. "Thank you both. Now, waste no time. Get my notes to the witch and wizard and bring the magical sword to me. I will not leave it behind again. I know, I wanted a normal week away for once, but I have come to realize it will never happen again." It was settled. Hopefully, she would not have to explain her decision to the Queen.

\*\*\*

Georgia watched the carriage leave. When it was past the gate and out of sight, she turned to go inside. It was then six riders appeared at the gate and trotted to the door. Behind her, Bea came out to the porch. "Georgia, riders from Grandhall, and at this early hour? It must be important," she said. "They wear the green heraldic swan. I think they are Earlsmen or Knights."

At the head of the group of riders was someone Georgia knew… or rather, met once. Mr. Lucas

Greenheart, 5th son of the Earl of Grandhall. "Get into the house before he sees you," Bea hissed.

The horsemen stopped. Sir Lucas saw her but looked down immediately. He was not the sort of gentleman to simply barge in, apparently, and gained a point of favor.

Georgia ducked inside. It would not be appropriate to be loitering at the front door. She went upstairs, followed by Bea. Downstairs, she heard the bell.

"Duchess, there is a Sir Lucas Greenheart to see you," the footman said, catching up to her.

"Thank you," Georgia answered. "Put him in the drawing room with refreshment. Urge him to get comfortable, as I will need a few minutes. If his entourage needs support, tend to them as well."

"Yes, Duchess."

"Perfect," Bea muttered. "Millie leaves and right away we are confronted with a potential suitor. What will you wear?"

"Millie set out combinations in the guest parlor," Georgia answered. "I need to fix my hair, so if you could find something simple but appropriate, I would be grateful."

Bea went into the parlor and returned with a pale green dress in hand. It was the kind of garment one would wear on a bright morning.

Millie had created a wig for Georgia; it was more of an extension to her real hair. If one looked closely, one might see it. That said, attaching the extension wig was a whole process unto itself. Following the process as best she could remember, Georgia put her wig on. From there, she carefully pulled the bulk of her real hair up to lay over the extension. All the while, she checked herself in the mirror, which was upsetting. She looked like a mad woman for a moment. Finally, she got her real hair under control and laid over the extension. How in the hell did Millie do this without ripping her head off? She almost gave up, but kept smoothing it out. Once the extension was in place, she was able to comb out her wavy tresses in a way that looked almost natural. She joined Bea in the bedroom and slipped into the green frock. When she was ready, they went downstairs.

Sir Lucas waited in the drawing room with a tray of biscuits and tea. When she entered, he stood and bowed. "Thank you for coming, Sir Lucas," Georgia said. She did not nod or bow but did pause in deference not so much to his rank as to his potential with her.

Sir Lucas kept his eyes to the ground. She saw him smile and blush, though. Then he remembered himself. "Thank you, Duchess Goldenheart. I am honored you will see me, and… uh… forgive me for appearing at your door at this hour. I am beyond happy to see you again," he looked up. "My mother received your letter and expedited the coroner's report. I have it with me. My father bade me and my men assist you in your investigation. He insisted I speak to you the moment we arrived. We are at your disposal. Oh, and my mother sends her fondest greetings." His left eyebrow danced upward a smidge. She felt vaguely dizzy. What was that about? He knelt on one knee the way one would present a ring and handed her a leather-bound bundle. It was the coroner's report.

"Sir Lucas, this is a surprise. A good one. You are welcome in my home at any hour." What? Why did she say that? Oh drat. Last time she saw Lucas Greenheart, he was covered in sweat from a bocce game on a sunny afternoon. Why did she remember that? She would not soon forget his smoldering grey eyes, tousled black hair, and alarmingly angled jawline. This time, he was clad in a very modern jade green suit but complemented with a hunter green sash. The sash had a swan embroidered on it, indicating he was in the formal regalia of an Earlsman of Grandhall. The swan was from his father's heraldry, so he must have been invested since their last meeting. He wore an epee blade in a green scabbard. He looked quite dapper, although she could see he was tired from riding. She could also see him sweating under the coat, and he smelled vaguely like cucumber and saffron oil. She had met the man twice, and he was always sweaty.

"Will you pardon me for a moment?" Georgia asked. "There is something I must attend to. I will only be a moment."

"Oh. Yes, of course," he answered. "I will just drink some tea, my lady."

"Excellent, sir. You do that." Georgia stepped out into the hall to find Bea standing there. "Were you listening at the door?"

"No, but I was considering it," Bea answered. "Did you leave Sir Lucas back in the drawing room?"

"I needed a moment. He smells like saffron oil and cucumber," Georgia muttered. "I needed a moment."

"You needed two moments, apparently. Why is he here?" Bea smirked.

"His mother received my letter and got the coroner to send the report right away. He delivered it in person. His father... er... sort of assigned him to me, I think."

"And now he is all sweaty after riding all night," Bea murmured. "I like where this is going."

"He is a bit unshaven too," Georgia said.

"Because he did not delay for any reason to come to your aid, but instead rode all night in his little green uniform and did not even shave," Bea whispered. "Is the stubble offensive?"

"It is the opposite of offensive," Georgia answered.

"As long as he is not turning into a frog zombie, I am all for it," Bea said with a chuckle. "You had best get back in there."

Georgia took a moment to smooth out her dress before opening the door. "Well, that is… um… taken care of."

Luke stood up. "Please forgive me for being so disheveled, my lady."

"Oh, that is all right. Have your men taken refreshment?"

"Yes, Duchess. They are resting in the stable," he answered.

She smiled. "Um, this would be easier if we dispensed with at least one formality. May I call you Luke and you call me Georgia… and will you look me in the eye?"

Luke looked up. "Oh, thank you. Yes, this is better. Looking in the eyes is better, I mean." He smiled. His cool grey eyes twinkled, and there was a hint of blush on his cheeks. Georgia nearly stepped back. The man had a charm about him. There was nothing plain about his features, and she was sure he knew it. He gazed at her. "Green."

"I beg your pardon?"

"Oh." Luke blinked rapidly. "Forgive me. Your eyes are green. Little flecks of amber. I mean, sort of like a forest floor. I am rambling, sorry."

She nearly went out to the hall again.

Instead, Georgia blurted, "You would be welcome with us if you prefer? I mean, if you and your men need somewhere to stay. I am sure the hotel is fine, but this place is so much more comfortable. This house has a plethora of unused rooms. There is a whole section on the first floor we did not open. You and your men could stay there. The ladies would be upstairs. We would all feel more comfortable with you here."

"We would be honored, my lady," he whispered, blinking. "Thank you. Uh, yes, thank you." He blushed but then smiled again and gazed at her with those remarkable grey eyes. Grey eyes. Who would have thought them that interesting? They reflected the colors of the room and changed as he moved. Oh dear. Georgia knew how to read a person. She watched this man look at her, almost flinch, smile, and then look again.

"Oh good," Georgia said.

Bea ducked in with a quick knock. "Sorry to interrupt."

Georgia turned. "Bea, you remember Sir Lucas Greenheart. Luke, you remember Miss Beatrice Irvingdale."

"Of course," Luke said with a bow. Bea curtseyed. "We met last Spring at your family's social." After saying that, he went pale. No doubt remembering the series of deaths at that Spring social.

"We seem to run into each other whenever there is a… um," Georgia stopped herself. Why was she rambling now? "I am sorry, that came out the wrong way."

Luke shrugged. "You said what I was thinking, but too nervous to…" He stopped talking, realizing where he was going with it.

"Good heavens. Both of you need to stop while you are ahead," Bea said in Cymbre Speak. She turned to Luke. "It is a pleasure to see you again. We are all glad to see you, Sir Lucas."

"Thank you, Miss Beatrice," Luke said with a slight bow.

"Please call me Bea."

"In that case, please call me Luke."

Bea turned to Georgia before anyone could speak. "Sorry, but I thought you should know Mr. Brown is about to depart in his balloon. Half the village is over in the western field to see it take off."

"We should join," Georgia said. "Luke, have you ever seen a hot air balloon?"

"I have never seen one," he admitted. "I think I will gather my men too. What an amazing sight it must be."

"Perfect. I just need to change my outfit, but first let us read the coroner's report." Georgia said, pulling open the packet. "Luke, would you like to see it too? After all, you rode all night with it."

"Absolutely," Luke answered. They settled in and Georgia laid out the documents on the coffee table. There were sketches of the dagger and shoe with notes. Alongside was a summary from the coroner and the fingerprint expert, which read as follows:

Official Summary of Grandhall Coroner's Office

*Dr. Filius Brownsable, Coroner*

*Dr. Thaddeus Whitesquall, Expert in Remnant Tracing (Fingerprint and other)*

*In the matter of the alleged blood pool, the description given by Duchess Goldenheart implies the loss of approximately 4 pints. Without further evidence, we may only assume it is the blood of a human. Loss of 4 pints of blood by a grown human would likely be fatal without immediate treatment.*

*In the matter of the knife (dagger), the weapon appears to be domestic to the Three Realms, common amongst volunteer militia (mercenaries) in the Realm of Findor. The design of the weapon is detailed in the sketch. Based on our inspection, the weapon was almost pristine, but by association to the scene of the crime, was likely the offensive implement. Based on the condition of it, we might assume this was the first time it was used.*

*In the matter of the shoe, the apparel is standard size for an adult man. The fashion appears to be a high-quality foreign slipper uncommon in the Three Realms and made of leather. In this land, we tend to reserve leather for boots with a higher lip. I found a stamp on the interior of the garment. It appears to identify the cobbler as 'Singuile', which is a surname more commonly found in the kingdom of Jendina. The shoe was well-worn.*

"Not a bad report for a country coroner," Bea said, looking over the summary. She looked up at Luke. "Oh, forgive me, I meant no offense."

"None taken," Luke said with a grin. "My mother says that Dr. Brownsable has the manners of a troglodyte, but his work is impeccable."

"What does your father think of his work?" Georgia asked.

"I would be shocked if my father even knew his name." Luke picked up the sketch of the dagger and squinted. "Interesting."

"What do you see?" Georgia asked.

"Well, the fingerprint expert says there's nothing on the hilt. He notes the wielder of the weapon was probably wearing gloves. Not uncommon. But the length of the blade is peculiar: it is only 4-inches in length," Luke looked up. "It looks sort of like a stiletto."

"Like an embroidery knife?" Georgia asked.

Luke showed her the illustration. "Almost. One could fit it into their sleeve and would be useful for a stealthy attack."

"Grim," Bea murmured. "So, our attacker wasn't simply carrying it around by accident."

"He could also use it as a letter opener," Luke said, gazing at the illustration. "Perhaps we should ask Mrs. Crauford if she is missing one."

"The maid would have recognized it, I suspect," Georgia answered. "She is the one who said it was a knife when she delivered it to the constables. That said, I will enquire."

"That brings us to the shoe," Bea said, holding the other illustration. "I had a thought."

"Tell us," Georgia urged.

"It is a slipper, as mentioned in the summary. See? No laces on it. One would not wear it out and about," Bea said slowly. "Also, no one wears slippers over to visit another person's house. They wear proper shoes. It stands to reason that someone in residence would wear slippers, though."

Georgia nodded. "Without other evidence, we can postulate that victim of the stabbing was wearing the slipper and lost it either in the scuffle or when he was removed from the library."

"You will want to ask Mrs. Crauford if she has ever heard of anyone named 'Singuile'," Bea said.

"I have to admit something," Luke said, looking embarrassed. "But I am finding all this very exciting. Being a detective is quite fun."

***

Above the gate hung a banner that read: *Farewell and Good Luck Luncheon for Mr. Brown!* The season was changing. In a week or two, the frost would arrive. Georgia wore her soft charcoal wool coat with matching wide brim hat as they stepped out of the carriage. Ahead was a field of people. It was the sort of gathering that normally happened in the summer. But this was a special occasion.

The grassy field next to Mr. Brown's cottage riffled with a low wind, even as great clouds rolled westward above. Tables and chairs spread across the field, just to the side of the great red balloon. Bea secured a large table for their party. To the north was a 24-piece orchestra. Along the west part of the field, an outdoor kitchen was set up. The scent of sausages, bread, spice, and tea filled the air. Someone paid to send Mr. Brown off in style. East of the balloon was the road, already jammed with carriages from around the county. Everyone wanted to see the balloon.

Even Nelda joined them, despite still being weak. Excited children got underfoot; even as cranky old men predicted the imminent winter. Lovers snuck kisses before their mothers could object.

Mr. Brown sat at the center table flanked by the village mayor, Constable Jenkins, and the woman who owned the café. The old man was clad in a short umber jacket, tawny trousers, and tall black boots. On his head he wore a white leather cap with a pair of goggles affixed. Georgia had never seen a balloon pilot, but imagined this was the appropriate ensemble. All around the old man were villagers and clusters of Cymbre girls from the baby shower. To one side, Georgia spotted Lady Rebecca Drake with her security entourage. They were near Harriet, Mr. Blackheart, and half a dozen of his dapper valets. Just beyond, Georgia spotted Mrs. Crauford sitting with the Greenstreets.

Mr. Darkleaf appeared, as if out of nowhere, and led them to their table, which was wide, circular, and laden with delightful foods. Bea sat to the right of Georgia. To her left was Nora, Nelda, and then Luke and his men. This put Luke almost precisely opposite her in the seating. When she looked up, he smiled almost impertinently. The footmen from the house served their table as they enjoyed sizzling sausages, onions with peppercorn, and tea. Every table on the field featured pitchers of ice water.

Nelda looked at Luke and his men. "May I ask you a question, Sir Lucas?" she asked.

"Of course," Luke said. "Mrs. Northbrooke, call me Luke."

"Very well, Luke. Call me Nelda if we are on such informal terms," she responded with a weak smile. "We have not been introduced to your associates. Are you all knights?"

Luke looked at the six men seated around the table. They were all dressed as gentlemen, but also wore the green swan sash of the Earldom of Grandhall, and epee blades on their hips. "We are Earlsmen. It is sort of a middle ground between a formal knight and a gentleman. My father granted us the title yesterday."

"Yesterday," Nelda gaped. "And here you are today. He put you to work right away, I see."

"Allow me to introduce, from left to right," Luke said with a cough. "Sir Callum Arnold, who is my second cousin." Sir Callum nodded with a broad smile. "Sir Ian Clark, whose family are bannermen to the Earl." Sir Ian waved. "Sir James Davis, Sir Rupert Agar, Sir Nicholas Blackflower, and Sir Ignatius Lavender. All are sons of baronial families in eastern Findor."

"All of us are second, third, and fourth sons without an entail," Sir Ian muttered.

"Speak for yourself. I am a seventh son with no entail. That said, we are Earlsmen now," Luke answered with an arched eyebrow. "This is an opportunity to prove our worth." The men chuckled, as if they were all in on a private joke.

"I see. Well done, all of you." Nelda said. "Your father formed your group only yesterday?" She spoke to Luke, who nodded. Even as he did, his fellow Earlsmen toasted their good luck.

"A bevy of new options for you," Bea whispered to Georgia.

Nelda overheard and leaned in. "What does that mean?"

Georgia leaned and whispered. "Nelda, last week the Queen-Regent told me I had to find a husband. But it is beyond complicated."

The Earlsmen were still laughing and clinking glasses. Nelda leaned into Georgia and whispered. "I do not understand. Are these men all your suitors?"

"Luke, the Earl's son, is the suitor," Georgia answered. "The Earl also anointed the excess sons of every significant family in his demesne. All of them have a peer title now. Something they could not have expected before. This is part of the Queen's plan. If Sir Lucas fails to impress me, the Earl is hoping I will find at least one of them suitable. It is political. He will want to link me to one of his banner families."

"Oh, my word," Nelda whispered. "I thought my family was complicated."

"Most of these men have no idea they are auditioning," Bea whispered. "Look at them. If they did, they would be quiet as mice." The Earlsmen were laughing and drinking. None of them were rude, but they were enjoying themselves. Bea looked at Luke. He was not drinking; he was watching Georgia.

Nelda nodded. "I see now."

"It looks like half the county showed up," Nora said as Mr. Darkleaf refilled her cup.

"These people love their ice," Georgia murmured.

"The ice caves are beloved here, yes," Luke said. "This whole region is famous for it. My father says they are the key to the local tourism economy."

"There is no staple crop in the area?" Bea asked.

"Dead Mourner's County has a different terrain from the rest of eastern Findor. It is rocky and forested with strange springs and small lakes," Luke said. "Many of the eastern provinces grow grapes and olives on dry lands. The temperature tends to be hotter in other places. The soil in this region is a bit different. It gets cold here, and the soil seems to resist growing anything but weeds. My father says nothing of substance comes from here other than old oak trees and even older hills. When I look at this place, I feel like there is more to it, but what do I know?"

"Oak trees," Nelda said, looking at Nora. "It is all oaks here. You remember what Mr. Brown said."

"They hold a grudge," Nora whispered. "Troubled waters run cold."

Constable Jenkins walked up. "Duchess, I wonder if I might talk to you?"

"Of course, Constable." Georgia hopped up, leaving her group to chat. "How can I assist?"

"Oh, I wanted to tell you, I gathered a posse of Constables early this morning. We raided the smuggling cave you and Miss Bea found," Jenkins said with a smile. "We arrested eight pirates, reclaimed more than a hundred barrels of olive oil, and ten crates of musket pistols. I think there was more in the cave, but some of it was taken before we arrived."

"Oh, well done, Constable," Georgia said.

"We also found the ice cave you mentioned. It had at least twenty jars of contaminated water."

Georgia jumped. "Oh dear. How do you mean contaminated?"

"The water was treated with *Akaphis*… a type of alchemical poison native in other countries," Constable Jenkins explained. "I would not have known, but the Earl sent a chemist to join our raid. He detected it on the bottles. He also told me *Akaphis* has a distinct metallic odor, but not when it is in the ice."

When Nelda was suffering, she had a metallic odor. Mr. Brown even told Georgia it was from poison. Surely, this could not be a coincidence. "Poisoned ice. How terrible. Many of those jars had a seagull symbol on them. I wish I had looked more closely when we were there, but we were distracted by the smugglers," Georgia remembered.

"All of the jars had that symbol on them," Constable Jenkins said.

"Can you trace them back to the owner?"

"We think it is part of a crime syndicate reaching up and down the coast and along the Findalon River," the Constable answered. "I finished the first round of paperwork before coming here, but we are still trying to learn who these people are. I do know this: they are not from the Three Realms. This is a foreign operation. We arrested the pirates in the cave. Most of them hail from Jendina and Phaedros. They delivered the jars, but that was not part of their normal routine. It was a special job, apparently."

"The usual overseas suspects," Georgia muttered. "Thank you, Constable. What happens now?"

"We increase vigilance." He shrugged. "Without your intervention, we would not have known about the cave.

You have our gratitude, Duchess. Thanks to your work, the olive oil market is saved."

"Something I never thought anyone would say to me."

Constable Jenkins tipped his cap. "I will keep you posted on our progress, my lady."

Georgia returned to her table in time for drunken pears in ice cream. The ice cream was delightful. The idea of frozen poison was not.

Mr. Brown stepped onto a platform near the hot air balloon and waved. Kenneth the oriole landed on the end of his staff and chirped. "Pardon me for interrupting the party," he called out. "I wanted to tell you something before I go. Well, also, it's about to rain, so I should not delay lest I miss the window of departure. My time in this sweet little village, all six years, has been a pleasure. Thank you for your kindness and friendship. Even though some of you still believe I am a sorcerer, you were never rude about it. I thank you for that, as it is important to maintain a polite disposition. Well, that is about all. Enjoy your lunch before the rain. I should go, as the wind is really picking up to the west."

People called out and waved as Mr. Brown climbed into the basket of his hot air balloon. He waved back and smiled. Just before he untied the rope he signaled to Georgia. She approached.

"Oh, Mr. Brown," she said, "be careful up there."

"I certainly will be, Duchess." The old man leaned in. "Just remember, having a magic sword is a very reassuring thing, but it is merely a tool in your hand. Your hand is the important thing. And, I suppose, your arm along with it. And, of course, your eyes. You get what I mean, I hope."

"I think I do," Georgia answered with a smile.

"Excellent," the old man said with a smile. "Oh, one other thing: there is definitely something strange and sinister in this village."

"Perhaps you should have led with that."

"Perhaps, yes. I cannot shake the feeling that what happened to Nelda will happen again, Duchess. Something supernatural tried to take her... it was transforming her. Be on your guard."

Georgia tilted her head. "I will be on my guard, Mr. Brown. Fly safely."

"I will do my best. I shall be off then. Do not worry, Kenneth will still be here. These woods are his home, after all." Mr. Brown unfastened the rope holding the hot air balloon down and tossed it to the side. Everyone watched in wonder as the massive red balloon sailed smoothly into the clouds. Once it was a certain height, the hot air balloon shifted and rode the breeze westward. They watched it sail over the house, and then over the woods gathering speed. Within moments, it was too far away to be seen through the rolling clouds. Just like that, Mr. Brown was gone.

# CHAPTER 11

# GODMOTHER? DID YOU SAY GODMOTHER?

As predicted, lunch in the field was cut short after Mr. Brown left. Within minutes, the rain began to fall in sheets. Everyone fled to their carriages and prams. "Just as well," Nelda announced. "You all need to get back and get dressed in time for the Godmother Naming Ceremony. I believe I will return to my bed for a long nap."

"That was fun," Bea said, following Georgia into the carriage. Nora and Nelda followed.

"If you are feeling well enough, we should move ourselves back to the resort," Nora said to Nelda.

"Nonsense," Georgia answered. "Nelda is only just starting to recover. Look at her. She needs to go back to bed immediately, Nora. I insist you stay with us for the duration."

"We cannot impose," Nelda said. "That said, thank you so much, Georgia."

"It is not an imposition," Bea said, joining in. "We have only a few more days. Why not make it a group affair, and we are well-protected by the Earlsmen."

Nora blinked. "Very well. Thank you both. I am quite beside myself."

They returned to Croft House with Luke and his men following on horseback. The party was at the hotel, but not for a few hours. Plenty of time for a nap, bath, and a change of clothes. Georgia received a few correspondences. One was from Mr. Stackhouse congratulating her on unprecedented profits in her tin mines. Good to know. Another letter came from Lady Amaris with an update. As promised, Amaris wrote to the six great houses in the Three Realms and was already receiving reassurances they would each seek potential suitors for Georgia. Amaris wrote a hopeful message, saying Georgia could expect to start meeting potential matches soon. She took a moment to write back to Lady Amaris about Sir Lucas Greenheart, and how he arrived that very morning with half a dozen newly minted peers in tow. She promised to keep the lady-in-waiting posted.

Georgia was just finishing when Bea popped in with the Redstone Journal. "I think I found something in the journal," Bea whispered.

"Let us have a look," Georgia said.

Bea showed her a page. It featured an illustration of an ornate ring.. Redstone wrote notes all around it, speculating it might be a powerful heirloom of an ancient family of sorcerers. "He says in the notes the stone in the ring is called *The Cabor Sarn,* which translates roughly to 'Stone of the Frog'."

"Frog?" Georgia asked.

"We cannot avoid them, apparently."

"Neat," Georgia said. "How does this relate to us?"

"It is the missing ring from Lord Redstone's house," Bea explained. "He was certain it was a talisman of incredible power… and value. However, he was unable to sell it to any museum. They all rejected it, saying it was just some old cheap jewelry, and that he was too blinded by his mission to see it for what it was. I think he was onto something, though. This may sound crazy…"

"Say it anyway," Georgia urged. "You should know by now that what sounds crazy one day can sound logical the next."

"I think this is Harriet's heirloom ring. The one her husband gave her, just a few weeks ago," Bea said. "Look at it."

Georgia nodded. "I see where you are going. Okay. Harriet will be at the party later. I will ask her about it."

\*\*\*

The Godmother Naming Ceremony.

This was the event of the week. Standing in her dressing suite, Georgia realized she sent Millie away the very morning when she needed her most. She gazed at the garment combinations laid out and felt overwhelmed. Then she noticed the note sitting atop a pale green ensemble. More green. Well, it was the color of the new season. The note was from Millie, and read, 'Follow the usual process: smooth the unders, pull the overs, flip the hair, then put on the baubles. This is the gown.'

She was just about to start dressing herself when there came a soft knock at the door. "Enter," Georgia said.

Two of the downstairs maids entered and curtseyed. "Good day, my lady," the first maid whispered. "Before she left the village, Miss Pepper asked us to assist you."

"Miss Pepper? Oh, you mean Millie of course." Georgia was relieved. "What are your names?"

"I am Angela and this is Kat."

"Are you lady's maids?"

Angela shook her head. "No, my lady, but Miss Pepper said we have the right… um… fingers for the job." She held her hands up for inspection. Her nails were clean and her fingers were delicate. "Last night, Miss Pepper checked all of our hands and decided we should be the ones to help you."

"Very thorough of her," Georgia said with a smile. "You have no formal training, though."

"No, my lady, but Miss Pepper said you might direct us. Both of us know how to sew, of course."

"That makes sense. Millie already laid out the ensembles. Very well, Angela, we will give it a try." The alternative was dressing herself. Georgia was a grown woman and when necessary, she could do that. Even so, the gown for that day was a complicated one. She would need help with some of the buttons and last-minute revisions to the fabric. Who knows when one might have to sew something down or cut something else off.

One hour later, Georgia walked into Bea's suite with her two temporary maids in tow. Bea was still in her robe, enjoying a cup of tea. Mrs. Macklin hovered in the background. Georgia twirled. "What do you think?"

"Well done," Bea said, checking over her waist. She looked at the two maids. "Nice work, girls. Thank you." Angela and Kat curtseyed and went away beaming.

"I need a little assistance with my wig," Georgia admitted.

"Mrs. Macklin, can you manage it?" Bea asked.

Mrs. Macklin hurried over. "I believe so, my lady. Miss Millie showed it to me a few times."

"Excellent." Georgia sat down. She felt regal in the light jade green gown, which was snug with a high waist and intricate piping down the arms. Instead of off the shoulder, the gown buttoned up the front to the throat, a choice Georgia was making more and more. Not only was it modest, but she could move faster. Buttons on the back of the dress might look fashionable, but one never knew what was exposed back there. Her skirts flared charmingly, and featured a rose cut to make them appear like the pedals of a flower. She opted for high quality shoes sans lift. No one could see her feet through the skirting, so she didn't see any reason to be taller. Besides, she was already the tallest woman in the room.

Her hair was up in Millie's wig and strung with green pearls. The effect was impressive.

Mrs. Macklin looked her over. "I must admit, my lady, when Millie first showed me the wig, I was dubious. I did not understand why you would need it when your own natural hair is so beautiful."

"I am still dubious Mrs. Macklin," Georgia admitted. "And yet here we are. Wigs are quite the fashion these days. Still, I may abandon this look. Thank you for your assistance." With that, Georgia returned to her suite and sat at the makeup table to fix her base and lips herself.

A few moments later, Bea was ready: elegant in a snug black lace tulle gown. She normally wore her garments clasped to the throat, but this time opted for a gentle V-Neck. The lace was stitched in elegant patterns of petals and stars. Instead of pinning her tight golden curls up, Mrs. Macklin convinced Bea to go another route. The final product was beautiful with Bea's hair coiled loosely backward. Mrs. Macklin secured a dazzling pearl beaded headband on top. It was designed to look like a juniper branch with pearls as berries.

"Mrs. Macklin, this is wonderful work," Bea breathed, reviewing herself in the tall mirror. Her golden hair caught the reflection of the headdress.

"Thank you, Miss. Ever since you started growing your hair out, I have been itching to try this coil."

"I have never seen that woman so excited," Georgia gestured in the secret language.

"I must say, we should do it again," Bea said. "You have convinced me, Mrs. Macklin."

Nelda and Nora joined them downstairs. The sisters were once again at their most sophisticated in nearly identical hunter green long-sleeved satin gowns. The design was simpler than the fashion, with a single row of buttons up in the center. Each dress featured a white lapel. Nora wore hers on the left, and Nelda's was on the right. It was all very modern, and odd... but so were the Brady sisters. The sisters highlighted the look with modest black caps and short white gloves. The effect was almost martial, but somehow, they pulled it off. "Very sharp, ladies," Bea said as they loaded into the carriage. "A minimal look with impact. I love it."

"Thank you, Bea," Nelda whispered, still weak from sickness. "I'm just happy to be up and walking, but I will take the compliment."

"Once we are done with this party, you are going straight to bed," Nora chided. She looked at Georgia and Bea. "Please agree with me, ladies? Today has already been exciting enough for Nelda."

"Nora is correct," Bea said to Nelda. "After this party, get home and rest."

"Oh, very well," Nelda said. "I know I said earlier I planned to rest, but I simply could not miss the party. It is a shame to get sick like this."

Twenty-five minutes later, Georgia walked into the lobby at the Dead Mourner's Resort with Bea, Nora, and Nelda in tow. Behind them, Clyde the footman carried their gifts and a few other things, including Lord Redstone's journal. Since it was a baby shower event, Luke and his men stayed behind. Just as well. She needed a break from the male gaze. These affairs were normally reserved for ladies, although today was a bit different. Harriet's husband was attending, but he kept to the outskirts of the room, in the company of his valets. There were a few odd footmen and valets in the room, all lurking at the edges. Georgia assumed they all worked for various guests of the party, since they were not in matching uniforms. The group of ladies gathered in the main solar room of the hotel, which was light and airy with a lovely skylight dome. Harriet had a quartet of violins playing, and the women mingled.

Once again, borage over ice was served. Georgia declined. She noticed her friend, Lady Rebecca Drake, was not present. One of the other ladies mentioned Lady Rebecca took a chill after the hot air balloon took off. What a shame. She was missing the best part of the baby shower week.

"You should visit her after the party," Bea suggested. "Perhaps bring her a cup of borage."

"Ew," Georgia laughed. "Still, not a bad idea. There is only one day left. I would like to see her again."

Harriet took center stage. She was the perfect hostess, calling for various ladies to re-enact their talent show offerings and doling out gifts. As per custom, she sat back with her husband while various ladies offered speeches of support and good luck. Early dinner was served. Not surprisingly, it was pheasant. The hotel dazzled with the most delicate and savory dish Georgia could remember. The sauces were perfect. Each dish was matched with a stunning red malbec blend. Georgia found herself enjoying the whole afternoon, but there was work to do. She made her way to Harriet, as she still had a mystery to solve, and questions to ask. None of it related to this baby shower, she hoped.

Harriet was resplendent in her own heather green gown and wearing her glittering heirloom ring. Once again, Georgia found herself staring at the stone. It was dazzling, odd, and compelling. She pulled her eyes away to look at Harriet. The woman looked so happy. Georgia noted Mr. Blackheart at the other end of the chamber signing some sort of document. He was up to business.

"Oh, Georgia, thank you for coming," Harriet said. "We are about to announce the godmother, and then I fear the fun will wind down. Such is the way of these things."

"The whole week was a success," Georgia answered. "Did you enjoy it?"

"It was fun. I will admit, I look forward to things getting back to normal. Also, I believe I am about to go into labor. I can feel it," Harriet admitted, "and I am nervous."

"What do you mean 'about to go'?" Georgia asked.

"Georgia, I think it will happen within a few days," Harriet whispered. "I could be wrong. I have never had a child before. But I feel it. Every fiber is calling me to lie down and let this sweet baby come into the world."

"Do we need to take you somewhere?" Georgia asked.

Harriet shook her head. "Tonight, I will rest, and then it begins. I have no idea how I would know this, but there it is."

"I believe you," Georgia whispered. "I must ask you a few questions, Harriet. When not attending your events, I have been working on an investigation."

"The incident at Redstone House. Yes, everyone is whispering about it." Harriet smiled. "I would love to be part of the adventure. How may I assist?"

Georgia signaled Clyde, and he opened the Redstone Journal to the page with the ring illustration for Harriet to see. "Does this look familiar?" Georgia asked.

Harriet smiled. "Yes, that is this ring right here."

"You know this?"

"Richard bought it, not long ago, from Lord Redstone," Harriet said, holding up her hand to show it off. "Redstone told us he thought it was a mythical item. But later learned it was worthless. I always liked it, though. We spotted it on Redstone's desk about a year ago, I suppose. I simply could not take my eyes off it, so he acquired it for me. It is lovely, don't you think?"

"I do," Georgia agreed. "When was the last time you spoke to Lord Redstone?"

"Oh, when he came to dinner," Harriet scratched her head. "Two weeks ago, I think."

"Wait. Lord Redstone was in the village within the last month?" Georgia blinked. "His sister said he has been gone for months."

Harriet shook her head. "No, we dined with him. Wait a moment." She waved to her husband, who detached himself from the valets.

"Richard, this is Duchess Goldenheart," Harriet said.

Mr. Blackheart bowed immediately. "Your Grace, it is a pleasure to meet you."

"The pleasure is mine, Mr. Blackheart," Georgia answered. She opted not to get into the whole 'Your Grace', 'Duchess', 'My lady' lecture. There were more pressing matters.

"Georgia is investigating the break-in at Lord Redstone's house. You remember reading about her in the paper. She solves murders with her friend the wizard," Harriet said. "You heard about that, dear."

Mr. Blackheart went pale. "I did, yes." He looked at Georgia. His pupils were dilating. Clearly, the man was not good at playing cards. He blinked rapidly but recovered quickly. "How is the investigation going?" He darted a glance at one of his valets, who began to hover nearby.

Interesting. He was up to no good, but she could not be sure what it was… yet. "I am without my wizard guide at the moment," Georgia said, her mind moving quickly. "Without him, I fear I am limited." It was a calculated lie, of course. The part about the missing wizard was true, but the rest was rubbish.

Mr. Blackheart looked relieved. "Oh, yes, of course."

"My love, when did we have dinner with Lord Redstone?" Harriet asked. "You remember when he gave you my ring."

Mr. Blackheart went pale again, and his hands shook for a moment. Georgia watched it happen, all the while appearing not to look interested. He pulled himself together and nodded, as if this were everyday conversation. "It would have been several weeks ago, my darling."

"About two weeks ago. Remember, Mr. Ridley found those lovely rutabagas at the market, and we served them that night. I remember saying to you the baby shower is less than a month away, and too bad we could not find more of the rutabagas. Redstone came to the house for dinner, and you went back with him to get the ring. After that you polished it yourself. I remember, because Ridley wanted to polish it and acted rather foolishly. He began to shout, and you sacked him." She looked at Georgia. "Sometimes, it is difficult to find good help. You probably have the same problem."

"Yes. Yes, of course," Mr. Blackheart agreed. "The rutabagas." *That answers that question.* Mr. Blackheart looked like he might lose his balance at any moment. His forehead glistened with sweat. Lord Redstone had certainly been in town, and Mr. Blackheart had followed him home. Circumstantial evidence, but it was a lead.

"Oh, too bad about the rutabagas. They would have been wonderful today. A little salad with vinegar. Oh, I do love a good rutabaga."

Mr. Blackheart trembled. "Yes, you silly thing. Yes. We will find more rutabagas," he said, raising his voice ever so slightly. It sounded like he was growing irritated, but it was panic.

"Forgive me," Harriet said, seeing his expression. "This baby has me craving the oddest foods. I am sorry, darling." She gazed at her husband in a combination of adoration and something else. Was it fear?

Mr. Blackheart smiled at his wife with his mouth, but his eyes were cold. "There is nothing to forgive… dear."

Georgia opted to go the silly girl route to try and diffuse the situation. She would follow up on this later. "Uh…where did you get that lovely borage? I find it quite refreshing." She intentionally raised her voice an octave. In her experience, men took women with high voices less seriously.

"Oh," Harriet said, blinking. "I, uh, we had it imported from the capital."

Mr. Blackheart regained his composure. "I will ask my man where he obtained it."

"Lovely," Georgia sing-songed. She had a bad feeling about this. Also, Harriet was no fool, despite her current fixation on rutabagas. Georgia could see she didn't believe the silly girl act but was unsure how to respond. Still, there was no going back. Georgia leaned in. "You have so much to think about right now, I wish you all the best. In fact, perhaps now is a good time to announce the godmother?"

Harriet blinked, about to say something, but her husband was elated to change the topic. "Oh, Lady Georgia is right," he said with enthusiasm. "Let's announce the godmother."

"Very well," Harriet said. Georgia watched as Harriet glanced at her husband. Her features went from worried to serene as her Cymbre training kicked in. "Help me up to the podium, husband?"

The Blackhearts climbed the podium in the center of the room, and Harriet held up her hands. "Hello, everyone," she said. "The moment has arrived. It is time to announce the godmother. First, I would like to thank you all for coming. This week has been wonderful. What a privilege to see so many old friends. I will cherish the memory of this week." She looked at Mr. Blackheart. He was looking at Georgia. Georgia smiled and waved, continuing the silly girl act. Mr. Blackheart smiled, then looked back at his wife. Harriet watched the whole thing, glanced at Georgia, then turned back to talk to the room.

"Ladies, I am so pleased to announce the godmother to this child: Miss Beatrice Irvingdale."

The room erupted. Cymbre girls stood and clapped, nodding their heads in approval. Bea was well-liked in school, and her prospects were to be admired. She walked up to the podium and hugged Harriet. The Blackhearts stepped back to let her speak, as was the custom.

"Thank you," Bea said. She wiped a tear from her eye and looked at Harriet. "I want you to know I am incredibly honored and humbled to accept the role of godmother. I feel a deep responsibility to be a source of guidance and support. Whether it is offering words of wisdom, lending a listening ear, or being a reassuring presence in the child's life, I believe being a godmother means being a true friend and confidant. I am grateful for the Blackheart family's faith in me, and I hope to live up to their expectations. Finally, I want to say being a godmother is not just about the formalities of the role. It is about the love, care, and devotion we give to our godchildren, day in and day out. It is about being there for them, no matter what. And it's about celebrating all their achievements, big and small. Thank you once again for this honor. I accept it with what I hope is the utmost humility." Bea hugged Harriet, and Mr. Blackheart bowed to her.

Afterward, Bea settled in and let the other ladies approach with their congratulations. Georgia watched with some pride. "She is really in her element," Harriet said, standing nearby. "I think I made the right choice. I mean, Bea is a bit of a social butterfly, but she comes from a solid background. Do you agree, Georgia? You think I made the right choice?"

"For godmother? Oh, most certainly you did," Georgia whispered. She looked at Harriet. "Forgive me, I have another question."

Harriet smiled. "Of course. Although, I do not think I will be much help with the investigation."

"This is unrelated," Georgia answered. "You see Nelda over there." Across the room, Nelda was standing at the edge of a group of young women. Behind her, Nora was fretting. After a moment, she guided her sister to a chair.

"I heard she was taken ill but recovered," Harriet said, gazing at Nelda with a smile.

"She is still recovering but keeping a brave face. Harriet, you were roommates with her in school, were you not?"

Harriet nodded. "Yes. We shared a dormitory cabin for six years. Oh, I must tell you, Nelda was a bit of a nightmare in the early days, but we came to peace and even became friends."

"I am glad to hear that," Georgia said. "You know, when Nelda was ill, she mentioned something. She called out your name a few times. There were several hours where she was delusional, I think."

Harriet clutched breast. "Oh, that's horrible. Was she in terrible pain?"

"I think she was," Georgia admitted. Harriet winced. It was not a wince of guilt, though. She was a person who felt the pain of others. Georgia knew Harriet had endured pain of her own over the years, and she did not wish it on others. Watching the woman, she could see it on her face. Harriet wiped a tear away, looking embarrassed.

"Forgive me," Harriet said. "I think this baby makes me emotional."

"Possibly, yes," Georgia responded quietly. "That is not my question, though. When she was in her fit, Nelda called your name and tried to warn you about something."

"Warn me?" Harriet looked at Georgia. "What would she warn me about?"

"She said the Shadow Man was coming," Georgia answered.

If it were possible for Harriet to go any paler than normal, she did. She took a step back. "The Shadow Man? Georgia, is that the name she used?"

"Yes," Georgia said, not taking her eyes off her. Harriet was terrified. For a moment, Georgia wondered if the woman would not start running for the door right then and there. "You know what she was talking about, Harriet. I see it in your eyes."

Harriet nodded. "I do know, yes. Oh Georgia, this is… ridiculous. But even hearing it said now is frightening."

Georgia guided Harriet to a chair, just away from the crowd. "Tell me about this Shadow Man."

"He was… something terrible," Harriet admitted. "You remember the winter of the plague when we were all trapped in our cabins."

Georgia nodded. "Yes. That was a hard year for all of us."

Harriet leaned in. "That whole winter, he was outside our window every night. Nelda saw him, and I had to explain to her what he was."

"What was he?" Georgia asked.

"A demon," Harriet whispered. "A curse on my family."

"Really?"

Harriet doubled down. "Georgia, I read the stories about you in the paper. If anyone will believe me, I think it is you. The Shadow Man haunts my family, although I admit I only saw him that one winter. Still, it was enough."

"Will you tell me this story?"

Harriet gulped, her eyes darting around the room. "For me, it all began when my older sister died."

"You had a sister." Georgia blinked.

"Now, I am what you might call an only child, but at one time I did have a wonderful, beautiful, brilliant older sister. Her name was Henrietta. She was radiant, and all the things I was not," Harriet whispered. "She had the flame red hair and pale white skin of my father, just like me. But in her case, those features worked a different way. All who saw her were enchanted. Father liked to say it was our legacy. He used to say it came from Gildernesse."

"Gildernesse," Georgia repeated. She knew the name from Lord Redstone's journal. "You mean the ancient island kingdom from mythology."

"You have heard of it," Harriet said with a sudden smile. "I think they call it Naurland now, but our family has its own legends. My father insisted it was called Gildernesse until the newer languages came along. I know this will sound silly, but he said we came from ancient royalty. When I was a very little girl, he would tell me and my sister we were princesses, descended from heathen kings of old. I know what it sounds like, but I thought the stories were wonderful. I felt special, and not quite so ugly."

"You are not ugly. You never have been," Georgia said in a tone louder than intended. A few nearby ladies glanced their way in surprise.

"Thank you," Harriet said, blinking rapidly.

"Are you parents here today?" Georgia asked, looking around.

"Father is too sick to travel. They live in Palas now where the climate is better for his condition," Harriet said, shaking her head. "After I deliver, we plan to visit them."

"Harriet, tell me the full story. Why would Nelda try to warn you?"

"I do not know, but she saw him too," Harriet answered. She looked embarrassed, then shook her head. "I will tell you the story my father used to tell. He said the Shadow Man was haunting us, and it was a harbinger from the old times. A spirit or a curse. I never quite knew what he meant. But he said it was a demon who took my sister with him to the grave as payment for the sins of our ancestors."

"Oh, my goodness," Georgia said, rubbing her head.

"There was nothing good about it," Harriet admitted. "When she died, we were stricken with a series of horrible events. My governess leapt from a window to her death, for no apparent reason. The flowers in my late mother's garden all turned black. They did not die, they simply changed color."

Georgia shuddered.

"My father developed a cough and used to spit up blood and bile at the dinner table," Harriet whispered. "There were other disasters, but at the same time, our fortunes as a trade family grew. We prospered in business. Father grew rich beyond measure, even as he suffered. He would tell me the two were related. We would prosper, but our misery would outweigh it."

"It sounds like one of those old fairy tales where people would make deals with dark powers," Georgia said. "Rich in the pocket, poor in the soul."

"It is not something I bring up at dinner parties," Harriet said in a low voice. "So, the Shadow Man... Nelda and I saw him that winter. He stood outside our window every night, and we were terrified. I knew if either of us went out there, the creature would kill us. Poor Nelda was innocent, but because she lived in my cabin, she would also be his victim. We stayed in, drew the curtains, and stayed alive. When winter ended, Nelda moved out and I lived alone. We never spoke of it again. Father told me one day, after the curse ran its course long enough here in the material world, each of us would be taken by the creature to suffer eternal torment in the Void. Such were the crimes of an ancestor I never met."

"Who was this ancestor?" Georgia asked.

"I do not  know even that," Harriet admitted. "All I do know, Georgia, is this: we each have a limited time in this world. The question is what do we do with that time?"

\*\*\*

Luke and his men were in the yard training when Georgia and her entourage returned. It was raining, but they were running from one end of the field to the other, picking up logs, and throwing them.

"What in the heavens are they doing?" Nora asked as they stepped out of the carriage.

"Maintaining endurance and strength," Georgia answered. Of course, the Earlsmen were dressed down for exercise, wearing only trousers, white shirts, and training boots. They were also soaking wet. The sight was oddly annoying. Luke spotted her and bowed, grinning like a fool. She waved. He turned back to his exercise.

"They do look strong," Nelda said, her eyes like saucers.

Once the men realized they had an audience, they picked up the pace a bit. One of them slipped in the mud, much to the amusement of the others.

"Time to go," Bea said. "Modesty, ladies. Modesty."

Georgia pivoted with the others and fled inside the house. She found Mr. Darkleaf going over the house accounting books in his office in the basement.

"Hello. Do not get up," she said, after knocking. "My lady's maid should be returning soon. Will you let me know when she does?"

"Of course, Duchess," Mr. Darkleaf said, looking uncomfortable sitting. "I should tell you, the roads to the capital and to Grandhall are both washed out."

"Oh?"

"We just got word," he said. "Cook had an order of fennel from Palas on the way. Apparently, the bridge at the River Findalon was damaged in a storm last night. It is likely Miss Pepper is stuck in the capital right now. They say all road traffic going into Findor will stop until repairs are completed. We also heard the forest road has several fallen trees. It looks impassable for now."

"Oh, dear," Georgia whispered. Hopefully, Millie and Mr. Reardon were not stuck on a wet road somewhere. She was not sure if it would occur to Millie to take the barge across the river. But even if she did, she and Mr. Reardon would still have to contend with the forest road. Hopefully, they were waiting.

"I'm sorry, Duchess."

"You do not control the weather, Mr. Darkleaf, so you have nothing to be sorry about," Georgia answered. "Thank you. If you do get word on Millie's whereabouts, please keep me informed."

"Of course, Duchess."

Okay. Magic Sword delivery delayed. She remembered what Mr. Brown said: she was strong and the sword was a tool. Good. Comforting.

Georgia made her way back to Bea upstairs. "Millie may be stuck in the capital. The rains took out the roads," she said. "I am going to pop over and see Lady Rebecca Drake while we still have light." It would be dark soon, so she would have to be quick if she were going to be back in time for supper.

"Very well," Bea said. "You were more quiet than usual in the carriage."

"I was mulling over the conversation with the Blackhearts." Georgia sat down and poured them a quick cup of tea. She told Bea about the conversation with Harriet, the former paper weight, the Shadow Man, and how Mr. Blackheart reacted when Lord Redstone came up.

"You covered a lot of ground while I was giving speeches. Do you think Mr. Blackheart did something to Lord Redstone?" Bea asked, setting her cup down.

"Possibly. For all I know, he was nervous about some unrelated business matter. There was a lot of talk of rutabagas, but yes, I think he or one of his henchmen is the cause of the bloodstain at Redstone House."

"We need to keep digging," Bea whispered. She glanced out the window. "It will be dark before we know it. You should go now or go see Rebecca tomorrow."

"I will go now," Georgia said, standing up. "I am concerned. Rebecca is not one to miss a party without reason."

Bea picked up the Redstone journal. "I am almost done reading this. We know the story of the ring, but it may still provide a clue."

"Agreed," Georgia said. "I have two errands to run. I will be back in a bit." She went down to the kitchen and found a fresh-baked loaf of rosemary bread. When visiting a sick friend, one should always bring something comforting. The bread was right out of the oven when she commandeered it. She apologized to the cook, of course. Georgia was not sure if it was going to the staff but took it anyway. The cook appeared to be delighted by her sudden bread heist. Something in the woman's demeanor reminded Georgia of her butler, Mr. Derry, who was always at his best when pushed to perform under pressure. Georgia watched as the cook wrapped the bread. The woman then included a small jar of salted butter.

\*\*\*

Georgia hopped out of the carriage at Redstone House while en route to see Rebecca, just as the rain started to fall again. She hurried up to the porch, where Mrs. Crauford's footman was already opening the door. "Welcome, my lady," he said, ushering her into a small den before her hair got wet. Then he settled her in with a cup of tea. "Do you mind waiting here for a moment? I fear we are short-staffed today. I will alert the mistress."

"Of course," Georgia said. "Convey my apologies for the abrupt visit. Thank you."

The footman bowed and hurried away. He returned a moment later and led her to the sitting room. Mrs. Crauford was just arriving as well. The woman looked flustered.

"Forgive the interruption," Georgia said. "I was in the area and had a few quick questions, if you do not mind."

"Oh, yes, certainly," Mrs. Crauford said. "I thought perhaps you were returning my brother's journal."

"We are almost done reading it," Georgia answered. "There were several interesting clues. Thank you again for loaning it to us."

"I am glad to assist," Mrs. Crauford answered. She gestured to the opposite couch. "Won't you sit?"

"Thank you, this will only take a few minutes." Georgia took a seat and waited for the footman to finish setting up the tea. Once he was gone, she looked up. "Forgive me, I will get right to it."

"Of course."

"You said your brother was on an island off the coast of Jendina, correct?"

"Oh, yes." Mrs. Crauford forced a smile. She was nervous. There could be any number of reasons for that, of course. Just having Georgia pop in this way might be ruining the poor woman's nerves. "Forgive me, I should tell you there was a reporter... er, a journalist... in the village. He came to see me this morning."

Georgia blinked. "Sorry about that. I fear my social calendar is a popular topic with the press."

Mrs. Crauford smiled. "Yes, he was an odd one. Forgive me, this may sound strange. He told me you were here to find a husband at the behest of the Queen herself, and asked if Lord Redstone was a suitor. He was rather blunt about it. I nearly fell off my chair."

"Oh dear," Georgia answered. "What did you tell him?" No wonder her nerves were raw.

"I told him to leave immediately. Now, of course, if such an arrangement were in the works, I would be delighted for all parties. But my brother is at least thirty years older than you, and while he is respected, the idea sounds far-fetched. Even if it is something being considered, I was not about to engage in a discussion with some news person."

Georgia nodded. "Gossip," she answered. "It sells newspapers. You are correct. There is no communication between Lord Redstone and me. You were right to throw him out. Did you happen to get a name from the fellow?"

"Mr. Tom Turner," she said. "I remember because it sounded like a made-up name."

"Oh." Georgia blinked. "Well, interesting. Mr. Turner is a friend."

"You are friends with a reporter?"

"I have friends everywhere, Mrs. Crauford," Georgia said with a smile. "You may be surprised to learn this, but my position puts me in contact with an odd array of people."

Mrs. Crauford tilted her head in thought, then sipped her tea. "That does make sense," she admitted in a quiet voice. "Last time you were here, you crawled around a couch. When it happened, I nearly fainted."

"You had a duchess under the furniture," Georgia answered in a droll tone.

Mrs. Crauford laughed and fanned herself. "Forgive me. I worry about my demeanor with you, Duchess. I never imagined someone from your station could be so… well, shall I say down to earth? Is that vulgar?"

Georgia shook her head. "If that is vulgar, then someone needs to redefine protocol. Now, I must ask you a few hard questions."

"Oh, yes, of course." Mrs. Crauford straightened up.

"Your brother wrote to you approximately two weeks ago. He told you he was going to be in Jendina for several months." Georgia looked the woman in the eye. "According to Mr. Blackheart, your brother was here in the village about two weeks ago. Blackheart says he purchased the ring from Lord Redstone at that time."

"Extraordinary." Mrs. Crauford scratched her head. "I cannot imagine it."

"Why not?"

Mrs. Crauford shrugged and scratched her head. "He would have left a note. There was a pool of blood, and those other things. He would have seen them and left a note. He would have said something." The woman held her breath a moment, then began to shake. "Unless your original concern was true. I could not make myself believe the idea of it…unless he…"

"Unless he could not leave a note," Georgia finished.

Mrs. Crauford was pale. "What do you mean?"

Georgia shrugged. "He could have been in a hurry, or perhaps it was a mere oversight."

"He would not come all the way back here to sell the ring without telling me," Mrs. Crauford announced. She touched her face and swayed in her seat. "My brother was fascinated by that piece of jewelry. The idea that he would even consider selling it to a... merchant like Mr. Blackheart is surprising. I can imagine him selling it to a university or museum, of course. That was his original plan. He would have to have been quite desperate."

"I see," Georgia said. "Just a few more quick questions if I may? We may need to have Marguerite here too, as she may be the only one to know the answers... that is, if there are answers to be known."

"Of course," Mrs. Crauford said, ringing her little bell. Marguerite arrived within minutes.

"The knife that Marguerite found. Could it have been a letter opener? Perhaps one that Lord Redstone owned?"

Mrs. Crauford looked at her maid blankly. Marguerite shook her head. "It was not one of his letter openers, my lady. At least, not one I ever saw before. I think it was a knife for poking. There was no sharp or slim edge, and that's what you want when you open an envelope."

"Right. It was a stiletto of sorts," Georgia said. Marguerite nodded.

Georgia looked at Mrs. Crauford. "One last question: does the name 'Singuile' mean anything to you?"

Mrs. Crauford smiled. "Oh, yes, Mr. Singuile. He's an older fellow who lives in the capital. He's somewhat retired now, but he used to make shoes. My brother met him years ago on some adventure. Why do you ask?"

"The word 'Singuile' was stamped on the inside of the shoe," Georgia answered.

Mrs. Crauford blinked rapidly.

"We need to find your brother," Georgia said.

\*\*\*

The rain was falling full-on when the carriage pulled up to the guard gate. Lady Rebecca Drake was not staying at the hotel, of course. A lady of her station would never submit to a hotel suite this close to the capital. Not if there were better options available. In the northlands or the mountains, she might rent a suite in a lodge or hotel. But not here. Rebecca also had to consider security. Fortunately, Dead Mourner's Grove was full of massive rental houses owned by lesser lords and wealthy trade families. It was a perfect getaway spot if one did not mind the constant rain.

Georgia waited a full ten minutes at the gate while they ran back to get verification. She was about to leave when they let her in. The carriage pulled up and a valet, armed with a musket pistol, escorted her to the door. Georgia made her way into the foyer where the butler met her. "I'm so sorry, my lady. The mistress is in bed," the old man explained. "She took a chill from the rain this morning." As he spoke, shadows danced in the corners of her vision. Not a good sign.

"I have warm bread, salted butter, and even warmer regards for one of my oldest friends," Georgia answered. "I do not mind going to her room directly. You know, Lady Rebecca and I survived the plague together. You have no reason for concern." She walked past him. Georgia was not raised to ignore a butler guarding the door. This time, she did. When she got to the stairs, she caught a faint odor of something familiar: a metallic odor. She hurried upstairs.

"Of course, Duchess," the butler said, following in defeat. The main room was full of luggage. Rebecca was preparing to leave the village. Probably not a bad idea.

The butler, surprisingly quick for such an old man, managed to hurry past Georgia up the stairs, and then led her to a wide suite of rooms. She found Rebecca in bed in a gorgeous solarium bedroom. One entire wall was made of glass and featured the rain and wind dramatically whipping the trees outside. Inside was cozy, though. A roaring fire kept the room warm, and everywhere was the scent of cinnamon and apples. "This is pleasant," Georgia said, entering without a preamble. "What a charming way to build a bedroom."

Rebecca was pale but brightened up. "Oh, what a lovely surprise. I love these Findorian windows. My father's house is grand, but the rooms are so dark."

"That probably helps in the winter," Georgia said. "We did not get to speak at the hot air balloon party, so I thought I might stop by before you left town."

"I am glad you did," Rebecca said. "What is this?"

"Hot fresh rosemary bread with salted butter. Our cook made it," Georgia answered, sitting on the side of the bed. "How are you feeling?"

"I'm afraid I fell into a classic Beatrice Irvingdale rain trap," Rebecca said, sniffling. "One moment we were waving to that odd old man in his balloon, and the next I was soaked. Now I think I am getting a cold. Hopefully, not to fall the way of Marian Quickwood."

"I seem to recall Marian met a rich lord and now spends her days in the lap of luxury."

"I always thought Bea made her up as a way to explain her unnatural fear of rain." Rebecca smiled. "Then, last year, I met Marian at a gala in Palas and she confirmed the story."

"Bea rarely lies about anything. She occasionally reenacts with flare, but that is not the same thing. So, you are leaving?"

"In addition to being my assistant, Miss Sweet is also a nurse. Father thinks of everything when he hires these people. She thinks we should go back to the city right away. I have a privy council meeting with the Queen next week. I will need time to get settled and recover," Rebecca said. "It is a shame. I was having such a nice time here in the country."

"How often are you in the capital?" Georgia asked. "You know, I live there full time now."

Rebecca nodded. "I have been meaning to reach out as I have been there at least half the year. The problem is your lifestyle."

"Oh?"

Rebecca looked away. Georgia knew that look. She was trying to think of a delicate way to approach something. She looked at Georgia again. "I must maintain a certain security. You have reporters and journalists following your every move. If they start including me in their stories, it might cause difficulty for the men who protect me."

Oh. "I see," Georgia whispered. "Yes. Of course. You must take Phaedros into account."

"I am so sorry, Georgia," Rebecca said. "If I had my way, we would be brunching every week. I hope you are not offended."

"Of course not," Georgia said. "Oh, Rebecca, I do not blame you at all. That is very wise. Tell you what, next time we visit, I will make sure to throw off the press before."

After a discreet knock on the door, Miss Sweet entered with a service tray in one hand and a medical bag in the other. "Forgive me for interrupting, my lady. It is time for your afternoon tonic."

"Oh. It's a bit early, isn't it? Never mind. It will only take a moment, Georgia. The tonic helps with my panic spells."

"Of course." Panic spells? Anyone who knew Rebecca in school would be shocked to find her fearful of anything. Then again, most people did not have active assassins following them. One more reason to hold Phaedros accountable.

Rebecca turned back to Miss Sweet. "That's fine, Emmaline. I will take it now. Where are we with the packing situation?"

Miss Sweet set the bag and tray on a side table. On the tray was a glass of apple cider, a spoon, and a linen napkin. She handed the napkin to Rebecca, then gave the cider a quick stir. "Mr. Pearson says we can leave as soon as the rain ends, my lady."

"The roads are washed out," Georgia said, glancing at the great windows along the wall. "You might have to wait another day. Although, looking at the storm outside, it could be longer than that." Outside the wall of windows, the rain was now flowing across the house. Beyond that, the trees were bent over with the force of the wind.

"I see." Rebecca grinned. "Maybe tomorrow."

Miss Sweet handed the glass to Rebecca. Georgia could see the efficiency of the woman's movements. It was very nurse-like. Rebecca was about to drink but turned up her nose. "Oh, it smells bitter again. Can you make this sweeter?"

"Of course, my lady. I have some syrup in my bag." Miss Sweet took the glass back, opened her medical bag, and fished out a small bottle. At that moment, Georgia detected the metallic odor again. It was coming from the bag.

"Oh, let me get out of your way," she said, stepping over next to the side table. As Miss Sweet poured a bit of the syrup onto the spoon, she turned her back ever so slightly. Georgia took that moment to pull the bag open and peek. Inside were several items: soft wool wrapping for injuries, tweezers, a roll of gatgut, tongs, a pair of scissors, and a small bottle of clear liquid. The bottle had a tiny seagull symbol on the cap. She knew that symbol. It was the same as the one on the tainted bottles in the smuggler's cave.

Georgia looked at Miss Sweet. The woman looked at her too. Miss Sweet blinked, then her features hardened. She said nothing, but Georgia had caught her in the act and they both knew it. The woman was up to no good.

With a shrug, a stiletto appeared in Miss Sweet's left hand. She was still watching Georgia when she slashed at Rebecca's throat.

Georgia shoved Miss Sweet away. The dagger grazed Rebecca's sleeve but did not appear to connect to flesh.

"Emmaline... what...?" Rebecca sputtered.

"Rebecca, get over there," Georgia barked, pointing at the other side of the bed. She looked at Miss Sweet. "You poisoned Nelda."

Miss Sweet was past pretense. "Not on purpose." She stepped away from Georgia. "How was I to know your friend would be so impressed with iced borage." So, Rebecca was the target, but Nelda was the only one drinking the borage that morning at the coffee shop. She drank three glasses... all of them delivered by Miss Sweet to her mistress. Georgia remembered Rebecca handing her glass to Nelda.

"Emmaline, what are you doing?" Rebecca asked, scrambling off the bed on the other side.

"Now we must do this the hard way," Emmaline whispered.

"You are from the Sicarium," Georgia said through gritted teeth. She tossed the loaf of bread to one side and moved parallel to the woman. "An assassin."

Miss Sweet sneered. "Phaedros forever."

Rebecca gasped.

Georgia and Miss Sweet circled one another. "You could have done this at any time. Why act now?"

"We did not know if you would take her with you," Miss Sweet answered. "You should leave. I will spare your life if you go." She crept toward Georgia with the stiletto out.

"You appear to have misjudged the situation," Georgia answered in a low tone.

Miss Sweet jumped at her and slashed with her stiletto. Georgia let her step in, bending backward to avoid the blade, then grabbed the woman's arm with one hand and her throat with the other. She lifted the woman, holding the weapon away, then brought her down in a body-wide blow to the floor. Miss Sweet gasped. The stiletto skittered out of reach.

"Fun fact," Georgia said, "you are the first real human person I have ever fought hand-to-hand. Not counting training sessions, of course. I always thought when it happened, it would be a man."

Unfortunately, Miss Sweet was a well-trained fighter. She might have been taken by surprise, but now she knew better. "Unexpected," she whispered, pivoting her legs upward. She kicked Georgia in the face. Georgia was knocked over, startled. On the other side of the bed, Rebecca ran for the door, but Miss Sweet caught her.

"Guards!" Rebecca screamed.

Georgia was right behind. She grabbed Miss Sweet. In a fluid movement, the woman dropped and swept Georgia's leg out. She spilled into a desk and fell on the floor. From the corner of her eye, she saw Miss Sweet produce a second stiletto from her other sleeve and turn back to Rebecca. Georgia was on her feet instantly. The woman was just about to bring the stiletto down when she caught her by the wrist. Georgia did not give her time to twist around this time. Instead, she yanked Miss Sweet backward.

The woman lost her grip on Rebecca, along with her balance. As she tried to regain footing, Georgia punched her in the side of the head. With a small cry, Miss Sweet fell to the floor and did not move.

"Guards!"

The door flew open as two of Rebecca's bodyguards rushed in. They gawked at the scene: Lady Rebecca was on the floor, Miss Sweet tossed against a wall, and Georgia stood over everyone. The men pointed their muskets at Georgia.

"Stop," Rebecca commanded. "Riley. Towson. The Duchess saved my life. Miss Sweet tried to kill me."

"What? Oh, my lady," said one of the men. They hurried over to help their mistress.

"Thank you, Georgia," Rebecca said, getting to her feet. "How did you know? It all happened so fast."

"I caught a look at the bottle of Akaphis, and she must have realized I recognized it," Georgia admitted. "Why act now? She could have poisoned you at her leisure."

"I do not know. She's been traveling with us for weeks. She could have done it any time," Rebecca said, pulling on a robe. "That was terrifying. Oh Georgia, you were amazing. All those wild stories about you fighting witches. Until one sees it up close, one cannot fathom it."

"Miss Sweet still lives," one of the guards said, checking the woman's breathing. "She is unconscious."

"Make sure she has no other weapons," Georgia ordered. "Get her in a chair and tie her to it. Make it tight enough to restrain, but there is no need for suffering. Send a footman to fetch Constable Jenkins. He will want to question her. Be wary, once she wakes, she will not hesitate to harm you."

The guard rolled his eyes.

"She will depend on your skepticism right until the moment she puts a knife in your back," Georgia told him.

"Do it," Rebecca said, trembling. "Do not let her out of your sight. I do not care if she must do her private business in front of you. Do not let her go unseen."

"Yes, my lady," the guard said, looking uncomfortable.

Georgia looked over the room and found the still-wrapped rosemary bread. She held it up. "Perhaps we can enjoy this with a spot of tea until the authorities arrive."

\*\*\*

"She will not talk," Constable Jenkins said, entering the breakfast nook. Georgia and Lady Rebecca settled in with tea, cakes, and rosemary bread. He looked at Georgia and then down. Her dress was a bit ripped up, but he was too polite to say anything.

"Constable, take a seat with us, please," Lady Rebecca said. She poured him a cup of tea herself. After the attack, she cried for several minutes. Georgia could only console her. After she got her wits back, Lady Rebecca was done with tears. Now she wanted answers. "What is our next step?"

"I think we should take her to Grandhall, to the Earl's Constabulary," Constable Jenkins said, sitting down. "I could try questioning her again, but she was unfazed by the threat of jail time. I do not know what else to do, other than deliver her to lockup. If she had accomplices or additional plans, I cannot know. Perhaps the Earl's Constables can convince her to give more information."

Georgia could think of several ways to loosen Miss Sweet's tongue, and none of them involved jail time, but she kept her thoughts to herself.

"I must know if she had accomplices," Lady Rebecca whispered. "How can I trust my staff now? What if she was not working alone?"

Georgia stood up. "I would like to question her, Constable. I suspect she will be as resistant to me as she was with you, but it is worth the try."

"Of course, Duchess."

\*\*\*

Miss Emmaline Sweet was a sight. Her eye was swollen, her nose bled dry, and her hair was a disaster. She was tied to a chair in Lady Rebecca's bedroom. Over by the window stood the two grey suited guards, Towson and Riley. Across the room, Constable Andre sat at the desk sifting through papers. For a moment, Georgia feared the men were mistreating the woman, but realized the bruising and blood were all her own work. This was no supernatural monster. Now she looked like any young woman in over her head.

"Are you thirsty?" Georgia asked. "Hungry?"

Miss Sweet kept her eyes down. Another chair was opposite the captive, so Georgia sat down. Miss Sweet also noticed how she looked. The woman blinked. "Your beautiful wig is destroyed."

Georgia pulled the wig off and shook her natural hair out. "Yes, it appears to be ruined," Georgia answered. "Now, I must question you, Miss Sweet. I assume that is not your real name."

Miss Sweet looked away.

"What is your real name?" Georgia asked.

Miss Sweet looked down again. She did not answer.

"This will go better if you cooperate," Georgia whispered. She locked eyes with Miss Sweet the same way she had seen Mr. Blue do it with hostile witnesses. "You must realize the situation you are in. At best, you will be put in a prison for the rest of your life. Attempting to murder any citizen of the Three Realms is taken seriously, but trying to kill the only child of the most powerful earl in the Realms? Well, that is a whole new story. The court will have you executed, but not before they... well, I would rather not speculate. Talk to me. Give me information. I can convince the authorities to let you live. You are still going to prison, but maybe that is all."

Miss Sweet smiled and shook her head.

"Do you have accomplices?" Georgia asked.

The woman looked up. "Of course."

"Name them," Georgia urged.

"The whole staff. All the bodyguards," Miss Sweet said, jutting her chin at the two men in grey. "We are in this together."

"Liar," one of the men in grey hissed.

Georgia held her hand up and he went silent. She tilted her head. "I think we both know that is not true, Miss Sweet. Otherwise, you would have died before the Constables arrived. They would have shot you and claimed you broke free. Trying to escape. You heard what I said earlier about prison. I can make your life more comfortable." Georgia had absolutely no idea if she could do anything to help this would-be murderer, but she wanted answers. Also, if the entire staff were Miss Sweet's accomplices, they would more likely have freed her and then all of them would have murdered Georgia and Rebecca. But there was no reason to get into all of that.

"I heard you. It does not matter."

"It matters," Georgia said. "I do not understand. Why did you choose to strike now? You could have done the same thing at a more opportune time."

"No, I could not."

"Why? Illuminate me."

"Forget it. Just get on with this. Lock me away, or finish what you started." Miss Sweet turned her head to show off the bruising.

"I am sorry about that," Georgia admitted.

Miss Sweet sneered. "I forgive you."

"Tell me what I need to know," Georgia urged, ignoring the woman's ugly tone. "Explain to me how someone like you would come to be. Tell me about the Sicarium. If you do, maybe I can help you."

"You want me to turn sides," Miss Sweet blinked.

"I want to know how far this has gone," Georgia answered. "Do you have accomplices? Is this more than an attempt to murder the heirs to Phaedros? How does the Sicarium work? How does a girl like yourself, stock Volusian by all appearances, come to work for an assassin's guild on the other side of the Eastern Sea?"

"If I told you that, my life would be over," Miss Sweet said, shaking her head. She glanced quickly at the two men in grey.

"Your life is already over," Georgia countered. "This is a chance to save yourself. Once I leave this room, you are at the mercy of everyone else."

Miss Sweet looked down. Georgia was not sure if she should wait or go, but a moment later the young woman looked up. "I panicked."

"I beg your pardon?"

"You asked why I chose to strike when I did… instead of waiting for another time. I knew who you were. We all know. I read the articles in the papers. You are a detective. I did not believe any of the nonsense about zombies and witches, but we know what the Order of the Blue is. If they were working with you, then you had to be legitimate in some way. When I came into the room, my plan was only to give her enough to make her sleep. You would go away, and I would be able to get back to work."

"I see. Please, go on."

Miss Sweet shook her head. "Nothing has worked correctly since arriving in this horrid village. I was trained by the best. In some circles, I am considered the best."

"The best at what?" Georgia asked in a quiet, respectful voice.

"Poisoning people very slowly," Miss Sweet answered. To her left, the men in grey suits shifted position. Her eyes twitched. She was watching one or both discreetly. Something was happening here that Georgia could not identify yet. "It requires a certain rhythm. The doses must be specific and timed. If the victim misses a window, she has a greater and greater chance of noticing."

"Noticing? Why?" Georgia asked. Furtively, she glanced at the men in grey, then back to the assassin. Then she lifted an eyebrow slowly. Miss Sweet nodded imperceptibly. One or both of the men must be the woman's accomplice. If he allowed her to keep talking, he would be discovered too.

"Administering the Akaphis poison on a regular basis requires a schedule. The point is not to cause pain, but rather to kill the victim with as little trace as possible. Eventually, the buildup of the poison will cause what appears to be a natural failure of the organs. If the victim misses even one dose, they will begin to feel discomfort," Miss Sweet said. "I have been poisoning Lady Rebecca for two weeks. Always on time, and always at the right dose. At that rate, I would have brought her to the end in about nine more days. Even a coroner would think it was a natural death because Akaphis is so subtle. In my nurse journal, I have been noting a concern over her anxiety. I have spent the last week confiding with the security men, telling them how I am concerned about her health and how she ignores it. The plan was to present my notes after her death. The authorities would absolve me, as I was the only one to notice her deteriorating health. But ever since we arrived in this stupid village, one event or another has arisen to disturb my work." What a plan!

"Disturb? In what way?"

Miss Sweet looked almost embarrassed. "The best way to subtly poison someone is in private. You need a controlled environment. You need consistency and a distracted or otherwise pliable victim. You need trust. Lady Rebecca's life is a busy one. She changes her schedule almost by the hour, what with privy councils and other obligations. She trusts no one. The woman surrounds herself with guards… half of whom are related to her by blood. She has a refined palate. In short, she is a terrible candidate for this type of murder."

Georgia blinked. One minute the woman stubbornly refuses to cooperate, the next she is talking shop. "What would be the best kind of… um… of murder?"

"In her case, a direct assault by a squad. Kill her and her guards in a staged attack. Slaughter everyone in the house and leave no witnesses. Burn the place to the ground and flee the country."

"I see. Why was that not the plan then?"

Miss Sweet gazed at the ceiling in thought. "No one asked my opinion. I was given an order."

"So you set out to poison her."

"I mistakenly thought that I could get the work done on this trip away from the capital. You see, she had only a few obligations here. I checked her calendar. It looked like a restful holiday, but there were still more complications than expected. I had to get easy access to a supply of the poison, taint the ice ahead of time and on schedule, and worst of all transport it to various locations while she traveled from party to party."

"This does not sound conducive to consistency at all," Georgia said. "What made you think this getaway was the right time?"

Miss Sweet shrugged. "We all have deadlines, my lady. I was about to miss mine. I was already rattled when you arrived at the coffee shop. I mis-measured the tainted ice. Something I never do. I was preoccupied trying to stay away from your attention, so I missed the trade of glasses when that other woman drank the borage. I thought I collected the poison glasses before she could, only to realize later I had the wrong ones. The dose was enough to make that woman sick."

"It nearly killed her," Georgia admitted. "Fortunately, there was an antidote."

"Sloppy work on my part. Who would have thought this area has a naturally occurring antidote growing in the woods," Miss Sweet muttered. She knew what had happened to Nelda. She knew all of it.

"Are you snooping on my rental house?" Georgia asked in a slightly indignant tone.

"We are snooping on everything and everyone, Duchess," Miss Sweet shot back without pause. "It is easier than you might imagine. Think of how many times you have wandered blithely through a drawing room and not noticed half a dozen maids and footmen. Before you ask, no, we do not have an agent inside your rental house. This afternoon, Lord Wyclef's seneschal ordered *Prince Robert Flowers* planted on each of his properties. Word is all over the village about it. That is how I learned about the existence of the antidote."

"Pure luck played a part in all of this then," Georgia answered. Of course, Mr. Brown knew about the antidote. If they had not called him in to assist, all would have been lost.

"I do not believe in luck. Or perhaps you are right. Lady Rebecca's schedule kept delaying the doses, which made them less effective. This morning, she missed her dose entirely when that old man showed up to invite her to his hot air balloon party." Miss Sweet shook her head. "Without an appointment, he simply appeared and away they went, no questions asked. Have you ever seen that happen? I have not. By the time you arrived, she was sick with withdrawal symptoms. I told her it was a cold, and somehow, she believed me. I was going to get her back on track and finish the job when we got back to her house in the capital. That's when you arrived, and I was sure you would take her away again. That is why I struck when I did. I saw you standing there, but I did not believe you were truly capable of fighting me. I saw only a very observant highborn lady, not the character they talk about in those papers. It was just the three of us in the room. I was running out of time and felt certain you were about to call the guards. I was taught to fight to the death against multiple opponents. Surely, I could handle two soft noblewomen if I acted fast."

"You give my detective skills more credit than they deserve," Georgia whispered.

"Then I deserve what I get," Miss Sweet answered. "When you lifted me by the throat, I knew I was lost. There was nothing natural about it. I knew I would be dead soon."

"Why did you continue?" Georgia asked. "You could have surrendered."

"Perhaps," Miss Sweet admitted. "But it is too late. You said you thought I was Volusian. I was. I am. I was born in Simsley. My parents died in the plague, and I was passed around different orphanages. The Sicarium took me in as a girl and trained me. I survived in their training school, even as others died. I learned about poisons, alchemy, combat, and stealth. I am not the only one. They took other Volusian children and trained them, too."

Off to the side, one of the men in grey, Towson, sagged to the floor with a groan. His side sprayed blood. The other guard, Riley, stepped away with a bloody dagger in hand.

"Duchess!" Constable Andre cried, jumping up.

Riley ran at Miss Sweet, who kept her eyes to the ground. Georgia caught him by the blade arm and twisted. He had so much momentum, his arm broke before he could stop himself. She held him down until the pain rendered him unconscious.

"My lady," Constable Andre whispered. "Are… are you all right?"

"I am fine, Andre. We need a doctor," Georgia said, stepping over to Towson and pressing one of her flared skirts into his wound to stop the bleeding. She would have used the wrapping wool from the medical bag, but it was now evidence. The Constable ran from the room, calling for help. She looked at Miss Sweet. "Thank you for warning me. Do you have any other accomplices I should know about?"

Miss Sweet looked up. "No. Riley was my handler. Um. Can you really help me?"

"I think so," Georgia said. She looked down at Towson, who was in shock, but alive. Riley was out cold, and probably in shock too. She returned her gaze to Miss Sweet. "If you tell us everything you know, I will do what I can to help you. If you explain how the Sicarium works, I suspect even Lady Rebecca will be willing to pull strings for you. I cannot promise you any sort of freedom. You are a trained assassin, and based on the way you speak, you have already murdered many people. But perhaps there is a way to atone for some of it. Maybe you can do some good."

Miss Sweet looked startled. "No one has ever asked me to do anything good before."

"I have another question," Georgia said. "I have a bad feeling I already know the answer, though."

"What is it?" Miss Sweet asked.

"Do you know anything about the break-in at Lord Redstone's house?"

Miss Sweet almost smiled. "I have to say, I honestly know nothing about that."

"Why was your equipment in the smugglers cavern below the Redstone archeological dig?"

"Was it? I had to have my supplies shipped in secret. I knew the poison was in a smuggler's cave somewhere nearby," Miss Sweet answered. "No one told me where it was kept. Riley brought it to me. We relied on the pirates to deliver it. It was safer that way. If Lady Rebecca's security found me carrying a bag full of poison, they would have taken me in."

# CHAPTER 12

# GIFT PARTY.

Millie was still gone. Georgia got back to the house and changed out of her torn clothes, tied her hair in a ribbon, and washed up. She was far from the height of elegance, but much more comfortable. Bea poked her head in. "Welcome back. You were gone awhile. I think we are still fifteen minutes out from dinner, though, so good timing there. Oh Lord, what happened to you? Is that a black eye?"

"Where to begin," Georgia said. "I need a glass of wine before I tell you about it."

Bea vanished, only to reappear a moment later with Mrs. Macklin. "Can you fix her up, Mrs. Macklin?"

"Heavens," Mrs. Macklin whispered. She pulled open the cosmetic bag and got to work repainting Georgia's face. Georgia drew a sharp breath when the woman started cleaning up her eye. "Forgive me, my lady."

"Nothing to forgive," Georgia answered. She could feel her face swelling where Miss Sweet kicked her. She had been hurt in combat before, so it was of no concern. It was troubling to see the look on Bea's face, though. Mrs. Macklin looked like she might cry for a moment. "I am quite well, I promise."

Bea returned with a glass of cabernet. The sound of the pianoforte drifted up from the salon. "Everyone is downstairs, but, of course, they will wait. I put Nora on social duty. She will keep them entertained. What happened?"

Georgia told her about the visit to Lady Rebecca and briefly described the fight, omitting several details. No need to panic anyone. "Both assassins are at the County Constabulary overnight. If the road re-opens tonight, they will be taken down to Grandhall. Lady Rebecca will try to leave for the capital tomorrow, too."

"What this world is coming to," Mrs. Macklin whispered. She gathered an appropriate outfit in the side suite while Georgia sipped her wine. Bea went back down to make sure things were moving. Once Georgia was ready, she thanked Mrs. Macklin and went down.

Bea, Luke, Nora, Nelda, and all six of the Earlsmen were loitering in the solarium. Nora continued to play. As they went into dinner, Georgia pulled Luke aside. "Luke, I wonder if I might ask a favor," she said.

"Of course, Georgia." He smiled and gazed at her, not realizing how banged up she was. Mrs. Macklin did her job well, it would appear.

"Tomorrow morning, the County Constable will be escorting two Phaedros assassins to Grandhall. I fear they are both quite dangerous. Would you be willing to send a few of your Earlsmen along for security."

"Of course," Luke said. "I will send four of them. Or do you think we should all go?"

Georgia shrugged. "The prisoners will be shackled during the trip. I think four Earlsmen is enough."

"As you wish."

"Thank you, Luke."

\*\*\*

Sunlight peeked through a canopy of leaves above. Georgia was on a blanket. It was spring. She could feel the balmy air upon her arms. Summer was coming. It would be here soon, and then the big parties would begin. She glanced to her left to see a canal barge passing. A man leaned over her. "Hello, sleepy head," he whispered.

Georgia opened her eyes.

The room was dark, and her fireplace was cold. She could almost see her breath, but under the sheets it was deliciously warm. Georgia stretched and poked a toe out of the covers to feel the morning chill. Outside, the rain hit the window in waves. A scullery maid opened the door and crept over to the fireplace. Georgia watched her sweep the ashes out, then build a new fire. She worked almost without sound; her movements were precise. When she finished, she noticed Georgia. "Sorry to wake you, my lady," the maid whispered.

"You did not wake me," Georgia whispered back. "Thank you for the fire."

A kitchen maid entered with tea and scones. Georgia lay still and let them work. When they were gone, she got up and poured a cup. It was the last day of the baby shower. As was tradition, they would have lunch, deliver their gifts to the mother-to-be, and everyone would be on their way. The last party was really a bit of an anti-climax, as the godmother had already been named.

Should she go home? No. There was one investigation still unsolved. Someone was attacked at Redstone House. Based on the description of the blood, it was likely fatal. Lord Redstone apparently made an appearance around the same time, and now he was missing. Georgia had a feeling it was not a coincidence. She had a strong feeling Mr. Blackheart was the culprit.

"What am I missing?" Georgia murmured.

Millie was still in the capital, or possibly stuck on a road somewhere. Georgia chewed her scone and wondered if she should stay put until her lady's maid returned. The problem: Mr. Reardon, if put on a road, would try every side road to get back. For all she knew, they could be trapped in some odd corner of the woods. She hoped Millie had more sense. If the rain washed out the roads, would she stay put in the capital? Georgia was not sure. Two years ago, she would have assumed her lady's maid would take the easy route. However, Millie was no longer the same girl. She might cross a river to find Georgia out of loyalty.

What if Millie and Mr. Reardon were stuck in the woods?

Georgia shook her head. "Trust them," she whispered. "If they are not here now, there is a reason. Worry too soon and you worry for nothing, Georgia." That last part was a favorite saying of her beloved late Uncle Raymond.

Talking to herself out loud was a sign of nothing good. Georgia shook her head, got up, pulled on a robe, and went down to the kitchen. Anything was better than fretting alone. She settled in the cook's office, after asking the staff to ignore her. They did not. Instead, the cook brought her a skillet-fried apple fritter sautéed in butter, and a cup of chicory coffee. Delicious. "I will not stay long, Mrs. Hensley," she said. "I hope you do not mind."

"Stay as long as you like, my lady," the cook answered. "I will check in again in a bit."

Georgia could not shake the feeling she was missing something. Some oversight.

Mr. Darkleaf, the young butler, was next to find her. "Duchess, I spoke with the Constables. They asked me to alert you when the south road to Grandhall reopened. They are escorting your prisoners to the Earl for judgment. The east road to the capital is still blocked, but there is a river boat that can transport you back. The boat arrives tomorrow."

"What if I need to stay a few more days?" Georgia asked.

Mr. Darkleaf nodded. "Of course, Duchess. According to our last note from Lord Wyclef, this house will not be rented again for another month. We would be most honored to serve you."

"Thank you, Mr. Darkleaf. I suspect Lady Blacklock and Mrs. Northbrooke will leave as soon as the road clears. Miss Irvingdale, the remaining Earlsmen, and I will be staying on for a few more days."

Mr. Darkleaf bowed his head. "Excellent, Duchess."

Georgia returned to her room. If she stayed any longer in the basement, they would likely keep feeding her... and she would keep eating. Instead, she changed into a day dress, pulled her hair back, and tied a modest cap on. The look was far from perfect, but she managed her hair well enough to make it. Of course, the outfit would never do for going out or an evening affair. But it worked well enough for early morning, even on someone at her station. She went down to the salon to find Nelda and Nora enjoying breakfast and the morning paper. "It is a copy of the *Vexbury Gazette* from yesterday," Nelda explained. "The roads are still washed out, but they deliver this paper from the other side of the lake by boat."

Nora flipped through her copy. "Not on a par with the papers in the capital, but not bad for a provincial rag. There's even an article on Sir Lucas and his men if you are interested."

"Oh, I think I need to read that, yes," Georgia said. Nora grinned and handed her a section.

"Be forewarned; there is a bit of speculation," Nora whispered. "Also, the printing is less refined in these parts. Mr. Darkleaf ironed both these copies twice, but the ink is still a little sticky."

Georgia flipped the paper open, careful not to get any ink on her dress, and read. The article started out well enough. It outlined how the Earl of Grandhall created a unit of Earlsmen for the first time in a decade and went on to explain the difference between them and proper knights. The explanation was a bit obtuse, but eventually made sense. Knights are created by the royals, or by other knights. The Earl himself is a knight, so he could have made them knights, but instead he made them Earlsmen, because he wants them to become knights. There was something about giving them the opportunity to aspire and earn their position. Ironic. The Earl himself inherited everything, and never aspired. Yet his seventh son must work for it because of an abundance of… other sons? That part did not quite make sense. "An awful lot of explanation about the Earlsman versus Knight thing here," she whispered.

"Fascinating, right?" Nelda was enthused. "Get to the part with the rivalry between Luke and the nephew of the Earl of Vexbury. That's my favorite bit."

"What?" Georgia scanned on. The article went on to talk about her, and whether Luke was a possible suitor. Overall, the language was more respectful than the papers in the capital. But it was still gossip. Then it took an odd turn, outlining how Luke was in competition with Sir Alfie Crighton, the nephew of the Earl of Vexbury. Alfie was the heir-presumptive for years, but then Alfie's older sister, Alvina, married the Baron of Nesbitt, and arranged for him to inherit Vexbury instead. This effectively left poor Alfie out in the cold, and according to the paper… he held Luke responsible for all of it?

"I do not understand," Georgia admitted. "I have met Sir Alfie. He and Luke know one another?"

Luke walked in and grabbed a plate of bacon and eggs. "Alfie is one of my oldest friends," he said. "We are the same age and went to school together. He does not blame me, nor does he blame his sister. Alvina and the baron were an enviable match, and their union is good for southern Volusia."

"We should not be reading gossip," Nora said, jumping.

Two of the Earlsmen wandered in and headed for the sideboard full of breakfast food. They were followed by a footman carrying a tray of still more bacon, eggs, and crumpets.

"Oh, do not worry about that, my lady. It is the way of the world. In fact, I suspect we third sons understand the plight of second daughters better than one might think." Luke glanced at his fellow Earlsmen. "All seven of us are spare sons. Some of us have come to accept it. In some ways, my father did us a great favor. We may not amount to much, but at least we have choices." He glanced at the other two Earlsmen, who both grinned.

"Well put. You do understand the plight of a second daughter," Bea said, entering from the servant's door. She set down the journal and went to the side table for food. "I see you already made the arrangement to stay longer." She directed that to Georgia.

"I did. I was up early."

"So, do you think the rain will delay departure?" Nora asked. "Today is our last day. Once we delivered the final gifts, I hoped to return home. I… miss my husband."

"You do?" Nelda asked her.

Nora blinked. "You know, sister, I really do. In the morning, he insists on having breakfast together before starting the day. I realized this morning he always waits for me, and he always smiles when I come in. No matter how long it takes me to get ready."

Bea sat down with a massive plate of bacon. "That is wonderful, Nora."

"Sorry. The road to the capital is still washed out," Luke interjected. "I fear we will all be here at least one more day. I must admit, I am not unhappy about it." He glanced at Georgia. She noticed his ears turn red.

She found herself blushing back. Oh dear. "You are all welcome to stay here," she said. "I arranged for at least another week at this house. Perhaps I should have mentioned it when I returned last night, but I still have the Redstone investigation. I will stay until it is solved, or until there are no leads left to follow. Each of you is welcome for as long as you feel comfortable."

"Obviously, I am staying until you leave, Georgia." Bea chewed her bacon as delicately as one could and winked. She gestured, "I suspect Luke will stay as long as you do."

Georgia gestured back. "I think you are correct."

"May I ask what is left to investigate?" Luke asked. "I assumed the Redstone break-in was somehow related to the plot to kill Lady Rebecca Drake. You found the tainted ice in the cavern next to the smugglers, who in turn were next to the Redstone excavation. I assumed that meant they were related. The culprits turned out to be the Phaedros assassins. Lady Rebecca is now safe, and the killers are on their way to Grandhall for justice."

"The Redstone break-in and Lady Rebecca's attempted assassination are likely two separate cases," Georgia answered. "Miss Sweet and her handler were storing her poisons in the cavern so the men in grey… er, the bodyguards… could not trace it back to her. She mentioned she herself did not go there. Her accomplice may have been to the cave, but they were relying on pirates and possibly another courier. It passed through several hands. She also told me that neither she nor her accomplice had anything to do with the Redstone matter. It is possible she lied about that, but either way I will need to find out the truth."

"So complicated," Bea said, shaking her head. "If I was going to poison someone, I would not rely on so many potentially unreliable partners."

"Miss Sweet lamented that choice herself," Georgia noted.

"If you were a poisoner, how would you go about it?" Nelda asked, looking amused. Ironic, as she was a victim of the assassin too, albeit without intention.

Bea thought about it. "Well, I would start with pickled herring."

"Of course, you would," Georgia said with a grin.

"Do you want to know my evil plan or do you not?" Bea asked, her eyes twinkling.

"I do," Luke said.

Bea leaned forward. "I would have a crate full of the smelliest pickled herrings with me when I visited and tell everyone how much I love them. Everyone would think I am a loon, but I would hide the poison in the crate. No one would look for it because they would get pickled herring juice on their skirts."

"So, you would bring pickled herrings to the coffee shop and sneak the poison into the ice there?" Georgia asked.

"Of course not," Bea said. "Poisoning someone in a coffee shop is ridiculous. What was that woman thinking?"

Nelda was giggling throughout the conversation until they talked about the coffee shop. It was about that moment it must have sunk in. She grew quiet. Nora patted her hand.

"We have to keep looking into the Redstone matter," Georgia said. "I just... I just feel like I either missed something or assumed something. I feel it in my bones."

"Evidence?" Bea asked. "Or a hunch?"

"Or both?" Luke asked.

"I do not know," Georgia admitted. "Lord Redstone allegedly returned two weeks ago and sold the ring to Robert Blackheart. Mr. Blackheart gave it to Harriet. We can discuss the ring itself later, I suppose. It is stunning, and I must admit I cannot imagine anyone thinking it so mundane as not to be what Redstone originally posited. It is a thing of supernatural craft. That said, events continued. After that, Lord Redstone may have left town before his sister, Mrs. Crauford, arrived. Mrs. Crauford was away from the house for at least three weeks, did not know he was there during her absence, only to return to find a pool of blood, a journal, a shoe, and a dagger of unknown origin. Except, she herself saw none of the evidence because her house maid cleaned it before she arrived."

"Forgive me," Luke said. "The blood must be from Lord Redstone. He's the only missing part of this. That is how it would go in a crime story. I hate to say it, but he must have met a grim end."

"Maybe," Bea said. "There are problems with that theory. Would Lord Redstone return home literally alone? Does the man have no staff?"

"Lord Redstone is famous for running off on adventures. It may be that he can pick out his own outfits. He may not have a valet," Luke answered.

Bea nodded. "That makes sense."

Nora shuddered. "What an awful and lonely way to live."

"Living a life of adventure and travel? Sounds like fun to me," Luke said.

Nelda grinned. "Yes. It would sound that way to a man of wealth and means."

"Oh, now, let's not be unkind," Nora chided.

"She is right, actually," Luke admitted. "My problems are fairly simple."

"May I ask how so?"

Luke shrugged. "I am a spare son who must find a lady of consequence to marry. There are rules, but otherwise I am free to do as I wish."

"No wonder you want to run off and have adventures," Nelda admitted. The other two Earlsmen nodded quietly. Georgia suspected their fortunes bore similar stipulations. On the other hand, they were sons of knights. If they ran out of options, their families would allow them to marry downward if the dowry was significant. They might even be allowed to marry daughters of wealthy trade families. Luke would not have that option. He must marry a significant landowner's daughter, or someone so lofty she could live outside of a category. There were maybe four women in the Three Realms who fit that description, and three of them were witches. That left only Georgia.

"It could be worse, of course. My entail will provide me with a quiet but comfortable life somewhere on my family's estates if I decide to remain alone. If I do not, I must find a way to excel."

"Excel? In what way?" Nelda asked.

"My father has certain ideas about what it means to be a gentleman and a Greenheart. He will expect me to build a proverbial, if not literal, empire of my own. What I cannot do is marry downward or bring a burden to my brothers." Luke did not sound too put out. Georgia could see he recognized his good fortune. Still, he glanced at her with a faint blush before looking down. They both knew his mother, Lady Constance, was angling for a match, although the pretense of assisting Georgia in the investigation might be legitimate. The Earl of Grandhall would have sent assistance anyway the moment she wrote regarding the Redstone affair.

Of all the noble ladies in the Three Realms, Georgia was the only one who could use him to her advantage. His pedigree was ideal, and if the arrangement worked, it could benefit them both. She discreetly looked him up and down, not for the first time.

Luke was healthy, smart, and handsome. He had coal black hair that despite combing, seemed to loosen every time he moved. A big lock kept falling over his eyes. He would push it back without thinking. She had a momentary impulse to swat it, just to see what he would do. That's not a problem, is it?

"So, today's plan is to attend the gift-giving ceremony," Nelda said, sipping her coffee. "After that, we may have to stay longer, due to the weather? Do we want to plan some sort of thing?"

"A thing?" Georgia asked. "You mean like a post-party party?" She really did not have time for more parties. There was still an active investigation.

"Maybe?" Nelda said. "I do not wish to presume, but as long as we are all still here, I thought I might make dinner myself."

"Yourself?" Nora asked.

Nelda shrugged. "Nora, since we have been here, we have been guests through my sickness. I thought it might be nice to give a gift back to Georgia and Bea for all of their hospitality."

"That is sweet, Nelda," Georgia answered, "but you did not know you were going to be poisoned, and I am glad we were here to help you. If you would like to impress us with a bit of cooking, I think that sounds wonderful. That said, having you back and walking around is enough for me."

"What would you make?" Nora asked with a grin. "Honestly, Nelda, you barely passed the culinary classes in school."

"I would make Mother's baked cheese and macaroni," Nelda answered. "The one dish you and I both know will impress even the most rigorous palate."

Nora's face lit up. "Oh." She looked around the room. "All right, forgive me. I think Nelda and I should join forces and make this dish for the group. If not today, then tomorrow for lunch."

"Cheese and macaroni?" Bea asked. "It sounds rather simplistic."

"It is a surprisingly obvious recipe, but making it special… that is another matter," Nora answered. "If prepared correctly, it is one of the most satisfying side dishes on the planet."

"Really?" Bea laughed. "Well, as long as you do not offend Lord Wyclef's cook, I am all for it."

Nelda clapped her hands in delight. "I promise she will not be put off. I gave her the recipe yesterday, and she was intrigued, to say the least. These Findorians love their spicy foods, but she is a true chef who respects the Volusian mastery of all things cheese. I made a pot of it for her. Yes, I was as nervous as if being presented at court. But I have a convert."

"You were downstairs cooking?" Nora blanched.

"I have been stuck in a room next to the kitchen for days," Nelda answered with a chuckle. "By the way, the kitchen in this house is a joy. They have everything, and enough counter space to feed an entire festival. When I get home, I am going to ask Mr. Northbrooke to renovate my own accordingly."

"Something to look forward to," Georgia said.

"In the meantime, we still have that last little gift giving party, and a mystery to solve," Bea said, flipping through the journal. "I finished reading the journal. Besides the ring, it is all about mythology and burial site information. I do not think there are any other clues. How much have you read of it, Georgia? What do you think?"

"We can return it to Mrs. Crauford tomorrow," Georgia answered. "I am going to check in with the Constables when they get back. I will take it to her on the way. I just wonder where Lord Redstone went. His sister was sure he would have left her a note when he was in the village."

One of the Earlsmen leaned in. "Are we talking about the pool of blood again? You must realize it belongs to Lord Redstone, right?"

"Sir Ignatius is not wrong," Luke said. "We do not know where he went. We only know he was in town because Mr. Blackheart admitted it after Mrs. Blackheart started talking about rutabagas and her ring. Who else could the blood belong to?"

Bea shook her head. "Oh, this is grim. Do you think his body is in the woods somewhere? If something happened, they… whoever they are… would have to hide it."

"I would imagine so," Luke answered. "I wonder why the culprit did not clean up the blood, though. It sat for weeks, did it not?"

"Another good question," Bea admitted. "If I stabbed someone in their own house, I would clean it up as soon as possible."

"What if Mr. Blackheart did not do the actual stabbing?" Luke countered. "What if one of his valets did, but somehow overlooked the mess? Perhaps the valet fled?"

"We still have no motive for Lord Redstone," Georgia muttered. "People do not kill for no reason, unless they are mad."

"The ring," Luke said. "You saw the thing. It is worth a fortune. He wanted to give it to his wife. Blackheart told Mrs. Blackheart he bought it, but he must have stolen it."

"According to Harriet, Lord Redstone himself told her he was selling it to Mr. Blackheart," Georgia corrected. "She said he was their dinner guest before her husband went back with him to fetch it."

"Could she be lying?" Bea asked.

Georgia listened to the speculation. All these people were serious in their own way. Bea was the most solid of minds, and it would appear Luke had a bit of the detective about him. Perhaps they could solve the mystery together? "We need a plan," she announced.

Luke nodded, understanding. "You and the ladies are about to attend the gift-giving party. That will take several hours if I am not mistaken? What can we men folk do to assist you detectives while you are detained?"

"Good question. We need to find Lord Redstone… or confirm he went back to the Kingdom of Jendina, yes?"

"He's dead," Luke said in a mordant tone.

"Luke, you have a sharp mind, and I suspect you are correct, but we do not know that for certain," Bea chided. "For all we know, Lord Redstone stabbed someone in his library and left it for the maid to clean up while he went off on another adventure."

"Very well, we need to find his body or some other evidence. Should we scour the woods, or his other properties?"

"What other properties?" Georgia asked.

Luke shrugged. "He owns the archeological dig site outside of the village. I guess we can count that out. You and Miss Beatrice searched it when you found the hidden cave."

Bea blanched. "Oh. We did not search it thoroughly. We were not looking for a body." She flipped the journal open, turning to a page. "In fact, we missed something glaring and, dare I say, a bit on the nose. Georgia, is this the thing, the tidbit, you were missing? We passed over all the dig spots to find the last one on the map. As it happens, Redstone even said in the journal… 'hole number seven… the perfect spot to hide a body'."

"What?" Georgia blinked. "You did not mention this before, Bea."

"I was excited about the secret door thing," Bea shot back. She shook her head. "I am sorry."

"No, it makes sense. You did not know, at the time, Lord Redstone might have been in town. You were looking for something else," Luke said.

"There was a giant pool of blood in Lord Redstone's house and dozens of giant holes and secret caves in the woods," Bea said, rubbing her eyes. "I missed the obvious."

"We both did," Georgia admitted.

"I will take Iggy and Nick back to the dig site. We will start with hole number seven, but we will check each of them. If Lord Redstone's body is not there, we can get Mrs. Crauford to write to him. If we find a body, we will report back. How does that sound?"

Georgia stood up. "Thank you. Yes, it sounds like you are going to have a terrible day climbing down chilly, wet holes in the ground while we ladies eat scones."

"I would not have it any other way," Luke said with an impertinent wink.

"Be careful of everything," Bea said in a serious tone. "Lord Redstone said some of the holes had ancient traps in them."

"Did he say which ones?" Sir Ignatius asked.

"No," Bea answered, shaking her head. "He was infuriatingly vague on that part. He mentions it twice in the journal. He said if one moves slowly and observes, one can avoid the traps. To be fair, he also said the place was cursed and to avoid frog zombies."

"Understood." Ignatius looked at Luke. "You will have to observe. You know we cannot."

"I have known that since we were 13 years old," Luke answered with a smirk.

"Okay," Georgia said after a breath. "Gentlemen, please take the utmost care on this expedition. I feel as if I should go with you, but then I worry you would look at me sideways."

Luke smiled. "Thank you, Duchess. We will do our best to stay safe."

Okay. We shall see where this goes.

\*\*\*

Millie was still away, but Mrs. Macklin was getting to the point where she might be a suitable, albeit temporary, substitute.

Somehow, Mrs. Macklin managed to repair Georgia's wig. How? Georgia had no idea. Last time she looked at the thing, it resembled a pillow or possibly some rodent akin to a mongoose more than a headpiece. That said, when the ladies arrived at the gift-giving party, Georgia was not embarrassed or unwilling to be seen. In fact, she looked amazing. Her fake hair was sewn with silver stars and strings of pearls. She wore a high-waisted jade green silk gown with long sleeves. It covered her completely. The construction was both complementary and something only a person with Georgia's slight figure could pull off.

The main room at the hotel was strung with garlands and ribbons. The floor was dominated by tables of food. Georgia, Bea, Nora, and Nelda took a seat at the end near the door. There were no directions. It appeared as if everyone was milling about. Finally, Octavia Potter took the center and shouted out. "Ladies! Hear me? Harriet has gone into labor. She is with the midwife now."

Bea blinked. "In labor?"

"That is what happens when one is about to have a child," Georgia answered drolly.

Bea smirked. "Yes. That is what they say. I mean, I am surprised no one told me. I mean, I am the godmother."

"It must have come on too quickly," Nora whispered. "And you know, I saw no other women in Harriet's group. It's all just Mr. Blackheart's valets. Men simply do not think of these things."

"We are on our own today," Octavia continued. "Obviously, we cannot present gifts to the new mother, but there is a spot on the table where you can leave your present. Thank you on behalf of the Blackheart family and have a good day."

Bea gestured to Georgia. "This means we do not have to sit for hours watching Harriet unwrap boxes."

"The day just got a bit better," Georgia gestured back.

After Octavia finished her announcement, the string quartet launched, and everyone sat down to enjoy the spicy sausages, potatoes, and rice. Georgia took her gift, a custom-made teak baby rattle of the most excellent craftsmanship, up to the receiving area.

"I do not see Lady Rebecca Drake," Bea whispered, looking around.

"She left town on the river barge," Nelda answered. "Octavia told me several of the guests are gone. The river is the only way to leave right now, so some of them took it this morning. They had their gifts delivered earlier."

Nelda looked at Nora. "I can send one of the footmen over to get us passage on the next barge when we are done here." Nora nodded.

"I believe I will fetch a drink. Would anyone like anything?" Georgia asked.

"Georgia, you are not going to serve us," Nora said in shock.

"Just watch me, Nora." Georgia grinned and headed for the bar.

On the way, she passed Clarisa Dulac and Mindy Stratford. "Leave it to Harriet to miss her own party. On the bright side, we can stop drinking this horrid borage."

"The cow has to have her baby someday," Mindy answered. "Might as well do it now and put the rest of us out of our misery."

"Speak for yourself, Mindy. You have always been so rude," Georgia said, passing them. Mindy literally flinched.

"See you in the capital." She watched as both women blanched.

They lingered for another hour, enjoying the music and small talk. Octavia Potter wandered past to talk about the weather and diplomatically gain reassurances of Georgia's patronage in the next season. When that was done, Georgia was ready to go. "Ladies," she said to Nora and Nelda, "We are going to check on the men at the dig site. See you at the house."

# CHAPTER 13

# AN UNEXPECTED TURN OF EVENTS... OR WAS IT?

Mist clung to the ground as Georgia and Bea exited the hotel. It was starting to sprinkle again. A serious rain was approaching. "I wonder where our driver is," Bea said, glancing about.

"Let us remain under the portico for now," Georgia suggested. She was not sure her newly repaired wig would hold up. They waited a moment before she spotted a fellow chewing sour gum. Another driver. For a moment, she thought Mr. Reardon had returned. No such luck, though. The fellow glanced their way and bowed. No, he was someone else's driver. Georgia nodded and looked away. Millie was still gone. It was not just inconvenient: Georgia was getting worried. Yes, the most logical thought placed Millie and Mr. Reardon back at home in the capital because of the rains. It was that time of year. She should not worry. But she did. At the edge of her vision, shadows were twitching. Cold dread clutched at Georgia. What if they tried to return and were trapped somewhere? Visions of trees falling on the coach to trap them while ice cold water rose all around made its way into her brain.

Georgia gazed at the mist for a while. Something flickered at the edge of her vision. It swooped back and forth and called out. She focused her eyes to find Kenneth the oriole. "Goldenheart," the bird called out, "Follow me. Danger comes. Follow me."

"Georgia, do you see that bird?" Bea asked. She looked over. "Do you hear him speaking?"

"You can hear him?"

Bea blinked. "He is *literally* speaking."

"We need to follow him," Georgia said, blinking.

They crossed the boulevard and followed Kenneth down the street. A moment later, they found a sign that read: 'Frog Prince Lane.'

"This is the other end of the trail we followed to the amphitheater," Bea noted. Kenneth circled above them once, then flew down the path ahead. "Follow!" he chirped.

"This ends at that creepy ruin," Georgia whispered. "Be careful. I have a bad feeling about this."

"Let us see where he takes us? I mean, how often does one encounter a talking bird?" Bea sounded almost cheerful, but Georgia could see she was afraid.

"More often than one might think, apparently. There is danger ahead.Perhaps you should go back inside, Bea."

"Absolutely not, Georgia." Bea turned to follow as Kenneth flitted ahead. Georgia stepped ahead of Bea. Eventually, they found the ring of stones and the ancient amphitheater. The rain was building up and the ground was like soup. Georgia turned to Bea. "The rain is getting worse. You should go home," she said.

"That is not going to happen," Bea answered.

"This could be dangerous," Georgia said. "There could be something supernatural happening. I mean, we are following a talking bird into an ancient ruin, after all."

"Life is dangerous," Bea countered. "Might as well get used to it."

Georgia smiled. "When did you get so brave?"

"My best friend taught me," Bea answered with a smile.

Georgia nodded. They followed Kenneth into the ring but stuck to the edge of the gnarled oak trees next to one of the standing stones. At the edge of her vision, shadows danced. She noted the little bird did not lead them directly in. Instead, he too remained at the edge. She gestured to Bea, "Hide."

Bea ducked behind the standing stone with her.

The grass was tall around the ring of stones, and they hid with ease. The scent of the ground was a receding memory of summer turning to the new reality of fall. Within the ring was the old amphitheater. From her vantage, Georgia could see inside with ease.

What she saw made her cold.

A circle of men in dark robes and masks was chanting. Harriet was sitting at the center, right next to the old well, on a chair. She was mumbling and looked terribly frightened. Georgia watched as her belly heaved and she screamed. Harriet was definitely in labor. On her hand, she wore the blazing ring. As she twisted, the stone seemed to grow ever brighter. As it grew brighter, the masked men chanted louder.

Bea saw all of it too. She turned to Georgia and gestured. "What are they saying? What is that language?"

"I do not know," Georgia gestured back.

"How do we help her?" Bea asked silently.

"It is a dark ritual of some kind. We must be careful," Georgia responded. The cold grip on her tightened. Without her magic sword, what could she do to stop these people? Kenneth landed on a nearby rock and watched her. Faintly, she could hear Harriet panting and crying. All the while, the mist around them thickened. Light was fading, and she began to shiver. Everything was crashing down.

Bea leaned over for a better look, then scooted back. "There are men with muskets walking around on the other side of the amphitheater. One of them looks like he is headed this way. They must be guards."

Suddenly, Georgia was not brave. She was strong and fast but was that enough? On the other side of the rock, mad cultists were gathering around a woman who was giving birth in an ancient glade. It all started to make sense now. The shadow spiders in the capital, the new millennia, the ancient prophecy about a Century of Evil. It was all related. They were using Harriet to summon something. "But without the sword…" Georgia whispered.

Bea laid a hand on her shoulder. Georgia looked at her old friend. "You defeated the winter witch and dozens of blood zombies," Bea whispered.

"I had the sword," Georgia whispered back. "I should never have left it at home. I sent Millie away to who knows where? For all I know, she is dead in a ditch with Mr. Reardon. Drowned on her way back, all because I was willful and stupid."

"What are you talking about?" Bea asked. "You left the sword at home because the Queen said so."

"What are we doing here?" Georgia asked no one in particular.

"We came to see Harriet. During that time, you rescued Lady Rebecca and we are close to solving the mystery of Lord Redstone. The clues were all in the journal, and this is part of it. Look at how the ring blazes.

They are using it to do something terrible to Harriet," Bea whispered with urgency. "Georgia, what is this doubt that grips you?"

Georgia blinked. Shadows moved in the trees all around. She heard something chuckling. "Shadows," she whispered. "They have been following me ever since we got here. I do not have the sword. Without it, I am…"

"What are you talking about?" Bea hissed. Above them, the rain grew worse. Georgia could feel it seeping through her ridiculous wig. Bea leaned in. "Listen to me. With or without the magic sword, you are a hero. You are *the* hero. The sword is… well, it is a weapon in your arsenal, but it does not complete you, nor does it take the place of the choices you make. Your mind is your greatest weapon."

Georgia looked at her old friend and blinked. "Someone else said something very similar recently," she whispered. "Mr. Brown, when he was getting on his balloon. He said almost that very thing."

"He was right," Bea whispered.

"Was he?" Georgia asked. "I mean, are we now taking advice on the nature of heroism from a veterinarian in a hot air balloon? Bea, I feel no confidence."

Bea shook her head. "That veterinarian is friends with a talking bird and he saved Nelda's life with a pot of boiled weeds. However quirky he might be, he saw you for who you are. Now, instead of debating this, I would urge you to get the job done: save Harriet and think it all out later."

"Right. Yes. That was good advice and surprisingly succinct for you."

Bea smirked. "Now I see the old Georgia."

"I want you to run back and fetch the constables or find Luke and his men," Georgia whispered.

"How are you going to stop the men in black robes?" Bea asked.

Georgia swallowed hard. "I do not know, but I am going to figure that out on my way down there using this brain you keep saying is so powerful. I do not know if I will succeed, but you must get away from here, Bea. Go get help."

Bea nodded. "You can do this, Georgia, and I will return with reinforcements."

Georgia stood up. "Thank you for the lovely pep talk... now go."

Bea hesitated a moment, then gathered her skirts and ran back down the path, keeping low until she was out of sight. Once she was gone, Georgia turned back to the amphitheater and stalked confidently in. To one side a man with a musket spotted her.

"Stop," he said to her. "Who are you?"

"Who are you?" she answered, in her most entitled Lady-of-Note voice.

He grabbed her arm and laughed. "A high-born lady. You have come to the wrong place on your stroll, missy…" he managed to say before she chopped him in the throat and watched him crumble. Georgia turned back to the center of the amphitheater. Harriet was still on her birthing chair and in terrible pain.

Behind Harriet, a man in a blood red robe appeared. He lifted his arms to the sky and called out, "*Il Malvagio*, we call you. From the blood of the ancient darkness, you were born. Come to us now. Take the child. We offer it for your power to bring about the Century of Evil. Come to me. I offer my child in exchange for your power." He threw his hood back.

It was Mr. Blackheart.

Georgia began to walk toward him.

One of Mr. Blackheart's valets stepped between them. He was in a dark robe, but she could see the collar of his livery peeking out. He grabbed her around the waist and laughed. "Dumb whore," he guffawed. "You are…" He would have said more, but she grabbed him by the head and flipped him over. Along the way, she heard the hem of her gown rip. Another dress is gone. She prayed she would one day see Millie again, so she could apologize. When he landed, she kicked him in the throat, and he passed out.

Georgia moved closer.

Two robed men with knives were next. She was unarmed. The man on the left jumped at her. She grabbed his wrist and waited. The man on the right moved forward. She punched him in the nose, shattering it. He fell back. She punched the other man in the side of the head and watched him spit teeth. He tried to rally, so she punched him again. At that point, he went down. She was getting better at fighting without the sword. Dusting her hands, Georgia looked at the other men in robes. There were still six of them left standing. "Anyone else care to fight me?" she asked.

One of the men in robes stepped backward. She noticed he had a gold fringe on his sleeves. He was probably Mr. Blackheart's butler, or perhaps dark cultists do not follow traditional service ranks. Either way, he was clearly second-in-command. "We must keep the ritual going. Kill her," he hissed. "I will help the master."

All five men drew knives and rushed forward. At the same time, she heard a twig snap from behind. Georgia leaned away just as another fellow tried to grab her arms from her blind spot. He toppled forward, losing his balance. She promptly grabbed him by the collar and shoved him into the oncoming attackers. Two of them were tangled for a moment. Another man tried to stab her, but she leaned away again. He was fast and jumped back as another one made a feint. She dodged yet again, letting him jump back. As they circled, other men in robes were trying to get around to attack from another angle.

"Hold her down," a man at the back shouted. "Kill her. Kill her before she spoils everything." Beyond him, Mr. Blackheart was still chanting. As he did, the ring pulsed in tandem. Every time it pulsed; Harriet screamed in pain anew.

Two men dropped their knives and grabbed her arms… one on each side, as another moved in to stab from the front. Using the men holding her for balance, Georgia kicked the stabber in the face. He flew backward and did not get up. A second stabber tried to get her from behind. She yanked around the man holding her right arm and used him as a shield. He screamed as his compatriot drove the blade into his shoulder. He could not stop her; she was stronger than him. A moment later he was gasping on the ground. The second stabber gaped in surprise. With her now-free hand, she grabbed the man holding her left arm by the neck and threw him at the second stabber. They sprawled across the ground together.

There was no time to catch a breath, though. Another robed man leapt on her back and tried to cut her throat. Georgia could see the knife coming around, almost as if time stopped. She grabbed his wrist and flipped him over her head. He hit the ground hard on his back and gasped. Without hesitation, she punched him and he lay still.

A knife sailed past her ear. Georgia snatched it out of the air with her bare hand, spun, and threw it right back. It landed in the chest of the next fellow so hard he flew backward, instantly dead.

"Cowards!" the butler in the back shrieked. Georgia turned to see the remaining two men... the second stabber and the left-arm holder... running out of the amphitheater. She stepped over the bodies and kept going. At the edge of view, the shadows writhed. She chose to ignore them.

Mr. Blackheart's butler had a musket pistol under his robe. He yanked it out. Gunpowder spilled over his shaking hands. "Ridiculous," Georgia said, swatting the pistol away. She glared at the butler. "It would take you at least another minute to load that thing. You should have at least had a knife." Before he could reply, she broke his jaw and he crumpled.

"Stop there, Duchess," Mr. Blackheart shouted. He had a knife to Harriet's throat. On the bright side, he was no longer chanting. The ring on Harriet's hand still pulsed, but not quite like before. "You really are everything the papers said. Look at what you did to my poor men." His tone was mocking.

"You are planning to sacrifice your child and maybe murder your own wife," Georgia answered. "What kind of cad are you?"

Blackheart laughed. "The worst kind, my lady. Sorry, dear. But I need the child for my master."

"Richard, why?" Harriet panted.

"You know why, Harriet. You have known why since your father told you about your family, all those years ago." He sneered at her as she trembled.

"The Shadow Man," Harriet gasped. "You serve him. How…?"

"The Shadow Man? Oh, come now, darling. Not that old tale again," Mr. Blackheart answered. Then he tilted his head, as if in thought. "My master goes by many names. Frog Prince. *Il Malvagio* in the ancient tongue… or perhaps he is this Shadow Man you feared as a child. You were right about one thing: you are the lost child of the Gildernesse. The last princess of their kind. The heirloom ring on your finger confirmed it when you put it on. I watched it light up at your touch, and I knew. That is why I need you. My child grows within your belly, and he will be the key to my power. When *Il Malvagio* sees the gift I bring, he will grant me power. I will be his hand, and together we will bring the Century of Evil to this world."

"In short, you are mad as a chair," Georgia muttered.

"You tricked me. How did I not see this?" Harriet was starting to sound more angry than afraid.

"I have been asking myself that same question for months, wife," Mr. Blackheart answered with a sneer. He was really good at sneering. "Did you really think a horrid cow like you could land one such as I? Oh, Harriet, you poor dull thing."

"I… I assumed I landed you with my father's wealth and my plucky spirit," Harriet shot back. She was about to say more but winced. She was still in labor, after all.

"Oh, that you did." Blackheart chuckled. "Not that I'll need his money. Not when I have you and the power of the curse on your family. I will miss that when you are dead."

Georgia shook her head. "Well, that answers that question." She snatched up a large rock and threw it at Mr. Blackheart's head. The movement was so quick, he didn't have time to react, and it hit him in the nose. Blood sprayed as Georgia crossed the distance between them in an instant. She grabbed him by the lapel.

"You are too late," Mr. Blackheart spat through bloody lips, his once beautiful face destroyed. Harriet screamed suddenly. She was about to deliver the child. "Behold, *Il Malvagio* comes. The spell is done. It matters not what you do now, for he has been summoned and his curse will remake the world."

The ground shuddered. Beside them, the old well filled with black water and a terrible odor. Georgia watched as it overflowed, staining the ground all around. Tiny black frogs were everywhere as the muck rose. Harriet screamed and tried to get up, but her labor was intense. On her hand, the ring flared with green fire. It was all connected. Lord Redstone *was* right. Harriet slid back into her chair panting. Another form appeared in the well… it was almost… human. A black gooey form. "*Vieni a me, mio signore…*" Mr. Blackheart chanted.

Georgia punched him in the chest and felt his ribs crack. "That is about enough of that, sir." She wondered why the ritual did not stop when she interrupted the chanting. The robed butler was quite specific about it earlier.

Harriet was gibbering. Her leg was covered with blood. She was out of time. Green fire coruscated around her. The almost human thing rose out of the murky well, its eyes blazing green to match the ring. "Blackheart," it whispered. "You summon *Il Malvagio*, mortal. I am weak from my captivity. Where is the sacrifice you promised?"

Mr. Blackheart flailed on the ground, gasping.

Georgia spoke instead. "He did summon you, foul thing. But I am sending you back." With a strength she did not even know she had, she used Mr. Blackheart as a sort of flail. With all her might, she picked him up and swung him around smashing the thing. He hit the creature with force enough to bend his legs in some odd directions. Mr. Blackheart screamed once and went silent. Georgia let him go, and he toppled into *Il Malvagio*. Together, they writhed in the well, and began to sink.

"No!" the creature screamed. "It has already begun. You cannot stop the coming evil."

Kenneth sailed overhead. "The ring! The ring! Destroy it!"

Georgia turned to Harriet. "Give me the heirloom ring," she said. "I have to break it."

Harriet gaped. "What? No. Georgia, it belongs to me." She gazed at it on her finger with a strange look on her face, even as flecks of spittle fell from her mouth. "It is precious."

"It is an evil artifact from a bygone age, Harriet," Georgia answered.

"Mr. Blackheart gave it to me," Harriet whispered. "It is an heirloom of our house."

"He gave you that ring so he could use you. Harriet, snap out of it. The man just tried to sacrifice you and your child to that thing." Georgia stepped toward the woman, but Harriet scrambled off her chair. She tried to run, but was too weak. Georgia caught her before she could fall over.

"Leave me alone, Georgia," Harriet snarled in a weak voice. Suddenly, she screamed and grabbed her belly. The ring flared to life again.

"Let it go," Georgia said. She could have taken the ring by force but was afraid she would hurt Harriet. "Do you not see what it is doing to you? You heard the monster when it said it has already begun. I do not know, precisely, what it meant, but I would not be surprised if this ring is tied to it in a profound way."

Harriet was crying and shaking her head. She wasn't listening.

"Think of your child," Georgia whispered. "Take that ring off."

Harriet looked at her. She was clearly exhausted, and Georgia could see the pain in her face. Slowly… excruciatingly slowly… she pulled the ring from her finger and pressed it into Georgia's hand. "Destroy… destroy it, Georgia." The instant it was in Georgia's hand, the ring stopped pulsing. The gem grew dark.

Harriet smiled, and promptly slumped over with utter exhaustion.

Georgia wasted no time. She squeezed the ring with all of her formidable strength. Perhaps she could crush it. Alas, that did not work. Behind, the sound of water sloshing grew. The creature was pushing the body of Mr. Darkheart off, and struggling to climb back out of the well.

Georgia hopped up. The ring began to hum again. She felt it grow warm in her hand and looked down. Instantly, the gem regained life. She remembered when she first laid eyes upon it and the desire to take it from Harriet she once felt.

Well, as it happened, Harriet had just given it to her.

"It is pulling at your mind," a voice called out from above. Kenneth the oriole was perched on a standing stone. "Resist."

Georgia hopped over to the well cap. It was a massive piece of granite. She slammed the ring down on it, and tried to crack the jewel. Nothing happened. She tried grinding it into the well cap, but all it did was scratch the granite. The ring itself remained undamaged.

Kenneth landed on her shoulder. "You cannot break it that way. No one can. Only magic can break magic."

The ring began to burn her hand. If she put it on her finger, she knew the pain would stop. She also had another realization: her magic sword could have broken the ring. The thought nearly brought her to tears.

"Put the ring on, Georgia," the creature in the well whispered in a hoarse voice. "I will make you a queen of the world. You will have everything you ever wanted."

"Don't listen to him!" Kenneth chirped.

Faintly, Georgia heard whistles. Earlsmen's whistles in the woods nearby. "I already have everything I ever wanted," she whispered. She looked down at the ring. "How do I destroy this thing without magic?"

"You cannot destroy it," the creature hissed. "As long as it is in the world, I will return. Even now, my power grows. This form I wear may still be weak, but my power is everywhere. I am in the soil, calling to the little things that burrow and dig. I will fill them with my malice, my hate, and my mission to corrupt all. They grow in the dark places, to emerge in the world and do my bidding. Even as they do, I feed on the weak of mind and take them. Petty grievances, rivalries, and mundane thoughts of regret. All of these are my province. All will fall to me, their faces sinking even as their hunger for flesh grows. I will corrupt all."

"Frog zombies," Georgia whispered, realizing what he meant. Lord Redstone spoke of them in his journal. She looked at the ring. It was glowing blood red. She had to do something, but the strength in her hands was not enough to crush it. Without the sword, she would fail.

"Yes, you will fail," the creature whispered.

"I do not know what to do," Georgia admitted. She looked at Kenneth, hoping the bird had a suggestion.

"Well, I have an idea," Harriet said in a weak voice, sitting up slowly. She pointed at the creature pulling itself out of the well. "Get rid of that thing."

"Right," Georgia said. "One problem at a time." She hopped over and kicked the creature in the face, knocking it back into the black tadpole pool.

"Close the well cap," Kenneth chirped. "The cap will seal it in."

It was something at least. Georgia stepped over to the well cap. With her remaining strength, she pushed. For a moment, nothing happened. It was a gigantic stone stuck to the ground surrounded by murky water.

"Push harder," Kenneth said. "Push with your legs."

"I… am… pushing… harder." She could feel the seams on her dress tearing. The well cap budged ever so slightly. On the other side, she could see the creature… *Il Malvagio* or the Shadow Man or whatever… poking its head back up out of the murky water.

"Stop," the creature hissed. "I will give you power, female. I will give you immortality."

"It is lying to you," Kenneth said.

"Do you think so?" Georgia asked dryly, putting her back into it again. She pushed so hard it felt like she might snap in half. The well cap came loose from the ground. Gasping, she gave it another great shove and it slid over the well. The creature was caught underneath and wailed for a moment before the cap settled. The wail became muffled, and then there was silence. Georgia fell backward into a pile of mud and little black frogs.

"Good work. Now go destroy the ring. The longer it is here, the worse it all gets," Kenneth chirped, and promptly flew away.

Georgia sat for a moment in the muck while disgusting little frogs crawled all over. Nearby, Harriet moaned softly and held her belly. "Oh, Georgia, the baby will be here soon."

"All right, I am coming," Georgia whispered, getting up. "Are you delivering now?"

"I think I might have some time. Perhaps we could get somewhere more comfortable?"

"Excellent idea," Georgia answered. She looked down at the ring in her hand. What to do with this thing. On the bright side, it stopped burning her the instant the well cap was in place and *Il Malvagio* was trapped under it. That prompted her to wonder how long he would be stuck though.

Once again, she heard the Earlsmen's whistles. They were getting closer. On impulse, she pulled her wig off and wrapped it around the ring. Then she tied the bundle to one of the strips of her ruined skirt like a sort of hanging satchel. Not ideal, but it would allow her to have her hands free to help Harriet up. As she helped her to her feet, Georgia felt the growing rumble of galloping horses.

Luke and his two men appeared on horseback at the edge of the amphitheater. Bea was riding sidesaddle with one of the Earlsmen. "Georgia!" Luke cried, leaping off his mount and running to her rather heroically. "Oh, thank heavens you live." Before she could speak, he hugged her.

In most situations, this would be a breach of protocol, but given the situation she was quick to forgive.

"Oh, Luke, I am a mess," Georgia said when he stepped back. She looked down at her torn-up gown covered in black mud and frogs. Luke's green livery was filthy. "And now I have made you a mess."

"It does not matter," he answered. "You look like you to me, whether dirty or clean. I do not mind."

"I knew you could do it." Bea ran over and hugged Georgia too. Now she was a mess. "We had better get Harriet somewhere warm and comfortable," Bea said.

"I think I can travel a short way," Harriet said. "Even so, this baby will be here soon."

"We will take her home," Luke said.

"No, take her to Croft House," Georgia answered. "Who knows what mischief awaits at her home. Two of Mr. Blackheart's valets got away."

As Luke helped Harriet onto his horse, Georgia double-checked her wig-satchel. The ring was safely stowed. Once she was satisfied, she allowed Iggy to help her onto his horse, and away they went.

\*\*\*

Harriet was panting as they got her into bed. The ride back to Georgia's guest house took only minutes, but it was touch-and-go the whole way. Luke carried Harriet inside. "We will have to deliver the child," Bea said to Georgia as they followed him in.

"Have you... have you ever done that?" Georgia asked.

"As a matter of fact, I have not, but Mrs. Macklin mentioned having grown children. I will enlist her."

Georgia nodded. "What can I do to assist?"

"Get the staff to boil water, fetch towels, and make her comfortable," Bea said with care. "I will find Mrs. Macklin."

"This has been some week," Young Mr. Darkleaf announced, bringing towels.

"I wonder what Lord Wyclef will say when he hears about it," Georgia answered.

"I imagine he will be as amazed as the rest of us, my lady," Darkleaf said with a grin.

"I will put in a good word for you all," Georgia said. Once Harriet was in bed, Georgia went to her suite to change clothes. When she saw herself in the mirror, she nearly jumped. The dress was utterly ruined. Best to toss it in the bin, as it was ripped all about and covered in black mud. Carefully, she pulled the ring from her makeshift wig-satchel. On the ride, an idea formed in her mind. She could take it back to the capital and give it to the Order of the Blue.

"Oh, you look a fright," Bea said from behind. Georgia nearly jumped out of her skin. She was either very tired, or so focused on the ring she did not even hear Bea come up. "What is that? Oh, Harriet's heirloom ring."

"Be careful," Georgia said. "It is... how do I say this?"

"A magic ring," Bea said. "It is just what Lord Redstone said it was: an artifact of some hidden power. He said so in the journal." She gazed at it intently without blinking.

"I have to take it to Mr. Blue," Georgia said. "Bea, I think this ring has the power to seize someone's mind if they look at it for too long."

"Oh, Georgia, I completely agree. I just had the strangest urge to snatch it out of your hand and run away. You do realize this is the third evil magic ring you have encountered in less than a year. I hope we are not seeing a trend. Give me a moment," Bea said, looking away. She went out the door but returned quickly with a finely embroidered stocking purse. "My sister Bonnie made this for me. It is rather plain, but remarkably useful. You can put all sorts of things in it: handkerchief, a small mirror, perhaps a snuffbox if that is your thing... and a magic heirloom ring. Put it in there. The purse ties around your waist like a belt. Keep it on your person at all times until we get back."

"Right. Good idea." She looked critically at the stocking purse. It was rather plain and black, but that meant it might go unnoticed. She wrapped the heirloom ring in a handkerchief and slipped it into the purse. There was a brass loop she could slide down to secure everything in one spot. There were also buckles on each end, designed to fasten it to one's waist. Georgia had seen other ladies on the street wearing stocking purses, but never understood the fad. The things looked bulky and odd.

"First, let me help you with that dress," Bea said. "Get cleaned up, and tell no one you have it on you until we are home."

"It is not reasonable for me to have that purse on me at all times," Georgia answered. "I literally change clothes three times a day."

"Well, when you do that, just keep the purse in eyesight and keep the contents of it secret. We will be leaving as soon as Harriet is safe, so it should not be long before you can deliver the ring to Mr. Blue and his friends," Bea said thoughtfully.

"Sound advice," Georgia said as they wiggled her out of her dress. She looked at Bea. "Will you be alright? I mean, you know where it is hidden."

Bea shrugged and smiled, but kept her eyes away from the purse. "I am fine. Something tells me that the ring is nothing but trouble. The sooner you are rid of it, the better. How are you feeling now? You had quite the moment of doubt without your magic sword, but you still won the day."

"I suppose we all have moments of doubt," Georgia answered. "Sorry if I frightened you, dear friend."

Bea grinned. "Toss that gown. It is ruined. You did not frighten me. Those men trying to murder Harriet were frightening. You were a human."

There was a knock on the door. "Who is it?" Georgia called out.

One of the maids poked her head in. "My lady, she is having contractions. Mrs. Macklin said to tell you they are only minutes apart." Harriet was getting close to delivering.

"I should go," Bea said, hurrying to the door.

"I will join you as soon as I get cleaned up." Georgia gave herself another look in the mirror. She was filthy. "Sometime tomorrow, I suspect." She grabbed the purse, went down the side stairs to the basement and found a tub. She could hear Harriet wailing upstairs, even this far below, but allowed herself a moment in the steamy hot water.

When she was clean, Georgia hurried upstairs purse in hand. This was going to get annoying before long, but it had to be done. Along the way, she encountered another maid. "Duchess, Sir Lucas is asking for you."

"Thank you," Georgia said. "I will meet him in the solarium as soon as I am dressed. Find Kat or Angela... or both. Send them to me."

"Yes, my lady."

"Unless they are helping Mrs. Macklin with the birth. If they are, come back yourself."

"Yes, my lady."

Kat and Angela arrived a moment later. Angela combed her hair back and tied it efficiently. It was not her usual spectacular look but would have to do. She slipped into a fine blue wool gown, which Kat buttoned up the back. Once the outfit was assembled, she slipped on her new stocking purse, and made her way down to the solarium.

Luke was waiting with a cup of tea and a plate of biscuits, clad once again in clean livery. When she entered, he stood and bowed.

"Hello, Luke," she said.

"You are looking much refreshed, Georgia," he answered with a blush.

Outside, the rain was pouring. The solarium was a perfect spot for observing the garden without getting involved in it. Georgia settled in with a cup of tea. "You wanted to see me, Luke?"

Luke nodded. "We went to the archeological site with the journal as our guide, you may recall. In hole #7 we found a body."

"Oh dear. Was it Lord Redstone?"

Luke nodded again. "I believe it was, yes. A middle-aged man of means. He was stabbed and bled out. He was also missing one shoe. I looked on the inside of the other shoe and found it was stamped with the name 'Singuile'. That said, there was found no proof of identity, but Iggy noted the indent of a signet ring on his hand. The ring was gone, of course. But there was evidence he wore it all the time."

"I think you found the remains of Lord Redstone. What did you do with the body?"

"We took him to the Constables." Luke said before sipping his tea. "I suggested they summon Mrs. Crauford to see if she could identify the body. As we were leaving, we ran into Bea and she led us back to you."

"Very good," Georgia said. "I suppose that is that, for now. Tomorrow, I will check in with Constable Jenkins and see if he has any news."

Luke smiled. "I will join you." He bowed again.

"Then it is settled." Georgia smiled. She stood to go upstairs when something caught her eye. Out in the garden, a lone woman stood with her back to them. She wore a tattered green dress, and her hair was in disarray. Despite that, Georgia recognized her. "Octavia Potter?"

"She will catch a fever in that downpour," Luke said. "I will fetch her." He stepped out through the solarium door and hurried over. Octavia turned to stare at him, but something was wrong with her face. Her eyes bulged out of her head, her skin was like loose leather, and her mouth drooped. She let loose a low gurgle. Octavia snarled and rushed at him. Luke fell backward. They hit the ground together and rolled around in the wet grass. All the while, she tried to bite his face but he barely held her at bay.

Georgia rushed out to help. "Stop," she cried. "Octavia, what has come over you?"

Octavia rushed at her. Georgia was quick enough to dodge, but Octavia was on her again in a flash. Slobbering and panting, she jumped on Georgia's back and tried to chew through her shoulder. Georgia threw her off. Octavia slammed into the ground with enough force to paralyze a grown man, but it hardly affected her. She was on her feet again. Luke drew his epee blade and stood between Georgia and the danger. Octavia lunged again. He swiveled and stabbed her in the shoulder with a rather precise move.

Octavia did not even wince.

Georgia could not help herself. She gasped. Not so much in fear as surprise. Surprised at what, though? Whether it was Luke's excellent swordsmanship or Octavia she did not know. She did know one thing, though: the blade was not slowing Octavia down. The woman growled at Luke, sounding very much like a wild animal. He dodged to one side and brought his blade around again. "Miss Octavia, you must stop," he said.

Octavia did not stop. Black blood pumped from her shoulder, but she crouched and ran forward on all fours. As she moved, Georgia noticed something else: her blood was writhing… with tadpoles. "Octavia?" The woman looked at her without recognition. As she scampered forward, the edges of the yard grew dark. The shadows were returning, and Georgia was still without her sword. Octavia's eyes were dead. On her hip, the ring began to pulse again. Dread began to consume her.

Luke stabbed Octavia. Howling, she tore at him with her fingers, which were much like talons. They tore his vest open. Fortunately, he was agile and stepped back. Octavia followed him, frantically trying to bite his face. Luke brought his elegant blade around and stabbed her in the arm and then the other shoulder, but it merely enraged her. Black blood spurted from her wounds, and Georgia's stomach nearly turned. Octavia was covered in slimy black tadpoles. They were coming from her veins. Luke stepped to one side, and expertly jabbed her in the face. He rammed the sword through her brain. She croaked, both literally and figuratively, on the spot. Georgia watched her slump to the ground. Slowly, she looked up.

"I am so sorry," Luke said, drawing his blade free and wiping the black blood on the grass. "She was going to kill you."

Georgia stared at Octavia. Her face was flowing black blood. She was not mistaken: the blood was writhing with tadpoles. "She was already dead," she whispered. "Look at the blood."

Luke leaned in to inspect. He shuddered and gulped. "What kind of devilry is this?"

"*Il Malvagio*, I suspect. I do not understand Octavia's connection to him, though." Georgia shook her head. She could feel the ring pulsing.

"The creature in the amphitheater?" Luke asked. "On the ride back, Harriet said you trapped it in the well."

Georgia gazed at poor Octavia's body. Her face was sinking into her skull. All the while, the ring continued to make its presence known, physically pulsing. "This is all tied together, but some of the strings are hidden," she whispered.

"Yet another mystery. Or simply dark magic," Luke whispered. "Let me take you back inside. My men will clean this up."

It was then they heard a scream on the other side of the garden wall. "What now?" Georgia asked. They hurried to the gate. Outside, one of the footmen was being dragged to the ground by two men in gardener's clothes. The gardeners' faces were sagging with bulging eyes, just like Octavia. Before Georgia could get the gate open, they tore the footman in half between them, not unlike toddlers playing tug-of-war. Georgia and Luke both gasped, drawing their attention. The gardeners leapt to their feet and charged.

Luke pulled her away from the gate. "Run," he hissed.

"Run?"

"You saw how powerful Octavia was on her own," he said, pushing her back toward the house. "Now there are two of them." The gardeners smashed through the gate. They could have opened it but were beyond thought. Upon breaking through, they howled with glee and gave chase. Georgia and Luke ran inside and slammed shut the solarium door.

"This will not keep them out," Georgia said, regaining her senses. "Follow me." She ran down the hall with Luke right behind. She heard the solarium door shatter. They passed one of the maids. It was Angela, one of the girls who helped Georgia get dressed in Millie's absence.

"Hide," Luke said to the girl. "Get out of sight. Do it now."

"Angela, hide yourself," Georgia shouted. She found the study at the end of the hall and threw open the door. Wyclef's family sword, *Winterthorn*, was still there, mounted on its little pedestal. She snatched it up. Behind her came a terrible scream that abruptly stopped. Luke was no longer beside her. She ran back into the hall to find him facing the two gardeners. At his feet was poor Angela. She was dead. Georgia stared at the girl's face, which was torn to bloody ribbons.

Luke jabbed at the two gardeners. "Stay back," he said through gritted teeth. She could see he had already stabbed both once, as blackish blood and tadpoles sprayed from their hearts.

Georgia swallowed hard. Magic sword or not, she had to do something. With an expert swing, she brought *Winterthorn* around and cleanly severed the head of the first gardener. In a spray of black blood, he toppled. The second gardener spun on her, but found himself skewered by Luke's epee, right through the temple. He dropped to the ground.

"The head is the best place to attack," Georgia whispered. She stared at the gardeners. Both were employees of this very house. She had seen them around the grounds. Now they were dead.

"What is going on?" Luke asked, stricken. "Three people taken with this malady. Did you see their faces? Georgia, they look like… like frogs."

At the end of the corridor, another maid entered carrying a stack of towels. When she saw them standing over the bodies, she screamed. Georgia snapped to attention. "Get the other staff members," she barked at the girl. "Tell everyone to stay inside. The solarium door is broken, so we will need to find a way to close that room off." Outside, she could faintly hear more people screaming.

The screaming stopped.

Georgia sat down next to the body of Angela. "I am so sorry," she whispered.

Luke went into the solarium but returned a moment later. "This house was not made to be fortified. All of the windows are wide and near the ground. Perhaps we can seal off the second floor for a time, but we have to get out of here," he whispered. "Something has happened in this village. I cannot see past the trees in the lane but could hear people running up the road. I sounded like a lot of people."

"Get out of here?" Georgia asked. "You mean leave town?"

"I would have thought this house safe enough tucked away on the side street and hidden by trees, but I would be wrong. Those men found their way in immediately. We should gather everyone and go," Luke said. "Although, how to do that? There are at least two dozen staff here, and that is not even counting the guests."

"Not to mention a woman giving birth upstairs," Georgia added. "I cannot imagine Harriet hopping into a carriage after what she just went through."

Luke stared at the dead gardeners and maid, just ten feet down the hall. "How do you think it works?"

"How does what work?"

"The malady. Forgive me, sometimes my mind jumps around. I remember a story I once read. It was about zombies and monsters. The zombies would bite their victims, and then the victims would become zombies." Luke rubbed his eyes, suddenly looking quite tired. "And then the new zombies would bite new victims… and so on."

"Right. That sounds familiar," Georgia muttered. She looked at Luke. "Mr. Blackheart said the curse of *Il Malvagio* would cover the world… or maybe the mud creature in the well said it."

"Forgive me, I was not there when you talked to the, um, the mud creature. I was just looking at those men. They bit that woman, but she did not change into what they are."

"Her name was Angela," Georgia whispered. "The men were gardeners here. I do not know the answer. We are speculating."

"Right," Luke said. "I jumped ahead again. Miss Beatrice would not approve."

Georgia nodded and got up. "That happens. Perhaps we can see the village better from the second floor. Either way, we need to talk to the others." Luke followed her upstairs. They found Mrs. Macklin in the hall with a handful of hot towels.

"How goes the labor?" Georgia asked.

"The child will be born at any moment," Mrs. Macklin said with a rare smile. "Mrs. Blackheart is a strong one, my lady." Georgia nodded, letting the woman get back into Harriet's room.

"I will look for a window with a view. On the south side of the house, we should be able to see the road to the resort from there," Luke said.

"Agreed. I will check in and see how things are going here," Georgia answered. She entered the bedroom to find Harriet panting and clutching at the sheets, her legs up to deliver. To one side, Bea was dabbing at her head and cheering her on. Mrs. Macklin set down the towels for later. To one side, two of the maids were preparing a spot for the child to rest when it arrived. Another maid, Janet, was staring out the window. When she saw Georgia, she gestured. Georgia went over to look where the maid pointed. The window looked out over the hedge at the edge of the property. Georgia could see the street leading to the resort. People were running everywhere. She watched as a man leapt onto someone's back. His face was sunken with his eyes bulging... just like Octavia and the gardeners. He was not alone. Two more men were chasing a woman down the street.

"Frog zombies," Janet breathed.

"I beg your pardon?" Georgia asked. Lord Redstone had mentioned frog zombies in his journal.

"They're back," Janet answered.

"Have you seen this happen before?" Georgia asked.

"They've been here ever since I was a little girl, but never so many at once. We used to see people change like this once in a great while. My aunt says it all started when they found those old ruins outside town." The maid answered. "When they dug it up, they let out the curse."

"How long ago was this?" Georgia asked.

Janet rubbed her eyes. "I was about six years old. So, I guess it was almost twenty years ago, my lady."

"And you have continued to live here despite it?"

Janet shrugged. "Home is home. This is where my family is."

Georgia was about to say more, but there was a commotion in the room. "One more push, Harriet," Bea said, stepping around the bed. Harriet huffed and made a low growl… and pushed. An instant later, the wail of a newborn child entered the world. Harriet wept as Bea cut the cord. She brought the baby over to the basin for a quick rinse in warm water, then back to Harriet.

"It is a girl," Bea said.

"Oh, she's beautiful," Harriet whispered. "She looks like her father. How unfortunate."

"What are you going to name her?"

Harriet looked up. "I think I shall name her Glenda."

"Lovely."

Georgia looked at the maid who was still gazing out the window. "You are very calm right now."

The maid looked at her. "My lady, this is Dead Mourner's Grove. You never know what will happen here."

"I wish I had known that before I came," Georgia said.

The maid grinned. "That is how we get you, my lady."

Georgia was about to answer but had to laugh. Behind them, Bea came over. "What is going on now? Georgia, why are you holding a sword?" she asked. "What is happening outside?" In the distance, Georgia could see smoke rising from a burning house. People were screaming.

"Frog zombies, and this time it is no joke," Georgia answered. "I think we should leave town before things get worse. We should take as many of the residents of Dead Mourner's Grove with us as possible."

Bea stared out the window, blanching, as the faint sound of gunfire reached them. She looked around. "Harriet is in no condition to travel, and the village is in chaos. We certainly cannot go down each street gathering people to flee."

"Very well, but we must leave before it is too late," Georgia answered. The idea of abandoning everyone out there was upsetting, but Bea was right. She thought about the Greenstreets possibly trapped in their adorable garden, but could see through the window several fires raging in that direction already. The junipers were burning. The thought of them made her eyes sting with tears.

Bea stood next to her, gazing out the window. "Amazing how quick the fire spreads," Bea whispered. "You would think with all this rain, it would be slower."

"My lady, we have a coach. It has cushions, but we can take more from the house to make sure that Mrs. Blackheart is comfortable," Janet offered.

\*\*\*

Outside the ground trembled. Smoke drifted through the front garden. The coach rolled down the driveway as the footman pulled the gate open. Inside were Harriet, the baby, Bea, Nora, Nelda, and Mrs. Macklin. Behind them, most of the staff was on foot, flanked on each side by an Earlsman on horseback. Behind them was a cart loaded with food and water. Luke took up the rear. Georgia sat in the front seat with Mr. Darkleaf driving, sword in her hand. The trouble started the moment they crossed on to North Street. A man with a musket pistol ran past, firing at something or someone in the distance. He was screaming. The horse nearly bolted, but Mr. Darkleaf kept it under control.

"Which road shall we follow?" he asked. "South to Grandhall, east to the capital, or west into the backcountry."

Georgia really wanted to go to the capital but had a feeling they would be lost in those woods. She was about to answer when Kenneth the Oriole appeared, flitting overhead. "Goldenheart!" the bird cried. "Follow Kenneth!"

"Follow that bird," Georgia ordered. "He is headed west, it would appear." Behind them, a commotion arose as two constables appeared on horseback. They rode past in a rush and turned down another lane toward a house on fire. Ahead, they spotted a small family huddled in the bushes. "Gather them. Leave no one behind." One of the maids hurried over to help. A moment later, they were on the road again.

Kenneth led them down the west road for almost a mile, where they passed out of the smoke haze to fresh air. It was then they encountered a frog zombie. A tragic young man with a half-melted face burst out from behind a large rock. One of the maids gasped and cried, "That's Bobby Redburrows!"

Georgia leaned out of her seat and kicked him square in the chest. He flew back into the foliage and did not return. She hoped he was not dead but wasted no time to find out. "Keep going." They rolled by without further interruption. Half a mile further they found Kenneth perched on a tree limb.

"Take that path," the bird instructed. Next to him was the sign denoting Lord Redstone's archeological dig site. "Go to the cave."

"You can hear the bird talking, right?" Georgia asked Mr. Darkleaf.

"The bird... talking?" he asked. "I, uh, no I cannot, my lady. I thought we were simply following it because, um, I don't know why." Bea could hear Kenneth talking, but Mr. Darkleaf could not? That was a mystery for another day.

"We are." Georgia smiled. "Everybody out. We are going to hide in a cave by the lake."

"Is this a good idea?" Bea asked. "What if the cave is full of frogs?"

"Let us keep our eyes open," Georgia answered. "I would have kept going down the road, but Kenneth says to go to the cave instead. He has not led us wrong yet."

Bea nodded. "Follow the magic bird. Got it." She and the maids helped Harriet out of the coach, grabbing loose cushions to take with them.

Georgia scouted ahead. She counted her blessings as the dig site was empty. Ahead was the line of holes. She counted fourteen before finding her way to the crypt with the secret door. Behind her, the staff followed, helping Harriet and the baby. Behind them, Bea trailed with Nora, Nelda, Luke and the Earlsmen. Nelda was still weak and stumbled on the stairs going down. Nora pulled her to her feet. They crossed through the secret door easily enough, and down the long corridor to arrive at the cavern. To Georgia's surprise, a barge was waiting on the underground shore.

She was not half as surprised as the barge crew and captain.

"Who the devil are all of you?" a man cried from the deck.

"I am Duchess Georgia Goldenheart," she answered. "Who might you be?"

"Captain Orsal Smith," an overweight fellow dressed as a boat captain answered. He bowed from the deck.

"How did a barge get in here?" Bea asked, looking around. "The cave must have another entrance."

"It does," Luke said, pointing. "They came in through that tunnel."

"Greetings, Captain. I fear we have an emergency," Georgia informed him. "The land above us is crawling with frog zombies and other madness. May we use your vessel to escape?"

"Frog zombies?"

"People driven to madness by a magical malady," Georgia explained.

"When did this start?" the captain asked.

"I think they began to change this afternoon," Bea said. "There was a dark ritual and some other mischief. Captain, let us come aboard."

"We do not carry passengers," the captain answered. "Only cargo."

"Surely, you have seen what is happening outside," Luke called out to the captain. "We are all in peril."

"We have been down here all night, Earlsman," the captain called back. "I have seen no… um, frog zombies of any kind."

"I think they are smugglers," Nora whispered to Georgia.

"Do you really?" Georgia answered dryly.

It was then a commotion arose from the back of the room. Georgia spun to find a dozen frog-zombie infected people bursting in. "We were followed," Luke cried out. "Everyone, get back." The staff pulled Harriet closer to the boat, followed by Bea. Georgia joined Luke and the Earlsmen at the entrance, pressing the frog zombies back. Georgia spun and severed the head of a man dressed as a tailor. His face was entirely deformed.

Luke and his men pressed forward with their epee blades, stabbing at various frog zombies with varying accuracy. "We will not last long at this rate," Luke observed.

Georgia called back to the captain. "Name a price for passage, Captain. As you can see, we are not safe."

"Come aboard," the captain called back. "We will discuss it on the lake."

"You heard the man," Georgia said. "Everybody on board." With that, she spun back to help the Earlsmen.

"Georgia, you must go," Luke cried. "Get out of here."

"Absolutely not," she answered, whirling around to decapitate two frog zombies at once before they could squeeze to attack the people getting on the boat. One of the frog zombies was Tula Chambers, a former schoolmate. Back in school, Tula used to get the hiccups whenever she drank milk. The memory popped into Georgia's head, and she almost cried. There was no time to mourn, though. Another frog zombie rushed her. Georgia stepped to one side, tripped him, and cut off the top of his skull in a spray of gore and tadpoles. Luke and his men skewered the last few frog zombies through their heads, and stepped back.

"I hear more coming from up the passage," Luke whispered.

"Let's get on the boat while we still have time," Georgia answered. They sprinted back and up the gangplank to find everyone else aboard. Georgia turned to see the cavern filling with frog zombies. How had they found them? Half the village seemed to be infected and following.

Then she realized: it was the ring. It was calling to the frog zombies.

"This is madness," Captain Smith muttered. His men pulled the plank up before the frog zombies could get onboard. "Forgive me, my lady. I am wary by nature, and we have been moored here since yesterday." Wary by nature. In other words, he was definitely a smuggler.

"You were awaiting a delivery?" Georgia asked.

"The less said about it the better, don't you think?" Captain Smith responded.

The barge pushed off. The crew brought out long oars and navigated into the darkness. For a time, they floated in almost no light. "It is a curving tunnel to the lake. Apparently, there are a few of these places around these parts. I read about it once," Luke whispered. "I wonder if it is natural or man-made." Georgia sat down next to Bea and waited. After a time, light glimmered ahead. They passed through an opening at the base of a bluff and floated onto the lake. Once it looked like they were safe, Georgia negotiated a generous price for passage to the capital, no questions asked. "We will cross over to the river, which will take us to the city," Captain Smith said. "It should take another day or so to get there."

\*\*\*

"And that, as they say, is that." Georgia sipped her wine.

"Amazing," Mr. Blue said. "What an escape. I wonder what will become of Dead Mourner's Grove."

"Most of it burned," Georgia said. "We could see that from the boat."

"I think the Witch of Findor must intercede," Lady Clara whispered. "If only we knew where she was. I fear the worst."

"What happens if she cannot assist?" Georgia asked.

"The Crown has already cordoned off the area," Mr. Blue answered. "It is some sort of zombie outbreak, as you guessed. From what I have heard, there were only a few survivors. You escaped with the lucky ones. Everyone else is dead."

"And the ring?" Georgia asked. Upon return, she had delivered it to the Order of the Blue immediately, thereby freeing herself of its evil.

"The Order sealed it in concrete at a hidden location. Once that was done, several magical wards were put in place. We could not devise a way to destroy it," Mr. Blue said, "so we did what we could. Hopefully, the power of the ring will be diminished, if not blocked altogether."

"I had a thought that I could destroy it with my magic sword," Georgia offered.

"It is possible the sword could do that," Lady Clara said, "but I suspect the sword would also have been destroyed. I think you chose the better course of action, Georgia."

"Oh, I meant to mention this. William told us that Constable Jenkins managed to save a few people," Bea offered. "Mrs. Crauford and her maid got out, along with the Greenstreets. Lady Rebecca happened to leave before the disaster, so she is safe. Alas, we lost several old classmates in the outbreak."

"We returned to find Millie and Mr. Reardon stuck at the house. The roads were washed out, so I need not have worried. Still, it was a great relief."

"No doubt," Lady Clara said. She sipped her wine and gazed at Georgia and Bea with fondness. "I am so relieved you both made it back in one piece."

They were all enjoying the evening, for once. The crisp air of autumn encircled the city, but there was still time for a few dinner parties before the cold snap came. After the adventure in Dead Mourner's Grove, Georgia was glad to be back to her old routine, albeit with a few new friends.

"Did you ever learn the truth about Mr. Brown?" Mr. Blue asked. "Was he a wizard?"

"I suspect he was some kind of magic person," Bea admitted. "He had a talking bird, after all. Oh, I hope Kenneth is okay."

"Birds have a way of flying away from danger," Clara said. "I think if you ever return to that region, Kenneth will turn up too."

"I hope so," Georgia said.

"And what of Sir Lucas?" Clara whispered, leaning in. Luke was, of course, right down the table from them, enjoying cake with Harriet. Next to Harriet was a crib with baby Glenda sleeping peacefully.

"That appears to be progressing," Georgia admitted. "I find him pleasant enough." More than pleasant enough, but time would tell. In the meantime, Georgia was fond of him, and the idea of other suitors was becoming less appealing. On the other hand, it had only been days since they escaped Dead Mourner's Grove.

"Excellent," Mr. Blue said. "One more question: was Lord Redstone the body in the ruins?"

"Yes," Bea said, shaking her head. "Mrs. Crauford identified him at the constabulary, just before the frog zombies arrived. Constable Jenkins said they apprehended one of the escaped cultists. They were all posing as valets and staff for Mr. Blackheart. The fellow filled in a few gaps." She took a sip of wine.

"All right," Mr. Blue said, blinking. He looked at Bea to continue and smiled. "So, what did he say?"

"Georgia, you are the detective here," Bea said. "I keep stepping on your skirt with the story."

"Bea, you are just as much a detective as me," Georgia countered.

"Oh, good heavens, one of you please tell us what happened," Lady Clara said, laughing.

"Mr. Blackheart was an evil cultist and a dark sorcerer. He needed a magical ring and the last heir of the ancient Gildernesse royal line for a ritual of power, and tracked down Harriet," Bea explained. "He knew about the coming Century of Evil prophecy and was convinced he could benefit from it. *Il Malvagio* is apparently some sort of evil monster from myth, well actually from ancient history. It was trapped in the ground, just like the shadow spiders you fought here in the city. The cultist… er, his valet… told Jenkins about it."

"Terrible," Mr. Blue whispered.

"Perfectly horrible, yes," Bea agreed. "That last bit about being trapped underground does raise a few questions."

"Ask them," Clara urged.

"Well, if the spiders and other creatures are simply underground… what is to keep them from digging up to the surface and eating all of us in our sleep?" Bea asked.

"There are several reasons they do not simply appear," Clara answered. "First, each of the Three Realms has a Witch who would sense something and try to stop them.

One reason I and my sisters exist is to maintain the natural order. We also have Georgia for that, and the wizards."

"And there are other good powers in the world. Evil does not simply crawl up on a whim," Mr. Blue added.

"So, they are just underground and that is that?" Bea asked, not quite ready to let it go.

Lady Clara shrugged. "In the dark places beneath the earth, there are other worlds. Perilous lands known only to a few, but they are not always able to find our world."

"Vague and menacing, but good to know. Blackheart needed a Gildernesse magical artifact if he was to use his evil spell to bring *Il Malvagio* into our world," Georgia said. "He was searching in museums, talking to everyone from scholars to smugglers and pirates… you get the idea. Along the way, he heard about Lord Redstone and the ring, and how the archeologist took up residence in Dead Mourner's Grove. As it happens, the village is located on the site of the ancient amphitheater with the well. Apparently, it was some sort of old-timey blood sacrifice spot."

"It was a coincidence," Bea said.

"There's no such thing," said Mr. Blue, Georgia, and Lady Clara in unison. Bea chuckled.

Georgia continued, "Anyway, the academics all thought Redstone was a joke, but Blackheart knew better. He bought a lovely mansion in Dead Mourner's Grove, arranged an acquaintance with Lord Redstone on one of the occasions he was in town, and eventually tracked down Harriet. All of this was done timed to the coming of the new millennia. Lord Redstone, despondent about the ring appearing useless, was eventually convinced to sell it to Blackheart."

"And that is when it all hit the dirt," Bea said. "Pardon my crude language."

"Do you want to tell the story, Bea?"

"Oh no, of course not. I have interrupted enough. Go on."

Georgia turned back to the others. "On the night of the sale, just after dinner with Harriet and the rutabagas, Lord Redstone guessed that Mr. Blackheart was not the friend he appeared to be. He had a revelation of some kind. In the library, he tried to cancel the sale. The valet said that he saw the ring in Blackheart's hand and demanded he return it. He even offered to buy it back at double the price. Mr. Blackheart stabbed him and left him for dead, ordering one of his other valets to clean up the mess. The valet in question was working on that very project when he was spotted by Mrs. Greenstreet. She thought he was one rider on two horses but failed to notice the body draped over the second horse. She yelled at him as he passed, saying she had seen his mischief. The cultist or valet or whatever he was, dumped Lord Redstone at the dig site and went back to Mr. Blackheart." She looked at Bea. "This is the perfect moment to interrupt again."

"Oh no, do not mind me," Bea countered. She looked at Mr. Blue and Lady Clara. "That said, the next part is delicious."

Georgia laughed. "The cultist who was supposed to clean up the blood was afraid to go back to Redstone House. He was certain the constables were waiting for him, so he lied to Mr. Blackheart and said he finished cleaning up. Then, weeks passed and there were no constables showing up at Blackheart's door. The fellow thought he was in the clear."

"And that is how you know he was only a dirty cultist, and not a proper valet," Bea inserted. "A real valet would have finished the job."

# CHAPTER 14

# WRAP-UP.

*THE WEDDING OF THE YEAR!*
*Youthful Ladies Journal Exclusive*
*Written by Mrs. Smythe-Turner*

If you thought this year couldn't get any more exciting, I would say you were wrong. Between shadow spider monsters in the city and frog zombies in the countryside, we have had quite a season. How fortunate it comes to an end, just in time for a lovely winter break.

But first, let's take a moment to celebrate the newest marriage of note in the Three Realms. After her harrowing ordeal in the frog zombie infestation of Dead Mourner's Grove, Miss Beatrice Irvingdale and her handsome suitor, Lord William Reade, Viscount of Simsley, were wed in a surprise ceremony. The Viscount, after hearing of his fiancé's near brush with the eternal, decided to forego the usual Volusian tradition of waiting at least a year to tie the knot. Instead, he and Miss Beatrice moved the ceremony up with alarming speed.

Despite the sudden date, the wedding was a lavish affair. Perhaps not as lavish as one would expect from ones of such a high station. But it was wonderful, nonetheless. The Queen herself was guest of honor. She wore a gown of silver and green and was the envy of all who saw her. Other prominent guests included Duchess Goldenheart, who was also Chief Bridesmaid. Other notables included the Dowager Countess of Vexbury, Lady Osibeth Crighton, her nephew Sir Alfie Crighton, and Sir Lucas Greenheart, a son of the Earl of Grandhall. They were accompanied by the most important Dowager Countess of Nisbitt, Lady Hermione.

Lady Hermione is a great aunt of both Miss Beatrice and her beau, Lord William. As per their marriage pact, she transferred to them her holding of the title to the House of Dale. From here forward, Lady Beatrice, whose station is raised, is the heir-presumptive of Dale, and a countess in her own right. She and Lord William took the new noble name of Dale as part of their vows. This is most appropriate, as the Irvingdales are a secondary house of Dale. Lord William's mother was Amelia Rosedale, who hails from another secondary house of that great family.

There were more guests at the ceremony, including the wizard Mr. Blue, and the Witch of Volusia, Lady Clara Gaye. Lady Beatrice's mother, Lady Breanna Irvingdale, was in attendance along with the bride's sisters, Bernadette, Bridgett, Bonnie, and Barbara who served as bridesmaids. Lord John Wickham, 9th Baronet of Irvingdale gave the bride away.

The ceremony took place at Cadwin House in the capital.

***

*Epigraph:*
*The Tale of the Frog Prince*

Once upon a time, there was a prince among frogs. He lived in a lovely bog surrounded by clingy mist and tall reeds. His friends included the Turtle and a fun Sparrow who flew high above. The prince was well-fed in that bog. He ate spicy mosquitoes, savory midges, and salty water bugs every day and was always happy.

Until one day a nasty dragonfly found her way into the bog. The prince was quickly stymied, as the dragonfly dived and flitted. She ate all the midges before he could, jumped on the water bugs, and even snapped up his beloved mosquitoes. It seemed as if he could find no food that she could not get to first.

Finally, out of frustration, he crept up on the dragonfly as she dozed on a lily pad. It took only a moment to stick her with his tongue, and before he knew it, he had the finest meal of his life.

And he lived happily ever after.

# APPENDIX

# PEOPLE, PLACES, AND THINGS.

## OUR HERO

Duchess Georgia Goldenheart

## THE BEST FRIENDS

Lady Beatrice 'Bea' Irvingdale

Lady Clara Gaye

Mr. Blue

## GEORGIA'S HOUSEHOLD STAFF

Mr. Reardon – coach driver

Miss Millie Pepper – Lady's Maid

## CROFT HOUSE STAFF

Mr. Darkleaf – butler, early teens

Janet – housemaid

Mrs. Hensley - cook

Clyde – footman

Mr. Tremble – gardener

## DEAD MOURNER'S GROVE RESIDENTS

Constable Jenkins
County constable in Dead Mourner's Grove

Mrs. Crauford
Sister of Lord Redstone

Lord Redstone
Archeologist who owns Redstone House

Marguerite
Housemaid at Redstone House

Mr. Robert Greenstreet
Redstone's neighbor

Mrs. Trudy Greenstreet
Wife of Redstone's neighbor

CYMBRE SCHOOL FRIENDS

Lady Rebecca Drake
Daughter of the Earl of Elton and
Princess Calliope of Phaedros.

Lady Nora Blacklock
One of the Brady sisters (maternal). An old friend from
school, Nora, is the sensible one.

Mrs. Nelda Northbrook
One of the Brady sisters (maternal). An old friend from
school and Nora's sister, Nelda is somewhat less sensible,
but in a charming way.

Miss Octavia Potter
Bea's old rival from school. She was salutatorian, but they
were a half-point apart, and the rivalry was real.

OTHER STAFF

Millie Pepper
Georgia's loyal ladies' maid

Mrs. Macklin
Bea's dour ladies' maid

Martha
Nelda Northbrook's ladies' maid

GEORGIA'S MOTHER'S FAMILY
THE WHITESTONES

Sir Roger Whitestone
Georgia's cousin, and heir to the earldom of Westfall

Lady Alice Whitestone
Sir Roger's wife

THE QUEEN'S COURT

Queen Frederica Hart
Queen and wife of King Robert Hart

Lady Amaris Bronte
Assistant to the Queen, noblewoman from Jendina

THE EARLSMEN OF GRANDHALL

Sir Lucas Greenheart
7th son of the Earl of Grandhall,
and potential suitor to Georgia

Sir Callum Arnold

Sir Ian Clark

Sir James Davis

Sir Rupert Agar

Sir Nicholas Blackflower

Sir Ignatius Lavendar

OTHER FOLK

Mr. Martin Edson
florist courting Millie

ANCIENT ITEMS OF POWER

The Lungimiranza
Ancient text written by the Gildernesse that
predicts a Century of Evil

Secolo del male
Gildernesse name for the Century of Evil

ACKNOWLEDGEMENT

How to thank all the friends, family, and odd encounters with human beings who may or may not have unknowingly helped me write a book?

My mother, Virginia Marie Duggan, told me from an early age I could do anything. When I said I wanted to write books, she maintained that position, and still does.

This book took 3 years to write. And then at least another year of editing. Many rewrites. During that time, I was not alone. Contrary to popular opinion, the writer's life is not lonely. I spoke to MANY people while developing this latest chapter in Georgia Goldenheart's story. There was a lot of research into knives, poison, blood spray… you know, the usual. And now we are here. I would most like to thank the following people for invaluable contributions: Alan Pierce, Rachel Fain, Rebecca Drake Eisel, Sheila Noonen, Matina Bevis, Chris Ingle, Nathan McHue, Sean Shelton, Samantha Mueller, Damon Bradley, and Joseph Naftali. I could not have written this book without you.

www.ingramcontent.com/pod-product-compliance
Lightning Source LLC
Chambersburg PA
CBHW051543250626
47157CB00001B/170